Praise for Sujata Massey's
THE FLOWER MASTER

"A fascinating foreign world. . . . The book is a delight."
— *West County Times* (Pinole, CA)

"What Sujata Massey excels in, as evident from two previous Rei Shimura thrillers, is the arranging of plot details, interwoven with sprays of scene and freshly cut dialogue."

— *Baltimore Sun*

"Her best yet. Intricate plotting and writing as beautiful as the ikebana described."
— Laura Lippman, author of *Butchers Hill*

"Massey not only fleshes out each of [the] subplots but weaves them together to illuminate conflicts of old and new in Japanese manners, morals, family, and love."
— *Kirkus Reviews*, starred review

"A harmonious mix. . . . The narrative is enhanced greatly by the richly detailed Tokyo setting, from ancient tea houses to arcane rituals involving the cherry blossom festival. . . . An appealing sleuth."

— *Publishers Weekly*

THE SALARYMAN'S WIFE

"Sly, sexy and deftly done. *The Salaryman's Wife* is one to bring home."
—*People magazine Page-Turner of the Week*

"Massey gives us a clear-eyed look at Japanese daily life. An impressive first novel."
—*Baltimore Sun*

"First-time author Sujata Massey has done better than other authors who have used Japan as a backdrop, from James Clavell to Jay McInerney."
—*Japan Times*

ALSO BY SUJATA MASSEY

The Salaryman's Wife
Zen Attitude

The Flower Master

Sujata Massey

HarperPaperbacks
A Division of HarperCollins*Publishers*

HarperPaperbacks
A Division of HarperCollinsPublishers
10 East 53rd Street, New York, NY 10022-5299

This is a work of fiction. The characters, incidents, and
dialogues are products of the author's imagination and are not to
be construed as real. Any resemblance to actual events or
persons, living or dead, is entirely coincidental.

ISBN 0-06-109734-9

A hardcover edition of this book was published
in 1999 by HarperCollins*Publishers*.

First HarperPaperbacks printing: April 2000

Printed in the United States of America

Visit HarperPaperbacks on the World Wide Web at
http://www.harpercollins.com

❖ 10 9 8 7 6 5 4 3 2 1

Acknowledgments

As usual, I am indebted to a brilliant team of experts on both sides of the Pacific. Any mistakes contained within these pages originated with me, not them.

I received entree into Japanese flower arranging through the Sogetsu School and offer sincere thanks to my first Sogetsu ikebana teacher, Atsuko Suzuki, who is also a past president of the Kamakura Chapter of Ikebana International; and my current teacher, Toku Sugiyama, the past executive director of Sogetsu U.S.A. I enjoyed learning about the history of ikebana from retired Sogetsu headquarters administrator and teacher Mieko Tanibayashi; Shizuko Asakura, second vice president of Ikebana International and a Sogetsu member in Kamakura; Jane Redmon, a Sogetsu teacher in Arlington, Virginia; and Stephanie Tomiyasu, past international president of Ikebana International and a student of the Ohara School living in Yokohama. Many more friends in Ikebana International gave selflessly, proving that the motto "Friendship through flowers" is truth and not fiction.

I thank the historic poets of Japan for giving me inspiring haiku clues, and Christopher Belton, the Yokohama-based translator and author, for his spooky translations and fact checking. For criminal matters, I am again grateful to National Police Agency Superintendent Naohito Yamagishi and our mutual friend, Koichi Hyogo, and Akemi Narita for introducing me to the Nezu Police Department. I received a crash course in ceramics from John Adair Jr., owner of Kurofune Antiques in Roppongi, and Seiko Behr, the sculptor-owner of Pottery in Chestertown, Maryland. Important assistance of myriad sorts was given by Dr. In-Hei Hahn; Dr. Gershen Kaufman; Manami Amanai; my beloved writers' groups, House Blend and Sisters in Crime, Chesapeake Chapter; Flower Auction Japan; and the Sawanoya Ryokan in the Yanaka section of Tokyo.

I am grateful to my husband, Tony Massey, for his love and support, and to Laura Lippman, a dear friend and talented author who has been at my side for more book-signing road trips than I can count.

Finally, I thank my agents, Ellen Geiger and Dave Barbor, at Curtis Brown Limited, and the whole gang at HarperCollins, especially my editor, Carolyn Marino, her assistant, Robin Stamm, publicist Betsy Areddy, and art director Gene Mydlowski.

Cast of Characters

REI SHIMURA: California girl turned antiques buyer in Tokyo

NORIE SHIMURA: Rei's aunt, who is married to Uncle Hiroshi and is the mother of Rei's doctor-cousin Tsutomu "Tom" Shimura

MASANOBU KAYAMA: *Iemoto* — or headmaster — of the Kayama School of ikebana. His daughter, Natsumi, and son, Takeo, are training to take over the business. His wife, Reiko, is deceased.

ERIKO IWATA: longtime Kayama School student who is Norie's best friend

MRS. KODA: senior administrator at the Kayama School

SAKURA SATO: Kayama School teacher

LILA BRAITHWAITE: a Kayama School student who heads the foreign students' association and is Richard Randall's cousin. Lila is the mother to Donald, David, and Darcy Braithwaite.

MARI KUMAMORI: amateur potter and student at the Kayama School

RICHARD RANDALL: Rei's close confidant; a Canadian teacher of English

CHE FUJISAWA: an environmental activist from Colombia

ENRIQUE: Peruvian barman who catches Richard's fancy

LIEUTENANT HATA: Tokyo Metropolitan Police detective

MR. WAKA: proprietor of the Family Mart convenience store

YASUSHI ISHIDA: antiques store owner who serves as Rei's mentor

MISS OKADA: receptionist at the Kayama School

PLUS a dash of environmentalists, antiques customers, and spoiled children

Chapter 1

Nobody runs in Japan. A nation of naturally fast walkers has no reason to pick up its pace—except for emergencies like a closing train door. During four years in Tokyo, I've found the only runners besides myself to be senior citizens chasing a better cholesterol count or teenagers trying to make the high-school team.

I was jogging at a pathetically slow pace, the better to weave between office workers without toppling them. The city is crowded, and there are unwritten rules about knocking people down. At the Roppongi Crossing intersection, I had to wait two minutes for the light to change so that I could cross over and go three blocks farther to the Kayama Kaikan, the landmark building that was headquarters for one of Japan's leading schools of flower arranging.

Being late was my fault. I had lingered over my morning coffee, watered all my plants, and found a half dozen other reasons to dither so that, in the end, I had to jog from the train station to the school. As my aunt Norie frequently points out, my job as a freelance antiques buyer gives me control over my time. Not making it to the Kaikan on time was my own passive-aggressive response to her demands.

Being half Japanese and half American, I sometimes struggle to fit in with my father's Yokohama relatives. I can understand most of the jokes in movies, drink tea correctly, and even prepare my own pickled daikon radishes. Still, I was clueless about ikebana, the uniquely Japanese art of flower arrangement. The last time I overstuffed an urn with plum branches, my aunt stared at it without speaking. Shortly after that, she informed me that I was enrolled as a part-time student at the Kayama School.

I'd only been to the Kayama Kaikan twice, but that was enough for me to learn that in ikebana, less is more, and I'd rather spend less time arranging flowers in an overheated classroom and more time outdoors. That Tuesday morning in late March was bright, with temperatures in the sixties—almost time for the blooming of *sakura*, the cherry trees that are Japan's premier symbol. A weatherman on the morning news forecast that Tokyo's cherry trees would be in flower within five days, remaining at peak condition for no more than two weeks. Viewers were encouraged to plan their cherry blossom viewing parties accordingly.

"But watch closely, because clouds over the moon may mean storms over blossoms!" the reporter added with a corny smile. He was making a double entendre—referring to the likelihood of rain as well as offering up an old proverb that meant misfortune is lurking even at times of great happiness.

Prediction is a risky game. During the time that I've lived in Japan, I've marveled at the number of people who insist that the future is determined by patterns held in the past. I'm not good at predicting things; that sunny spring morning, I had no idea what I was running toward. The next fortnight's cherry blossoms would bring a storm of death and revelation that none of us—my clever aunt, the proverb-quoting newsman, and especially not I— would have expected.

The Kayama Kaikan was erected twenty years ago, as Japan soared toward the bubble years of vast economic expansion. The mirrored asymmetrical tower spoke of innovation, wealth, and power, the traits that had made the Kayama family successful in teaching ikebana from the start. Aunt Norie had told me that the land-owning family began the school in the 1860s, when the second son in the family abandoned training as a Buddhist monk but decided to teach others the flower-arranging skills that he had learned in a temple setting. The students of the first iemoto, or headmaster, were the socially ambitious wives of Japan's growing merchant class—similar to today's students, almost all the wives of salarymen.

The Kayama School, and many other ikebana schools like it, prospered into the twentieth century, but following World War II there were few Japanese women with the money and leisure to continue flower-arranging studies. Not ready to shut down, the *iemoto* invited an American general's wife to see his work, and after she enrolled, many other officers' wives followed. The Kayama ikebana philosophy became more avant-garde and international, spurred on by the new student body and the current headmaster, who traveled the world. By the late 1960s—a full century after the school had opened its doors—the small cement building where my aunt had trained had grown into a low-rise, which was demolished in turn to give space to the shiny new tower.

Walking through the school's giant glass doors, I faced the school's signature artwork, an installation of jagged sandstone boulders. It would have been interesting to climb through the rock garden to examine the flower arrangements peeking from various crannies, but I didn't have the time. I stepped into the large elevator with mirrored walls and a polished granite floor and sailed up to the fourth-floor classroom.

Outside the classroom doors, tall containers sat filled with a lavish assortment of flowers and branches. At my previous class I'd learned that each student was allowed to choose a bunch of line materials—branches that would give a dominant shape to the arrangement—and another bunch of smaller, decorative flowers to use as an accent. Today I took the last bunch of cherry branches and some white asters and slipped into the classroom, where a dozen women were working at the two long tables. Aunt Norie was snipping loganberry branches with her best friend, Eriko Iwata, at a table close to the teacher's lectern. Norie and Eriko were like two peas in a pod: both slender housewives in their early fifties who looked about thirty-five. They wore their hair in pageboy styles and had chosen similar gabardine slacks and silk blouses with the sleeves folded over, exposing their hairless forearms. Why the two of them felt it necessary to shave their forearms, let alone wear silk blouses to a flower-arranging class, was beyond me. I was dressed in a short-sleeved striped cotton sweater over a pair of flared jeans I'd picked up at a teen boutique in the Harajuku district. Even though the jeans were a nice deep black, I doubted my aunt would be fooled into believing they were proper ladies' trousers.

"Ah, at last it is Rei-san!" chirped Eriko, who had known me long enough to greet me by my first name.

Aunt Norie put down her ikebana scissors with huge, scary blades and looked me over. "Did you have some trouble getting out at the correct subway station?"

"No, I'm just late. Sorry," I said, perching on a hard stool next to her.

"Your hair looks nice. But such big, ugly shoes!" Norie winced as she regarded my running sneakers. I'd once pointed out that trendy teens were wearing Asics like mine with everything from jeans to dresses, but she countered that a twenty-eight-year-old antiques dealer had no business looking like an eighteen-year-old.

"If it weren't for these shoes, I'd be even later. The shoes allowed me to run," I said defensively.

"You haven't missed anything," Eriko soothed. "There is plenty of time to make an arrangement before Sakura-san starts the lecture. Just take a container from the shelves the way you did last time."

If I'd been at home, I would have arranged the three branches of cherry within a few minutes. But the school environment made me nervous, and the branches wouldn't lean the way I wanted. In the narrow earthenware vase I'd selected from the classroom shelf, they fell against one another instead of stretching up gracefully the way Aunt Norie's and Eriko's flowers did. Was I the only one who couldn't do it? I looked over at the next table.

Lila Braithwaite, a tall Canadian who was president of the foreign students' association, had mixed cherry with azalea in a very professional arrangement. Nadine St. Giles, her French friend, had chosen the same materials but wasn't quite as confident using them. I most admired the work of a student called Mari Kumamori. Mari was working with heather, its pale purple blossoms making a delicate contrast with a celadon bowl.

"I like Mari's bowl. Are there any more?" I asked Norie.

"It's not the school's property. She makes her own pottery and must have brought it from home. Anyway, the container you have is correct for your particular arrangement. Just make a slanting fixture, and your branches will stand straight."

Slanting fixtures, I'd learned the week before, had something to do with cutting a gash into one of the branches before inserting a second, shorter branch into the cut. It was an act of precision that I barely managed before turning to my aunt for help with the next step. After all, she had earned a Kayama teaching degree more than thirty years ago and was in class primarily to be with her friends.

"I can't get it to look like the picture in my book. And I can't read the directions." Because I was a beginner, I had to form my arrangements after models in the Kayama School's handbook, earning a stamp for each of them before I could progress to the next one. I could understand the diagrams but very few of the words.

"Oh, I didn't know you couldn't read Japanese!" Eriko sounded mournful. "Let me see if I can find a lesson book with an English translation. That's how Lila-san and Nadine-san are able to study."

"Rei-*chan*, it's up to you to make your arrangement," my aunt reproved. "If I move the branches for you, you will not have the confidence you need. There is nothing wrong with making mistakes. And very soon, when you progress to freestyle, you will have to follow your own intuition."

I was working slowly, distracted by my aunt's conversation, when the class was called to order by Mrs. Koda, director of the teaching program.

"Sakura Sato has graciously agreed to demonstrate to us today the challenges and joys in working with one floral material. After she speaks, I will provide an English translation for our visitors." Mrs. Koda spoke English loudly, as if the foreigners in class were not only language-impaired but deaf. I was pretty sure this wasn't meant to be malicious, but it was unfortunate that she'd labeled Lila and Nadine visitors instead of bona fide members of the school. I could understand why Aunt Norie had been adamant that I sit with her and Eriko. She didn't want me to get stuck in the *gaijin* ghetto.

I hastily finished off my arrangement by throwing in a few asters. My aunt was smiling at Mrs. Koda—she had known her for more than thirty years, ever since my aunt began studying ikebana. I'd seen photographs of Mrs. Koda at that time and found it amusing that she still had not updated her hairstyle from the hard black beehive of her younger days. Despite her thick, upswept bouffant, Mrs. Koda had a drawn, weary-looking face. She had moved slowly when she gave me a tour of the school the previous week, using a cane to help her along. She'd been apologetic that the school's headmaster, Masanobu Kayama, was away in Luxembourg, and she promised I'd have the chance for an audience with him soon.

Mrs. Koda bowed deeply to Sakura Sato, a woman of Aunt Norie's age dressed in a pale pink suit. As Sakura stepped briskly to the lectern and slapped down a notebook, her elbow flew out, causing Mrs. Koda to lose her balance and bump the edge of a student table. The crowd of ladies murmured with concern, and Aunt Norie came forward to take Mrs. Koda's arm. Seeing no more stools in the classroom,

I jumped up from mine so that the elder lady could have it. Aunt Norie gave me an approving glance. Feeling vindicated, but realizing that I no longer had a place to sit, I retreated to the back of the classroom. A young Japanese man in a Greenpeace T-shirt and jeans was rummaging through a drawer containing ikebana supplies. I perched in a corner that was not in his way and offered a clear view of the teaching demonstration.

"Could someone please lower the blinds? The sun distracts me," Sakura said, and Eriko, who was close to the window, slipped over and drew the venetian blinds across the view of the Tokyo skyline.

"As many of you have heard already, the *iemoto* chose the name Sakura for me when I was selected to become a teacher twenty-four years ago." Miss Sato delivered a thin, superior smile to us, cementing my instinctive dislike of her. "I had made an arrangement entirely from cherry blossoms that actually was contrary to the mixed materials required for the lesson. I could not help myself—the cherry was so beautiful. It was as if nature had entered me and taken hold."

Everyone in the room appeared rapt. Some women were writing down her words in their Kayama School notebooks.

"Kayama-*sensei* laughed when he saw my arrangement and said that since I liked cherry blossoms so much, he would give me the formal teaching name Sakura, to celebrate the flowering cherry tree that is our national treasure. And whenever *sakura* is in bloom, he asks me to come up with something special to decorate our headquarters."

Aunt Norie had been given the flower name Hasu, which means "lotus." She used it only for identification in ikebana exhibitions. I doubted I'd be in the Kayama School long enough to receive a flower name. Dealing with my own Japanese name, simply pronounced "ray," had been an enormous complication during my California childhood. There were even troubles in Japan, since the name was written with an unusual *kanji* character meaning "crystal clarity."

"As you know," Sakura said, breaking my meditation, "it is a great challenge to communicate the essential essence of ikebana—heaven and God above man—when the flowers in question are all identical. How does one guard against massing the same color and shape? That is our question for today." She glanced at the table in front of her, which was bare except for an industrial-looking black container. "My flowers do not seem to be here, nor are my ikebana shears. Could someone please bring them?"

I glanced at the casually dressed young man, since he looked to be the most likely candidate for gofer in the room. He wasn't bad-looking, with his high cheekbones, golden skin a little darker than mine, and eyes the color of espresso. He stared back at me blankly when I gave him an inquiring look. He clearly didn't feel obliged to help Sakura.

Slightly embarrassed, I looked away but stayed put. I wasn't doing Sakura any favors, not when she'd caused Mrs. Koda to trip.

Mari Kumamori, the woman who had brought her

own celadon dish from home, stood up and spoke softly, using a supreme honorific. "Please, Sakura-*sama*, what may I bring you?"

"Cherry," Sakura barked. "Or have you been sleeping while I was talking?"

Mari blushed and hurried to the outer room, where I'd chosen my flowers. She was gone for a long minute, and Sakura filled the time by chattering about how the headmaster had personally asked her to arrange flowers for a big installation in the lobby of the Imperial Hotel.

When Mari came back, she hurried up to the front of the room and whispered something to Sakura, who laughed shortly and addressed the room.

"Apparently cherry is such a popular flower that all of it has been taken for use by the class members. Well, I shall improvise. That is the challenge that faces us when we create ikebana. Remember, the term literally means 'living flowers.' We must endeavor to make the most realistic arrangement with the natural materials to which we have access."

Her curt words made me feel guilty. I'd been the one to take the last bunch of cherry blossoms from the bucket in the hall. I could race to my flower arrangement and retrieve the few inferior branches I hadn't cut up, but I could imagine how nastily she'd accept them.

"I shall use forsythia," Sakura said to Mari, who ran out again to bring a big bunch of green-and-yellow branches to the head teacher.

"Please strip the bottom foliage," Sakura commanded her volunteer assistant. Mari had given her own scissors to Sakura, so she was forced to rip off the offending leaves with her bare hands.

"With this design, I am creating a contrast between light and dark," Sakura lectured. "The container is a length of industrial drainpipe that I painted black—an unorthodox material that reflects Kayama innovation. Any material, from drainpipe to wire netting or paper, may be combined with fresh materials. In all situations, the characteristics of the materials must be vividly expressed. If the container and flowers do not truly relate, the work will not be beautiful."

I was skeptical about whether Sakura could succeed in making the crude drainpipe beautiful. She thrust forsythia branches into holes she had punched at various places in the pipe, and in the end created something that looked remarkably like a black centipede with long, furry yellow legs. Had the cherry branches been available, the centipede would have been pink.

Sakura showed her versatility by arranging more forsythia in an antique stone container, a fairly classic arrangement that made everyone sigh in relief. She took a few softball questions from the audience, then set out to evaluate each student's arrangement, the entire cluster of women following her to hear the verdict. She praised the first few students profusely but was surprisingly cool to Lila Braithwaite.

"By stressing the idea of shape, you are losing the truth in the flowers' nature," Sakura told Lila, who nodded, looking unhappy when she heard Mrs. Koda's translation of the words. On the other hand,

Lila's friend Nadine's lopsided arrangement of cherry blossoms received a sweet smile and a compliment on her sense of color. Both women had identical flowers. Why did one get praise and the other criticism?

Sakura dismissed Mari Kumamori's heather arrangement by saying the pale green of the celadon was wrong for the flowers. Mari bowed very low and thanked Sakura for her wise criticism. I was curious what Sakura would say about Aunt Norie's arrangement. Last time Norie had mentioned that she, Eriko, and Sakura had begun studying together the same year, but Norie and Eriko had both taken off for more than a decade to care for their young children. Sakura had never married, so she stayed active in the school, rising to become a staff teacher. My aunt had a second-degree teaching certificate, and Eriko had a third-degree one, which meant that both of them were entitled to teach classes in their homes but not at headquarters.

Aunt Norie had assembled a mass of fluffy white rhododendrons accented with loganberry vines. The arrangement in a blue glass container had a snappy feeling, like my aunt herself.

"Well, Shimura-san. You used rhododendron." Sakura paused. "It is such a common bush."

She bowed slightly, and Aunt Norie responded in kind. When Norie's face came up, I read the irritation. Sakura had not criticized her outright, but she had refused to give anything that could be regarded as praise. She had said rhododendrons were common. Nothing more.

Eriko received similar treatment. "What a classic container," Sakura said, tapping the smooth length of bamboo springing with long grasses and camellia blooms. She moved on, not saying anything about the flowers. It was hard for me to understand why my aunt and Eriko even bothered with the class, except that Sakura Sato wasn't always the lecturer. The previous week Mrs. Koda had given an interesting talk on hanging arrangements, and her comments when she'd come around the room had been helpful.

Now it was my turn.

"You are Norie Shimura's niece from California? I see the family resemblance." Sakura took in my clothing, then the cherry branches I'd arranged. I wondered if she'd deduced that I'd taken the last bunch.

"May I touch your arrangement?" Without waiting for my answer, Sakura reached in and touched the branches making up my slanting fixture. They fell apart, but she wasn't interested in that. "The parts of these branches that are underwater still have some foliage." She tapped the tiny cherry blossom buds that I hadn't removed.

"I didn't want to cut off anything that might bloom later," I explained. There was such a deathly silence in the room, I wondered if I'd accidentally used an impolite word. Then I realized my flaw: I was the first person who had even tried to make an excuse for doing something wrong.

"As you arrange more flowers, you'll notice that water contaminated by plant matter will begin teeming with bacteria, thus cutting short the life of your arrangement." Sakura whisked sharp scissors out of her suit pocket and began snipping away the buds. "The lines are wrong in this arrangement. Isn't this lesson eight, basic slanting style?"

"It's lesson three, actually. Basic upright style," I said.

"How far your branch leans! Much greater than fifteen degrees."

She removed my branches and rearranged them according to her desire. "It's surprising to have junior-level students in this advanced class. Normally one must have completed the beginner's book to enroll in this class. I suppose family connections make such things possible, *neh*?"

Without bowing, Sakura moved on to the next person. She'd kicked the stuffing out of me, but I knew that she was right. I'd been admitted because Aunt Norie had sweet-talked Mrs. Koda.

But my aunt couldn't let things go. In a pleasant but firm voice, she called after the teacher, "Sakura-*sensei,* is there a problem?"

Without turning around, the head teacher said, "I'm afraid I must discuss the next student's arrangement. If you have questions, please see me after class."

"The school's teachers certainly have changed their attitude since I was a young student. I apologize to everyone present for you," Norie called out clearly. With her falsely courteous manners, Aunt Norie was picking a fight. Everyone knew it. The other women in the class started studying the floor.

Sakura finally decided to face my petite aunt. She had a six-inch advantage and a voice that carried a cool, menacing authority. "Norie-san, you know the motto for the school is 'Truth.'"

"'Truth in nature!'" Norie interrupted. "Flowers should be the focus of our class, not personal situations."

All the women began talking at once, as if to cover up the breach of etiquette that had occurred. Only the sharp crack of a wooden stick stopped the verbal explosion.

"Be quiet, please!" Old Mrs. Koda returned her cane to her side and spoke up in her quavering voice. "It is time for our class tea break. It is time for everyone to be quiet and drink tea!"

Chapter 2

J'm not going back. It was like a Wild West showdown, only the gun-toting cowboys were replaced by ladies wearing silk and carrying scissors," I told Richard Randall later that night at the Mister Donut near Sendagi Station. In the time I'd taken to tell the details of my dreadful class experience, I'd accordion-pleated my paper napkin into something like origami. I was still upset.

"Your aunt sounds like she has a split personality," Richard mused. "Why else would she speak out like that? Japanese people have the best manners. They would sooner die than cause a scene."

A teenage boy two tables away suddenly decided to stand on his chair and begin singing an Oasis song.

"You were saying something about the Japanese?" I reminded Richard.

"He's not the norm. He's drunk and sixteen," Richard said, looking the boy over a little more carefully. "Hey, do you think he's interested in improving his English?"

"He's got a girlfriend." I inclined my head at a teenager with dyed red hair and a Hello Kitty lunchbox.

"How do you know? They could be like us, a pair of asexual soul mates."

When I'd first arrived in Tokyo, Richard and I had shared a miserable apartment while we taught English to kitchenware salesmen. We drifted apart during my intense, short-lived liaison with a Scottish lawyer. Like most foreigners, Hugh Glendinning eventually left Japan for home. He become deeply involved with organizing the new Scottish parliament and with the Honorable Fiona Somebody, according to the gossip pages in *Tatler* magazine. I'd called up Hugh's international toll-free number to find out the details, but the number had been disconnected.

Feeling abandoned, I'd plunged into work. Eventually I had enough money to rent a small one-bedroom apartment in a historic inner-city neighborhood called Yanaka. The apartment was on the ground floor of a seventy-year-old, barely renovated wooden house. To most Japanese, it appeared to be a nightmare dwelling, but I thought it was charming. I'd painted the walls the color of dried persimmons, laid fresh tatami mat flooring, and installed a brand-new peach bathtub and matching tiled wall and floor. There was no central heat or air-conditioning, but I loved the place, which had the benefit of proximity to Richard's language school in Ocha-no-mizu. After Richard finished teaching he often dropped by for dinner, and even occasionally could be persuaded to spend a Sunday morning shopping the antiques flea market with me. I valued him more for his company than his muscle power. At five feet four inches, Richard was exactly my height, but skinnier. His slight frame, combined with white-blond hair and blue eyes, gave him the look of a delicate angel, the kind of doll that filled Tokyo department-store windows at Christmas. Ladies would beg to help carry his load, which worked out well for both of us.

"I think you should go back to that flower-arranging school just to see what happens next week. And it could only improve your social life."

"What do you mean? It's all women, except for one lazy young man who might have been a florist, given the way he was dressed. If the worker could have found Sakura some more cherry blossoms, maybe she wouldn't have gone off on such a tear in the classroom."

Richard raised his eyebrows. "Think he's gay?"

"Just because a man works with flowers doesn't mean he's gay. You, of all people, should be ashamed of yourself for your stereotyping." I couldn't help admitting, though, that I'd wondered the same, since the florist had looked right through me.

"I'm looking to meet someone, okay? Don't be so uptight," Richard said, his mouth full of bean-paste doughnut. "So what's the reason for the long-simmering vendetta? Did your aunt tell you in the end?"

"Of course not. She went into the ladies' room for ten minutes and came out with red eyes and a little white mask stretched over her nose and mouth. She said she had to go home because her allergies were acting up."

The excuse had been almost plausible because a sizable number of Japanese people wore gauze face masks to avoid cedar and cherry blossom pollen. However, Aunt Norie had all those kinds of trees in her garden at home, so I gathered she was not allergic. She probably was carrying the mask around in her purse because it was left over from the last time she suffered a cold.

"Sakura's more involved than Norie in school politics. That could be cause for friction," Richard said.

"Sakura's already on top. Her behavior to my aunt and the others before her was incredibly rude. I don't know why the school lets her carry on that way."

"You could complain to the headmaster."

I laughed in astonishment. "Richard, I've only been to the school twice. I'm not even supposed to be in the advanced class, but my aunt convinced Mrs. Koda to allow me to work at my beginning lessons with my aunt at my side. Given such privileges, I really have no right to complain."

"Maybe my cousin could say something." Richard sipped his coffee, staring pensively at the young couple kissing each other at their table.

"Don't tell me you have some secret Japanese relatives," I teased.

"No, but my cousin Lila takes classes at the Kayama School. She moved here a year ago, but you were too busy with His Hugeness for me to introduce you."

"Lila Braithwaite? The president of the foreign students' association? There's not much resemblance between you two." I decided to overlook his cruel joke about Hugh's name.

"Her father was French-Canadian. She inherited dark hair, height, and a taste for Hermès scarves. She's also got three little kids who are a lot of fun. She recruits me to baby-sit when her nanny can't take it anymore."

I didn't know Richard was a baby-sitter, but it made sense, given his playful nature. I asked, "What does Lila tell you about the Kayama School?"

"Lila started studying flower arranging when she got here. Her husband's pretty high-ranking at some Canadian steel company, so she gets asked to chair various ladies' committees. But for expat society, she's not bad. She shops a lot."

"Antiques?"

"Rei, they have a cost of living allowance. Of course she buys antiques. You should hit her up."

I would do as he suggested. Newcomers to Japan were wonderful customers because their apartments were bare and their sponsor companies often provided generous expense accounts. That had been Hugh's situation—I'd transformed his apartment into a veritable showplace. When he gave up his apartment, he asked me to sell everything. Then he wouldn't take the money. Unable to bring myself to spend it, I threw it into the U.S. stock market. It was a smart move. But as the dividends grew, so did my sadness.

The next morning I left a message on Lila Braithwaite's answering machine about the interesting assortment of antique Japanese china I had for sale. Then I called a country auctioneer about an upcoming sale I needed to attend. When the other line beeped, I switched lines.

"My dear niece!" It was Aunt Norie.

"May I call you back? I'm on a business call. Are you home?" I knew my aunt's morning schedule, and since it was only 9 A.M., she probably hadn't yet hung out the day's laundry.

"You don't want to talk to me." Her voice broke. "Well, I can understand that, after my appalling performance yesterday! You must want to disown me."

I told Norie to hold on while I got off the phone with the auctioneer. When I came back, she sounded more cheerful.

"Rei-*chan*, we are going to make amends. This afternoon we will go to the Kayama School and present some gifts to Mrs. Koda and Sakura Sato. We have to do it. The school is going to invite its top members to do a big exhibition at the Mitsutan department store, and I cannot have bad feelings during that time. I also want to save your chance to make a good impression in the school."

"Sakura was being honest when she said I didn't belong in that class," I reminded Norie. "Ikebana is just not something I'm good at. Let me work in your garden or something. I like flowers, but I don't want to stay in the Kayama School."

There was a long silence. "You mean you want to quit your study of ikebana? That is unlike you."

She was right. Since I'd come to Japan, I'd never quit studying *kanji* characters. I'd never stopped learning new dishes, new vocabulary, new ways to survive and thrive.

"I'm just not talented, and it's so expensive for you to pay my way. I'd pay for the classes myself if I wanted to go on, but I really don't want to!" As I made my excuses, I was aware of how lame they sounded.

"I prepaid your classes through July," Aunt Norie said flatly. "That's how I managed to get you enrolled in that special class with me."

"Let me reimburse you."

"Inside a family there is no such thing as reimbursement. Tell me, what would your father think about you quitting your studies prematurely? I believe he would be very disappointed."

My father, who practiced psychiatry in San Francisco, had emigrated to the United States in part for a greater sense of personal freedom. If I told him what Aunt Norie was putting me through, he'd recite a soliloquy on the manipulative power of Asian families, then tell me to come home—that is, to the United States.

"I cannot force you to go," my aunt continued. "However, I would like you to speak to Mrs. Koda. Otherwise she may think you were pressured to leave the school, and that would be very bad for morale."

"I'll go with you," I said at last. "But not today. At three I've got to see a client."

"We'll meet after your appointment, at five o'clock inside My Magic Forest in Roppongi. I'll pick up the gifts there. I'll be wearing my yellow Hanae Mori suit, so please dress yourself accordingly."

With that fashion directive, my aunt rang off.

That afternoon I made some quick yen appraising the porcelain collection of an old woman who was handing her house over to her children, minus its contents. As I admired Mrs. Morita's pieces of old Imari porcelain, I listened to the story about how she had acquired them as trousseau gifts in the 1920s.

"I can photograph the pieces, if you like, and try to find some buyers," I said. "It's much nicer that way—no chance of damage or theft, the way you would have in a shop."

"What kind of people are these buyers?" Mrs. Morita sounded suspicious.

"High-class ladies who want to treasure Japan's past. I have many contacts in the international community," I said, thinking of Lila Braithwaite.

"You should find a Japanese buyer, not a foreigner," Mrs. Morita told me.

"Foreigners are the only people who would buy a set like that," I said, indicating some dinner-size round blue-and-white plates decorated with a little bit of red, green, and gilt overglaze. The plates were pretty, showing a rock garden with a plum tree, small chrysanthemums, and bamboo. The china wouldn't attract Japanese buyers, who usually insisted on buying plates in sets of five. Foreigners didn't know the importance of having a good-luck number for their dishes.

"Yes, I know it's an odd number of dishes," Mrs. Morita said, grimacing. "I had them buried away, so I'd almost forgotten about them. You may as well take them with you. If you can sell them, I will consider giving you the chance to sell my other things."

That was a pleasing bit of serendipity. I carefully wrapped the plates in tissue paper and placed them in their original container, a sturdy pine box. Then Mrs. Morita surprised me by wrapping the box in a pretty pink scarf, creating a *furoshiki* carrier that I could take with me on the street.

"Keep the *furoshiki,*" she told me. "It is cherry blossom pink, and you can always use it as a scarf around the neck of that lovely dress."

Having taken Aunt Norie's fashion hint, I was wearing a dress, pale pink pique with white collar and cuffs. The A-line shift came only to midthigh, but the white collar and cuffs made it almost schoolgirlish, a perennial hot look in Tokyo. I caught a few glances while walking through Mrs. Morita's expensive neighborhood. The dress was one that my mother had worn at the end of the swinging sixties. I imagined she was a startling vision of glamour to my father, a young resident struggling hard to stay awake at Johns Hopkins Hospital. My father's parents had been unhappy when he announced his plans to marry a white American woman, but his younger brother, Hiroshi, who eventually married Norie, had been supportive. Beginning when I was very young, Uncle Hiroshi and Aunt Norie had invited me to stay with them in Yokohama every summer. These regular visits made me fall in love with my father's country, something that ultimately backfired on my parents. I'd gone home to San Francisco only once in four years—and that was because I needed knee surgery.

I glanced down at my left knee, which looked sturdy under the sheer nylon stockings I was wearing. I'd been hit by a car the previous summer, and fortunately my knee had healed well. Otherwise I never could have managed the many flights of stairs involved in Tokyo living. I was slightly out of breath when I climbed out of the correct subway exit at Roppongi Station and set off for My Magic Forest.

When Japanese retailers appropriate English names for their businesses, the results are often comical. But My Magic Forest really did fit its fairy-tale name. Stepping inside, I passed between thirty-foot faux Greek columns draped in ivy and Christmas tree lights. From there, I could spend an hour happily wandering through the dimly lit fantasy flower market. I strolled from a Dutch tulip farm with a small windmill to a cheerful English cottage garden and then into Tuscany, where lemon trees sprang from terra-cotta pots and white roses spilled out of an antique-looking urn.

The Kayama School ordered flowers from the same suppliers who served My Magic Forest, but the materials I'd seen at the school were less lavish than the shop's regular stock. I bent over the $500 verdigris urn and inhaled the scent of the luscious roses, $15 apiece. In this place, the Japanese philosophy of less is more had been thrown out of the stained-glass window.

"Rei-*chan*! Isn't this a lovely place?" My aunt had crept up behind me. She was holding a wicker shopping basket already filled with a porcelain flowerpot painted in a lively Portuguese style and a pair of cast-iron ikebana shears with oversized circular handles.

"Lovely." I faltered at the ten-thousand-yen price tag. At the current rate of 145 yen to the U.S. dollar, the shears cost about seventy dollars. "Are you sure you want to give such expensive presents? There are other things on sale. Look at the iris."

"The teachers receive all the flowers they want at school. Quality tools are a better gift. Don't you remember how Sakura needed a pair of shears? It would be thoughtful to give her a brand-new pair. And Mrs. Koda has a small window garden at her apartment, so a nice pot would be very welcome."

"I owe you five thousand yen for the shears. How much for the other?" I asked dutifully.

"You owe nothing, although I'm going to say the presents are from both of us, *neh*? I'm the one who caused the embarrassment. Besides, I have a frequent-shopper card, so these two purchases will take me a little closer to choosing a ten-thousand-yen gift for myself."

By the time Aunt Norie had paid for the gifts, the

weather outside had changed. It was raining, but a large group of people had gathered at the shop's entrance. There's nothing unusual about crowds on the Roppongi streets, especially outside the record store on the day a new Namie Amuro disc is released. But this time several dozen denim-clad young people had congregated directly in front of My Magic Forest, barring the door. They waved signs in Japanese, English, and Spanish. I rarely used my high-school Spanish, so I had to think a little before I could translate the messages. BEAUTIFUL FLOWERS KILL PEOPLE, one sign read. A ROSE BY ANY OTHER NAME STINKS. END PESTICIDE USE.

"It's an antiflower group," I said, looking closely at the young protesters. About half were Japanese; the others looked Latino, or had a combination of Japanese features and darker skin. I guessed that the last group were descended from Japanese people who had emigrated to Latin America at the turn of the century. Their offspring often returned to work in Japan. Japanese pay, even for lowly jobs in restaurants and construction, was higher than in their home countries.

"The signs in Japanese say 'Blossoms Bring Storms' and all that nonsense. Come, let's look for a taxi." Aunt Norie, small as she was, plunged into the solid wall of people, leading with her left shoulder weighted with her school tote bag.

"Buying flowers from Colombia supports an industry that is killing its workers. Madam, you surely don't want to kill?" a young woman implored my aunt.

"I'm afraid I don't understand." Aunt Norie gave her the kind of benevolent smile one gives preschoolers blocking an escalator.

"Japanese people demand extremely fresh and beautiful flowers from overseas. For you, the flower ranchers in Colombia spray their flowers with ten different pesticides. Female workers cut the flowers, and they become ill. Their babies are born deformed. At least twenty-eight people have died from pesticide exposure!"

Aunt Norie's face fell, and I imagined she was thinking about the many bunches of imported flowers she used weekly for ikebana. In a halting voice, she asked, "Which flowers are these?"

"Roses and carnations are the most common imports from Colombia, but there are others. If you boycott the store with us, it will force the flower ranchers to change their ways."

But if the flower shipments to Japan decreased, the ranchers would need to grow even sturdier, longer-lasting blooms, and so they would have to use stronger chemicals, wouldn't they? I wanted to ask the young woman, but she was blocked by a young man with Japanese eyes and thick, curly black hair. The man wore a denim jacket embroidered with the name CHE on one side and STOP KILLING FLOWERS on the other.

"Will you join our boycott? Are you a flower lover or a people lover?" Che demanded.

Aunt Norie retorted, "Actually, I respect all forms of life. I would like to hear more, but I must hurry to make it to the Kayama Kaikan."

"The Kayama School's headquarters? That school is completely amoral! They spend a fortune on flowers from my homeland. There are babies being miscarried or born without arms, all because the Kayama School ladies love flowers more than people!" Che's face was inches away from Norie's, and I could see her begin to cower.

"The Kayama family are the Nazis of the flower world!" another protester chimed in.

"Yes, indeed." Che was a small man, but he thrust his body forward aggressively. "Since you honorable customers buy flowers from the Kayamas and this wretched retailer, you're as good as double murderers!"

"But I didn't buy flowers. Look!" Aunt Norie tore the seal off the top of her shopping bag and pulled out a gift-wrapped box. When the crowd still did not part for her, she unwrapped the box and pulled out the ikebana scissors, holding them high in the air.

"She has a weapon!" Che bellowed. "Comrades, employ passive resistance!"

Of course, the crowd broke into pandemonium. People cried things to one another in Spanish and Japanese: "Be careful!" "Call the police!" "Remember passive resistance!"

Aunt Norie kept the shears in the air, and I tightly clutched the package of Mrs. Morita's plates as we scurried through. She was shaking, and I had a run in my panty hose, when we finally settled into a taxi that stopped for us a block away.

"I cannot believe that. I was sympathetic to those people, but they turned on us! Can you believe they thought I was violent?" Aunt Norie sniffled into her handkerchief.

"They shouldn't single out the Kayama School. There are hundreds of flower-arranging schools in Japan. I'm sure all of them use Colombian flowers!" I was surprised to hear myself defending the ikebana school, but Che and his gang had been pretty frightening.

"Our *iemoto* is one of Japan's ten wealthiest individuals. That makes him an easy mark, but it is unfair to target him. If those young people spent half an hour with Masanobu-san, they would learn what a great man he is."

I guessed that Aunt Norie could use the headmaster's first name because she had been one of his students long ago. She had been part of the inner circle. As we got out of the taxi and stepped up to the Kayama Kaikan, the doorman who had watched me enter without lifting a finger the previous day rushed to open the door for Aunt Norie.

"Shimura-san, you must be here for the Mitsutan exhibition planning." The young woman receptionist in a green suit beckoned my aunt over to her polished paulownia desk. The table was bare except for a vase with a sole white calla lily that looked as suggestive as the ones Georgia O'Keeffe had made famous.

"I'd forgotten about the meeting. Miss Okada, can you tell us where it is being held?" Aunt Norie asked.

"In the fourth-floor classroom," Miss Okada replied. "They'll be glad you are participating. Your arrangements are always among my favorites."

"Oh, my work is just average," my aunt said. "Actually, I have an inconvenient request—I must wrap up a gift in some nice paper. Do you have wrapping paper anywhere in the building?"

"I have a roll of *washi* paper in my office. It is flecked with dried cherry blossom petals, which makes it appropriate for this season!" Miss Okada beamed at this opportunity to help out. "Please come back in ten minutes and I'll have it wrapped up for you."

"*Ara!* How can the ladies be glad to see me when I was not invited?" Aunt Norie fumed when the elevator doors had closed and we were heading up to the second floor, not the fourth. "That meeting is surely a gossip festival. Well, our troubles will be over after we deliver these gifts to Koda-san and Sakura-san."

"I hope we find them, because I don't want to have to come back another day." My knee was beginning to throb. I'd twisted it during our dash through the picket line.

We passed a section of secretaries working at computer terminals; all of them wore heavy aprons, the protective kind of garment I'd worn when my knee was being X-rayed the year before. In Japan, it was believed that computer monitors gave off radiation that could harm women's reproductive tracts.

Suddenly my aunt said, "Oh, look down the hall by the administrative offices. It's Natsumi Kayama, the headmaster's daughter. I've been wanting to introduce you to Natsumi and her twin brother, Takeo."

We approached Natsumi Kayama, my aunt beaming while I kept a neutral expression. Natsumi was dressed in a sunny yellow and orange Lilly Pulitzer dress—a highly exclusive label, sold only at Mitsutan—with orange stiletto-heeled pumps that made her slim legs look marvelous. I remembered the run in my own stocking but couldn't think of a way to hide it. Natsumi had smiled automatically at Aunt Norie but was gazing at me as if she'd discovered a long-lost friend.

"Courrèges?" Natsumi breathed, and I realized she was talking about my dress.

I nodded. "It's my mother's. I took it out of her closet when I was last home."

"Natsumi-san, may I present my niece Rei Shimura? Rei was born in San Francisco but lives here now. Natsumi arranges flowers with a very youthful spirit," my aunt said to me.

"I'm really bad at it," Natsumi tittered. "They say I have been studying for a long time because I am slow."

"Nonsense! You have arranged some very special floral displays in fashion boutiques—Rei, I'm sure you saw the one that was photographed for *Hanako*," my aunt said.

Being unable to read standard adult-level Japanese, I rarely bought young women's magazines like *Hanako*. So I smiled politely and asked Natsumi if she'd seen Mrs. Koda. We could at least get that part of the business done before picking up the wrapped scissors to give to Sakura Sato.

"Ah, Koda-san! I was looking for her, too.

Nobody's seen her for at least an hour, but she must be nearby. Because of her cane, she cannot walk too far."

"Maybe she is in the meeting taking place on the fourth floor?" I asked.

"That's finished. The ladies are drinking tea in the restaurant," Natsumi said.

"Where is Sakura-san? Maybe she can help us," Aunt Norie suggested, and I could envision the wheels turning as she tried to get us back to our agenda.

"Mmm, she's probably still inside the fourth-floor classroom. You have missed the meeting about the Mitsutan exhibition, haven't you?"

"Thank you, Natsumi-san. Give my regards to Takeo-san and your esteemed father. Let's go up to the classroom, Rei." My aunt seemed annoyed at the second mention of the meeting from which she'd been excluded. As I started to follow her toward the elevator, Natsumi stopped me.

"You've got a hole in your stocking," she whispered. "I have an unopened package of stockings in my desk that you could have."

I smiled at her. "Thanks, but it's okay."

"Sakura will notice," she warned. "She is so very critical! I don't want your feelings to be hurt."

Judging by the sheen on Natsumi's long, slender legs, I imagined she was wearing something pretty expensive. I'd probably get a snag putting on her spare stockings, and replacing them would break my budget. I shook my head and said, "Please don't worry. And thank you very much for your kind offer."

I swung away from her worried face and went to the elevator. The doors had closed, and it appeared that my aunt had gone up to the fourth floor without me.

I pressed the call button and waited for a while, watching a panel of lights over the door tell me where the elevator was traveling. It went all the way up to the ninth floor and then slowly descended, stopping on each floor before the empty elevator finally arrived. I got in and used the mirrored wall to do a quick lipstick touch-up. Natsumi's perfect looks had made me self-conscious.

I took the elevator to the fourth floor, where I stepped out into the foyer where I'd picked up my cherry branches for the previous day's class. I did not see Aunt Norie. She might have gone into the classroom. The door was closed, so I knocked on it.

A soft noise coming from within sounded like a cat's meow, and I recoiled. I associate cats with death because of a bad experience from a year earlier. Since then Richard had tried to get me interested in adopting a kitten, but I'd always refused. Cats scare me. To be on the safe side, I laid down the package of antique plates and opened the classroom door.

My aunt was at the distant end of the room by the blackboard and teaching table. I heard the mewing again and realized it was her voice. I drew closer and saw she was bent over a long white boulder. A woman was lying on the ground. Somebody had fallen, and Aunt Norie was staying with her until help arrived. I rushed forward to see what had happened.

Aunt Norie looked up at me, and her face was wet with tears. She croaked, "Stay away, Rei-*chan*! Don't come near. Don't look, I beg you!"

But I'd already seen Sakura Sato laid out on her back as if in slumber. Her eyes were closed, but her mouth gaped, revealing a few gold fillings. Blood trickled in a sticky red river down the neck of her white silk blouse. At the source of the river was an instrument: the ikebana scissors. I recognized the oversized black handles and looked to Aunt Norie for confirmation.

She was gone.

Chapter 3

J fled into the hall, the door knocking against
the package of plates I'd left outside. The
row of lights above the elevator showed it was on the
ninth floor, so I ducked into the emergency exit
staircase and began running downstairs. I heard
footsteps a few flights down from me. When I burst
out on the second floor near the administrative
office, I found my aunt collapsed in the arms of Miss
Okada.

"Sakura," Aunt Norie moaned. "Sakura . . ."

When the police came, I was stunned to see among
the stern-looking blue-suited men a young Japanese
officer with unruly black hair and warm brown eyes
that I knew well. Lieutenant Hata, of the Tokyo
Metropolitan Police, had helped me through a series
of adventures the year before. I shouldn't have been
surprised to see him there, since Roppongi was his

territory. He raised one eyebrow slightly as a sign of greeting but didn't say anything more, probably due to the presence of an inspector from the National Police Agency. The inspector was a bossy-looking man in his forties who was loudly asking questions of the doorman, the only male Kayama employee in sight.

When the inspector started querying Aunt Norie, she broke down sobbing on the shoulder of Miss Okada. Lieutenant Hata urged her to sit down, and the inspector began grilling me.

I was going over the sequence of events as carefully as possible when the school's elevator announced its arrival with an electronic chirp. As the doors parted I saw Natsumi Kayama's bright yellow and orange dress. She had her back to us and was arguing loudly with somebody in the elevator.

"I cannot stand the way you behave," she was saying to whoever was with her. As her companion hit the elevator door to keep it from closing and stepped around her, I recognized the cool young man who had been at the previous day's ikebana class. Instead of jeans, he was wearing a loose-fitting linen suit. He looked elegant and intensely annoyed as he stepped around Natsumi and headed down the hall.

"You can't do it. Don't try!" Natsumi hustled down the hall after him, but at seeing all of us, she stopped and bowed. "Oh, I'm sorry! My brother and I had a slight disagreement. I hope we didn't disturb you."

So the insolent-looking young man who'd been lounging in the back of the class was a Kayama. It made sense; even though women made up the vast majority of the millions of ikebana practitioners in Japan and throughout the world, men were almost always the school headmasters. It seemed unfair that Takeo would automatically inherit most of the money and all the praise.

"Why aren't you at the front desk?" Takeo asked Miss Okada. "If the police need help, you should have telephoned Mrs. Koda."

"She's not here! I looked everywhere!" Aunt Norie spoke shrilly, her first real sentence since the police had come.

Lieutenant Hata's attention turned from me to the Kayama heir. As he began introducing himself to Takeo Kayama, the young man cut him off.

"Nice to see you. We already donated money to the neighborhood beautification campaign."

Lieutenant Hata smiled tightly and told Takeo that he was not there to solicit funds. He explained to him that Norie and I had found Sakura Sato upstairs, and that the medics who had tended to her had declared her deceased.

At this retelling of the cold, hard facts, Natsumi gave a small bleat and swayed as if she was going to faint. Takeo caught her by the arm just as the elevator door opened once more and a half dozen flower-arranging students filed out. The ladies stopped short at the sight of all the men in blue.

"I thought the school was officially closed! How many people are in the building?" The National Police inspector sounded furious.

"I don't know exactly," Takeo Kayama said. "With

staff and other students, perhaps thirty."

"In a ten-story building? That is relatively few."

"Floors six through eight are vacant space," Miss Okada explained. "Ten is the Kayama family penthouse, and as you can see, the *iemoto*'s children are here."

"Seal the exits," the inspector directed two assistants. "Miss Okada, please help them."

"But our families are expecting us to come home to make dinner," Eriko said. She obviously had no idea of what was going on. The other Japanese women began murmuring, and the two foreigners in the group, Lila Braithwaite and Nadine St. Giles, looked toward me for help. Mari Kumamori, the student with a talent for pottery, seemed frozen in place.

"Sakura Sato is dead," I said in English. Lila gasped and Nadine reached toward her, inadvertently knocking against the receptionist's table. The calla lily arrangement fell over, spilling water across the glossy rosewood surface. The spreading water on the red wood reminded me of Sakura's blood, which by this time had probably flowed enough to make a red sea.

The National Police Agency inspector tapped the slate floor impatiently with the tip of an umbrella. "Shimura-san, we need you and your niece to accompany us upstairs and retrace your steps toward the scene of the death."

"I can't. Oh, please." Aunt Norie began sobbing, and Eriko rushed to embrace her friend.

"She is in shock. She must take a rest," Eriko said sternly to Lieutenant Hata.

"Yes, I've been trying to get her to sit down for the last five minutes. Can you help with that? In the meantime, the niece will accompany me upstairs," Lieutenant Hata said. I followed him into the elevator, admiring the way he hit the door-close button so swiftly that the inspector had no chance to follow us. Well, he would probably be busy enough questioning all the ladies.

"The National Police Agency heard what happened over a scanner. Murder is big enough news for them to get involved in Metropolitan Police business. Especially in this neighborhood." He raised his eyebrows at me. "I'm sorry, Shimura-san. How are you?"

"Pretty upset. Do I have to look again?"

"Not so much at the body, but at the scene. I want you to explain again what you noticed before and after you entered the room. I'm hoping that will help you remember more details than you told us downstairs."

I'd thought that I'd done a pretty thorough job of talking. I didn't respond, just stared at the elevator floor. There were a few cherry blossoms in a corner that had probably fallen off the bundle of flowers a student was taking home.

"It will take only a minute, Shimura-san." As we stepped off the elevator, Hata and I took off our shoes, leaving them with a line of footwear that had been taken off by crime personnel already collecting evidence in the room.

I walked forward in my sheer stockings with the worsening run in them and looked at Sakura's body.

To my relief, her blood hadn't formed a lake. It had not dripped much further than her collarbone. A police photographer tiptoed around her taking photographs, while three other officers crawled on the floor collecting pieces of dirt for later analysis.

Sakura looked the same. The scissors were still buried in her neck. But there was something different about the lighting. I said, "The window blinds were open when I walked in and saw my aunt and Sakura. Somebody closed them."

"We did that for the lighting. And to keep people outside from looking in," the photographer said.

The Kayama Kaikan was covered in mirrored glass; you could see out but not in during daylight hours. I supposed the photographer hadn't thought of that. In fact, the only reason the blinds were ever used was because the midday sun could be blinding. The day before, Sakura had asked for the blinds to be drawn so that she could see her work better.

"Sir, there is a suspicious package outside the classroom door." Another officer came in from the hallway to Hata, and we followed him out to Mrs. Morita's *furoshiki*. I explained the package contained a box of plates that had been consigned to me.

"Just in case, may I check inside?" Hata asked me.

"Sure."

"Dust for prints," Hata said, and the young officer untied the *furoshiki* and spread powder over the wooden box, quickly tracing the fingerprints I was sure would prove to be mine and Mrs. Morita's.

When the box was carefully opened, the other officer became very excited. "Someone must have stolen one of these antique plates. The box with ten spaces has only nine filled."

"I was given nine," I explained. "That's why I'm trying to sell them!"

From the way he and the photographer exchanged glances, they obviously thought it was a lost cause.

Lieutenant Hata rode the elevator down to the second floor with me.

"Do you need assistance getting home?" he asked.

"You mean you'll let me go free?" I was amazed, given my previous experiences with the Japanese police.

"You're not going to flee the country, are you?"

I shook my head. "I'm just going to northeast Tokyo. My new address is on this business card."

"We will keep you and your aunt informed about everything. This was a terrible thing for you to witness, but I know you will have the strength to get through."

Lieutenant Hata let me use his pocket phone to call my cousin Tsutomu "Tom" Shimura at St. Luke's International Hospital. Aunt Norie was too shaken to travel back to Yokohama alone, but she insisted that I not go out of my way to accompany her home. After I told Tom the facts, he said he would get another doctor to cover his shift and come to the Kayama Kaikan to take his mother home.

True to his word, a half hour later Tom had arrived, still wearing a white doctor's coat over a nondescript gray suit. A few of the ikebana students looked at him approvingly; he was in his early thirties, handsome, and without a wedding ring, perfect for somebody's daughter.

"How did this happen, Rei?" Tom's face was red, as if he'd run for miles instead of just stepping out of the taxi I saw waiting outside.

"We were in the wrong place at the wrong time," I said to him in English, which he understood well. I was tired of all the ladies listening. At first they had been upset at being detained by the police. Now they were fascinated, taking in every word for gossip broadcasts of the future.

But Tom had turned his attention away from me and was staring hard at Takeo Kayama, who was standing in his glamorous wrinkled linen and talking to the National Police Agency inspector in a voice too low for us to hear. I wanted to ask Tom if he knew Takeo, but there wasn't a chance. He was busy shepherding his mother into the waiting taxi for an insulated, expensive ride home.

Chapter 4

The Chiyoda Line was jammed with evening rush-hour commuters. Just twenty minutes, I promised myself. Twenty minutes and I'd be home. The afternoon before, people on the subway had steered clear of me because of my armload of cherry blossoms. Now I had been contaminated by murder, but there was no outward sign. Office ladies and salarymen were molded against my back, while schoolchildren filled the spaces under my arms. Following subway etiquette, we pretended not to be aware of how closely we were touching. Nobody noticed me as I silently began to cry.

Outside Sendagi Station I wiped my damp eyes with some tissues given to me by a young woman hawker wearing a doctor's coat similar to Tom's, but in the style of a minidress.

"Cherry blossom allergies, *neh*," the hawker commented sympathetically. "These tissues are distributed with the compliments of Nezu Natural Medicine Clinic. Please give the clinic a try!"

I sniffled a thank-you and began my walk up Sansaki-zaka into Yanaka, the Edo-period village that had survived World War II's bombings with many of its buildings, and almost all of its charm, intact. I adored my neighborhood, where there was a traditional cracker or tofu shop on almost every street, and the residents decorated the narrow pavement with potted plants and unchained bicycles. Yanaka had security and warmth and history like no other place in Tokyo.

Once inside my apartment, I double-chained the steel door and turned two deadbolt locks. Despite the safety of the neighborhood, I couldn't shake patterns that I'd learned growing up in San Francisco. I curled up on my futon couch and gazed around the room, lit only by two paper-shaded lanterns. They filled the room with shadows, a look I used to think romantic. That night it felt spooky.

Even though the police had let us go home, I knew that my aunt's future was not secure. Norie was the one who had bought the ikebana scissors that had been in Sakura's neck. We'd been in the school just fifteen minutes before the pruners had found their way into her throat.

How could my own flesh and blood be a killer? It was unfathomable. Still, I hadn't seen what had happened when Norie first stepped into the classroom and found Sakura. My father had told me that a person suffering a psychotic break could commit acts and not have any recollection of what had happened. When Aunt Norie finally spoke a few words to the police, she moaned about not being able to remember everything that had happened inside the classroom. She also had not mentioned her argument with Sakura. I doubted that would stay secret after the other flower arrangers had talked to the police.

I felt too shaken to make dinner, so I drank a cup of green tea and took a few bites out of a *senbei*. The salty-sweet cracker soothed my stomach and made me crave another. Before long I had finished the four-pack and walked into the closetlike space that qualified as my kitchen to throw away the wrapping. The blinking light on the answering machine stopped me, and I pressed play.

"Rei? This is Lila Braithwaite, from icky-bana class." The Canadian woman mispronounced the word for flower arranging the way many Americans did, instead of pronouncing it correctly as "ee-kay-bah-nah." I listened as Lila continued in her brisk, happy voice. "I'm glad you called, and I'd love to talk with you about antiques. I'll be at home tomorrow morning until eleven. I live in Roppongi Hills, number seven-oh-two. Call me if you can stop in for a visit."

Obviously she had made the call before Sakura died. I wrote down the apartment number but not the street directions. Roppongi Hills had been my last address. No doubt her apartment was even larger than the comfortable two-bedroom model I'd shared with Hugh. Going back would be horrible. I imagined walking past the concierge, who would remember me, and then having to ride upstairs in the elevator, stopping a few floors short of the place where Hugh and I had lived in unmarried bliss. I couldn't go back.

I dialed Lila, thinking that she probably wouldn't want me to come, not after what had happened at the flower-arranging school.

"Oh, it's you!" Lila sounded out of breath when she answered. "I just got back from the Kayama School. The police talked to all of us. It was absolutely awful. I wish that I could disappear into a hot bath for a few hours, but my little ones need dinner, and I'm going crazy."

"I'm sorry to disturb you. I was just calling back about tomorrow morning. You want to cancel, I assume."

"Tomorrow morning? Goodness, that call I made to you. I almost forgot." Lila paused. "I don't want to cancel."

"But you said that you were wiped out from the police—"

"I like to have lots of things going on! It keeps life from being dreary."

She was too lively for me. "Sorry, but Roppongi is hard for me to get to. Could we meet elsewhere?"

"The Kayama School is in Roppongi. You were there yesterday and today," she reminded me.

"Yes, but, well, the circumstances are a bit difficult. . . ." I was making a typically Japanese excuse. It worked well in the original language, but sounded pretty phony in English.

"I need to talk to you," Lila insisted. "Not about

antiques. About the Kayama School."

Why talk to me instead of Lieutenant Hata? I thought of how Lila had seen Aunt Norie break down crying in front of the police. Maybe Lila was afraid that things would be worse for a foreigner such as herself.

"All right," I said, compassion rising. "Can we meet somewhere besides your apartment?"

"Oh, I can't leave. I have three small children, and my nanny doesn't arrive until eleven. Then I have aerobics class, and after that it's a women's club luncheon. Every second after eleven is completely booked." Lila sounded desperate.

I buckled under.

You look so different, Miss Shimura!" Mr. Oi, the Roppongi Hills concierge, greeted me with a startled expression when I walked into the sun-filled marble and glass lobby.

"It's my hair," I said gloomily. My hair had once been short and chic, but I was letting it grow. The ends had crept over my ears, and it would probably take another year for all the different layers to match up. For now, I used gel and bobby pins and slicked everything back behind my ears. Richard Randall said the style looked like a low-budget Isabella Rossellini, but I didn't believe him.

"No, not the hair. It is your eyes. You look tired and almost sad."

I had good reason to feel sad. But I didn't want to tell the concierge about the murder at the Kayama

School six blocks away. No, he could find out on television or through a tabloid.

"I'm here to see Lila Braithwaite," I told him. "Apartment seven-oh-two."

"She is expecting you? Feel free to go ahead. I trust you in the building." He sighed heavily. "Is Mr. Glendinning returning to Tokyo?"

"No," I said flatly, realizing that was the reason Mr. Oi thought I was so blue. The death of an acquaintance was worse than the decamping of an ex-boyfriend, but I didn't want to get into it. I just said good-bye and went to the seventh floor.

Lila's door, unlike the others, was decorated with a few hand-painted children's works of art. I knocked carefully so that I wouldn't disengage the taped pictures, and Lila opened the door. She was dressed in her aerobics gear, turquoise leggings topped with a short Tokyo American Club T-shirt. A three-year-old girl was clinging to her slim thigh. I could hear the sound of *Doraemon,* an animated cat video, blaring from a nearby room, and two children were screeching somewhere else.

"What are the proper words of welcome?" Lila asked wearily. *"Irrashai?* The maid hasn't come in yet, so I apologize for the clutter."

"Mummy, I want crackers *now,*" her daughter demanded, and as Lila went to get her something, I spent a moment looking around the apartment, which had a similar layout to the one I'd lived in but felt so different. An army of plastic dinosaurs lay scattered across a Chinese rug, and sippy cups and brightly colored plastic bowls were ringed around an arrangement of cherry blossoms on the glossy paulownia tea table. A handsome Meiji-period *tansu* chest stood in the dining alcove, a protective plastic sheet draped over the top. Hugh had wanted marriage and children. I felt a slight pang, remembering.

Lila stuck a cracker in her daughter's mouth and carried her into the room where the television was blaring. She then shut the door and came back to me.

"It's too chaotic here. Let's go in the kitchen."

I cleared a few cereal pieces off a chair and sat down at a scrubbed wooden table decorated with a pitcher of pink and white roses. They probably had been bought at My Magic Forest, which was only two blocks away.

Lila dithered around, microwaving us two cups of tea. She put milk in both our cups without asking, but I had to ask her for sugar. She put it in for me herself, as if I were one of her children, while prattling about Richard Randall and how glad she was he had a suitable girlfriend, because his parents worried endlessly about him, and she'd not been able to introduce him to any girls who worked out. I rolled my eyes at that but figured now was not the time to tell her we weren't romantic partners.

"What is it about the Kayamas?" I put down my overly sweet cup of tea. "I mean, that's why you wanted to talk to me, isn't it?"

"I was wondering . . ." She trailed off, looking uncomfortable. "How is that you already knew one of the policemen at the scene?"

"Lieutenant Hata gets around," I said, adding, "There was a burglary in Roppongi Hills last summer."

"A burglary in Roppongi Hills? My God!" She glanced toward the closed door of the TV room, as if to make sure her children were still safe.

"The break-in was an extremely rare, isolated event," I reassured her. "Did Lieutenant Hata interview you yesterday? His English is good, isn't it?"

"I don't think I understood him, and I misstated the facts. I'm afraid I left a wrong impression."

"Did you tell him about the argument Norie and Sakura had in class?" I asked. That was what had worried me.

"No. He just wanted to know our movements in the school that day, and I guess I told him that I was somewhere that I wasn't. Now I realize that he's probably going to find out the truth, and I'm a bit scared."

As Lila spoke, she lifted clean glasses from the dishwasher up into the kitchen cabinet. Her cropped T-shirt rode up, exposing her slim back, which was marred by a few scratches. She must have gotten them roughhousing with the kids. Motherhood really was a formidable task.

"Don't be scared of Lieutenant Hata. He's a very kind person, and he's young, like us, without the excessive formality of the older generation. You can tell him what you told me."

"Couldn't you do it?" She made a slight grimace. "You understand both cultures, and your Aunt Norie is very influential in the school. By the way, I don't want to forget about the antique dishes you have for sale."

The transition, and its implications, were rather crude. As much as I wanted someone to buy Mrs. Morita's unlucky plates, I wouldn't tell the lieutenant stories that might not be true. In a cool voice I told Lila, "I'm afraid I already have a buyer for the plates. And as far as my aunt being influential, she certainly wasn't told about the Kayama students' private meeting yesterday."

Lila looked away. "It wasn't our idea to meet alone. You and your aunt left the Kaikan early yesterday. After you were gone, Sakura said we had to come back the next day to go over the final layout for the flower exhibition at Mitsutan. We assumed Mrs. Koda or another staff member would call Norie with the details. I'm surprised that it didn't work out that way."

I could accept that, but I still watched Lila, waiting for more.

"I told your lieutenant that I arrived at the school at four o'clock and went upstairs with my friend Nadine to the classroom. Sakura talked to us for about half an hour, and then a group of us decided to stop in the school's restaurant for tea. When we were leaving for home, we took the elevator down to the main floor and ran into the police." She took a deep breath. "What really happened is that I didn't join the others for tea until the last five minutes. I went looking for Mrs. Koda."

"Mrs. Koda wasn't around," I said. "My aunt and Natsumi and Miss Okada all couldn't find her."

"Oh, could that help me? That nobody could find her?" Lila asked eagerly.

"Lila, I'm sure that if you walked around the administrative office on the second floor, a dozen secretarial workers would have seen you. There's your alibi." I looked at my watch, thinking I'd wasted my morning.

"But nobody saw me! I didn't go to the second floor. I went up to the Kayama family's penthouse." Again her face flushed. "I know where it is because I'm president of the foreign students' association and was invited to dinner."

Until the day before, I had not known the Kayamas lived in the school building. Norie had mentioned they had a lovely country residence. I asked, "How does one reach the penthouse level? The elevator doesn't list any floor above nine."

"You ride the elevator to nine and go into a small hallway just off the main one. There's a private staircase leading up."

"Why did you think Mrs. Koda would be in the personal apartment? She's an employee, not a family member," I asked as a piercing screech came from beyond the kitchen.

Lila bolted, and I followed. The daughter who had wanted crackers was lying on the floor. A little boy of about four was sitting on top of her. He was flexing a pair of scissors in his sister's wispy blond hair.

The scene of Sakura lying dead with scissors in her throat came back to me. I gasped, and Lila's third child, a seven-year-old boy, looked up from the television to my face.

"Mummy, you said no more Japanese baby-sitters!" he cried.

"I'm not from Japan," I said, trying to gain composure. "I speak English, just like you do. We're from the same continent but not the same country. Can you think of where that is?"

"You're . . . you're from a weird place!"

"Hush, Donald," Lila implored while trying to pull the scissors from her daughter's hair. I saw now that the scissors were child-safe, made of blunt plastic pieces that couldn't cut flesh. I relaxed, but Lila was still upset. "You children are impossible. If you don't behave, I'm going to run away!"

"You already do. Aerobics, shopping . . . ," Donald, the television watcher, cataloged nastily. Had Richard really said Lila's children were fun?

"I'm so sorry, Rei." Lila didn't even look up. "We're going to have to finish later. Darcy's hair is so tangled she's going to need a cream rinse. And David, you need a time-out!"

David, the four-year-old who had done the bad deed, started to cry as loudly as his little sister. Donald aimed the remote control at the TV, turning up the volume to rock-concert level.

"When can we finish our talk?" I shouted over the din.

"Oh, I don't know! Come to the exhibit tomorrow at Mitsutan. Maybe I can slip away, get a moment of peace."

Would the Kayama School go on with Friday's exhibition after the death of a star teacher? It seemed callous.

I left Roppongi Hills with my old, troubling memories and a few new ones.

Chapter 5

J telephoned Aunt Norie in Yokohama, but
she didn't answer me personally.

The machine spoke in her soft voice, requesting
me to leave a message. I did that and spent the rest
of the afternoon at an auction, wandering past tables
laden with old prints, but I was too distracted to
make any bids. In midafternoon I left the auction
house and went out onto the street. A newsstand was
loaded with copies of *Asahi Shinbun*. The front page
bore Sakura's face, and right underneath it was a
photo of Aunt Norie posing next to a flower arrangement that had won Best in Show at an exhibition in
1996. The story jumped to an inside page, where
there was a recent photograph of Takeo and
Natsumi Kayama in formal dress and a year-old snap
of me with shorter hair than I had now, wearing an
equally short evening dress. How could I have

dressed like that? The dress was no longer fashionable, and looking at it now made me feel half naked. Since I couldn't read much of the story, I returned to Yanaka and stopped in at the Family Mart. Its owner, my friend Mr. Waka, had had so much success with his first convenience store in Nihonzutsumi that he'd opened a second one in Yanaka.

"Shimura-san, welcome!" my friend called when I stepped through his spotless glass doors decorated with cheerful green and yellow cartoon figures. No matter where you went in Japan, Family Marts were all the same, bright and sparkling and filled with comic books and good things to eat. The difference in this particular shop was a proprietor who ate half of the candy display when he was bored, giving rise to his gently rounded stomach.

"Oh, the wide world's ways. Cherry blossoms left unwatched even for three days!" Mr. Waka said when I came up to the counter.

"Is that another cherry blossom proverb?" I asked.

"No, it's a haiku by the poet Ryota. It means that when a cherry tree is not observed for a few days, the blooms will disappear. Just as a person who has been away from one's eyes can also suffer great change. In the short time I have not seen you, you have come close to the face of death."

"You know a lot about poetry," I said.

"My surname, Waka, literally means 'poetry.' Perhaps that's why I have a fondness for the literary form." Mr. Waka beamed.

"Well, I came to ask you more about news articles

than poetry," I confessed, holding out the *Asahi* that I couldn't read.

"You look hungry as well as unhappy," my friend said gently. "Go to the candy shelves and choose something sweet to perk up the afternoon."

I came back with a box of Pocky and chewed the chocolate-covered pretzels slowly as Mr. Waka translated. The *Asahi* reported that Sakura Sato, a high-ranking teacher at the Kayama School, had died of knife wounds. Police investigation was proceeding at priority speed. The death had been reported by Norie Shimura, a flower-arranging student, to the police.

"My aunt is a teacher, not a student," I objected.

"'Miss Rei Shimura, a civilian homicide investigator, assisted Lieutenant Hata of the Tokyo Metropolitan Police at the crime scene. The niece of Norie Shimura is of mixed Japanese and American blood. She is permitted to live in Japan because she has a cultural work visa. Her antiques-buying business had a gross of two million yen last year.'"

I didn't know what to be more upset about, the ridiculous labeling of me as a civilian homicide investigator or the revelation that I'd made less than fifteen thousand dollars in my first year of business. I had thought it was a decent start—at least I wasn't losing money—but the small figure might turn off some of my well-heeled clients. Then I shook myself. What was I doing worrying about business when I was caught up in murder?

"'In a related story, witnesses report both Shimura women were involved in a savage altercation outside

My Magic Forest, a trendy flower shop in Roppongi. See inside page for details.'" Mr. Waka turned the page. "The headline reads, 'Terror at My Magic Forest Is a Prelude to Murder.'"

The *Asahi* reporters had worked hard, interviewing almost everyone on the scene. A salesclerk at My Magic Forest recalled that Aunt Norie and I argued over a pair of ikebana shears, which Norie purchased with her credit card, taking the time to request a proof-of-purchase stamp on her frequent-buyer card. Outside the shop, Stop Killing Flowers director Che Fujisawa alleged that Aunt Norie had waved the scissors in a threatening manner at people participating in a peaceful protest. Che went on to declare that Aunt Norie was a typical example of the Japanese bourgeoisie, unafraid of the human costs of selfish pesticide use. Norie's violence did not frighten him, he said. In fact, he would give his life if it would stop harmful pesticide use.

"He's exaggerating, and he makes my aunt sound like a madwoman! She's not. You've met her," I reminded Mr. Waka. "We came in together when I was buying supplies for my new apartment."

"That's right. She said the food in my take-out section was not fresh, and my household goods were overpriced!"

"I'm sure it was a misunderstanding—"

"Probably not! Should I keep reading? Do you want to hear the official comments from Mr. Kayama?"

"Do you mean Takeo?"

"No, Takeo is only the heir, not the leader of the

school. And did you know the meaning of the *kanji* that spells his name?" Ever the teacher, Mr. Waka showed me the paper.

"Bamboo?" I guessed, looking at the character that was usually one of the first hundred students learned.

"That's right. Apparently the flower family's children all have flower-related names. The sister's name, Natsumi, means 'flower gathering.' And judging from her picture, she is the very flower of young womanhood."

"Mmm," I said. "What's the rest of the article about?"

"The report says that Masanobu Kayama, the sixty-five-year-old headmaster of the school, was preparing for a major exhibition at the Mitsutan department store when the incident occurred. In a late evening interview at his penthouse apartment in the Kayama Building, he expressed sorrow at the loss of one of the school's most prominent teachers. Headmaster Kayama said, 'Sakura Sato gave twenty-five years of her life to ikebana and had been awarded *riji* status, the highest possible teaching certification, two months ago. Her flower arrangements were creative and an inspiration to all, and her thoughtful essays on flower arranging were published in *Ikebana International* magazine and the Kayama School's semiannual publication, *Straight Bamboo*. Miss Sato performed demonstrations throughout Japan, England, Australia, and the United States, spreading the school's motto, "Truth in nature," to a global audience.' In honor of Sato, members of the Kayama School will plan a special memorial at the Mitsutan exhibition, to be held Friday through Sunday, ten o'clock to eight o'clock daily."

Now I had the answer to whether the Kayama School would go on with its exhibition. I was stunned. At the same time, I was intrigued by the fact that Masanobu Kayama had listed Sakura's accomplishments without saying anything nice about her personality. Maybe he hadn't liked her. She could have been a thorn in more than one side.

"So what are you going to do about your situation?" Mr. Waka asked.

"What can I do except pray the police don't arrest my aunt?" I was walking around the store, trying to find something to buy.

"You are an amateur investigator. Surely you can help," my friend insisted.

"I'm an antiques buyer, not an investigator. Oh, you've got *sakura mochi*." I selected a package of glutinous rice cakes wrapped in fresh green cherry leaves. They'd be good for a business visitor I had scheduled for the weekend.

"You must help your aunt. It is your filial duty as a niece," Mr. Waka lectured as he rang up my purchase.

I'd thought Mr. Waka didn't like my aunt. Either he was more forgiving than I'd thought or he was hungry for a continuing stream of gossip. I figured the latter.

❀   ❀   ❀

At home I listened to my answering machine. Richard had left instructions on where we should meet for drinks on Friday night. My mother wanted to know why I hadn't telephoned in a month, and gave me the number of the estate she was redecorating in Southern California.

I dutifully wrote down the number, but I knew that I wouldn't call. If I did, I would wind up having to say something about Aunt Norie's and my trouble, and that would lead to another push for me to come home. My mother was like that.

I turned the page of my message pad and on a blank sheet wrote "People at the Kayama School at time of death." Lila Braithwaite, and her friend Nadine St. Giles; Mari Kumamori, the pottery artist Sakura had been rude to; Eriko, who was Aunt Norie's best friend. Then there were Takeo and Natsumi Kayama, and Miss Okada, the school receptionist. There were a few other Japanese women students whose names I could check with my aunt.

Under "People missing" I listed Mrs. Koda and the headmaster, Masanobu Kayama.

Lieutenant Hata probably possessed this information. Maybe he had cleared everyone on my list and was looking for a serial killer. Of course, there have been very few serial killers in Japanese history.

I turned to look at Mrs. Morita's nine blue-and-white plates, which I had displayed in a kitchen *tansu* that took up the length of a wall. Each shelf of the cabinet had a door with a railing that protected the china inside from falling out should an earthquake hit. I wondered how long I'd be responsible for the unlucky group of plates.

I put away the notebook and dialed my aunt's telephone number, hoping against hope that she would answer. The recorded greeting came on, but as I began leaving my name, Aunt Norie answered.

"Thank you for calling so many times, Rei-*chan*." She sounded weary.

"How are things in Yokohama?"

"The reporters are outside the house," she whispered, as if they might be able to hear. "It is absolutely awful. Somebody even brought a futon and slept on the street! They are waiting for me to come out. My husband was going to come back from Osaka tomorrow afternoon, but I warned him not to, for fear of what will happen. Are the press doing the same to you?"

"No, it's all clear." Looking out my window, I saw a couple of drunken university students staggering down the street, but nobody else. I was glad again for having an unlisted address and telephone number. I had purposely left my name out of the NTT telephone book because a feminine name was an invitation to obscene callers. The only concession I made for running my business was listing a fax number under Rei Shimura Antiques. I'd actually received eight media messages that day on the fax and simply turned off the machine.

"Why don't you stay with me?" I suggested. "I'm not listed in directory information. My sofa folds out into a bed."

"When one is in trouble, she should seek shelter

under a big tree, not a seedling," Norie said. "Besides, I could not leave without being followed. They are stalking me, and I know they will catch up, because I have to leave the house tomorrow to help put together the exhibit at Mitsutan."

"That doesn't sound wise," I said.

"We need to be there. There is an allotted three-meter space with the Shimura name on it. To have it empty would be disgraceful."

"We? I would ruin your arrangement. Remember what Sakura said about my skills?"

My aunt spoke in the wheedling tone that she used whenever she wanted me to dress in kimono to show off to her friends. "If we hide from the other school members, it sets us apart. It is like an admission of guilt. We need to carry on proudly, as the Shimuras have done for many centuries. Our surname is common in Japan today, but please remember that my husband and your father are descended from an important family. We must defend the family name."

Maybe it wasn't a good idea to have Aunt Norie stay with me. I could imagine her lecturing me around the clock on my samurai heritage.

"Aunt Norie, I love you. If it's that important, I'll work with you on the installation at Mitsutan."

"It will only take a few hours," she said, sounding happy for the first time. "It will make such a big difference for everyone there. And . . . for me."

We hung up and I had dinner: a glass of Asahi Super-Dry beer and some old rice that had hardened in my tiny refrigerator, with a bit of pickled *daikon* radish and plum on the side. The meal seemed lacking. When living with Hugh, I used to cook elaborate dinners of grilled fish, stir-fried vegetables, and perfect sticky rice. These were the dishes that Aunt Norie had begun teaching me to make as soon as I was old enough to use a kitchen knife. She'd been very strict on how to cut swiftly but safely.

I flashed quickly to the vision of Sakura with the shears in her throat. My aunt had nothing to do with her death.

Then why, when I fell asleep, did I dream of my aunt slipping like a wraith into the room? In the dream she stood at my window, begging me not to look outside. I looked out and saw a carpet of lilies and chrysanthemums tossed haphazardly over the tarred street. The flowers were dying, their petals and leaves turning brown and ugly. I could smell the stench.

"It's a funeral!" my aunt cried. "My funeral."

In the weird, jerky way that one travels in dreams, I was suddenly standing in front of a coffin covered by white brocade. Tom was weeping. My father and mother were dressed in their travel clothes with luggage at their sides.

"No!" I gasped, and woke up with a horrible start.

My small apartment was peaceful and dark, lit only by the small red pinpoint of light on a water heater in the kitchen. I stared at the red dot, willing my heart to stop thumping, trying to get beyond the dreadful feeling that Aunt Norie needed me to save more than her family name.

Chapter 6

It's hard to pick a favorite department store in Japan, but Mitsutan has always been mine.

From the giant doorway on Shinjuku-dori, I entered a dazzling space lit by chandeliers and the bright smiles of young women dressed in pink suits and pink-and-white hats. I passed the Prada, Gucci, and Coach leather boutiques to take the slow route up the escalator. The store was made up of two eighteen-story buildings joined by walkways on four different floors, creating a gigantic maze of consumption. Six floors alone were devoted to women's fashion. Cruising past the foreign designer level, I ignored Chanel, not my taste, but sneaked a glance at the sleek little spring dresses on mannequins surrounding the Nicole Miller section. My eyes stopped on a familiar pair of lissome legs, and I recognized Natsumi Kayama in a short blue dress. She bent over to sort some roses, revealing the lacy edge of her white girdle—regardless of size and age, Japanese women adore girdles. Natsumi was making an elaborate bouquet, perhaps to go in the mannequin's hands. I wasn't surprised that Mitsutan would go to the trouble of using real flowers in a mannequin's arms, but I hadn't expected that Natsumi would be working two days after her big shock at Sakura's death.

My escalator ride took me past menswear, then the children's department, then an entire floor of restaurants. Finally I was on level twelve at Musée Mitsutan, the department store's in-house museum. A ticket to a show of Matisse paintings in the north gallery was a whopping four thousand yen, making the thousand-yen admission for the upcoming Kayama School show a relative bargain at about $7.00 U.S.

The cream and gold gallery was crammed with long florist boxes full of flowers and buckets overflowing with long branches. The women were so busy arranging that they didn't notice my arrival. When I found the area marked with the Shimura name, I was greeted by Mrs. Koda.

"Miss Shimura, how nice to see you. You've arrived before your aunt and Eriko-san," she chirped, as if I'd truly accomplished something. "The bamboo and lilies are here. I removed them from the florist boxes, cutting the stems under water and allowing them to rest in this bucket, where they can enjoy a nice long drink."

Did she think the flowers were human? I nodded,

as if I agreed, and pushed on with my agenda.

"My aunt and I came to see you the day Sakura died," I began.

"I heard," Mrs. Koda said in a soft voice. She didn't look over her shoulder to see if anyone was listening, but her thin shoulders jerked, as if she wanted to do that.

"Where were you?" I asked, belatedly realizing how aggressive the question sounded.

"I was in the building," she said, but didn't look at me, concentrating instead on moving a flower stem that had popped up out of the water.

"In the Kayamas' apartment?" I asked, thinking of Lila's suggestion.

"No! I was on the ninth floor, working in the *iemo-to* designate's office. You should have asked Miss Okada."

It would be impolite to bring up the fact that the receptionist hadn't known where Mrs. Koda was. I changed the subject, trying to cover up my uneasiness. "I think I'll walk around and see if I can learn something. By the way, have you seen Lila Braithwaite?"

"No, but she called to say that she was running late. Some problem with the nanny," Mrs. Koda said. "Well, as you walk around, take your time, but remember that we are supposed to be finished making our arrangements by six o'clock tonight."

I eyed the lilies, which were the same yellow as the flowers in my nightmare, and decided I wanted to avoid working with them at all costs.

Mari Kumamori, the student whose work I'd

admired in class, was winding a long green vine around a tall earthenware jar. There were four jars behind the one she was working on that needed to be filled.

"Did you make those containers?" I asked, recalling what Aunt Norie had told me about her talent.

She nodded, looking embarrassed. "They are very poor quality, but I tried to model them on some sixteenth-century Bizen ware."

"Do you work from photographs?" I was amazed.

"No, I collect as many old pieces as I can, and then when I've got them in my hands, I try to reproduce something similar."

I blinked. Bizen ware was very expensive. I wondered what her husband did to bankroll her collecting, and then chastised myself for being sexist. Mari's money might very well be her own.

"Your work is extraordinary," I said, wishing there were American-style assertiveness-training courses in Tokyo that Mari could benefit from. "If you made more of them, I'm sure lots of people would buy them."

"Ceramics is just a hobby," she demurred.

"You're more of a professional than a hobbyist," I insisted.

"Not many people share your opinion." Mari kept winding the vines as if she wanted to avoid my eyes. "Actually, I don't feel like talking today. I am mourning Sakura-san's passing."

Sakura had been so unfriendly to her, but I could understand why Mari was upset. I was apologizing for my intrusion into her grief when Aunt Norie suddenly appeared.

"Your friend Eriko hasn't arrived yet," I said.

"Then that leaves the two of us!" Norie said. "I'm so glad you came to help."

"If there's anything I can do, please tell me," Mari said. "My work is almost finished, and I have plenty of vines."

"We'll see," Norie said, striding back to our designated site. Once there, she bowed and greeted all the women working around her. She was making a tremendous effort to appear normal, and it was all for nothing. All the women bowed back, but they didn't answer her with any customary pleasantries.

"I don't like these lilies," Aunt Norie said to me when it became clear that nobody was going to talk to her. "They look too old. I'm glad I brought some extra flowers from my garden."

She showed me a pail of Japanese irises: dark, velvety purple blossoms still tightly furled. I breathed a sigh of relief at not having to work with the yellow lilies from my bad dream.

But first we had to thoroughly wash the bamboo, then cut each stalk to a prescribed length, removing the membrane inside so it could be filled with water. It was two hours of backbreaking work in a large tub set up in a staging area behind the main gallery, but at least it put us out of the eyes of the silent flower arrangers working around us.

When we came back to the front of the room, we arranged the bamboo in an upright semicircle, and I used an electric saw to trim the bamboo into a wave-shaped design. The easy part would be to fill each bamboo stalk with irises, then add a few harmonizing curves of Mari's vines.

"This isn't what you planned, is it?" Natsumi Kayama pointed a French-manicured fingernail at the rippling lines of bamboo. "Koda-san told me about your original plan, but this is different."

"The florist sent lilies that were not worthy of the exhibition, so we have improvised," Norie said in the falsely cheerful voice that had been driving me crazy.

"Somebody's going to have to rewrite the place card that's going in front of the flowers, because it says lilies, while you're really working with rabbit-ear irises." Natsumi sounded aggrieved.

"Actually, the flower is roof irises," Aunt Norie corrected.

"How many kinds of irises are there?" I was amazed.

"Our school's ikebana handbook lists seven. There's dwarf iris, fringed iris, and Dutch, German, and Japanese varieties," my aunt counted. "Anyway, I will take care of changing the place card."

"Oh, no, the calligraphy must be consistent!" Natsumi would not relent. When I'd first met her and she clued me in on my ruined panty hose, I'd thought she was being kind. Perhaps she'd done it because she delighted in pointing out flaws.

Striving to distract her, I said, "You have so much to do, Natsumi-san. It must be really tiring to be here after all your hard work in the women's designer section—"

"The Nicole Miller dress display." She made a face. "The bouquets I made for it are supposed to make shoppers aware of the exhibition. It's rather pointless work."

"I don't think so!" Norie said, as if to make amends.

"Young women aren't going to want to spend the time or money to walk around our exhibit." Natsumi had begun filling out a new place card for our installation, drawing clear *kanji* characters with a green marker. "They'd rather spend a thousand yen at Mister Donut."

I thought of my own recent meal at the local chain. Was Natsumi also a fan of their French crullers? Her stomach was so flat, it didn't look as if there was room for even one.

"Attracting young students is a challenge," Aunt Norie conceded. "In my generation, most girls in their twenties had to study ikebana."

"That was because they had to get married," Natsumi said. "Didn't you study in order to catch your husband? And then once you had your children, you stopped. Because your nest is finally empty, you've come back like all the others."

"I have always loved ikebana." Aunt Norie's voice shook slightly. She was not afraid to show her displeasure with me, but it seemed that she was being very careful with Natsumi Kayama. "Even when I could not travel to the school, I practiced at home."

"My aunt has her own group of students," I said, feeling defensive of Norie. "Several women come to her house to study each week. She's a real professional."

Professional. I had just used the word with Mari Kumamori. Even though Mari and Aunt Norie were called housewives, they were certified teachers of flower arranging. The problem was that they gave the token payments from their students straight to the Kayama School. From listening to some of the other flower arrangers' conversation, I'd learned that everyone making flower arrangements in the exhibition had paid a fifteen-thousand-yen "creative fee" to the school. I would have to figure out a way to reimburse Aunt Norie, who had paid my fee in advance. It pained me to think she had spent close to $250 just to be twitted by this bitchy young woman into whose pocket the money was headed.

When I was leaving Mitsutan an hour later, I caught a glimpse of a TV camera crew outside the main doors. They must have been denied access upstairs and were simply waiting for Kayama School flower arrangers to emerge. Fortunately, my cousin Tom had brought the family car to the store's underground parking lot. I said good-bye to him and Aunt Norie, sure that they'd escaped media scrutiny.

Now it was my turn to be evasive. I turned around from the main entrance and found a discreet employees-only exit.

"No hablo japonés," I said loudly, deciding to pass as a Japanese Latina when the guard tried to stop me. I was in a Latin mood, thinking of my plans for the evening. Richard had insisted we meet at Salsa Salsa, a Brazilian bar that had just opened on the edge of Nishi-Azabu, a posh neighborhood slightly east of Roppongi.

At home I changed into a short, flaring red slip dress appropriate for Salsa Salsa, if not my emotional state. I hunted for a pair of sheer stockings without any snags; not finding any, I went bare-legged. This was a bit unusual for Tokyo, where women wear panty hose under shorts in ninety-degree summer heat. The temperature had gone down into the fifties, so my legs were chilled, and my bare feet stuck to the lining of the black patent sling-back pumps, making squishy sounds as I walked. With luck, the bar would be noisy and nobody would hear.

Salsa Salsa was in the basement of a dull, boxy retail structure that looked like many other buildings on the southeast side of Roppongi-dori. Stuffed parrots guarded the turquoise doorway, which was appropriate given that the band playing that night was called the Lovely Parrots. A Japanese Latino man looked me over before waving me inside. The cover charge was normally two thousand yen, so I was glad to get in free. Entering the room, which was gaily decorated with bright wooden carved animals, I pressed my way past the salsa band and through the mix of good-looking, young Japanese career people and foreigners.

At the small, polished teak bar, Richard was talking animatedly to a handsome bartender who looked barely twenty-one. There was a queue of people waiting to place drink orders, but the bartender's ear remained close to Richard's mouth.

"You're early, Shimura." Richard looked annoyed when I gave him a friendly punch in the biceps.

"You're wearing my favorite dress. You must want something from me."

I ignored his meaningless flirtation and asked, "What's good to drink here?"

"The *caipirinha*. It's a Brazilian drink made with lemon and sugar and lots of love, right, Enrique?" Richard spoke in Japanese to his new friend.

"The liquor is called *cachaça*." Enrique shook his head, making the large gold hoops in both ears dance.

"Do you speak Spanish or Portuguese?" I asked Enrique in Spanish.

He looked surprised. "Spanish. I'm from Peru, not Brazil."

"That makes you a *Perujin*, Enrique?" Richard asked.

"They call me *nikkei Perujin*—Japan-related Peruvian. I'm not a regular *gaijin* like you, little blond one."

"I find dark men attractive. Rei doesn't. For her, it's always been the whiter the better."

"That's not true! I've had three Japanese boyfriends, but none of them worked out," I explained to Enrique in my high-school Spanish. "May I have a *caipirinha* as well?"

"A good stiff drink after finding a good stiff body," Richard said to me in English. "Hey, you told me that was a cutthroat class, but I didn't know you were speaking literally."

"Let's discuss it elsewhere." I didn't want the whole bar to hear my sad story.

"He doesn't speak English. Just Japanese."

Enrique went to the other end of the bar to get lemons and was immediately accosted by his long-suffering line of customers. Richard gave me a quick embrace.

"Sorry. I joke like that, you know, to make things seem better."

I let myself be held for a minute, relishing the human contact that I had so infrequently these days. "Well, things are terrible. And as for my aunt—you should see how she's covering things up, coasting along and insisting on taking part in that ikebana exhibition at Mitsutan."

"That sounds smart," Richard said. "What do you want her to do, hide in the suburbs? If she stays isolated, she could have a nervous breakdown."

The Lovely Parrots were doing a loud cover of "Macarena." A group of office ladies jumped into a line and began dancing in front of the band. The young salarymen at the bar surveyed the women moving like a line of matched dolls, arms rising and falling to reveal perfect bosoms, bodies turning to show off slim behinds. They watched without approaching. Only a gauche foreigner with a telltale Marine crew-cut dared to jump in the middle of the girls and dance along.

"Norie's all alone out there. My Uncle Hiroshi is still in Osaka, and my cousin Tom's always busy at the hospital. I invited Aunt Norie to stay with me," I told Richard.

"She'll drive you crazy!"

"Well, she's not coming. She thinks it will draw the press to me, and she's probably right. Tom drove her home from the Mitsutan exhibition. I can only hope they don't get ambushed."

"Did they attack you?" Richard gestured to my hands, which he had been stroking. They were criss-crossed with tiny scratches I'd gotten while stripping the bamboo.

"No, this is from working with bamboo. I need to go back tomorrow to make sure the arrangement still looks okay."

"Poor baby. You shouldn't let your aunt boss you into doing things like that."

"In a Japanese family, you have to listen to your elders," I reminded him.

"I don't let my family control me," Richard said.

"Oh, really? Then why does your cousin Lila Braithwaite think you're straight?"

Richard flushed deeply but didn't say anything. When Enrique came back with the drinks, Richard began whispering in his ear. Feeling like the prover-bial third wheel, I gazed around the room until I caught a glimpse of a booth with a coat peg on the side. Hanging from the peg was a denim jacket dec-orated with distinctive embroidery. I craned my neck and saw the environmental activist Che Fujisawa sit-ting in the booth, staring at, but not touching, a plate of food in front of him.

I stared at Che, thinking about how he had criti-cized my aunt for being a member of the Japanese bourgeoisie. According to the menu, the rice and beans he was going to eat cost twenty-three hundred yen. He was a real hypocrite.

All thoughts of social class faded when I saw Che

rise and greet the person he was going to have dinner with—someone I'd considered his enemy.

Takeo Kayama wasn't in his corporate drag, but a black T-shirt and what looked like 1950s Levi's—the kind Japanese people pay $700 for. Being in the antiques business, I could evaluate old textiles pretty well.

As Che filled Takeo's glass with beer, I watched incredulously. Then I realized I'd better get out.

I nudged Richard, who was writing down Enrique's phone number on the back of his hand. "I've got to go. I see two men who mustn't see me." I envisioned Che leaping up and coming after me and Takeo sneering at the ensuing melee.

"Which men?" At last Richard raised his head. "You haven't dated in months. Of course you should let these men see you."

"*Αδιόs,*" I said, standing up.

"No, I'm not letting this opportunity slip by. Enrique and I will make you look popular." Richard slid off his barstool and grabbed me around the waist. "Recognize the song?"

"I don't know how to do the lambada. Seriously!" The only thing worse than having Che and Takeo see me hanging out at the bar was being spotted making a fool of myself.

"I adore serious, clumsy girls. Enrique, can you help?" Richard curled his index finger toward the bartender.

"He's working," I pointed out.

"This is my break time for relax," Enrique said in English, no doubt learned from Japanese. He laid his cocktail shaker aside and swept out from the bar to join Richard and me.

"Oh, God." Before I knew it, they were sandwiched on either side of me in the middle of the dance floor. As they gyrated toward each other, grinding me in between, some of the office ladies looked envious. I looked stupid standing still, so I danced awkwardly on my three-inch-high patent leather pumps.

I tried to escape when the song ended, but another one began. Enrique tried to teach us both the merengue, holding hands with Richard and trapping me in the middle. The other customers were laughing and clapping. Then the music changed abruptly to U2. Or rather, the Lovely Parrots slowed down and began singing "Discotheque" in a mixture of English and Spanish. The shift in rhythm gave me a chance to slide out from between Richard's and Enrique's sweaty bodies. Richard pinched my arm hard but whispered in my ear, "Good luck. Now you're the belle of the ball."

Completely mortified, I ran straight for the door and into the massive Latino-Japanese bouncer who had let me in for free.

"Your drinks are not paid," he said.

I felt for the shoulder strap of my purse before remembering Richard had swept me up so fast I'd not been able to take it to the dance floor. I made some pleas, and the bouncer followed me back to the bar, where my purse had been perched next to my glass. Both the glass and the purse were gone.

I glanced toward the dance floor, but enough people had stormed the floor at the change in music that I couldn't see Richard and Enrique. I would have to handle things myself.

"Somebody in your bar is a thief," I said to the bouncer.

The man laughed. "*Sí!* You are talking about yourself, trying to sneak out like a *bandido.*"

"I had a bag with twenty thousand yen on the counter, and it's been taken!" Credit cards, address book, my MAC lipstick—all those things were also lost.

"Is this what you want?"

Takeo Kayama was suddenly standing next to me, dangling my small purse on its long chain like a used tea bag.

I grabbed it from him, wondering if he had taken it in the first place. I glanced toward his booth and saw that Che had vanished.

I opened my bag. The money, lipstick, and address book were all there. "What do I owe you?" I asked the bouncer.

"Two thousand fifty," the bouncer said, slightly mollified.

Takeo watched closely as I handed over two thousand-yen notes and one hundred-yen coin.

"I will get change," the bouncer said.

"Don't bother." I hastened toward the door.

"People don't tip in Japan," Takeo said, following me.

"I'm not standing around for fifty yen, okay?"

"You're dressed up like a little gladiolus. Where are you going?" There was laughter in Takeo's voice.

It was obviously the way a headmaster-in-training could speak to his underlings.

I didn't answer, just kept walking. I was furious about his participation in my little drama.

"Maybe you're going home. Twenty-five-fifty Shiomodai, apartment one. Yanaka is a rather old-world neighborhood. I didn't know any young people lived there."

"So you went through my address book? Either you want to date me really badly or you're planning to kill me." I stopped. What would have normally sounded like a snappy comeback was suddenly inappropriate.

Takeo stopped smiling. In a lower voice, he said, "Let's go around the corner. There's an *izakaya* where we can talk."

He was suggesting we go to a pub on the spur of the moment, as if I were some kind of pickup. Or because he was worried that I'd seen him with Che Fujisawa.

I shouldn't have gone, but looking over Takeo's lean frame, I decided that, angry as I was, I could still stand having a drink with him. Especially if he paid the bill.

Chapter 7

The *izakaya* around the corner was packed but, to my eye, disappointingly bright and ordinary. Students, young salarymen, and office ladies were squeezed into booths, the tables between them filled with bottles of beer and small plates of grilled sardines and rice balls. We had to wait in a line in the vestibule with everyone else. So much for being with the son of one of Japan's ten wealthiest men.

Takeo seemed blasé about the wait. He lifted a pack of Mild Sevens out of his jacket pocket.

"Smoke?" he asked.

I shook my head and said, "I wouldn't have thought you'd smoke, given your interest in environmentalism."

"Nicotiana is a marvelous plant. I became interested in it when I was studying horticulture in

California. But you're right, smoking is a bad habit. I've been trying to quit."

After five more minutes, a waitress with a pierced eyebrow led us through the rowdy front section to the back section, where we had to take off our shoes and step up to a floor covered with tatami mats. Here the low tables were made of pine, and the seats were blue-and-white print cushions. It was nicer than the booths, but I felt embarrassed to take my shoes off and reveal that I didn't have stockings on. I swiftly tucked my feet under me in the traditional *seiza* kneel and watched Takeo lower himself into a careless cross-legged position. Men could get away with that.

"Is this your old college hangout?" I asked.

"No. In fact, I've never been here before. I've just walked past."

"I won't ask you for any recommendations then." I studied the laminated menu.

"Are you able to read Japanese?" he asked, sounding honestly curious.

"Sure," I fibbed. Fortunately, enough was written in *hiragana* that I could make a selection. "I think I'll have the green pepper and scallion *yakitori*. Do you want to share a large bottle of Kirin?"

Takeo looked startled. "That's very Japanese, to anticipate the taste of the person with you. To understand without asking is very good."

I smiled, allowing him to enjoy his fantasy. I knew which beer he liked because I'd watched him drink with Che.

Takeo gave the waitress my order and requested *edamame* for himself. When he saw my eyes light up at the mention of the dish, lightly steamed soybeans still in their green pods, he ordered a double.

"You're a vegetarian," he said.

"Well, I eat fish. But I'd rather eat it somewhere a little more . . ."

"Classy," he finished for me. "This place isn't good enough. I'm sorry. I wanted to get you somewhere alone to talk about, well, the incident that happened the other day."

"Really," I said, playing for time.

Takeo was silent, but I figured it was his turn to speak. In short order the food and drink came. He poured the amber lager into my glass with a slow, relaxed tilting of his right wrist. His motion was so methodical, it reminded me of the tea ceremony.

"It seems unbelievable that it happened. I just cannot believe she is gone," Takeo said, his tone leaving no doubt as to whom he was speaking about.

"What was your relationship with Sakura like?" I asked, sensing that he wanted me to take the next step.

"It was very close. She became practically a member of our family after my mother died."

This item of information startled me so much that I spilled a little beer on the way to my mouth. "I'm sorry," I said, for want of something better. "I hadn't heard about your mother."

"It was twenty-two years ago," he said. "I was just six."

So he was the same age as I. My aunt had been studying ikebana at that time. I wondered why she hadn't mentioned that Mrs. Kayama had died.

"Was it a car accident?" That was the most likely way to die before your time in Japan.

"No. She fell down the steps in the garden at our country house. I remember the ambulance coming to take her away. Everyone called it *jiko,* the word meaning 'accident.' I believed it was something that could be fixed, like the time I ran my bicycle into a curb, or when I pinched my fingers hard with ikebana scissors. I did not understand that she had died until Sakura explained it."

"So how close was Sakura, exactly? Did she live with your family?"

"Just for a few months after the accident. She slept in my bedroom or Natsumi's in case we had bad dreams."

I wondered at the detail about bedrooms. Was he trying to make a point that nothing had gone on between Sakura and his father? Sakura's helping with the children might have helped her rise in the Kayama School, but I wasn't going to pursue that with Takeo seeming so sad.

"That's interesting about your family," I said, sliding the *yakitori* off its wooden skewer.

Takeo frowned, and I could practically see the storm clouds move in. "Why? Does it give you a different impression of me?"

"Yes." I had been surprised that Takeo was so forthcoming. I could understand his awkwardness with people now, given that he'd lost his mother and had only Sakura to guide him. I still was suspicious about his association with Che. Now was probably as good a time as any to reveal my hand. I cleared my throat and said, "One thing I wonder about is your relation-ships with others. Che Fujisawa, for instance."

"The environmentalist at Salsa Salsa? We talk from time to time." Takeo didn't bat a sooty eyelash.

"Don't you think it's a conflict of interest?" I asked. "His group is rabidly anti-Kayama. I have to assume that you, as heir to your family business, are pro-Kayama."

"I want our school to do well." Takeo snapped a soybean out of its pod. "At the same time, I want to support flower workers' health and the environ-ment."

I thought about my own mixed reactions to the message of Stop Killing Flowers and to the actions they'd taken. "Could you make peace between the two sides?"

"Creating cruelty-free flowers?" he said sarcastical-ly. "The MAC lipstick that you carry in your handbag is promoted as cruelty-free. From Canada, isn't it? I know it's very popular in your country and Japan, too."

"You went through my bag pretty thoroughly." I was outraged.

He laughed. "Don't worry, I didn't try it on. And I think the cosmetic industry is actually smart to latch on to things that young people care about. Protect the eyes of little bunnies from dangerous chemicals, protect beef from becoming somebody's dinner . . . it all goes together."

We paused as the waitress arrived with a second bottle of beer. I hadn't noticed that we'd drunk so much.

When she'd gone, Takeo picked up the conversation again. "Remember how I mentioned nicotiana?"

"Oh, right. The tobacco plant." I sipped the new glass of Kirin he had poured for me with the same hypnotic slow movement.

"I've been growing it in my country garden. It thrives there without any pesticides or much irrigation. It's a fantastic plant. I'm growing more of what I call humble plants—Japan's native grasses, wildflowers, and what many consider weeds. These are ideal materials for ikebana."

"What's your school slogan, something like 'Truth in Nature'?" I couldn't quite translate what was written in the front of my Japanese-language ikebana textbook.

"That's right. I think that going green really would be a way of expressing truth in nature, but unfortunately, my father doesn't agree. He says that if we stopped using imported or hothouse-grown flowers, we would alienate distributors, florists, and students. After a pretty bad argument we had last year, I stopped talking to him about it. He doesn't even know about my garden of humble plants."

"Why did you tell me?" I looked at him steadily. Again, not a shadow of discomfort flickered across his handsome features.

"I'm trading information with you. I told you something interesting in the hopes that you will do the same for me."

"You want me to go over the crime scene? I really don't think I should do anything that might, ah, compromise the investigation. If you care so deeply about Sakura, you would want her murderer to be found."

"That's not what I require. I need you to give me information about a certain woman. Her family life, her interests, her assets."

"Is this a girl you're seeing?" For some reason I felt slightly deflated. "Hire a private detective. There are a lot of them around."

"You'd be better. You are much closer to the person I'm interested in, and you actually have experience in criminal matters. I read that in today's newspaper."

"Who is the woman?" I asked, running through a mental list of attractive women I knew, Japanese and foreign.

"Norie Shimura."

My fingers tore through the soybean pod I'd been trying to open and sent the pale green orbs flying. "My aunt?"

"Yes, the one who brought you to the school in the first place. Don't worry—it's not that I suspect her in Sakura's death. The homicide investigation is entirely the business of your Lieutenant Hata."

"I'm not going to spy on my aunt." I felt myself begin to sweat through the thin silk dress.

"Hey, all I want is something you already know. Family history."

"Well, I don't live with her. I've only been in Japan for a few years. You should ask your father. They've been friends since before you were born!"

"I mentioned earlier that my father and I do not

communicate." Takeo picked up the bill that had been brought with our meal.

"I'll split it with you," I said, reversing my original plans. There was no way I wanted to feel beholden to him now.

"Sorry, that's impossible," he said.

I struggled up to a standing position. One of the feet I'd tucked under me had gone to sleep, so I had to wait a minute before I could hobble after Takeo, who had already paid the bill at the restaurant's register.

"Next Tuesday I'll pick you up to go to Izu. I want to show you my garden, and we will talk more about your aunt."

I was beginning to realize that Takeo automatically expected me to go along with every plan he suggested. I didn't like it, so I said, "No, thank you. I have work to do that day."

"You're freelance, which means you make your own schedule, neh? Look for a Range Rover outside your apartment building at ten in the morning. I imagine that parking is impossible in your neighborhood, so look out for me, please."

"I won't," I said, but he would not listen.

Takeo insisted on escorting me to the subway for my safety. I'd walked the streets of Tokyo many times past midnight, so this gallantry was ridiculous. The only seedy part of the walk involved passing by an "image club" outside of which Russian women dressed in short fur coats and high heels draped themselves over Takeo, cooing of the pleasures within. As he tried to hand their free-drink coupons back to them, I took advantage of the confusion to cut across the street and dash downstairs into Nogizaka Station. I didn't want him following me all the way home.

Once I had worked through my anger at how aggressive he'd been, I thought about the irony of the situation. If Aunt Norie knew that Takeo Kayama had asked me to his country house, she would be beside herself with delight. She had been trying to find me a decent Japanese boyfriend for years. Here was someone beyond her wildest dreams of economic stability—and he liked to garden.

But Takeo was interested in Norie, not me. Even though he said he didn't suspect her of killing Sakura, there was no other reason for him to be interested in Norie. He'd made a snap decision, given the circumstances of the crime.

Of course, there was the chance his belief could be replaced by something better, like the truth. Maybe if I elaborated on the boring details of Norie's life—the laundry washed every morning, the multiple-dish dinners cooked for hours, the conversations she had with neighbors about eliminating black spot on roses—he would reject her as a suspect.

I could even get him to sit down with Norie over coffee and cake, maybe my aunt's famous *gâteau au chocolat*. He would be overcome by sweetness.

I went on plotting as I disembarked at Nezu Station and headed home.

Chapter 8

Richard Randall telephoned on Saturday afternoon, just as I was in the middle of negotiations with a dealer who had come from Kyoto to my apartment.

"Enrique and I lost sight of you at the bar, and we heard later there was some problem with the bouncer. Mea culpa, babe," Richard drawled over the line. "Let me apologize at a cherry blossom viewing party tonight. It's bring-your-own-bottle, on the street running through Yanaka Cemetery—"

"Certainly. May I return your call later?" I said as pleasantly as I could. I didn't want Mr. Noe to think I was making a date for a drinking binge during a business meeting.

"Just tell me, did the lambada strategy work? My spies tell me that a young tycoon followed you out of the place."

"Yes, I understand you are interested in the screen with cranes, but I have another buyer right here. It's such a shame, but another piece will come along. Good-bye, Mr. Randall. My best to your family in Toronto." I hung up and smiled at Mr. Noe.

"Your customer from Toronto is calling at . . . midnight? Overseas customers are strange."

I should have pretended the call came from Los Angeles. I improvised, saying, "Mr. Randall always takes my schedule into account. He's a very gracious customer."

"Well, I have no interest in the nine plates you are trying to sell. If only they were a full set of ten, *neh*? I would consider the crane screen. I don't believe it's from the Edo period, of course, judging from the gilding on that corner," Mr. Noe said.

"I never made a claim of age; however, the work was stored carefully for many decades in my client's *kura*. That's why the gilding is still so attractive," I said. It was true. When antiques were protected from light and wind in the traditional storehouses known as *kura*, the quality often remained exquisite.

"Well, I could only give you two hundred thousand yen for the screen. I understand if you would prefer to go with your Canadian customer."

I hadn't meant to pretend there was a second buyer for the screen; that wouldn't be ethical. I thought two hundred thousand yen, a little under fourteen hundred dollars, was an okay price. But prices were always worth testing.

"I think if you check the price a similar screen went for at the last Sotheby's auction, you would find two-forty to be a very reasonable figure."

Mr. Noe studied me, and I tried not to flinch.
"What are the terms?"

"Payment due within thirty days. If you'd pay me
today, though, I could give you a discount of five
percent."

Mr. Noe scratched his chin. "I do like dealing in
cash. Very well, Miss Shimura."

We concluded business amiably over cups of green
tea and the *sakura mochi* cakes that I'd picked up at
Mr. Waka's Family Mart. Instead of serving the
sweets on my mismatched antique Imari, I used pale
green plates decorated with a pattern of pink cherry
blossom petals. Aunt Norie had given them to me for
my last birthday.

"We have had our cherry blossom season in Kyoto
for the last two weeks," Mr. Noe told me. "It's such
a shame that Japan's most beautiful city is no longer
its most visited. Whereas you certainly have the
cherry blossom lovers enjoying parties under the
trees in Ueno Park."

"Are the cherry trees in bloom?" I had been so
consumed with the Kayama School problems that I
hadn't noticed.

"Of course! But your *shoji* are closed," he said, ges-
turing toward the paper shades drawn over my window. "How can you enjoy nature?"

I had trotted downstairs for a jog earlier that
morning but had not opened the door when I saw a
Fuji TV truck parked in the road. It lingered all
morning, and I was careful to keep my blinds drawn
and my lights dim. It could have been there to report

on cherry blossom parties—or to report on me.

Now, as I discreetly moved the *shoji* aside to look at the avenue of trees running through Yanaka Cemetery, I saw that they were fully afloat with pink blooms and that the television van was gone. After Mr. Noe left, I would be able to travel unhindered to Mitsutan to refresh the bamboo and iris installation. I'd told Aunt Norie not to bother driving in from Yokohama to add water to the arrangement, thinking that it would be better for her not to face the coldness of the other flower arrangers again.

Mr. Noe gave me a fat envelope of cash that I deposited at my bank's cash machine on my way to Mitsutan. Saturday afternoon meant school was out, so the streets were packed with shopping families. The crowd was particularly thick around Mitsutan, and when I drew closer, I saw a familiar embroidered denim jacket. Once again Che Fujisawa was leading a Stop Killing Flowers protest.

A YELLOW ROSE MEANS DEATH TO PEOPLE OF ALL COLORS, one sign read, referring to Mitsutan's official yellow rose emblem. THE FLOWERS YOU ADMIRE POISON OUR YOUNG, said another. WHEN IS DEATH A BARGAIN? was the final cryptic message. The signs, lettered in Japanese, Spanish, and English, moved up and down as the mix of Japanese and Latin American–Japanese young people slowly circled the store entrance. A number of uniformed guards stared down the protesters but appeared unable to do more. Customers headed for the store merely bypassed the main entrance and entered through side doors. The protest was visible, but it wasn't stopping shopping.

Che didn't hold a sign; he was too busy handing out leaflets. When I came up, he didn't recognize me, perhaps because I had sunglasses on and was wearing jeans instead of a dress. Maybe I looked like a likely convert, because he murmured, "Sister, please join our fight against the death fields of flowers. Boycott the Kayama killers' exhibition!"

I took the leaflet and ducked into the store, which didn't seem to be suffering any from the protest outside. Mitsutan was packed with housewives hefting large shopping bags decorated with the yellow rose that Stop Killing Flowers was railing against, as well as affluent teenagers clutching Prada totes and toddlers with Sanrio backpacks on their backs. Everyone had a status bag of some sort. I was carrying a slim wallet tucked into my jeans, having been sobered by the near loss of my tiny handbag the night before.

Riding up the escalator to the gallery floor, I stopped off on the young designers' floor to look at how Natsumi Kayama had decorated the mannequins in the Nicole Miller boutique. The mannequins were dressed in orange and green silk dresses, and Natsumi had given them bouquets of fat yellow roses mixed with orange striped tiger lilies and trailing ivy. The flowers were undoubtedly imported.

A long queue of people was waiting to get into the Matisse exhibit in the north gallery. There was no line at the south gallery, which housed the Kayama show.

"How are things going?" I asked Miss Okada, who was in charge of admission.

"Mmm, not so well." Miss Okada sighed. "There is a protest outside. We've had the same ones outside our school building, but it is really embarrassing to have them make trouble at Mitsutan. And we're losing lots of money."

Once I entered the hall, I could see why she was worried. The spotlighted floral wonderland was a lonely country unto itself. Kayama School students dressed in matronly, expensive-looking suits or kimono treaded softly between the spotlighted arrangements. I viewed Mari Kumamori's ceramic urns draped simply with vines, and then Lila Braithwaite's arrangement of showy white orchids. So Lila had come through and put some flowers together.

Aunt Norie's bamboo and iris installation appeared like a graceful purple and green wave. The iris had been tightly closed the day before but had opened under the warm spotlights. Thank God I wouldn't have to do much more than adjust the flower that was falling out of one of the bamboo stalks.

Lila Braithwaite cut across my line of vision, rushing toward her arrangement. She was wearing a dark blue suit with an Hermès scarf tied into a big ruff around her neck.

She stopped when she caught sight of me. "Oh, hello, Rei. I'm just here for five minutes—my children are waiting with the nanny outside." She lowered her voice. "Did you tell Lieutenant Hata about me?"

"Not yet." I was struck by an idea. "Lila, you should be with me when I talk to him."

"With my schedule, that's impossible!"

"You can make it to a flower-arranging show but not to police headquarters?"

Lila's face reddened. "Well, nice seeing you. I'm on my way out."

"You can't go," said Nadine St. Giles, running up to both of us. "He's here. You've got to stand by your arrangement and take the criticism!"

"He?" Lila and I asked in unison.

"The *iemoto*! Mr. Kayama has come, and I believe he's going to critique everybody's arrangement."

Aunt Norie would be sorry she was missing this. Or maybe it was better that I was there instead of her—if he didn't like our arrangement, she would be devastated.

Nadine, Lila, and I ran into the herd of Kayama students, who had assembled in complete silence by the door to await the headmaster. He was entering the gallery with Natsumi.

Masanobu Kayama looked like an artist, from his long silver hair tied into a low ponytail to the ascot tucked into the neck of his cream-colored silk shirt. My eyes ran over the black corduroy Levi's covering his long legs and settled on his extraordinary footwear, a pair of Japanese flip-flop sandals worn with white cotton socks called *tabi*.

The man was a walking cultural contradiction. I wanted to gaze at him longer, but the student group had collectively swept themselves into a knee-grazing bow, and I figured I'd better follow.

The headmaster bowed back, stretching his back into a less-demanding angle, as befit his rank.

Afterward his eyes traveled over the students and came to rest on the small grouping of Lila, Nadine, and myself. He smiled with a tenderness that seemed completely out of place. I was too surprised to smile back, but Lila and Nadine beamed. They had been blessed.

"My dear students. I am humble before all you have done for me." Masanobu Kayama spoke softly, without an ounce of arrogance.

"On the contrary, we have done a very poor job. Excuse us," Mrs. Koda answered for the crowd.

"Your kind words are comforting in our time of sorrow, Koda-san. I can only wish our Sakura-san were here. Let's explore the work together. And we will start with the memorial flower arrangement. Who are the arrangers?"

"We are," Mrs. Koda said softly, indicating herself and Natsumi. Natsumi screwed her face into an unconvincingly humble expression and mimicked Mrs. Koda's deep bow. It must be odd to bow to your father, odder still to have him criticize your work in front of a few dozen people.

I regarded the grouping of Sakura's black drainpipes, standing upright instead of lying flat as she'd done in class. White magnolia stretched heavenward, with the soft pink tendrils of cherry woven through the branches, giving the feeling of a fairy forest arising from factory smokestacks.

"Of course, it is just an awkward attempt to recall the grace of Sakura-san's work. We beg your forgiveness for our poor arrangement," Mrs. Koda murmured, pro forma.

The *iemoto* walked around all sides of the arrangement, his sandals softly slapping against the polished pine floor.

He returned to the front of the arrangement and addressed his comments to all of us in a sonorous voice. "When one loses a loved one, it feels as if winter has arrived. There is a numbness, a sense of unbearable cold. Perhaps an arrangement marking a death should be one without leaves, without beautiful flowers?" He paused theatrically. "I think not. To remember the grace and style of Sakura, one thinks of our school motto, 'Truth in nature.' But that does not mean nature cannot be fantastic. This arrangement captures the unearthly quality of the ikebana that Sakura-san loved best."

The women in the audience murmured their agreement.

"However," the *iemoto* continued, "my daughter still needs to learn ikebana. She should have chosen some cherry branches that are not in flower yet. Because she chose branches that offer complete fulfillment today, this will lead to a less beautiful viewing for our guests who come tomorrow."

Natsumi smiled as if she was grateful for the criticism and bowed in perfect harmony with Mrs. Koda. I thought it was significant that the *iemoto* had blamed the arrangement's flaws on his daughter and not on Mrs. Koda. It was traditional for parents in Japan to speak disparagingly toward their children when in public. I wondered, though, if the *iemoto* was especially hard to please. Takeo had tried to suggest a green approach for the school and he'd been shot down.

The *iemoto* moved on to the next arrangement, which was by the arranger I admired most, Mari Kumamori.

"Kumamori-san, may I ask if you made these urns?" Headmaster Kayama asked her.

Mari Kumamori was already hanging her head. With the headmaster's words it just sank a little more deeply, her small chin hitting her chest. The flexibility of polite women was amazing.

"What a skilled artisan you are. The urns are influenced by the Bizen period, but their use here today reflects a modern sensibility. Nothing is too precious to contain our flowers," he said, making me glow with pride for Mari.

"And—nothing is too precious to be altered." Headmaster Kayama carefully unwound the vines from the first urn in the arrangement. He murmured something to Natsumi, who reached into the basket she was carrying and handed him a small towel.

The headmaster spread out the towel on the gallery's polished hardwood floor, then placed the urn on top. I wondered if he was nervous about spilling water on the floor. I'd watched Mari make the arrangement, so I knew there was no liquid inside. No need to worry.

"Hammer," Masanobu Kayama said to his daughter. Out of the gardening basket came a steel-headed tool that I wouldn't have expected a flower arranger to use.

Masanobu Kayama brought the hammer down, breaking Mari Kumamori's beautiful urn into a few

large pieces. I recoiled, as did some of the other
ladies around me. Mari just looked frozen.

"You will find that by integrating some broken
pottery, we will add a sense of movement to this sta-
tic arrangement," Kayama said, already moving the
urn pieces into the foreground of Mari's flower
arrangement. He trailed a few vines here and there
over the pottery shards.

The women began murmuring about how wonderful it looked, but they shut up quickly when the
headmaster made it apparent he was not finished. He
asked Mari, "Are these urns watertight?"

She nodded.

"Good," he said. "Mrs. Koda, could you bring me
some roses?"

Mrs. Koda hobbled to the back of the gallery, dis-
appearing behind an unbleached linen curtain. She
came back holding a bundle of white roses.

"Just what we need." Mr. Kayama took the flowers from her. Natsumi handed him a pair of ikebana
scissors and he snipped off the stems. My aunt had
taught me to cut flowers under water, but obviously
the headmaster had rules of his own.

Masanobu Kayama slid the roses into the mouth
of one of the urns. The vine-draped urns had
seemed serene and unpretentious before. Now there
was a bizarre contrast, the showy white roses out-
lined starkly against the dull pot. And the broken
shards in front looked to me as if they needed
sweeping up.

"What does Mrs. Braithwaite, head of our international students, think of the arrangement now?" Mr.

Kayama said in English, surprising me—and Lila, too, as I gathered from the way she stiffened.

"Oh!" Lila paused, her eyes darting from the flowers to Mari's bowed head and then to the *iemoto*. "I am struck by the contrast between black and white. Between clarity and illusion."

"I agree." The headmaster looked at Lila for a long moment. "Well, let's move on."

Mari Kumamori appeared so dejected that I wanted to stay back and squeeze her shoulder, but Mr. Kayama was already standing in front of Aunt Norie's and my bamboo fence. I had to be there to take whatever he hammered out.

"Well!" Masanobu Kayama laughed heartily. Natsumi joined in with a few giggles, but from her face I could tell she didn't know what was going on.

"At our country house we have a bamboo fence," the *iemoto* explained. "When my children were young, they once decorated it with some flowers from the garden."

"They were very naughty, completely beheading the iris garden on the day some people from the French embassy were visiting," Mrs. Koda said, smiling as she spoke. "I remember it clearly. Sakura sent you to bed early."

"She *always* sent us to bed early," Natsumi said, startling me.

There was an awkward silence until the *iemoto* said, "This arrangement certainly is enjoyable. You're playing with the concept of heaven and earth, placing the iris up so high. I like that."

He moved on to the next arrangement, but I

didn't really hear anything. I was too busy trying to decode what had been said. Did the headmaster really like the arrangement, or was he telling me that it was as clumsy as a child's work? Natsumi had looked at our arrangement when it was finished the day before. She hadn't said anything then about it reminding her of her childhood. But maybe that was what had upset her enough to argue with my aunt.

In the time since Masanobu Kayama had begun the critiques, a few more visitors not affiliated with the school had entered the show. One of them had brought a camera and was starting to photograph the arrangements.

"We are getting some business at last!" Mrs. Koda said. She had surprised me by coming up to me after the headmaster had passed on to critique the next arrangement. "Shall we have a cup of tea? I don't think the *iemoto* needs me."

"I would like that," I said, walking slowly with Mrs. Koda toward the beverage service. There were only two tables with chairs, and I wanted to be sure to find one for Mrs. Koda.

"Did you know that our school has its very own boxed tea and cookie sets imported from France? The black tea is perfumed with cherry, and the madeleines are flavored with almond. I know because I ordered the refreshments myself. Let me show you."

"Please just sit down and relax," I urged her, picking up a tray for both of us.

I made Mrs. Koda sit down and set off for the tea

service. A cast-iron teapot, the kind that imbues tea with a lovely flavor, was waiting, along with a tray of Wedgwood teacups and dessert plates. The madeleines lay on a tray with silver tongs next to it. I picked up a few cookies and poured two cups of tea.

Miss Okada appeared from behind the linen curtain. "Ah, Shimura-san! You are the first to try our refreshment center. I'm afraid there is a fee—the cookies are two hundred yen and tea is five hundred."

"Please keep the change," I said, giving her fifteen hundred yen. Once again the Kayama School was forcing its students and teachers to tithe. I realized part of my irritation was due to the fact that it seemed like I had almost stolen the tea and cookies. Well, there had been no sign telling me about the fees.

"The *iemoto* liked your arrangement. You should tell your aunt," Miss Okada said.

"I'll try. She'd probably be more likely to believe the comment if it came from you," I said while lightly sugaring my tea. Japanese people didn't usually add sugar or milk to tea, so I left Mrs. Koda's cup plain.

"Certainly. But she hasn't been to the school since the accident."

"Yes, it's been hard. The ladies aren't speaking much to her." Beyond Miss Okada, I saw the back of a woman wearing a fancy kimono and carrying a hot-water heater. As I spoke, the woman stopped in her tracks and then scurried off in the same direction from where she had come. The woman was probably one of the Kayama School members who had been ostracizing my aunt. It was a shame that I didn't get a look at her face. I could only imagine that she was blushing.

"I've been here all morning, and can you believe you are the first person to buy a cup of tea? Thank goodness! If only more people would come!" Miss Okada was refusing to stay on the uncomfortable topic I'd broached.

Feeling resigned, I said, "There are plenty of people in the department store, but apparently they aren't interested in ikebana. Natsumi Kayama told us she thinks the younger generation doesn't care about flowers."

"It is true, Shimura-san. That is why we need you to become part of our circle. You will be a wonderful ikebana artist. I can tell by your sense of commitment." Miss Okada smiled with what looked like phony approval as I picked up the tray of tea and cookies and brought it to Mrs. Koda.

"Ah, how delicious-looking. *Itadakimasu*." Mrs. Koda offered the brief Japanese grace meaning "I shall receive," and we both took sips of our tea.

"So how was it for you to undergo your first critique by the headmaster?" Mrs. Koda asked.

"It was Aunt Norie's work, not mine."

"How Japanese of you to give your senior credit. That is polite, Rei-san, but I have not kept my eyes closed. I watched you handle the irises yesterday and today. You are growing in confidence. You cut each flower to the right length without hesitation."

I had been working fast because I wanted to get out of the department store and back to my antiques work. I couldn't reveal that, so I said, "I'm not skilled. Mari Kumamori is much better."

"Mrs. Kumamori did an arrangement without flowers, just vines that are considered by the headmaster to be weeds," Mrs. Koda said.

"But she was doing freestyle!" I protested. "Doesn't freestyle mean free choice?"

"It lacked emotion," Mrs. Koda said. "Your work was exuberant. Hers was too quiet."

"I always believed quietness was considered a Japanese virtue," I said, draining my cup. Despite the amount I'd drunk, my mouth felt dry. Still, I wasn't going to shell out five hundred more yen for a second cup.

I turned to look at Mari, who was on her knees, touching the broken shards of pottery. She had remained beside her arrangement, even though the headmaster and his flock had moved closer toward the refreshments area, examining Lila Braithwaite's arrangement.

"I liked Mari Kumamori's arrangement *before* the headmaster broke it," I told Mrs. Koda.

"Shhh," she cautioned me, inclining her head toward Eriko. "You don't want rumors spreading that you are undisciplined."

I decided Mrs. Koda wasn't as sweet as my aunt had told me. In fact, I felt sick listening to her. I put a cookie in my mouth. If I could finish the snack, I'd have a good excuse to get away from her.

"It was interesting that your bamboo and iris

arrangement brought to mind the prank the Kayama children played so long ago," Mrs. Koda said. "With a memory as sharp as his, the *iemoto* will probably run the school for twenty more years!"

"Really? You think that Takeo won't be able to take over until he's"—I quickly calculated—"almost fifty?"

"Of course. Usually the takeover does not come until the death of the headmaster. That was the way it was for Masanobu-*sensei*. His father practiced until seventy, and then he took over. It was just twenty years ago."

"A few years after his wife was killed," I said, fighting the queasiness inside me. Maybe I was coming down with change-of-season influenza. If so, I should really consider buying a little white half mask for my subway ride home. Mitsutan probably sold them in their toiletries department. Or maybe Eriko had one in her purse. The thought of shopping seemed impossible.

"Not killed," Mrs. Koda corrected. "Mrs. Kayama died because of an accidental fall."

"Takeo told me," I said, putting my hand over my mouth as I felt myself start to gag. Yes, I definitely was coming down with something.

"You must say Takeo-san, or Takeo-*sensei*," Mrs. Koda corrected me. "I know that he is your age, but you must still show respect."

The nausea was overpowering me. I stumbled to my feet, preparing to run to the ladies' room. Headmaster Kayama and the knot of ladies were between me and the gallery exit.

"Rei-san? Is something wrong?" Mrs. Koda asked.

"*Chotto shitsurei shimasu!*" I bleated the traditional words of departure. They translated as "I'm going to be a bit rude," and for once in my life, I figured this might really be the case.

I was too dizzy to move in a straight line. I tripped over Mrs. Koda's cane and glanced off the side of the café table. I heard the porcelain teacup smash just before I vomited. A bizarre hallucination flashed through my brain, a vision of myself as some kind of grotesque watering can. I had never been so embarrassed in my life. Then I blacked out.

Chapter 9

When I opened my eyes, I focused on cherry blossoms so big and dazzling that they looked fake. I blinked and moved my head slightly. More flowers. Daffodils, azaleas, lilies. Was I lying in the middle of a huge flower arrangement? Beyond the flowers was a wall of familiar wood-block prints. I was at home, albeit with an extremely sore throat and a dull ache in my buttocks, thighs, and shoulders.

"Rei-*chan*! You are awake!" My Aunt Norie spoke, brushing her hand across my forehead. "Tsutomu, come and look at her."

I adjusted my head until I was looking straight up into my cousin Tom's face. When he began shining a flashlight into my eyes, I threw an arm over my face for protection.

"That's obnoxious," I muttered.

My cousin smiled. "Good verbal skills. Apparently there's no brain damage."

"I wanted you to wake up at home surrounded by beauty," Aunt Norie said.

"I couldn't possibly arrange all these flowers. Why not potted plants? They live forever," I said, feeling strangely weak.

"A potted plant is bad luck for a sick person. It suggests that you would grow roots and never get out of bed. Now, how would you like that?" Aunt Norie tucked a thermometer under my arm.

"The flowers are get-well wishes from your friends and colleagues," Tom added. "Everyone was so worried after you collapsed at Mitsutan."

"I got sick there, didn't I?" I suddenly remembered my image of the watering can.

"That's putting it mildly," Tom said. "You vomited and fainted on Saturday afternoon. It's now Tuesday. You were at St. Luke's until yesterday afternoon, when you insisted on signing out. I promised to coordinate your follow-up care, and you would ordinarily be at our house in Yokohama, but my mother decided it would be better for you to be away from the media."

I did have a dim memory of being in a bed fitted with starched white sheets. Another memory of an overflowing bedpan and a taxi ride with a lot of people around me. What else had I missed?

"I telephoned your parents to tell them about the crisis. They also agreed that it would be best for me to nurse you," Aunt Norie said. "I'm here for as long as you need me."

Now that my eyes could focus past the flowers, I

saw unfamiliar quilts, two suitcases, and an extra-large rice cooker. Aunt Norie appeared to have moved in for a while.

"This is rather a lot of fuss," I said. "What do I have, a bad case of the flu? My throat still hurts. . . ."

Tom shook his head. "Your throat is sore because we had to put a tube down in order to do the stomach pumping. And you received a series of intramuscular shots over the last forty-eight hours. You've been through quite a bit, Rei."

"Stomach pumping? Are you saying I overdosed on something?"

"You were poisoned, and we are still trying to determine the poison. I have my own suspicions, because grocers and home cooks do not always store food hygienically. I have seen patients who became seriously ill after eating grilled fish left out overnight on the kitchen table, or even mixed rice dishes left in the rice cooker too long."

"To refrigerate would ruin texture!" Aunt Norie chided, pulling the thermometer from under my arm. She handed it to Tom to read.

"Normal temperature," Tom said. "Did you eat some very old leftovers, Rei? Or perhaps you accidentally bought tainted food at a shop or restaurant?"

I'd had my usual breakfast of toast and tea. I'd skipped lunch but had eaten a few rice cakes that I'd bought from Mr. Waka. "There were some *sakura mochi* cakes I ate with my client. They came from Family Mart."

"The police found the *mochi* package in your trash and took it for testing. That seemed to be all right."

"The police went through my garbage?" Even though I imagined it was in my interest, I felt violated.

"Yes, and I promised to call Lieutenant Hata to allow him to question you once you awakened," Tom said.

"I've been telling you all morning that Rei's too weak. Just because she opened her eyes doesn't mean she's ready to speak," my aunt defended.

"If we don't find out where she bought the poisonous food, more people in the city could become ill or even die," Tom lectured. "It is her citizen's duty to share information."

I agreed with him, although I wasn't a Japanese citizen, and I didn't particularly feel like seeing Lieutenant Hata. All I really wanted was a hot bath. Standing up, I was still so unsteady that I had to have Aunt Norie help me to my bathroom.

"But, Rei, you should shower first. Please, I'll help you," Norie protested when I stepped directly into the tub that she was filling rapidly with hot water.

"I can't stand up long enough to shower." It was true. My poor, shot-up buttocks were screaming in protest. I didn't care that stepping into a bath unclean went beyond the limits of Japanese etiquette. It was my own bathtub, and as long as I didn't use soap I wouldn't damage the heating mechanism.

"Ah, you really do need me. Don't worry. I will take care of everything." Aunt Norie placed a warm washcloth on my forehead and left the room.

My gaze went around the tiny peach-colored room. As was traditional in Japanese bathrooms, the tiled room worked like a giant shower stall, with a small but very deep bathtub taking up one side.

Aunt Norie had shaken some bath salts into the water; a quarter cup of powder turned a plain bath into a bright yellow scented one.

I lay back, letting my hair get wet and fan out like strands of seaweed in the surreal yellow sea. I couldn't believe that I'd vomited in front of everyone at the ikebana show. I had felt fine before I went to Mitsutan. I could not have poisoned myself with leftovers.

"Rei-*chan,* I am coming back in." Aunt Norie poked her head through the door. "Tsutomu has gone away, so you can dress outside. But do it soon, *neh*? The lieutenant is on his way, and it would not be good for you to be undressed."

Not even my bathroom was private. But when I limped out of the bath, I realized I needed Aunt Norie to help me. I allowed her to bundle me into tights and a wool skirt and jacket, clothing that was slightly warm for the season, but what Norie considered appropriate for a police interview. She had also tucked away my futon.

"There, you sit in that chair and wait for the lieutenant. I feel terrible taking you out of bed, but it's not appropriate for a lady to receive a gentleman that way."

"But I thought you told Tom I was too weak to see the police," I protested, longing for the soft quilts and cushions.

"Tsutomu is the man of our family, Rei. What he says must be done." Norie sighed. "At least he won't be here for a little while. If you feel well enough, you can use your free time to write thank-you letters for your beautiful flower gifts."

My aunt whipped out a pad of stationery for the purpose: pale yellow sheets patterned with flowers. At the top was inscribed the word FLORESCENCE in capital letters, and following it was the Keats quotation "A thing of beauty is a joy forever; its loveliness increases; it will never pass into nothingness." Only in Japan, the country that had invented the word *salaryman,* could a word like *florescence* pop up on ladies' stationery. I could never make it up. The message didn't make sense to me, either—the words about beautiful things remaining joys forever. It was a vast exaggeration. All one had to do was consider the flowers around my apartment, which would no doubt be wilted within a few days.

Most of the participants in the ikebana exhibit had sent a bouquet. I wrote to Lila Braithwaite in English, and to Mrs. Koda, Mari Kumamori, and Natsumi Kayama in Japanese, with Norie serving as my handwriting coach. It turned out the cherry blossom bouquet that I'd immediately noticed upon waking was as artificial as I'd thought. The cherry blossoms came from Richard Randall, who either was being ironic or didn't have the cash for anything fresh.

Aunt Norie stamped the letters when I was finished and put them in her handbag to take out to the post office. Lieutenant Hata was due any minute now, so my aunt bustled around the kitchenette, turning on the small water heater on my counter to boil water for tea.

"You know how sorry I am about everything, Rei," she said.

"You mean about not being on hand when I vomited? Obasan, that was something you really couldn't have prevented."

"No, I mean that I feel regret about the whole business of asking you to study flower arranging when you didn't want to do it. I had the best of intentions, you know." She took a deep breath. "I enrolled you at the Kayama School in part because ikebana is known to lead to, well . . . marriage."

"But it's all women there!" I couldn't help laughing, although it hurt my stomach.

"Well, I thought the nice ladies who study there could introduce you to their sons or nephews."

"How can you talk to me about arranged marriages when you and Uncle Hiroshi didn't have one?"

"I did meet Hiroshi myself, and if you would be as lucky as that, I would not worry. But consider your life! You were with the nice Scottish lawyer for a little while, but then he left. Now you are twenty-eight years old and alone. As you lie ill in bed, only one man in Tokyo sends you flowers, and those are made of cheap polyester. Artificial flowers, when all of Japan is in bloom!"

I wasn't going to bother explaining that Richard wasn't interested in me that way. I think she already knew that, although I'd never explicitly said to her that Richard preferred men. I steered us away from the topic by saying, "Growing up means relying on yourself, not your parents or relatives."

"I can tell you about that!" Aunt Norie muttered, turning her back to me and searching my kitchen for something.

"Please do." I adjusted myself in the chair, bringing my knees up to my chest, which helped a bit with my stomach cramps. Takeo's request for biographical information on Aunt Norie floated into my mind, but I pushed that memory away. I was listening for my own benefit, not his.

"I was a first-year student at Ocha-no-Mizu Women's College, very shy and unsure of myself. Our school was holding a dance and I had no boyfriend to invite. In the end, I invited a male friend I knew from high school who had gone on to study at Keio University. At that time, women could not enroll there."

These days it was still hard for women to gain admission to top schools such as Keio and Tokyo University. I'd thought about trying for a fellowship there but, considering my poor *kanji* knowledge, had decided not to bother.

"My friend asked me to find a girl who would be good for his friend Hiroshi Shimura, who came from an old samurai family. I begged my friend not to bring Hiroshi, because I hadn't met many people of that class. I was afraid that I would use the wrong words or manners. We are no longer a nation of masters and servants, but I felt too insecure to spend time with a samurai."

"You were one of the wealthiest young women in Yokohama," I objected. When my father had told me that, I'd been very surprised, because Norie was the kind of person who did her own cooking and cleaning and never put on any kind of airs.

"Not upper-class," Norie said swiftly, and I sensed

an old hurt. "My father was only a pharmacist, and with his savings he bought some cheap parcels of bombed-out land in downtown Yokohama. During the rebuilding he was able to sell them for higher prices. Whereas the Shimura family had lived for five generations in a large house in West Tokyo—you could have built six homes with gardens on the property they had!"

"Dad never told me about that. All I ever knew was the apartment where Grandmother forbade me to touch any furniture," I said. Part of the reason I'd built a career in Japanese antiques was because I had been so resentful about not being able to touch such things in my grandparents' apartment.

"Your grandmother had to sell the house and move to an apartment to pay off the high inheritance taxes that were levied when your grandfather died. This happened around the time Hiroshi was an undergraduate at Keio and your father was already doing his residency in the United States." The water heater beeped its readiness, and Norie poured some into an Arita teapot to get the ceramic properly warmed. She turned on the water heater again and continued. "Hiroshi wanted to be part of Japan's industrial future as soon as possible, while your grandfather had wanted him to work in a more scholarly area."

That didn't surprise me. Although I'd never known my grandfather, my father had told me that he'd been a professor of classical literature at Keio. After the war, my grandfather had found it difficult to abandon the idea of Japan as the world's supreme culture. He had been forced to retire and, until his death, spent his time working on a manifesto that was never published but probably rivaled Yukio Mishima's work in terms of right-wing ideological passion.

"So what was Uncle Hiroshi like when you met him?" I asked.

"Well, let's get back to the dance. My friend insisted on bringing Hiroshi, and so I set up my friend Eriko, whom you know from ikebana class, to be his date. She didn't like Hiroshi because he was two inches shorter than she was. She danced off with somebody else. I felt sorry about her behavior and stayed next to Hiroshi, talking nonstop so he couldn't ask me what had happened to her. It turned out that no young woman had ever chatted so long to him. He asked me to go for a walk the next day to see if I would have anything left to say!"

"You almost lost your husband to Eriko?" I was stunned by the implications. How lucky that Eriko had been a snob about height.

"Actually, Eriko blames herself for making a poor choice. The tall, handsome man she married became a heavy drinker. Last year his company fired him. But don't worry about that. Here, please try the tea."

"Is this some kind of meat broth?" I had been expecting smooth and subtle green tea, but this brew was reddish brown and surprisingly salty.

"No, it is tea made from the beefsteak plant. It's very good for invalids," my aunt told me.

Regarding the mound of shopping bags on my kitchen table, I had a feeling I was going to be exposed to more foods for the sickly. I tried to suppress the feeling that I was drinking beef bouillon and took another sip.

"So you and Uncle Hiroshi decided to marry."

"*Decide* is a strong word for it. We asked our parents for permission. Mine were delighted, but they were too obvious in their pleasure. Mrs. Shimura and her high-class relatives thought we were trying to better ourselves." Norie sighed. "It became very painful. When Hiroshi's parents said no, he was very discouraged and said that it would be impossible to go against them. My parents decided that if they had several proposals for me from other families, that would build my value in front of the Shimuras. So they contacted a matchmaker who suggested I study ikebana and tea ceremony to become more cultured. These activities took so much time that I was forced to drop out of college. And I was afraid that in the meantime my parents would find somebody else for me to marry."

"Ah, so you didn't want an arranged marriage. Like me, you wished your relatives would stay out of your business—"

"Actually, I found that through their clever thinking, I was being called to drink tea in hotel lobbies with many interesting men." She smiled coyly. "The girls studying at the Kayama School had brothers, and of course at that time Masanobu-*sensei* was a young teacher supervising us, and he was very attractive. I kept in touch with Hiroshi through occasional telephone calls, and when he called once and my mother greeted him with the name of one of my other suitors, Hiroshi became jealous. He told me that he wanted to marry me as soon as possible, and he threatened his mother that if she would not allow me to join the Shimura family register, he would change his name and join mine. Mrs. Shimura decided they could not afford to lose their name."

"How were things with my grandmother after you married?"

"My family was worried that I'd be treated badly by Mrs. Shimura, so they built us a house all to ourselves in Yokohama. As a matter of pride, Mrs. Shimura never visited us there, not until Tom was born. A grandson who would perhaps earn a doctorate from Keio! She could not stay away."

"But what about girls? I met my grandmother when I was four. I wonder if she'd ever have guessed I'd come here to live for good," I said. What I mainly remembered about that first visit was how funny it was to lie next to my parents on a futon spread underneath a grand piano because there was no spare room in my grandmother's place.

"It was hard at first. You actually first visited Japan when you were one year old. Your father and mother tried to visit your grandmother, but she refused to see them. She made an excuse about being too tired. Your parents were devastated. They stayed with us that year, and each year after that until you turned three."

"Why was my grandmother so hateful?" I felt as if I'd been slapped.

"Your father had married out of his racial group. He was removed from the family register. And she really didn't want to see the issue. I'm so sorry, Rei-

chan. I don't mean to hurt your feelings. But that is the truth about your grandmother."

I turned away from my aunt's concerned gaze, trying to compose myself. This was a major shock. I never really had warmed to my grandmother, but I thought it was because she was so old and formal, so different from my beloved Aunt Norie, who had gone to the effort of enrolling me in summer kindergarten and primary school classes so I could learn what it was like to be a Japanese child. I asked, "How did it ever come about that my parents were allowed in my grandmother's apartment?"

"I mailed your grandmother a photograph of you wearing a kimono at age three, when you participated in a coming-of-age ceremony at the Meiji Shrine. I dressed you in a kimono similar to one she'd worn for her own childhood celebration. You were the exact image of her at that age. Her heart softened, and she invited your parents to see her the next time they were in Japan."

"She cared about how I looked. The surface," I said.

"She was a strong woman," Norie said. "But think about things from her side. After the war, she and her husband lost their entire world. All they had was their name, and neither of their sons married women befitting it."

"And now you are the champion of that name." The conversation that started off as an idle diversion had wound up making me feel bitter. I shouldn't have felt angry at my grandmother, who had died from a stroke years earlier—but hearing these stories, I was.

Chapter 10

The buzzer at my door sounded, signaling a visitor.

"That must be Lieutenant Hata," Norie said. "Sit politely, Rei. Yes, with your skirt over your knees and your feet on the floor."

I had pulled my knees up to my chest because it lessened my stomachache slightly. I rearranged myself into decency as Lieutenant Hata came in, murmuring the customary words of apology for disturbing the household. He looked around swiftly, then smiled at my aunt.

"You've been busy cleaning, I see."

"Just a little dusting. My niece is not one for housekeeping. How about a cup of tea?"

"Oh, please don't go to the trouble of making tea," Lieutenant Hata said.

"It's ready. You must have some." Aunt Norie

carefully poured three cups of the beefsteak tea and brought them to the tea table.

"You have been sleeping a long time. You probably do not know that it has been raining heavily since last night," Hata said, pushing back the damp hair that had fallen into his eyes.

"The rain is terrible for the cherry blossoms. They're barely opening, and now they are being shaken off the trees!" Aunt Norie complained.

"In an odd way, the rain actually helped our investigation of your poisoning," Hata told me. "Our pathology unit was scheduled to enjoy a cherry blossom viewing party yesterday, but it was called off because of the weather. That meant there were lab technicians available to run many different analyses."

"But you don't know everything I ate on Friday and Saturday," I cut in. "There's still a lot of work to be done."

"Actually, we have concluded that your stomach contained traces of a heavy metal." Lieutenant Hata said the *itadakimasu* grace under his breath and reached for his cup of tea.

"You mean I ate a bit of foil somewhere along the line? I'm sure I didn't eat anything that tasted like it contained metal."

"We found a particular heavy metal. It is a poison called arsenic. Have you heard of it?"

I nodded as my stomach went into a spasm. Psychosomatic, I hoped.

"Arsenic is serious! It is supposed to work over a long period of time. Can it still hurt my niece?" Aunt Norie demanded, as if the bearer of bad news was the one who had perpetrated the act.

"Too little was ingested for that to happen."

"Rei-*chan*, have you been eating in bad restaurants?" Aunt Norie asked crossly. "How terrible, when you could be living with me and having my home cooking."

The lieutenant and I exchanged glances. She didn't get it.

"The poisoning took place at Mitsutan, when Miss Shimura drank a cup of tea," Lieutenant Hata explained. "The sugar she added to her cup contained granules of ant killer. The ant killer itself is a mix of sugar and arsenic meant to attract and kill ants crawling on flowers."

"I know that product," Aunt Norie said. "I feel terrible about using it, but my peonies would be destroyed if I didn't use it."

"How interesting that you mention it." Lieutenant Hata turned his penetrating gaze on my aunt. "A container of ant killer was discovered in the staging area at the flower exhibition. Particles of dust and pollen on its surface matched that in your garden shed. Our tests make it seem that the ant killer container had been in your shed originally."

Aunt Norie swallowed. She opened her mouth, though nothing came out but a soft moan.

"It's all right, Obasan. I don't believe that you poisoned me." To Lieutenant Hata, I said, "Don't even hint at something like that! If you knew how my aunt has been the only true friend to my family since my birth— the one who made everything possible for me—"

"Let your aunt speak," Lieutenant Hata said.

"It is obviously my fault." My aunt paused. "I never keep the door of the shed locked. Anyone could have gone in."

"I don't know why you got the idea to snoop around my aunt's garden," I said, feeling fierce. "Are you searching all the garden sheds in the Kanto region? Surely others have pollen and dust that are similar."

"Her son gave us permission to search. We were there yesterday when you were at the hospital. It was not a matter of trying to sneak in, but speedy discovery of the poison was very important in this case of attempted murder."

"Am I a . . . suspect?" Norie breathed the last word softly.

"Do you think you should be?" Hata asked swiftly.

"I am guilty of carelessly leaving my shed open, and certainly guilty of not being with my niece to protect her against the poisoning person at Mitsutan. And I am guilty of disliking Sakura Sato, even speaking unkindly to her—"

"This is ridiculous." I interrupted my aunt's litany of self-blame. "As we all know, my aunt wasn't even at the exhibition the day I was poisoned. She wanted to come, but I told her not to. And I know the ant killer wasn't at Mitsutan on Friday, because I saw everything she brought in. Two buckets of irises. That was it!"

Lieutenant Hata held up his hand in a stop gesture and spoke softly, as if trying to calm down two unruly children. "We're not putting you in prison, Shimura-san. But we do need to keep track of you and your niece, as much for your own safety as that of others."

Norie nodded unhappily. Her mood was probably as low as mine. My throat still ached, so I bent forward to pour myself some more tea. As I did that, I caught sight of one of my antique kimono hanging on the rack behind Lieutenant Hata's raincoat. The early-twentieth-century robe, made of geometrically patterned orange and white silk, was hung in a manner displaying its beautiful deep sleeve. Now, staring at the sleeve, I had a startling thought. Mrs. Koda had been wearing a kimono with similarly capacious sleeves. Could she have tucked a packet of ant poison in her sleeve, flicking it into my cup when I wasn't looking? She, more than anyone, had had the opportunity to hurt me. I told Lieutenant Hata what I had just remembered.

"How can you say such things, Rei-*chan*?" my aunt said when I was finished. "Mrs. Koda is my lifelong friend! She would never hurt you."

"A lot of people you consider your lifelong friends haven't been very kind to you," I reminded her. "Remember the way the ladies didn't talk to you when we were arranging flowers at Mitsutan?"

"That theory about Mrs. Koda poisoning you in the individual manner is doubtful," Lieutenant Hata said. "The poison was placed in the sugar bowl for all to use. Therefore the intent might have been to poison many people at the exhibit."

"A terrorist act?" Tears came to Aunt Norie's eyes.

"Why not?" I asked. "Che Fujisawa and the Stop Killing Flowers group were in front of Mitsutan when I went in."

"We know that, but we doubt they are involved, because the poisoning at the flower show bears similarities to the poisoning death of Sakura Sato."

It drove me crazy how Lieutenant Hata chose to reveal bits of information at his leisure. But I wasn't going to complain about his conversational style, since this was the first time I'd heard that Sakura had been poisoned, and that raised a host of new questions.

"We saw her with scissors in her throat. Was the poison on the scissors?" I spoke loudly, because somebody in the street was honking a car horn.

"This is where the situation gets complicated," Lieutenant Hata said. "I would like to discuss it with you, but I'm afraid my language might be disturbing."

"Nothing could offend me," I assured him.

"When you found Miss Sato, you may have become shocked by the sight of the blood," Lieutenant Hata said. "But the truth is that there was only a modest amount of fluid on her neck and blouse. That is because blood had stopped flowing to and from her heart before the incision was made." Hata paused, looking toward Aunt Norie as if he was worried she would break down. She nodded at him, silently telling him to go on.

"Miss Sato was poisoned with the same type of ant poison as Miss Shimura, but she was not quite as strong. She went into a seizure and died. We believe she drank an individually poisoned cup of tea in the lounge and soon began suffering ill effects, because she excused herself to the other students and went into the ladies' room. The tea drinking broke up shortly after that, so someone could easily have gone into the ladies' room and found her. Or perhaps she met her killer before she reached her destination. In any case, her killer must have taken her into the classroom and stabbed her as a final gesture."

Why would someone bother with such superfluous details? I thought, but then reminded myself that flower arrangers lived for details. Flowers were first killed through cutting, then twisted and further altered to make a beautiful arrangement. Whoever had killed Sakura seemed to have made a grisly allusion to the art of ikebana itself.

"A flower arranger probably did it," I said.

"We aren't ruling anyone out," Lieutenant Hata said. "However, it is very important for you to think of anyone at all who might have a reason to want to cause you and your aunt trouble."

"I thought people liked me." Aunt Norie was weeping in large, gulping sobs. "Everyone except Sakura-san."

The doorbell buzzed again.

"Are you expecting a guest?" Lieutenant Hata asked.

"No." Aunt Norie sniffled. "My son advised that Rei couldn't have visitors until tomorrow."

"We can't face anyone right now," I said to Lieutenant Hata.

Lieutenant Hata walked softly across the room in his stocking feet and went to the window, moving the *shoji* slightly so he could see. He swore under his breath, then said, "I didn't expect this. Miss Shimura, why didn't you tell me?"

"Tell you what?" I asked with a sinking feeling.

"That you're involved with Takeo Kayama. He's waiting outside the door with a bouquet of flowers."

Chapter 11

Don't answer the door," I pleaded. "I'm not supposed to have visitors." Normally I wouldn't have been such a wimp, but the thought of having to smilingly receive flowers from someone with a hostile chorus surrounding me was too much. Why couldn't Takeo have sent his bouquet to the hospital, as everyone else had done?

"Let's sit in complete silence, and maybe he will think nobody is here," Norie said, surprising me with her shyness.

"But that would be a shame, as I want to talk to him. Hello, Kayama-san!" Lieutenant Hata said as he pulled the door open.

"Sorry. I must have the wrong address," Takeo said hastily.

Lieutenant Hata's solid frame kept me from getting a glimpse of Takeo, but it sounded as if he was turning around to leave. Relieved, I slumped back down in my chair.

"Just a minute, Kayama-san. Rei Shimura is here, if you want to speak with her."

It was too late to hide in the bathroom. I sat miserable and immobile as Takeo gazed past Lieutenant Hata's shoulder and into the small room crowded with flowers, Aunt Norie, and myself.

"Oh, you've got visitors. I'll be off. I have a Range Rover double-parked outside." Takeo bobbed his head at me in apology.

"A Range Rover? My street's only ten feet wide! How did you get it in?" My embarrassment turned to outrage. The neighbors would see Takeo coming out of my door and think that I'd taken up with a real space hog. For an environmentalist, he was pretty insensitive about issues of space.

"My niece has just come out of the hospital. She is so weak she cannot use the bathroom by herself," Norie said acidly. "She could not survive a car ride with you. Where were you planning on taking her?"

"Please stop, Obasan!" I was dying a thousand deaths again.

"I'm sorry," Takeo said, looking at me with new interest. "I didn't know you were ill."

"You brought flowers," Lieutenant Hata said.

"Not because I thought she was ill. I wanted to show her the kind of plants I'm growing—you know, to give her an advance look at my country garden."

"Please come in," Hata said, holding out a hand for Takeo's beaten-up-looking leather jacket. Takeo laid a bundle wrapped in handmade gray *washi* paper atop one of my *tansu* chests but kept his jacket on. However, he did take off his shoes and step up from the cement entryway onto the *tatami* flooring.

"Didn't you hear about what happened at the Mitsutan flower show?" Hata asked.

"I stopped in early Saturday morning for a check before the show opened. I couldn't stay. With Sakura's death, everything has been so chaotic." He gave a helpless shrug.

"So chaotic you were planning a romantic getaway this afternoon with Rei to the country?" Hata said in an almost-mocking tone. "Didn't your father and sister mention Miss Shimura's violent case of poisoning?"

"I haven't spoken to my father and sister all weekend," Takeo said.

"Or to me. I've been trying to have an interview with you for a while," Lieutenant Hata said meaningfully.

"Right. Well, let's plan on talking first thing tomorrow, *neh*?" he said briskly. "Rei-san, give me a call when you feel better."

"My niece does not telephone young men," Norie said acidly.

"Actually," I said, rebellion flaring in me, "I'd like to talk to Takeo-san right now. Lieutenant Hata, if you want to have your interview, why don't you wait a few minutes? If you go into the kitchen with Aunt Norie, I'm sure she can make you another cup of that nice beefsteak tea."

*   *   *

When they had gone into the kitchenette, which was only three feet away from my chair, Takeo jerked his head toward the door.

"Over here," he mouthed.

Let the crown prince come to me, I thought. I smiled in what I thought was a feeble manner and said, "I'm too weak to stand."

Takeo came over, covering the length of the small room in five strides. He got down on a knee and whispered in my ear, "You should have called me to cancel. I wasn't expecting to see *her*. Or him."

"I never said I'd go to Izu with you! How dare you show up uninvited?" I whispered back.

"Hey, I understand that pain may be making you ruder than usual. But don't worry. I ate some bad chicken once, and the whole drama was over within a few days. I certainly didn't make anyone take me to the hospital!"

"I was poisoned by arsenic, not salmonella!"

Takeo drew back and stared at me. As this happened, I felt a sharp tinge of regret at having spoken. Maybe it was information that Lieutenant Hata wanted to keep quiet for the purposes of his investigation.

"Why—why would anyone want to kill you?" Takeo practically breathed his question, his voice was so low.

"That's what we were trying to figure out before you interrupted us." I looked at him hard, deciding to withhold Lieutenant Hata's hypothesis that a large group of shoppers and flower arrangers at Mitsutan were the intended victims. Let that come out in their interview if Hata wanted. For the time being, Takeo remained on my list of potential slayers, and I would be careful what I said.

"Strange things are happening. I wanted to tell you in the car. Now taking you out to talk seems impossible."

"What strange things?"

"Not so quick. I'll tell you in exchange for information from you. About the matter we discussed." He jerked his head toward the kitchenette. "When are they leaving?"

"They aren't. I mean, Lieutenant Hata's going to have to go back to his office, but my aunt's staying. I can't take care of myself. After all, I nearly lost my life."

Takeo looked down at the *tatami,* and I imagined that my poignant statement had made an impact. But no—he was only picking up a white rose that had dropped from one of the many vases of get-well flowers.

"I hate these stupid imported flowers," he said quietly. "Compare their blowsy, over-the-top fullness with the simple beauty of the bittersweet I brought for you."

I looked over at the paper-wrapped bundle and saw a few branches extending outward that had tiny yellow flowers. So that was bittersweet. It looked more like a weed than a flower.

Takeo carefully inserted the fallen rose in with its fellow flowers in a vase on the tea table. As he did this, I saw dirt under the fingernails of both hands. It seemed odd for someone of his rank. I doubted his father or Natsumi had ever done a bit of weeding.

❋   ❋   ❋

Rei-*chan*, let's agree that from now on, you will not see Takeo Kayama."

I could hardly believe what I was hearing from the aunt who so desperately wanted me to be married. Ever since Takeo had shot out of the apartment, my aunt had been on a tear: I should have nothing to do with the Kayamas, Natsumi was a rude girl, and her brother was even worse.

"You don't understand," I said, shutting my eyes against the sight of her angry face. "I'm not interested in Takeo."

"But he's interested in you!" Norie cried. "To have brought you flowers!"

"I think he brought them to make a political point," I said. "He's trying to expose me to all those weedy things he believes in."

"I'm sorry that I didn't ticket his illegally parked car," Lieutenant Hata said. He'd run outside after Takeo but had come back alone, wet and grumpy. "I ran behind the Range Rover for two blocks, but he would not stop. Now I'll have to go to the Kayama Kaikan and confront him."

"Just a minute, Lieutenant! I want to show you something." I smiled at Norie and said, "Obasan, would you bring me the papers in my top desk drawer?"

When I had the list I'd drawn up earlier in hand, I put an asterisk next to the names of the people who had been present both at Sakura's slaying and also at my poisoning at the Mitsutan exhibition. There were only a few names that crossed over both ways: Lila Braithwaite, Natsumi Kayama, Eriko, and Mari Kumamori. I hated to mention Mari's name, given that she'd suffered so much discrimination, but I was trying to be complete.

"You forgot to list Takeo Kayama," Lieutenant Hata said. "He and Natsumi rode down in the elevator together at the school right after I arrived with the other police. And he just now admitted to being on the premises earlier in the morning. He could have tampered with the sugar."

"Okay, count him in." I felt a bit shaken at the thought of Takeo as a murderer, but Lieutenant Hata was right.

"May I say something?" Aunt Norie asked. Without waiting for a response, she said, "I've been thinking about something the lieutenant said before we were interrupted. If the killer's goal is to disgrace the Kayama School, he or she must be an outsider. There is every chance that an environmental terrorist could have walked into the Kayama Kaikan and Mitsutan to conduct the crimes."

"Environmental activist, not terrorist," I corrected my aunt. "And if you're thinking about outsiders, what about considering members of rival ikebana schools? Wouldn't you say that the Kayama School is competitive with the Sogetsu School? Could one of their people be envious of the Kayamas?"

"How do you know about the Sogetsu School? I thought you didn't like flower arranging!" Aunt Norie demanded.

"Obasan, their headmaster is very famous. He

made a film in the sixties called *Woman in the Dunes*."

"Still, he's not as artistic as our headmaster!" Norie sniffed.

"*Your* headmaster is too cold for my taste," I said. "During the critique session, Mr. Kayama smashed up Mari Kumamori's pottery and called it an improvement. I thought that was a terribly cruel thing to do. No wonder Sakura was so mean to her students. She learned from him."

"I also learned directly from Masanobu-*sensei*. You have seen me teaching classes in my home. Do you believe I'm cruel to students?"

"Of course not. I was just saying—" I cut myself off, realizing that I was on the verge of fighting with my aunt.

Lieutenant Hata cleared his throat. "Ladies, I think we have covered all the necessary business. Miss Shimura, I will examine your suspect list. However, the most important thing you could do for me would be to try to remember what happened at the Mitsutan exhibit—particularly any people going to and from the refreshments area. You may recall a detail that is important to the investigation."

After he left, I tried to make peace with Aunt Norie. I started by saying, "Please understand that I did not invite Takeo here to see me. But what's so wrong with him, in your opinion?"

She pressed her lips together. "Rei, he's not the right one for you."

I agree, I should have said, but couldn't, as I recalled the memory of Takeo's lips moving against my ear. He had gotten that close in order to keep

Norie and Lieutenant Hata from hearing his words, but just participating in the act had made me feel disloyal to the memory of Hugh Glendinning.

"Obasan, just forty-five minutes ago you were saying that you wanted me to get together with a Japanese man from a good family," I reminded her. "I thought you adored the Kayamas."

"As Lieutenant Hata pointed out, he could be the killer! And even if he is innocent, he is bad for you."

"We're acquaintances—not even friends. Actually, at some time I did want to have Takeo over for tea, and I would love for you to be there, to get to know him a little better. . . ."

"I've known him since he was a baby," Norie said shortly. "I don't need an introduction. Now, how about doing something to take our minds off the Kayamas and their troubles? Let's rearrange the flowers that were sent to us. Don't strain yourself by moving from your chair, Rei-*chan*. I will set up everything on the tea table in front of you."

Because I didn't own any proper ikebana vases or dishes, Aunt Norie rummaged through the china in my cabinets looking for flat-bottomed bowls that would have enough room for an arrangement. She picked up one of the plates I had taken on consignment from Mrs. Morita.

"The tenth plate doesn't exist," I said, answering the unspoken question. "It's an odd set that I'm hoping to sell. Do you know any likely clients?"

"I'll think about it. Too bad you didn't invest in some ikebana containers. I suppose we could put some flowers in those small hibachi." She gestured toward some sizable blue-and-white urns that had been used as charcoal braziers in earlier times. "The daffodils will look handsome against the blue and white pattern, but of course it would wind up being more of a Western arrangement than an Eastern one."

"I don't like to use things I hope to sell." I should have saved my breath. She placed the two hibachi in front of me with an extra bowl of water, a pair of scissors, and a *kenzan*, a small iron weight topped with short spikes that held flowers firmly upright. In the West, a *kenzan* was called a "frog," a name that had never made sense to me.

"I'm going outside to mail your thank-you notes and to pick up some groceries for supper. With the telephone at your side, you should be safe for a few minutes."

"Yes, yes," I agreed, waving her toward the door.

"Don't answer the door to anyone." With that final warning, she left.

As soon as my aunt departed, I painfully made my way to the telephone. I took the cordless receiver, and when I was rearranged in cushioned comfort, I dialed Richard Randall at the office.

"It's me. Can you come over and save me from my aunt?" I pleaded.

"Oh, you're finally well enough! When I called to find out why you didn't show up Saturday night, your aunt said you had to go to the hospital because of food poisoning. So what did you eat, pasta primavera past its prime?"

"A tasty spoonful of ant killer. Could you come over right now?"

"I'd love to, Rei, but I can't. I'm running late."

I looked at my watch. "Five o'clock? It's still early."

"I'm supposed to go to the Cherry Blossom Blowout party at Salsa Salsa. Enrique is expecting me. I couldn't possibly cancel." He paused. "We could stop by afterward, maybe bring you their special cocktail to go. It's vodka served on the rocks, and the rocks have cherry blossoms frozen within. Of course, the ice will have melted by the time I get to Yanaka, but I could add more vodka if the drink is weak."

"Have you forgotten my stomach already?" I didn't hide my irritation. "The last thing I want is vodka. And I'd really like to talk things over with just *you*."

"Rei, you're going to have to get used to my spending time with Enrique. We're deeply involved."

"Isn't that rather sudden?"

"We just *know*," said Richard, with the infuriatingly smug tone of a man in love.

"So when are you going to introduce him to Lila?" I said, still on the offensive.

Richard lowered his voice. "I don't think she could handle it."

"Richard, she's a pretty sophisticated woman. So sophisticated, in fact, that I've got a few questions about her myself."

"Well, I could stop by, but it couldn't be before midnight. And the trains stop after that, you know, so I'd have to sleep over."

•

"That won't work," I said grimly. "My aunt is using the spare futon. And even though she knows your orientation, she'd hardly approve of us sharing a bed."

"It sounds as if your apartment has turned into a Catholic-school dormitory," Richard snorted. "I'll try and sneak by sometime. But I'm sorry, I absolutely have to leave for Salsa Salsa now if I'm going to catch the early-bird drinks special."

My aunt was staying away longer than I'd expected. I made a small arrangement with the roses, and then I managed to limp over to the *tansu* to retrieve the bouquet of bittersweet that Takeo had brought me. I decided it wasn't as weedy as I'd first thought. The slim branches had plenty of elegant, natural curvature—I did not need to bend them into tortuous angles.

I made an arrangement of bittersweet with the azaleas Mrs. Koda had sent, but their trumpetlike shapes seemed wrong next to the demure bittersweet. I decided to work with the bittersweet alone. Aunt Norie had left my lesson book handy, inspiring me to follow an assignment from the middle of the book that required the use of one material. I was just doing it six months early.

As the hours went by, my apartment grew dark. I turned on a lamp and wished that I hadn't put away my small portable gas heaters in a fit of confidence about the spring weather. The day's dampness left me positively chilled. I wasn't feeling strong enough to retrieve the heaters from the top shelf of my closet, so I slipped on two sweaters and an extra pair of socks and settled in to watch the nightly news.

The anchorman reported that over the past three days, 150 people had been treated at Tokyo hospitals for alcohol poisoning that occurred during cherry blossom viewing parties. The day's rain would provide a welcome lull in emergency room admissions. The weather was expected to improve the next day, though, and that might bring in a new rash of crashed-out cherry blossom drunks.

Following the news, a game show came on in which the contestants all wore cherry blossom headgear. Feeling bored, I switched to the next channel, which was showing a documentary about cherry tree farming. The camera zoomed into the center of a pale pink flower, revealing a crawling bug of some sort. Disgusting. I switched off the television. I didn't want to see another cherry blossom.

I heard a scraping sound outside my door and thought, *At last*. I watched the doorknob move and stop. Well, of course. The door was locked. Aunt Norie would have taken the key. Or maybe she'd forgotten?

"Just a minute! I'm coming," I called as loudly as my sore throat would allow. I stood up and began a slow progression toward the vestibule.

There was no affirmative response from the other side. Well, perhaps it was hard to hear my voice against the street noise.

In the gap between the bottom of the door and the

floor, something white shot under the door toward me. An envelope.

I was struck with a feeling of dread. Who would send a letter this way instead of putting it in the mailbox? And if the letter was some kind of neighborhood cleanup reminder from Mr. Waka's brother, who was the president of the neighborhood association, he would have rung the doorbell first. Whoever had pushed the note under the door surely knew that I was home but didn't want to have contact.

It took me a long minute to decide whether or not to open the door and look for the person with the note. Taking a deep breath, I did so. Nobody was out there but some schoolgirls on their bicycles, and they were cycling toward my building, not away from it. I closed the door and put the letter on my desk under a bright lamp. Putting on the white gloves I sometimes wear when handling old paper, I used a letter opener to delicately slit the envelope open. I imagined Lieutenant Hata congratulating me on my care as I pulled out a sheet of thin white rice paper patterned with cherry blossom petals. The message was written in three lines in *hiragana*, so it was fairly easy to understand.

> *Yotte nemu*
> *nadeshiko sakeru*
> *ishi no ue.*

I knew that *nadeshiko* were the flowers known as pinks and *sakeru* meant "to bloom." The poem was something about sleeping, pink flowers, and rocks.

Weird. The three-line format made the message seem like a possible haiku.

I crawled to my telephone and called Mr. Waka at the Family Mart.

"The strangest thing happened," he said after I identified myself. "Your aunt came to shop in my store."

"Well, it all goes to prove what I said: She doesn't think your food is bad," I reassured.

"She carefully checked the date on the eggs and asked if I had any that were refrigerated. Refrigerated! Who refrigerates eggs?"

"When did she leave your store?" I asked.

"About two hours ago. And it's cold enough outside that you don't need to worry about her groceries spoiling, *neh*?"

I didn't want to explain my true worries. Instead I brought up the message I'd received.

"Oh, that's a poem by Bashō, the most famous haiku poet of all," he said after I'd read aloud the text. "I had to memorize his works when I was in junior high school."

"How can it be a haiku if the first line has only four syllables?"

Mr. Waka gave an explanation that there were five *kanji* and *hiragana* characters used to compose the first line. I couldn't have known about the kanji used to originally write the poem, since the letter I'd received was written completely in *hiragana*.

"I just can't put together the meaning," I said. "The verbs in the first line, *yotte nemu*, don't seem to go together."

"You don't know *yotte? Yotte nemu?*"

"I know that *nemu* means 'sleep.'"

"*Yotte nemu* means getting so drunk that you fall asleep, like the cherry blossom drunks that are spending all day and evening in Yanaka Cemetery! If you want to practice *yotte nemu,* go there."

Now I could fully translate the message. I wasn't going to bother with an English five-seven-five formulation because I wasn't teaching a poetry class. I came up with:

> *Intoxicated*
> *Slumbering amid pinks*
> *Laid out on a rock.*

Chapter 12

My first feeling was anger that somebody assumed I'd fainted at the ikebana exhibition because of alcohol intoxication. But I thought it over, and my conclusion was frightening. Somebody wanted to see me laid out on a rock. Perhaps even dead—amidst flowers decorating my coffin. I remembered the coffin in my dream from a few nights before. Obviously my subconscious was trying to tell me that I was at extreme risk. The coffin had been mine, not Aunt Norie's.

I ended my conversation with Mr. Waka and telephoned Lieutenant Hata. He was out, so I left a message with a secretary. I placed the letter and envelope in a plastic bag, the way I'd seen it done on *Furuhata Ninzaburo,* a cop show that used to run on television. I hid the bag in the *yukashita,* the cut-out hiding place in my kitchenette's floor. I was on my knees, just putting down the lid, when Norie came back.

"I shouldn't have left you!" she exclaimed. "Are you hurt? Where is your gas heater? It's cold in here."

"In the closet. And I'm fine. It's just that my stomach hurts too much to stand up straight." I would tell her about the ominous poem later, but not immediately, when she was so worried about my health.

"I'm going to give you some more of the painkillers Tsutomu left for you. I'm sorry I didn't make up the futon for you to take a rest. I've been such a terrible caretaker, but I'll try to make up for it with a very good dinner."

"What's that going to be?" Was she talking about her light-as-air vegetable tempura or my favorite noodles dipped in sesame dressing? I was beginning to see the advantages of having my aunt in-house.

"*Okayu.*" She was talking about a very bland rice porridge. The last time I'd tasted it was at a Zen temple. While the monks and old people had eaten it with relish, I'd barely been able to get it down my throat. "I found some of the ingredients at your Family Mart, but I also had to travel to Seibu department store to get the right kind of pickled plums. It will be a small meal, because Tsutomu said that we must not test your weak stomach."

I would have to eat a lot of it—and show dramatic improvement in energy—if I was ever going to taste the kind of cooking my aunt did best. I offered to help her remove the stones from the pickled plums and she accepted, helping me sit down at the tea table with a knife, a cutting board, and the jar of pickled plums. Reaching into the Seibu shopping bag, I pulled out the receipt, gaping at the amount my aunt had spent.

"Now I have enough goods to cook for you for a week! The question is, where will I store it all? I'm going to have to use the *yukashita*."

"No! It's a bit crowded down there," I said, thinking of the haiku letter I had hidden in its depths.

"Oh dear, and I definitely need a cool place to leave the vegetables. Tsutomu was pointing out that we Japanese must change our food storage habits. Eggs should be stored under refrigeration, and rice should not be left warm in the rice cooker for longer than a few hours. I must remember all these things, or Tsutomu will send me away and send you back into the hospital."

"Wouldn't the back garden be cold enough for the vegetables? I left a *tansu* out there that I'm refinishing. If you wrap up the vegetables, you could just put them in a drawer. I don't think insects would get in."

"But it's been raining! How can you possibly leave furniture outside?"

"It hasn't been refinished yet, and it's under plastic." All wrapped up, like the secret I was not ready to share with her.

The next morning I felt much better. In fact, I had rolled out of the futon and started walking toward the bathroom before I remembered how I hadn't been able stand up straight the day before. Tom's painkillers had worked.

After serving me a breakfast of properly refrigerated *okayu* that I hadn't been able to finish the night before, Aunt Norie began a big cleanup of my apartment, using a rag duster she'd brought from her home and a trusty bottle of My Peto household cleaner.

I was feeling pretty firm on my feet, so I pitched in, and at the end of it all I asked Aunt Norie whether she'd be taking an afternoon train home.

She shook her head vigorously. "I planned to stay the entire week, *neh*? It does me no good to stay in Yokohama, where criminals broke into my garden shed! No, I'm not returning until Uncle Hiroshi comes back from Osaka."

"But you have a life in Yokohama. Students who take flower-arranging classes in your home, a son who needs you to cook for him—"

"All changed," Aunt Norie said cheerfully. "I've given my students your address. In fact, at one o'clock this afternoon a few students are coming by. Do you have your lesson book? You can work with us as well."

"Aunt Norie, I made three flower arrangements when you were gone yesterday," I pointed out.

"Yes, and from looking at them I can tell that you were under the influence of painkillers. Today, since you're so nice and strong, you can rearrange them. Although I suggest you let me dispose of the bittersweet. It's drooping, and I found some nasty insects on it."

That's because Takeo gave it to me, I thought. She was as paranoid about him as he was about her. But instead of saying that, I told her, "I'll try to make your class, but Tom—Tsutomu— wanted me to follow up with an appointment at the hospital. Then I have a couple of work appointments."

"Just because you can walk to the bathroom, it does not mean you can walk to the train station. Especially up and down stairs."

"I'll be fine," I said.

"But you catch motion sickness so easily. You've been that way ever since you were a toddler."

"Not with your good breakfast in my stomach." I patted it for emphasis. "If Lieutenant Hata calls, please tell him to try me this evening."

I set off with my aunt's worried blessing, a plastic bag, and a fresh handkerchief. As the TV news had promised, the sun was shining, and the cherry trees that lined the road going through Yanaka Cemetery were in full frothy splendor. A pink carpet under the trees revealed how many blossoms had been knocked down by the rain. A shame, but it was the way of the season.

I took the stairs down to the station slowly, which was easy since rush hour was over, and rode out to St. Luke's for my checkup. After a lab tech took a blood sample, an internist poked at various places and told me I was in recovery. After he was done, I went to the emergency room to find my cousin.

"You look so much better today than yesterday!" he greeted me with a wide smile. "Are you ready for lunch?"

After nothing but *okayu*, I certainly was ready for a real lunch. Tom exchanged his white coat for a suit

jacket and we walked a few blocks to Tsukijī, the
wholesale market where huge fish were laid out in
the early morning, then sold off to Tokyo restaura-
teurs. By this hour everything had been sold, but
there were a number of modest, bustling restaurants
open for business.

"The best thing for you is well-cooked food," Tom
said sternly. "I know a good *ochazuke* shop. My colleagues and I eat there regularly, and I'm sure they
observe proper food hygiene."

Soon we were sitting at a well-scrubbed counter
with the dish in front of us. *Ochazuke* was a bowl of
bouillon with rice and seaweed floating inside. It was
only slightly more interesting than my last two meals
of *okayu*.

A small green blob of *wasabi* paste accompanied
the dish. As I used chopsticks to mix it into the soup,
Tom shook his head.

"You will aggravate your stomach, which is temporarily weak. Don't do it."

"The dish is so mild otherwise," I protested.

"I'd think that after your poisoning, you would
want things that are mild."

"It wasn't any particular food that made me sick, it
was ant killer! If I stay out of the flower-arranging
business, I should be okay."

"Yes, I've heard the final report from Lieutenant
Hata. Still, it's better for you to eat meals that have
been prepared by my mother using hygiene guide-
lines, or to ask our opinion of the restaurants you
visit. You must be careful where—and with whom—
you eat."

"Whom do you mean, with whom?"

"Takeo Kayama." He curled his lips around the name, looking as if he had tasted something bad. "My mother says that he came to your apartment, hoping to take you on a date to the countryside."

I smiled at my cousin and said, "Tom, you and your mother are disturbed anytime anyone shows interest in me. You can't expect me to believe this one's any worse than the others. At least he's Japanese!"

"Rei, I know Takeo from my time at Keio University."

"How? You're six years older."

"Yes, but I was working as an intern at the campus hospital. I knew him well."

"What, from his medical record? Did he have a sexually transmitted disease or something? If so, I can tell you not to worry. We haven't done more than have a beer together, okay?" I snapped.

"Rei-*chan*, you know that, by law, I cannot violate the confidentiality of a medical record. I would also never judge a person's morality by his or her health. But I received the true picture of Takeo's character on the night I was called to give first aid at a campus riot."

This made me sit up straight, almost forgetting the nagging ache in my belly. "A riot at the sedate private university that our family so admires?"

"Yes. Grandfather certainly would have been furious, had he still been alive. It all happened when some undergraduates protested a rise in tuition. They decided to cause the administration trouble by eliminating the university's water supply. A large group planned to flush all the toilets on campus simultaneously so that the university's water supply would be gone."

"So Takeo flushed a toilet. That sounds like a fairly harmless prank."

"No, he was on the other side. He was the president of the students' environmental club. In the interest of water conservation, he asked the students to protest in some way other than toilet flushing. The group would not, so in a last-ditch attempt to stop them, Takeo and his friends borrowed weapons from the kendo club and stormed the lavatories, threatening to hit the students who flushed the toilets."

"Wow! Isn't that really dangerous?" Kendo is a martial art that involves charging against an opponent with a length of bamboo bound with cord that makes a terrible cracking sound when a hit is scored. The bamboo weapons are powerful enough that kendo athletes are required to wear protective helmets.

"Yes. And because Takeo was the ringleader, he was the one charged with responsibility for the fights that broke out between students in several lavatories on campus. Many students were hospitalized, including one who was in a coma for a week." Tom looked at me. "Takeo was never charged with attempted murder, although I thought he should have been. However, he was kicked out of Keio. I don't think he has any kind of university degree."

"He must have finished up in California," I said, remembering the horticulture program he had mentioned.

"No offense to you, Rei, but an American degree doesn't carry much weight here. After leaving Keio, nobody would hire him but his father, I'm sure."

"Thanks for the intelligence, Tom." I looked away from his scowling face.

"You'd never guess a guy who played with flowers all day could be so violent, *neh*?"

"He certainly does break the stereotypes." I toyed with a few grains of rice that were stuck on the side of the bowl. "Do you think he could have killed Sakura?"

Tom sighed. "I don't know. But seeing him at the Kayama Building, he spoke so arrogantly to the police—the same way he spoke after the lavatory riots. There's a saying that a mature rice plant lowers its head, but he certainly didn't. He hasn't changed."

"I wonder if that's why your mother doesn't like him."

"I didn't tell her. She has always admired the Kayama family so much. I could not be the one to break her illusion."

"She must have heard something somewhere. She definitely doesn't like Takeo." I still wanted to know the rest of the story. "So what happened at Keio with the toilet-flushing protest?"

"Actually, the fights provided enough of a distraction that only fifty or so toilets were flushed at once, so there was no crisis in water supply. Takeo's idea worked, but at a terrible human cost."

I was silent for a minute, digesting the story. "What happened to the other students who were working with Takeo?"

"Nobody else was expelled. Takeo even admitted the riot was his fault."

"That's very Japanese," I said, thinking about a news story from a year ago about three companies facing bankruptcy. The three CEOs, all friends, had gone to a hotel, taken a last drink together, and then hanged themselves, taking responsibility for the failure.

"How can you call that Armani-wearing hypocrite Japanese?" Tom snorted.

"It wasn't Armani, it was Issey Miyake, who just happens to be a Japanese designer. I know because I saw his suit in the *Tatler*, the magazine you gave me expressly to show me the photograph of Hugh Glendinning and his new girlfriend."

"You're attracted to well-dressed men, Rei. It's your personal weakness. But the outside is not an accurate reflection of a person's inside."

I could have told Tom that I thought Takeo's stomach looked amazingly lean under the stretched cotton of his worn Greenpeace T-shirt, but that would only bring more ire. So I turned back to the thought that made me the most unhappy and fearful. Clearing my throat, I confessed, "I saw Takeo talking with Che Fujisawa, who is the leader of Stop Killing Flowers. I wonder if they're planning something."

"Do you think they were involved in Sakura's death?" Tom asked.

"Only if Sakura did something against the environment. Something really terrible," I guessed.

"Rei, you're not thinking of getting involved in

this, are you?" When I didn't answer, he went on in the needling tone that I hated. "You've had some chances to help the police before, but that doesn't mean you should make it your unpaid part-time job. You've been poisoned. You need to recover and get on with your life."

"Thanks for taking care of me. I'm already feeling much better."

I'd given a perfectly appropriate answer, but I could tell from my cousin's scowl that he knew I was being evasive. Sakura Sato and Takeo Kayama were my problems. Not his.

Chapter 13

On the way home, I visited some antiques shops to show Polaroid photos I'd taken of Mrs. Morita's plates. The negative responses I received confirmed my fear that I'd taken on a real albatross, but I couldn't bear to return to Mrs. Morita with a failure. Enough had gone wrong in my life lately. I was determined that at least one thing would work out.

Norie's ikebana class was in full swing by the time I reached my apartment. Three women I didn't know were fussing with flowers on my newspaper-covered tea table, and Norie's friend Eriko was working at the kitchen counter.

I'd never seen so many people at one time in my small apartment. Everyone bowed when I entered, but I was struck with an odd desire to excuse myself. Norie introduced me to her students, but I was too tired and stressed to remember their names. At least I knew Eriko, who patted a cushion for me to rest on. She alone seemed to understand that I was exhausted.

"You're in good time, Rei. We saved an extra portion of flowers for you," Norie said.

I deduced from the unfamiliar shopping bags bulging with bubble wrap that the students had carried their own ikebana containers from home. However, the chrysanthemums and ferns going into them looked oddly familiar.

"Where did the flowers come from?" I asked.

"The florist down the street. Because of the cemetery up the hill, it turns out there are many places to buy flowers," Norie said. "Of course, they are not of the highest quality, but I needed something fast."

They were flowers meant for dead people. That made me shudder. Perhaps my aunt understood my feeling, because she said, "We're getting ready for the certificate examination next month. Chrysanthemum is often a flower the students must arrange, so today is good practice."

"What's this about examinations? I thought students automatically received a certificate of completion after finishing each book." I'd read in the foreign students' handbook that I needed to complete twenty lessons and pay ten thousand yen to the school to receive a fourth-grade certificate.

"That is the way it works for international students. Japanese have to create two flower arrangements for a formal examination," Norie explained. "They have no choice in materials, and one arrangement will be assigned, while the other can be freestyle. Then the highest-ranking teacher judges the arrangement."

"Does the judge watch them and then make an oral evaluation?" I asked, remembering how nerve-racking it had been to wait for Sakura and Masanobu Kayama to deliver their verdicts.

"No, the students arrange their flowers first in a room by themselves. They place a number next to their arrangements and leave the room. The judge comes inside and inspects their work. It's a way of judging on merit and not personality," Norie said. "I was actually hoping that you would want to take the examination, Rei. Not next month, of course, but by next year's time."

"Yes, you did very well with your arrangement at Mitsutan," Eriko assured me.

"Really?" Norie turned to her friend. "Please tell me what the *iemoto* said."

"It wasn't that much of a rave," I said. "He started talking about a memory of the time Takeo and Natsumi stuck irises inside a bamboo fence. I think he was saying our installation was like a child's work."

"Oh." Norie's face fell, and I realized suddenly that I shouldn't have said anything so negative with Norie's students listening. Not only had I disappointed my aunt, I'd caused her to lose face.

"I think the master liked the arrangement and was just nostalgic," Eriko said. "Rei didn't understand the nuance of his language."

"Yes, of course I have trouble with Japanese," I

said, accepting the correction for my aunt's sake. "Anyway, your students' upcoming examination is much more important. Who will be the judge?"

Norie paused a moment too long, and one of her students piped up, "It used to be Miss Sakura Sato!"

"She and sometimes some of the school's other grandmasters," Norie corrected.

"Could you ever be a judge?" I asked my aunt.

"No, because your aunt and I are not high-ranking teachers," Eriko reminded me. "My guess is the judge will be either Mrs. Koda or, for family reasons, Natsumi Kayama."

"I hope it's Mrs. Koda. She has so much experience, and she's very kind. I'm sure that some of the more experienced foreign arrangers—Lila Braithwaite, for example—would be willing to take the examination if they had the chance," I said.

"Foreigners don't need a real degree," Eriko insisted. "It's just a pretty hobby they do for the year or two they're in Japan. When they go home to the West, they have something to show off to the ladies in their garden clubs!"

"Have you been to the West? To these garden clubs?" I asked Eriko a bit sharply. I didn't like the way she was talking about my countrywomen.

"Of course not. But I've met the women." Eriko raised her eyebrows, which were shaped like two perfect half-moons.

"We should never forget that foreigners saved the Kayama School." My aunt surprised me by speaking up. "After the war, most Japanese people did not have enough money to buy rice and certainly not flowers. The only people able to afford ikebana classes were the Americans. A navy admiral's wife became a student at the Kayama School, and after that many foreigners joined. These women made many generous donations to keep the school alive until Japanese women were again able to afford classes and flowers."

I followed my aunt as she turned her attention to her students' work. She suggested small things: the turning of a branch so that the arrangement would be beautiful viewed from all angles, or the rearrangement of a clump of ferns so that they looked as if they had naturally grown from the middle of an ikebana dish. The students did not bow their heads the way they had before Sakura or the headmaster. They seemed eager for Aunt Norie's guidance, moving the flowers as she suggested.

While my aunt concentrated on her students, Eriko whispered to me, "I didn't mean to upset you about the foreign students, Rei-san. I think of you as one of us. It was wrong of me to make you feel bad when you are still so weak from your illness."

"I'm making a good recovery, thanks to my aunt and people such as yourself," I said. In standard Japanese etiquette, you were supposed to attribute good health and success to whomever asked after you. Remembering what Norie had said about the financial hardship in her marriage, I added, "Thank you very much for the beautiful white roses. They are such a luxury."

"I first brought them to you in the hospital, but you were too sick to notice then. But look at this charming room! Full of flowers from many well-wishers—Takeo Kayama even." Eriko gave me a tiny, sparkling smile.

My aunt must have complained to her about Takeo's visit. Nervously I said, "It isn't anything, really."

"Because your aunt doesn't want it to be." Eriko kept her kind, knowing gaze on me. "Do you want to talk about it later on? I understand how difficult Japanese relatives can be."

"I'll be fine. There's nothing to talk about." As I rejected her offer I felt glum, although I didn't know why.

The class ended an hour later. After moving the furniture back to its proper place, Norie made up my futon so that I could lie down. Nestled in the soft quilts, I slept solidly all afternoon. I awoke to a room gray with the onset of evening. Aunt Norie sat close to the *andon*, using its weak light to illuminate the sewing that she was doing. She was obviously trying not to disturb me.

"What kind of embroidery are you doing? *Sashiko* work?" I raised myself on my elbow to get a better look.

"No, I'm darning your brassiere! The band is almost worn through." She stood up, snapping on the harsh overhead light and dangling my bra so that I could see all its faded glory.

"I was meaning to throw it away," I said.

"Actually, you wore it under your clothes at the

Mitsutan exhibit. I saw it when the nurses undressed you at the hospital."

My groan was interrupted by a ringing telephone which Norie answered. "Oh, Richard-san! How nice of you to call again." She paused, listening to whatever he was saying to her. Richard spoke very good Japanese. After a few moments she laughed and said, "*So desu, neh!*" They were in agreement over something.

"Your aunt's a sweetie. Why are you so scared of her?" Richard asked when my aunt finally handed the receiver to me.

"I'm not! It's just that I occasionally feel stifled," I said in English I thought she wouldn't understand.

"I suggested that I take you out for a health drink at the tea shop. She strongly believes in homeopathic remedies, did you know?"

"Yes." So Richard wanted to see me tonight. I was still smarting a little over his rejection of me twenty-four hours earlier.

"I'm just recording a few more lines on an English tape for a student. By the time you get dressed, I'll be ringing the doorbell." Richard seemed to become aware of my stillness. "That is, if you still want to go."

"Okay," I said. "I could use the break."

I dressed quickly, not wanting a debate with Norie about what I was wearing. I chose a pair of leggings that didn't constrict my bruised bottom, and a large DREAMS COME TRUE sweatshirt—"large" in Japan meaning the equivalent of a women's size six. As I sat in the entryway, tying my beloved Asics sneakers, I thought sadly of the many miles I'd run in the shoes over the past year. Now I could barely toddle to a tea shop.

Richard blew into the apartment like a small black bat. His tattered leather jacket glistened with rain, and the small ring in his lower lip trembled as he spoke to my aunt in super-polite Japanese.

"Shimura-*sama*, I apologize for my disturbance. I see you are embroidering a garment!" Richard moved in for a better look. "How lovely your work is! I wish that I could sew. With a needle and the right pair of scissors, I could have the perfect wardrobe."

Norie quickly buried my bra in her sewing basket. If my futon was considered too intimate for outsiders' eyes, underwear was even more taboo. Waving me off, she admonished, "Come back quickly. Dinner will be ready soon."

"She didn't invite me to dinner," Richard complained when we were on the street.

"Japanese never invite anybody home for dinner. Not because they're unfriendly, but because they think their homes are too small and the menu won't be good enough," I said as we passed a *yakitori* shop with its traditional welcome curtain flapping in the chill breeze. The tantalizing, smoky smell of grilled chicken made me almost wish that I weren't a vegetarian.

"Mmm, *yakitori*. I don't suppose you want to change our plan, maybe have a beer and a few skewers?"

"I worry that my aunt would smell the evidence.

Besides, I'm surprised you would have time for something other than a quick cup of tea. Don't you normally see Enrique at this time?"

"Jealousy rears its ugly head," Richard teased. "Well, you should be glad I saw him last night at Salsa Salsa."

"Why?" The pavement was wet with some kind of slop from the tofu-maker, and I skidded as we rounded the corner.

Richard caught my arm protectively. "I'll wait with my news till we're sitting down."

"How exciting can it be?" I asked, consciously trying to slow down as we turned into the narrow alley that housed the Yanaka Tea Shop. Mr. Waka's Family Mart notwithstanding, this was my favorite neighborhood business. The small wooden shop, built at the turn of the century, still had most of its original exterior, including an exquisitely carved panel over the door showing a samurai gentleman and lady taking tea. Inside, old wooden placards hung on bright red walls, advertising teas that could help with everything from constipation to a broken heart. Shelves full of boxed teas available to take home lined one side of the store; on the other side, a few tables were available for those who wanted to drink their potions in-house.

"Special of the month is a snake-blood beverage. It's supposed to be very powerful against hangovers, but it's too expensive." Richard, whose *kanji* knowledge was far greater than mine, paused while reading the menu. "How about *sakura-yu*? That's a tea made from pickled cherry blossoms. That would be salty, right?"

I nodded, although the last thing I wanted was a taste of cherry. Luckily, our waiter advised that I drink ginseng tea for energy and matters of the heart. Since he had no troubles with romance, Richard tried *kombu-cha*, which was made from a type of kelp that was supposed to ensure long life.

The tea was served in small tea bowls, with a smooth glaze on the inside and a rough outward surface that was similar to the urns Mari Kumamori had brought to the ikebana exhibition. I put the small bowl to my mouth and, after a few sips, decided it tasted similar to green tea. I looked around at the other tables and noticed that a significantly large number of young people were drinking tea. Was tea becoming trendy?

"So, tell me about last night." The tea's heat had poured down my sore throat, making it feel better.

"Well, Enrique was still tending bar when I arrived, so I got a drink and circulated a little. My ears perked up when I heard the Kayama School mentioned."

"I can't believe the flower-arranging ladies would go there!"

"These gossips were guys, both of them Spanish-speaking. One of them had a jeans jacket embroidered in Spanish and English. Actually, it gets me thinking: Could your aunt do a cherry blossom appliqué on my favorite pair of Levi's? It might be a good way to cover up the hole you say is obscene."

"Che. Was that the word you saw on the jacket?"

"That's it! Is it a name, or what?"

"I think it's a nickname that means something like 'good friend.' It's an informal form of address. Didn't you ever hear of Che Guevara, the Argentine activist who led various Latin American government overthrows?"

"Whoever thought I'd need Spanish to live in Japan?" Richard snorted. "Actually, it felt really odd. Aside from a few words, I understood nothing." Richard's face puckered as he sipped his tea. I guessed that he didn't like it.

"Why didn't you ask Enrique to translate?" I asked.

"Like I told you, he was behind the bar, and I wasn't sure whether the conversation was really worth anything. Still, I thought of you, and I wrote down the words I heard on a cocktail napkin." He whipped out a wrinkled piece of pale blue tissue pock-marked with words.

I read through them. *Kayama School. Mitsutan. St. Luke's Hospital. Rei Shimura. Yanaka.*

"They know about my poisoning. Look at all these linked words!" I was nearly beside myself with a mixture of rage, fear, and elation. At last I had some proof of a connection.

"Cool down, Rei. Lots of people knew you got sick."

"Not really," I said. "It wasn't in the papers. Did you tell anyone about it?"

"I told Enrique. He wanted to know why you weren't at the party Saturday night."

Could Enrique have been the leak, speaking to Che at an earlier point? Or was the leak Takeo

Kayama, who had gone through my address book and knew where I lived? "The men you overheard mentioned this neighborhood. Did you hear any numbers? Were they discussing my street address?"

"It's hard to tell. Like I told you, they were speaking mostly Spanish. There were a couple of Japanese guys who seemed to understand as well. Or maybe those guys were Latin Americans of Japanese heritage. It was difficult to tell."

"If only I could get Lieutenant Hata and a Spanish translator to stake out Salsa Salsa," I thought aloud.

"Don't do anything to cause Enrique trouble." Richard glowered at me. "He's my everything."

"Shouldn't you be spending your time getting to know Enrique outside the bar? It sounds as if everything that's going on between you is washed down by too many *caipirinhas*."

"At least I have a relationship. That's more than I can say for you, Miss Congeniality."

"Does Enrique know Che?" I ignored his insult. "Was there any sign of familiarity?"

"I saved the best for last. It turns out they know each other slightly, so I asked Enrique to introduce me on the way out. Che's a pretty friendly guy. He even offered us a kind of short-term job, but we said no."

"What kind of job?"

"He said it had something to do with garden work. Enrique assumed that it was off-the-books—you know, illegal. He's got a legit job at Salsa Salsa and a visa in good standing, so he obviously wouldn't take a risk like that."

My heartbeat felt stronger all of a sudden. Either I had gotten a case of jitters from the ginseng tea or I had a terrific idea brewing. "Do you think you could convince Enrique to find out more about that job?"

Richard shook his head, making his pewter crucifix earring fly out at a ninety-degree angle. "Enrique's adamant about spending all of his free time with me."

"If it's short-term, why don't you do it? Just once?"

Richard ran a finger around the edge of his moist tea bowl. "I suppose that I wouldn't mind taking off my shirt and getting a tan. Enrique makes me feel so white."

I took Richard's tea bowl from him. "Did you know I could read tea leaves?" I asked. As I stared at the dark pieces of sea vegetable clumped on the bottom of Richard's empty bowl, I said, "The pattern here reveals that it would be good for you to do something outdoors."

Richard sighed. "You sound like Lila. But the option she always presents me with is taking the kids to Tokyo Disneyland."

"This will be so much better than that phony playland," I promised. "All I'm asking you to do is dig up a little dirt. An afternoon's worth."

"For you, babe, I'll dig it up in spades," Richard said, taking his bowl and clinking it against mine.

He was in.

Chapter 14

There are times when I think my actions make perfect sense. Then, a few hours later, I realize that I'm crazy.

As I walked out of the tea shop with Richard, I was caught up in the heat of the moment, the certainty that Enrique and Richard were the perfect moles to infiltrate Che's organization. I went to bed stoked on ginseng and the promise of discovery.

I woke up the next morning with an unbearable need to use the toilet and a feeling of doom. Richard could no more carry off an underground sting than I could pass a flower-arranging exam. And there was the question of whether Enrique could even be trusted, given that he'd fallen into my friend's arms just a few days earlier.

"Do you want me to answer the telephone, Rei-*chan*?" Aunt Norie murmured from her futon, spread

a few inches from mine. I had just flushed the toilet
and was coming back into the bedroom, not having
heard the telephone's first few rings.

"No, I'll get it." As Lieutenant Hata's voice began
speaking into my answering machine, I took the
cordless receiver back into the powder room.
Running the water in the sink so that Aunt Norie
couldn't hear my voice, I began the saga, starting
with the mysterious haiku I'd received two days earlier.

"That was written by Bashō," he said after I'd
recited the three lines. "I had to learn that poem in
school."

"Do you understand why it makes me nervous?" I
asked.

"Not particularly. It is a tradition in Japan to present poetry to others as a gift. In fact, during the
classical period, young men would send poems as
thank-you letters to the courtesans they had affairs
with. I'm surprised that you cannot guess who sent
it."

I was silent until I realized the implication of his
comment. "I'm not having an affair with Takeo."

"Well, then, why did you deploy me to the kitchen
so you could have a private conversation? And you
aided in his escape," Hata added, his bitterness practically cracking the telephone line.

"Takeo left the apartment on his own. It's not like
he's a fugitive," I said. "The one you should be suspicious of is Che Fujisawa. There's a good chance he
or one of his gang poisoned me."

"Miss Shimura, you may need to return to St.

Luke's Hospital, because it sounds as if you are having delusions! Since when has an environmental group become a *gang*?"

"Two nights ago, at a nightclub called Salsa Salsa, Che and a friend were overheard talking about the Kayama School, Mitsutan, St. Luke's Hospital, and my address in Yanaka."

"Really?" He sounded wary. "There was no news about your sickness in the newspaper."

"Yes, they would have no reason to know. Obviously they are involved."

"What did you hear exactly?" For the first time in our conversation, I heard the scratching of a pen. He was taking notes.

"Well, it was overheard by a friend," I said, mindful that Richard hadn't wanted me to identify him or Enrique. "The conversation was in Spanish, so only the few Japanese words spoken were noted."

"Where is Salsa Salsa?"

"On Roppongi-dori, heading toward Nishi-Azabu. But you can't just walk in, you'll stick out terribly. And you'll need a Spanish interpreter." All of a sudden I was worried.

"We have plenty of those. And I do have plain clothes." I could hear the smile in his voice.

I thanked Lieutenant Hata for his time and hung up. Aunt Norie had been knocking on the door for a few minutes, and I could no longer ignore her.

"You don't have to hide your telephone calls from me. I know it was that policeman." Aunt Norie leaned in the door frame, her *yukata* robe snugly belted over flannel pajamas. Her hair was tousled with sleep, and the pale blue traces of her nighttime beauty face mask clung to her skin, making her look like a sci-fi character out of a comic book.

"I didn't want to disturb your sleep," I said.

"Leave things to him," Norie said. "He can find out better than you, and it is dangerous to get close to the Kayamas. I know."

"Did something happen between you and the Kayamas? Tell me."

"Water washes everything away," Norie said. It was one of her favorite proverbs, one that meant it was better to forgive and forget. "Speaking of water, are you going to bathe before breakfast? If you do that now, I'll prepare the *okayu*."

Over large bowls of the last of the leftover gruel, I searched for ways to get Norie to open up about the Kayamas, but it was impossible. She wanted to talk about my Uncle Hiroshi, who was at last returning from Osaka for a visit. I couldn't understand the stamina of *tanshin funin*—absentee husbands who accepted their company's orders to work far from home but didn't take their families with them. Norie had gotten caught up in a murder a week ago, and Hiroshi hadn't been available to offer her support. I supposed his homecoming was better late than never.

The Japanese press said my generation had a different attitude toward work, but I doubted it. As I rode the Hibiya subway line into Roppongi, I checked out a few good-looking young businessmen.

I had long ago identified a Hibiya Line type—a species of tall young man with cheekbones like razors and slicked-back hair, usually dressed for business in a European suit. An English wing-tip shoe might bounce gently as he rested in his seat. It was a law of nature that HLTs never had to stand on trains. I watched a twenty-something guy who fit the profile sit down across from me, then dash my fantasies by opening the latest edition of *Jump*. How could I ever get involved with a grown man who reads boys' comics? *Sorry*, I said in my thoughts to the HLT, *it's not going to work*.

Takeo Kayama lived within walking distance of the Hibiya Line, but I didn't think of him as an HLT. He had the height and bones, but his hair was long and floppy—all wrong. As was his dark wardrobe of jeans and T-shirts. Even the business suit he had worn on the day of Sakura's slaying had been wrinkled. Besides, HLTs had jobs. Takeo was a puppet in the Kayama administration, hanging around to collect cash from students and teachers. No, Takeo Kayama was not my type.

You're lying, the voice inside me said. To still it, I stared all the harder at the good-looking guy reading *Jump*. He must have felt it, because he eventually looked up. He hissed a single word at me: "*Hentai*." It meant "pervert."

He felt sexually harassed! I shouldn't have giggled, but I did. I put my hand over my mouth and looked down at my knees until I reached Kamiyacho Station. Then I strode out of the subway car without a second glance at the poor abused businessman.

❊   ❊   ❊

Ishida Antiques was located on the grounds of the family home where my seventy-five-year-old friend Yasushi Ishida had been born. Since World War II, the structure had been rebuilt every ten or twenty years, metamorphosing from a wooden house similar to the one I rented in Yanaka into a neat stucco box similar to the other shops around it. Mr. Ishida lived alone upstairs, having turned the ground floor into a crowded showplace for old furniture. The only item not for sale was a miniature shrine set above the door, decorated with miniature paper prayer strips and today's fruit offering to his departed parents, a fragrant peach. The fruit was changed daily, so the aroma was always fresh.

Today he had a customer, an elegant Japanese woman in her late fifties. Mother of a Hibiya Line type, maybe. Mr. Ishida sent me a swift glance that said to look around quietly while he completed his sale.

Mr. Ishida's shop reflected the same cherry blossom fever as the rest of Japan's commercial world. He had decorated a lacquered stand with a mauve kimono patterned with pink cherry blossoms. On a *tansu* chest, he had a cherry blossom arrangement in a large black *suiban* container. Surrounding it were similar ikebana containers of the same vintage. These weren't filled with water or flowers, so I turned one over to look for an artist's mark. Stamped into the ceramic were two simple *kanji* I recognized: those for "flower" and "mountain." Together the words were pronounced "ka-yama."

I wondered if someone in the Kayama family made pottery but dismissed the idea. Most likely the dish was made to order for the school, just like the minimalist modern stoneware that currently filled the shelves of the Kayama classroom. What was surprising to me was how these ceramics reflected a 1930s art moderne feeling. The colors of the ceramics — happy shades of orange, pink, and green — reminded me of American Fiestaware. At the same time, one could argue that these were the same colors that decorated typical Japanese kimono.

As I tried to figure out whether the containers were more Japanese or American, things were proceeding well for Mr. Ishida. His lady customer was on the verge of buying a *tansu* priced at a cool seven hundred thousand yen, about $4,800. She stroked the smooth lacquered finish, and I wondered what it would be like to buy something in perfect condition that was practically guaranteed to rise in value. Nice, I imagined. Very nice.

After the business was concluded, the lady left to deep bows from Mr. Ishida. He was still horizontal when she slipped out the door, and he took his time coming up, rubbing at the small of his back.

"I missed my tai chi practice for only two days, and it has turned me into an old man," Mr. Ishida grumbled.

"Never." I smiled at my mentor and settled down at the tea table crowded with papers and books, the prime spot where Mr. Ishida liked to serve tea and gossip.

"What a good day this is, Shimura-san. That *tansu* has taken up space for the last eight months. I was worrying that it would never sell."

"I have a problem like that," I said, and told him about the plates.

"I'm sorry, but I couldn't buy them from you," Mr. Ishida said. "I've got a set of twelve dishes like that upstairs—let me see, they've been around for five months. This market really is terrible."

"That's what I'm learning." I was going to have to find storage for all the brilliant consignments I'd taken on. I held up a shallow pink ikebana dish and asked, "Can you tell me about this?"

"That is a *suiban* made to order at a kiln on the island of Kyushu for the Kayama School. So much was made in the early part of the century that it was known widely as Kayama ware. I have a lot of them right now. I'd say the piece you're looking at was made in the thirties."

Mr. Ishida didn't seem to catch on to the irony of the fact that he was selling china from the death-marred flower school, but then again my guru did not own a television or read anything except antiques journals. A murderer could be running around Kamiyacho Station, but unless the killer committed his acts with a vintage samurai sword, my friend would be oblivious.

I examined the *suiban* again, thinking the pink color would not set off every flower to advantage. I held the dish up and asked, "This isn't as old as your usual merchandise. Why did you take it?"

"I took it all because I realized that I would be the

only dealer in Tokyo, perhaps Japan, with such a large collection. I hope that a Kayama enthusiast will come and buy the whole lot."

"I've been taking classes at the school. Unfortunately, I'm not an enthusiast." I smiled wryly.

"Nevertheless, you will meet very cultivated people through the world of ikebana." He paused. "I don't suppose you know the Kayama who sold me all the dishes?"

"One of the family came here?" I was stunned. Well, the shop was only a few blocks from the headquarters. I supposed it was convenient.

"The Kayama who came here was a woman the age of your aunt."

"There aren't any older Kayama women," I said. "There's just Natsumi, who is exactly my age."

"This lady was in her fifties, and I only say that because Japanese women have more luxuries to help keep their skin looking young these days," Mr. Ishida opined. "The lady was pretty but a bit unfriendly. I expect that she found it hard to part with her collection. These days, with the financial instability, I am receiving many more consignments from private people, and I imagine the tension of the situation added to her manner."

But the Kayamas weren't in financial trouble. Or were they? Intrigued, I asked, "What did the woman do that made her seem cold?"

"She demanded an immediate answer about whether I wanted a collection of two hundred pieces or she was going to leave. And then, when it came to the terms of our arrangement, she wanted to keep eighty percent of the sale price and give me twenty!"

Consignment agreements were usually sixty-forty in the consignor's favor, so this was an outrageous request. I asked, "What did you do?"

"I told her I would offer her sixty-five percent of the sale price, but no more than that. And if the goods were not sold within two months, she would need to take them all back. She agreed to that; no doubt she had been to other antiques dealers and had her terms rejected. But the pieces she'd brought were special." He ran a finger over the smooth glaze of the *suiban* that I'd placed on the table between us. "Somehow I felt that I should take them."

He'd fallen victim to antiques lust. It was the reason I'd taken Mrs. Morita's dishes: a hunch, a desire, an urge to have something with me for a little while. I'd thought that I took the plates in order to sell them for a profit, but now I was beginning to wonder. Maybe I just wanted to give a dinner party for eight guests of my choosing.

"I understand," I told him.

"Well, I was very stupid. I must have been distracted during our conversation, because I took the details of her telephone number, and that number is disconnected. And even more unfortunate is the fact that the woman has not called me back. It has been almost three months since she came in and I have sold nine containers. Yet I cannot give her any payment."

I made up my mind. "I'll be happy to do what you asked me to—that is, I'll find out whether there's a middle-aged lady in the Kayama family."

"But you just told me you are not enthusiastic about ikebana. Why are you so interested?" Mr. Ishida sounded skeptical.

I looked straight at him and said, "Well, I want to know who the lady is, too."

"You think you can find her telephone number?"

"Maybe," I said. "Takeo told me that his mother died, and unless some distant relative has come into Tokyo to pawn family wares, an impostor visited your shop."

"That sounds . . . unlikely." But there was a hint of uncertainty in Mr. Ishida's voice that told me he was worried. He needed my help.

"I promise you that I'll be discreet. Let me buy the *suiban,* and that will make my interest in the issue seem more natural." I really did want to buy the container. I thought that I could give it as a thank-you to Aunt Norie. In fact, presenting her with the *suiban* would help communicate that her job taking care of me was complete—and that she should return to Yokohama and continue her flower-arranging classes there in peace.

As I walked into Roppongi I bought a copy of the *Japan Times.* At least the English-language press had lost interest in the Kayama School murder. All the news was about the banking crisis. Japan's stock exchange had sunk to number three, behind the United States and England, although government officials remained optimistic. So what else was new?

After finishing the depressing news, I stuck the newspaper in my backpack, which was already bulky thanks to the *suiban* I was carrying. When the whole thing was mounted on my back, I caught sight of myself in the reflection of a window and decided that I looked like the youngest woman on earth suffering from osteoporosis. Turning onto Gaien Higashi-dori, I was glad to find My Magic Forest did not have any protesters outside. I was determined to buy a large bouquet of flowers to use as a prop at my next destination.

Stepping through Grecian pillars, I entered the shop, which smelled of earth, moss, and exotic blooms. I walked through the lavish international garden displays that I'd seen with Aunt Norie and toward a sale bucket of long-stemmed pink roses. I noticed the petals' dryness.

"These roses, where are they from?" I asked a shop girl who was fussing with some jasmine nearby.

"Latin America. I'm not sure which country, but I assure you that our supplier says that nobody who picked them was the victim of any pesticide poisoning!" She looked as nervous as she sounded.

"Actually, the roses look a little brown around the edges."

"They arrived two days ago. They did not sell, so we have dropped the price. If madam does not like the roses we have today, why not consider some Dutch tulips? Or Thai orchids?"

"Do you have any locally grown flowers?"

"Oh, yes, but they're very expensive." She glanced at my overstuffed backpack, which must have given

me the aura of a budget shopper. I slid the backpack
off my shoulder and shook out my Burberry so that
the clerk could see the plaid lining. Even though my
coat was from my mother's 1970s wardrobe,
Burberry was a major status brand in Japan.

"Cost is no object," I said, madness clearly kicking
in. "Not when it comes to ikebana."

"Oh, is madam a teacher?" she asked in a friend-
lier manner, leading me through a mini-park of cherry and white plum blossoms. Entire trees, with their
roots protected in earth and burlap, were available
for sixty thousand yen and up. I vetoed cherry due
to my blossoming hatred of the tree, and in the end
chose branches of mock orange that had pretty white
flowers. I added some lotus leaves and a few sweet
little purple cosmos. I handed over five thousand
yen—about thirty-five dollars—without too much
pain.

"We offer a choice of wrapping in either recycled
newspaper or our signature silver paper. What
would madam prefer?"

I debated the choice and decided to stick with the
My Magic Forest paper. With luck, it would make
me look like a regular at my next stop, the Kayama
Kaikan.

Chapter 15

To avoid having the doorman recognize me as the harbinger of illness and death, I shielded my face with the bundle of flowers as I entered the Kayama Kaikan. I needn't have worried. He was occupied holding open the door for a German tour group. I squeezed in behind them and stayed with the group until they got to the elevators. At that point, I melted up the stairwell marked EMERGENCY ONLY.

I knew from the Kayama School schedule that on Tuesday afternoons the administrative office was closed so that the employees could engage in continuing ikebana education or free activities of their choosing. The time was perfect for what I wanted to do.

At the second-floor landing, I stepped out into the gray-carpeted hallway that led to the administrative office. As was typical for a Japanese office, it was a large, open space filled with desks, each completely void of clutter or personal artifacts, but emblazoned with an employee nameplate.

Fortunately, I knew how to read the names Koda and Sato. I located Mrs. Koda's desk next to one of the long window-walls. At first I hung back from the window, but then I remembered that it was the kind of glass that couldn't be seen into from the outside during the daytime. I surveyed the sweeping view of office buildings and trees, thinking that although the desk seemed to be in a good position, it actually reflected Mrs. Koda's declining role in the school. If she really was functioning as the head administrator, her desk would have been in the center of the room so that she could call out orders to the minions around her. Sakura's desk was squarely in the center of the room; she had been the queen bee.

The police had been through Sakura's desk already. I noticed a thick black powder on its stainless steel surface and the drawer handles—a powder I guessed had something to do with dusting for fingerprints.

I turned back toward the windows, seeing Mrs. Koda's desk from a different angle. A slight shadow caught my attention. There was a gap between the top drawer's edge and the desk. The drawer was open.

Temptation bit me as sharply as one of the tiny bugs that live in old tatami mats. Couldn't I just slide the drawer a bit farther open? I wouldn't be breaking into her desk, just checking it. I would simply look for any address book that she might have, go straight to the *K*'s, and see if I could find anything on the mysterious Mrs. Kayama.

The drawer slid open soundlessly, revealing a few slim notebooks, a case of pens, a case of pencils, and a tissue box. No address book. I flipped open both notebooks and found them unreadable, except for a few flower names and locations in Tokyo. A roster of teacher names and addresses was printed in both English and *kanji*. Deciding that the teacher list might be nice to examine later, I went to the photocopy machine. It had been turned off, and when I pressed the on button, it groaned to life with a frighteningly loud noise. I hoped nobody else was on the second floor to hear it.

The machine was very slow. By the time I was finished copying the list, the clock on the wall showed ten minutes to two, the time when the staff flower-arranging session would be over.

I returned to Mrs. Koda's desk with the master list. As I slid it into the drawer, I noticed that I'd gotten black powder on the drawer handle. I must have brushed against Sakura's desk. I reached into Mrs. Koda's tissue box for something to clean the handle, and my hand knocked against a small plastic container. With the tissue around my hand, I pulled out a small bottle made from orange plastic, the kind that protects medications from light. The label was typed in English and said MOTRIN 800 MG. How ironic it was that the medication I used to tame occasional cramps was something that could help an older woman with arthritis.

The lid was half off—in Japan, childproof lids are

not mandatory on medicine bottles—and a tablet fell into my hand. It was small and white, with a cameo of a woman's head carved into its surface. There could be a chance that Motrin had a different design here, but the woman's head seemed an unusual feature. I turned the tablet over and saw that it was inscribed NOLVADEX 600.

Mrs. Koda was taking something stronger than Motrin but was using a Motrin bottle to hold it. It was either for her own use—or for somebody else.

Like me, Sakura had been poisoned. Lieutenant Hata had told me that it was arsenic. As I stared at the little tablet with the woman's profile on it, I felt the same nausea that had hit me at the Mitsutan ikebana exhibition. What did Nolvadex contain? Could it be something that could cause a fatal overdose?

I wrapped the tablet in a fresh tissue and stuck the ball in my raincoat pocket. I closed the desk drawer, wiping off the remaining traces of black powder, and turned off the photocopier. Before I left, I threw both tissues into a covered bin that said, in English, LET'S ENJOY RECYCLE. Takeo's project? If so, he should have corrected the English. I thought about that while I walked down the stairwell. Then I heard a set of footsteps a few flights behind me. Someone else was using the stairs.

I hurried all the faster, taking a corner so sharply that a few stalks of patrinia caught against the railing. I was dropping flowers, but there was no time to clean up. With a burst of speed I made it out to the building lobby.

I hefted the flowers protectively in front of my face again and proceeded to the door.

"Excuse me, madam, but we need to check your bags."

The doorman's command forced me to stop. From behind the flowers I murmured, "You mean my flowers? I never unwrapped them. You see, I had a mixup about there being a class this afternoon."

"No, just your backpack. I apologize for the inconvenience, but we are conducting examinations of all visitors as part of our new security system."

I laid my backpack and the wrapped flowers on a polished walnut table.

"Shimura-san! How is your health?" Miss Okada left the reception desk to greet me.

"Fine. As you can see, I'm up and around, and I made the silliest mistake about class time!" I kept my eyes on the doorman, who was slowly proceeding through my backpack. I hoped that he wouldn't notice the roster of teachers, its pages still warm from the copier, tucked between the pages of the *Japan Times*.

"Won't you take these flowers?" I blurted in an attempt to get Miss Okada to look at me and not the sloppy assortment of goods coming out of my backpack. "I went to the administrative office to present them to Mrs. Koda, but she was not there."

Miss Okada nodded absently, because she was staring at the doorman. I followed her line of vision to the doorman's hands, which were opening the box containing the ikebana container. Once the *suiban* was revealed in its pink glory, he started to cover it again.

"Just a minute," Miss Okada told the doorman. "May I see that piece?"

"Certainly," I said, although I wasn't sure whether she was asking permission of the doorman or me.

She turned the piece over immediately and looked at the Kayama seal on the underside. "Why, this is Kayama ware!"

"That's right. I wanted to show it to somebody here. I was thinking of Natsumi-san."

"She is not here today. Won't you sit down for a minute, Miss Shimura? I will telephone Mrs. Koda to come downstairs and assist you."

Settling down on a steel bench, I stared at the Kayama School's massive sandstone sculpture, sensing that I was between a bunch of rocks and a very hard place. I should have stuck to one excuse for being in the school instead of making three. Now it was up to Mrs. Koda to figure out the truth. Perhaps she would go straight to her desk, count the tablets in her medicine vial, and realize I'd stolen one. If not, she'd see the smudged tissue I'd foolishly left in the recycling container or notice that the photocopier was warm. Or was I being paranoid?

Miss Okada was still on the phone, keeping her eyes on me. The receptionist bowed slightly, signifying the end of one telephone call, and then made another call to somebody. She kept her eyes on me the whole time. I looked away, trying to seem fascinated by the sandstone sculpture.

After five long minutes Mrs. Koda arrived via the elevator. She was wearing a skirt and sweater topped by a traditional quilted jacket, and with her slightly bent posture, she looked like a cozy grandmother out of Japanese folklore. She smiled comfortingly at me and bowed but did not come close. She was intent on examining the *suiban*, which Miss Okada had moved to her receptionist's desk—the same place where Norie had left the pruners to be wrapped up.

Her eyes brightened, and she half smiled when she turned over the *suiban* and looked at the seal. Mrs. Koda said something to Miss Okada that I couldn't hear before she came to me.

"Please!" I jumped up and offered her my place on the bench.

"There is room for us both to sit down," she said. "First of all, thank you for your kind letter. I felt so bad when you became ill at the exhibition. I was such a terrible person to suggest you drink the tea! I never would have dreamed it was tainted by poison."

"The poison was in the sugar, not the tea, so it actually was my sweet tooth that was at fault." I usually disliked the back-and-forth exaggerated apologies that were key to Japanese etiquette, but today I wanted to do it for a while.

"No, my selfish demand led to your violent illness. There is no doubt about that." Mrs. Koda looked at the flowers I'd laid on the table. "Those are much lovelier than the azaleas I sent you. It is difficult to get quality flowers outside our regular school supplier."

So she hadn't bought the azaleas at My Magic Forest? Maybe she was secretly environmentally conscious or she was living on a tiny salary. It was likely that the Kayamas paid their employees poorly, keeping their fabulous wealth to themselves.

"Oh, the azaleas were outstanding." I tried to manufacture a compliment soulful enough for someone who believed that flowers were conscious beings. "I made an arrangement in a blue-and-white hibachi, and the freshness and beauty of your flowers set against the old pottery made up for my poor skill as an arranger."

"Do not doubt your ability. You see into the hearts of flowers, remember?" she chided. "Although I agree that the container one chooses adds a grace note to any arrangement. The *suiban* you were carrying today, for instance, was designed in the 1930s, breaking with the ornate nineteenth-century tradition of Japanese ceramics."

"Oh. Is it valuable?" I'd thought the price Mr. Ishida had charged me was reasonable.

"I think so. Only one thousand of these Kayama ware containers were fired at a kiln in Kyushu that did work for our school. Then came the war, and our school kiln was turned over to make military goods. After the war, there was no money for making or buying ikebana containers until the late 1950s, when we began using different techniques in order to illustrate the school philosophy, 'Truth in nature.'"

I nodded, wondering where she was leading me.

"It is impressive that you managed to find one of the 1930s containers."

"It was just blind luck, and it wasn't expensive at all," I assured her, before realizing that my careless words made it sound as if I didn't value the school artifact.

"Did you say that you bought the *suiban*?" She sounded surprised.

Just then the door to the stairs banged open. Takeo Kayama emerged in his old Greenpeace T-shirt and Levi's. He looked as if he was planning to do manual labor of some sort. The thought of Che's garden work opportunity flashed in my mind, but of course Takeo didn't need to work for money.

Takeo spoke to Mrs. Koda without even looking at me. "She had it in her backpack?"

"I believe so. We were just talking about how she bought it," Mrs. Koda said.

"I'll take care of it now." He shifted his gaze to me as if that were painful. "Come up to my office. We'll take the elevator this time."

So he'd seen the broken flower heads I'd dropped on the stairs. Connecting me with them was pretty easy, given that the opened bouquet was lying on the table by the door.

"Takeo-*sensei,* will you excuse me? I'm feeling rather tired," Mrs. Koda murmured.

"Of course. Do you want me to take you upstairs?" His voice softened.

"No, I will just have a cup of tea and then return to my work. Don't worry about me."

I picked up my backpack and smiled an artificial thanks at the doorman for setting off the whole annoying chain of events. Then I followed Takeo, who was carrying my *suiban,* into the elevator. We stepped in, and I kept my eyes on the floors lighting up. Three, four, five . . . soon we were at nine, the floor that Lila had told me had a private entrance to the Kayamas' personal penthouse.

"Get out," he said when I didn't move.

"I was waiting for you. In this country, it's customary for men to step in and out of elevators ahead of women."

"Were you planning on hitting the door-close button and escaping? Perhaps sneak out on one of the middle floors and switch to the stairs? Unfortunately, you'd run into the doorman again, and he's not going to let you leave without my permission!"

"Not if I get the right exit." I stalked out of the elevator ahead of him. "In a building this size, you need more than one staircase to meet the fire code and more than one exit to the outdoors. There are other routes through the building that are less well marked."

"That's right," he said as he followed me off. "In fact, you're about to discover the route to my office."

"Is it in your family apartment? There's a set of stairs that can be reached from a smaller hallway that stems off this main one—"

"I live in the country, not here." He looked at me hard. "Walk to the left. It's the fifth door."

This section of the building was more elegant than the efficiently decorated administrative office on the second floor and the bare, sunlit classrooms on four. The walls in the hallway on nine were a deep cinnabar color and decorated with small spotlights that fell upon small framed paintings. I recognized an infinity net painting by the Japanese artist Yayoi Kusama and a small striped picture that looked like something by Mark Rothko. Could it be? I stopped dead in my tracks.

"Yes, it's a Rothko," Takeo said. "I'm surprised you didn't take it."

"What?" I continued down the hall.

"Don't play games. You know the off-limits sections of this building very well."

"I heard about the path to your apartment from a fellow student. She'd been invited up for a dinner once."

"Lila Braithwaite," he said in a flat voice as he opened a nondescript door. I went into what looked like his office. I didn't really believe anything was going to happen to me. Mrs. Koda, Miss Okada, and the doorman all knew I was in this jumbled-up office with walls lined with framed photographs of weeds and wildflowers, a desk with a computer terminal, and a couple of club chairs upholstered in ancient brown cotton. The room was the antithesis of the spare, minimalist design of the Kayama Kaikan.

Takeo picked up the stack of *National Geographic* magazines towering on the seat of one of the chairs and motioned for me to sit. I did, falling deeply into the chair, the springs of which had probably been broken thirty years ago.

"You and I have something in common. I also buy old furniture," I said, unable to hide my amusement. "So which is your favorite Sunday shrine sale?"

Takeo's voice rose an octave. "It's not from a flea market! This is furniture from the original building my family lived in. The chairs were in my mother's suite."

Once again my American openness had gotten me into trouble. I felt terrible to have knocked his family heirloom.

"You're not here to appraise the furniture, anyway. I want to hear from you about what you were carrying in your backpack."

"I presume you're interested in one thing in particular?"

"You were carrying an art moderne ikebana container that was manufactured for our school during the 1930s. Only a thousand vessels were made. To find one today is rare," Takeo said.

"That's what Mrs. Koda told me." It would improve Mr. Ishida's spirits to know this fact.

Takeo swung his legs over the side of his armchair, as if he was planning on staying there for a while. "Out of the one thousand containers produced, there were two hundred different styles. Five samples were made of each. Some of them were given to teachers as gifts, while others were used at the school. Of course, some of them broke in daily use or disappeared."

I stared at the reddish earth on the bottom of his Frye boots, wondering why they remained so popular in Japan while the trend had died long ago in the United States.

"Then the war came, and the military government seized many of our things. Metal containers were melted down for bullets, but most of the ceramics— particularly the ones without any gold leaf or elaborate painting—were left. The art moderne containers survived the war, but in the late forties there was no interest in mass-producing the collection. They weren't in fashion anymore, and even if they were, nobody had the money to invest in new ikebana containers."

"The American officers' wives who studied ikebana might have."

"No. In the 1940s, leftover things from the thirties were regarded like clothes or furniture from the seventies are for us. Tacky. Besides, my father told me the American women wanted antiques, pieces of old Nippon to take away with them. Just like you."

The 1970s had been the major fashion influence on Japan for the last five years, but making that point would have muddied what I needed to say. "I'm not trying to take things out of Japan! I'm helping to raise the value of and appreciation for Japanese decorative art treasures. In a sense, my work is cultural consciousness-raising."

Once the words were out, I could have bitten my tongue. Cultural consciousness-raising. I sounded stupid and Californian.

Takeo stared at me coldly. At last he said, "It amazes me that you would use the excuse of cultural consciousness-raising to justify theft."

"Theft?" I asked.

"The only reason the police aren't here is because I can't count on them to tell me everything that you confess. After all, they didn't tell me anything of value after Sakura died."

"What's this about theft? Somebody stole something from the school?"

"You did, Rei. That's why you're here. I want to ask you how you stole the entire Kayama ware ceramics collection and why you cared to do it."

Chapter 16

*T*akeo." I stressed his first name, given that he had used mine without invitation or even as much as a *-san* ending to show respect. "Takeo, you certainly have a vivid and creative way of looking at the world. I guess that's why you're going to be the school's next headmaster."

"You stole that *suiban*, along with our entire art moderne collection. I don't know how you pulled it off, but you did it. Bravo." Takeo spoke in the authoritative manner he'd used when the police arrived at the building after Sakura's murder.

"Go ahead, call the police," I dared him. "I'd be happy to take them to the shop where I bought the *suiban* this morning."

"You're fabulous at lying, Rei. Your lies are almost as fabulous as your dancing."

That was as blatant an insult as I'd ever received.

But I merely raised my eyebrows and said, "Look at my sales receipt." Taking my time, I withdrew my wallet and found the paper Mr. Ishida had given me.

"Don't tell me that your accomplice is old Mr. Ishida!"

"You sound familiar with him," I said.

"Yasushi Ishida was named in several articles that were written about you last year. I think the fact that the venerable expert is now trafficking in stolen antiques will be even more newsworthy, don't you think?"

The issue of theft was being raised again. Trying to sound reasonable, I asked, "Stolen? From where?"

"Our school's archives."

"When did it happen?" I asked.

"About six weeks ago. But you know that already. Why are you asking?" Takeo snapped.

"Six weeks ago I was in Sapporo appraising an estate." There, I was in the clear.

"Well, I don't know the exact date. You or your friend could have taken the Kayama ware earlier. It's just that I noticed it at that time."

"My first step into this building was two weeks ago, when I came for a students' orientation with Mrs. Koda. She took me all over the school, but not to any archive. Ask her." My words were braver than I felt, as I remembered how suspicious Mrs. Koda had seemed when she'd asked me about the Kayama ware.

"If you weren't on the premises, maybe your aunt was," Takeo said. "She has easy access to the building."

"So do hundreds—thousands—of other teachers and students. But go ahead and blame my aunt. She thinks that finding Sakura's body ruined her image here forever, so I'm sure this new bombshell won't make a difference." I was really angry at him. "What about you? You could have taken the Kayama ware a while ago and had somebody fence them to Mr. Ishida. You knew that I was friends with Mr. Ishida and that I'd go into his store sooner or later and be drawn to buy one. Then, presto, I get caught with a piece and take the fall for your crime."

"Do you know what my personal net worth is?" He paused. "More than one billion yen. That's seven million American dollars at this week's exchange rate, and you know I've got much more money coming when my father dies. Why would I be interested in fencing an insignificant collection of 1930s ceramics?"

"Earlier you told me that the ceramics were rare. Now you say they're insignificant? What is the truth?" I seized on that as a way to hide my annoyance that someone my age had such a revolting amount of money.

"The Kayama ware is important to me because it is my family property. That's all." He looked at me hard. "Even if you unsuspectingly bought the *suiban* at Ishida Antiques, it's still stolen property. Ishida-san could be charged for selling it. I could report him with one telephone call to the police."

I envisioned my seventy-five-year-old friend being forced to kneel for hours in a harsh prison cell, and a wave of depression swept over me. I couldn't look at Takeo's triumphant face anymore, so I looked at my lap. How was I going to get out of this room and this terrible situation?

I heard a creaking of chair springs and then felt a

hand on my shoulder. Takeo was touching the place where a bra strap would have been, had Aunt Norie not decided to confiscate most of my underwear for mending.

"I'm not calling the police yet."

"Oh?"

"Yes, a murder and a poisoning within one week's time are about all the school can handle."

I sat up straight in the sagging chair, shaking Takeo's hand off my shoulder. "I'm not against talking to Lieutenant Hata, but please let me be there with you. I think the theft of the containers is probably related to Sakura's death. But it's not a case of Mr. Ishida trying to make money from your family's treasures."

"Then what is it?" Takeo was studying me in the same intent manner as a crow watching the garbage being put out in my neighborhood.

I told him about the woman who had swept into Ishida Antiques, arranged for a consignment ratio strongly in her favor, and left a phony telephone number. Takeo's expression didn't change, but at the end of my recitation he walked to one of his crowded shelves and removed something. He handed me a framed photograph of a slender young woman in a garden holding two infants. Both babies were wearing blue-and-white cotton kimono and were absolutely adorable, with small heads bristling with thick black hair and big eyes peering from sweetly round faces. They were much cuter than Lila Braithwaite's sniveling children.

Takeo made an irritated sound. "Don't waste your time staring at Natsumi and me—you know us already. This is my mother. The one and only Mrs.

Kayama—excepting, of course, my grandmother, who died five years ago."

"This woman who came to Mr. Ishida was in her fifties," I said.

"Hmmm. My mother would have been fifty-three this year. I don't think there are any other Kayama women in the same generation." Takeo kicked at some lint on his junk-covered rug, and the stack of *National Geographic*s toppled. He didn't pick them up.

"I want you to talk to Mr. Ishida about her," I said. "But the only way I'll introduce you to him is if you promise to be polite. You cannot go into his shop blazing with the outrage you showed me."

Takeo pressed his lips together. "Blazing with outrage? Is that how you see me?" When I nodded, Takeo said, "I'll try to stay in control. Will you take me there now?"

"Better not," I said, thinking that I needed to warn Mr. Ishida about the situation ahead. "Mr. Ishida's shop closes at six. Maybe I could get him to meet us for dinner."

Takeo shook his head. "You and I can't be seen together."

Feeling insulted, I said, "What about the *izakaya*? You took me there for a beer right after the murder."

"Nobody knew me in that dive."

"I see. Well, I've enjoyed the interrogation, and I wish you luck in your ventures. I'll be leaving. Would you be kind enough to call off the Rottweilers downstairs?" I waved and headed for the door.

"Rei." He looked at me with his bottomless-cup-of-coffee eyes.

"What is it?"

"The reason I can't be seen with you is that you are the blood relation of a woman who is the chief suspect in a murder committed in my family business. If you want me to meet you and Ishida-san tonight, I'll do it. But not in this neighborhood."

While sketching him a map showing the directions from Sendagi Station to the tea shop, I said, "The best place to go is the Yanaka Tea Shop. If you put on a decent suit and trade those hiking boots for wing tips, nobody will recognize you as the Kayama School's billion-yen boy."

"Look like a salaryman, you mean?" Takeo sounded annoyed.

I picked up my *suiban,* silently defying him to tell me that I couldn't take the property I'd paid for.

He let me go.

In the lobby downstairs, I was met with deep bows and apologies from Miss Okada and the doorman.

"I am so sorry that I did not know about your special historical project. Takeo-*sensei* just telephoned to tell us about it," Miss Okada said.

"I apologize for delaying you, madam." The doorman's eyelashes were practically grazing his green polyester knees.

I could give as good as I got. "Oh, please don't apologize! It was my fault for not explaining the situation."

"We are so looking forward to reading your article on the historical significance of ceramics in the Kayama School," Miss Okada said.

"What's that?"

"I'm speaking about the article that will be published this fall. Takeo-*sensei* said you will be writing about the Kayama ware for *Straight Bamboo* magazine. How lucky for us."

I smiled faintly and headed out into the spring afternoon. Takeo had provided a believable excuse for having the *suiban,* but he wouldn't be the one who would have to explain months later what had happened to the article. I wasn't a writer, and even if I was, I wouldn't waste my time writing about the Kayamas.

Still, I knew that Takeo had let me off easily. He could have tried to have me arrested for buying stolen goods. Instead, I'd made it out of the school with my flowers, the *suiban,* the list of teachers, and Mrs. Koda's mysterious white tablet, as well as an evening appointment with Takeo and Mr. Ishida that could prove fruitful.

Half an hour later, as I turned into my street, I heard the cheerful calls of children racing on bicycles. Expecting little ones on bikes with training wheels, I was almost knocked over by two girls in their late teens riding mountain bikes. I should have remembered that girls tried to sound childlike as long as possible; it was considered very cute. Funny how Lila Braithwaite's seven-year-old son had sounded considerably more world-weary. Western kids grow up faster, even in Japan.

Inside my apartment, I shut my windows against the squawking girls. The air was heavy with the smell of My Peto cleaning spray. My aunt had cleaned recently, but she wasn't around.

I played back the messages on my answering machine to see if she'd called me. However, both of my calls were from overseas, the first a message from my parents asking about my recovery, and the second from my ex-boyfriend Hugh Glendinning. He'd seen a photograph in a newspaper somewhere of cherry trees in bloom and thought of Japan, and of me. *Too little, too late,* I thought, and erased the message.

I called Mr. Ishida to book him for the evening, and once that was done, I called my cousin Tom. He said that he had heard of Nolvadex but would need to check the *Physicians' Desk Reference* to get more details.

Disappointed he wouldn't give me a quick answer about the drug's toxicity, I hung up. I stared at the freshly vacuumed tatami, spotless except for a crumpled paper lying near the door. I must have dropped it on my way in, because Aunt Norie would never miss such a thing.

As I picked it up, I realized it was an envelope folded in two. I opened it and saw the same cherry blossom paper decorated with three lines of text. The poem was once more written in *hiragana,* so I could read it.

> *Haru kaze ni*
> *Osaruru bijo no*
> *Ikari kana!*

> *The breezes of spring*
> *push the beautiful girl*
> *arousing anger.*

I focused on an image of a rough spring wind whipping a girl's hair into her face. Perhaps the poet was saying that the girl was irritated by the wind. But like its predecessor, this haiku could be read in a more sinister way. A girl pushed. Was someone threatening me?

Although I was certain both poems had come from the same person, I still wanted to compare this new haiku with the other one. I pried up the lid of the *yukashita*, where I'd placed the first haiku letter for safekeeping underneath a box of Belgian chocolates. I lifted up the box and stared down at the storage drawer's bottom. It was no longer grimy, and the letter was gone.

Damn my cleaning-genius aunt. I jammed the latest haiku in my raincoat pocket, which was the only safe place that I could think of, and left. I moved as if I was on automatic pilot through Yanaka Cemetery's road, bedecked with cherry trees, to my favorite temple.

Although the sky threatened rain, I wanted to be outside. Sadly, the tranquil small garden was now littered with cherry blossom petals, leftover sake bottles, and sushi boxes. I sat down anyway on a small bench and took the papers out of my pocket. I first studied the haiku and then read the Stop Killing Flowers flyer that Che had given me outside Mitsutan. It was printed in three languages, and the English text was well written and easy to understand. Colombia, the world's second largest cutflower producer, employed young female workers to

grow and cut the flowers to be shipped for overseas
sale. The flowers were heavily sprayed with pesticides, including the highly toxic methyl bromide,
endosulfan, and parathion, pesticides that were
banned in most parts of the world. Making matters
worse, some flower producers sprayed the flowers
while the women were working in the greenhouse,
giving them only torn masks and gloves for protection. The effects of the pesticides on the women
ranged from fainting and skin irritation to respirato-
ry and neurological problems. If the women workers
became pregnant, miscarriage, premature births,
and birth defects often followed. The pesticides also
had a possible link to breast cancer, based on evidence from a study done on female agricultural
workers in Hawaii.

Because Colombia had laws on the books against
use of these pesticides, environmental activists had
tried to get the government to force flower ranchers
to change their practices. However, there were only
two health inspectors for the region, and some companies denied the inspectors access to their sites. The
inspectors quietly went away, and the dangerous
practices continued.

I shut my eyes, imagining what it would be like to
work in a thick fog of chemicals, snipping flowers for
women to arrange in their ikebana classes. They
were my age, but they just happened to have been
born into the wrong country and economic situation.
The dash of ant poison I'd tasted was nothing com-
pared to what they had to endure on a daily basis.

I watched a middle-aged couple ladling water over

their hands, a step symbolizing purification, before they approached the temple to worship. My thoughts turned from pesticides to the way that money was running through my own hands. I hadn't brought in any income since the gilded screen I'd sold to the dealer from Kyoto—yet I'd just bought flowers at My Magic Forest and an ikebana container. At the rate at which I was going, in a month's time I wouldn't have money for rice, let alone pesticide-free flowers from My Magic Forest.

There was something familiar about the couple who had washed their hands. They stood praying a few feet away from the main religious building, a wooden structure with its doors open to reveal a bronze figure of Buddha. After studying the woman's familiar lavender coat, I realized the worshiper was my Aunt Norie. Her male companion had a light suitcase on wheels at his side. The man's bowed head revealed the same light thinning as my own father's. I recognized Uncle Hiroshi, back at last from Osaka. He and my aunt had come to the shrine to pray before they even dropped off his luggage at my apartment.

They had walked straight past without noticing me moping under the cherry trees. I was not certain whether I should stay put or interrupt their prayers.

When Aunt Norie finished the prayer by throwing some money into the wooden box in front of Buddha, she turned around and saw me. She beamed and called out my name. Uncle Hiroshi bowed, not a formal, waist-deep gesture, but a quick inclination of his head and shoulders.

"Welcome home, Ojisan. It's so good that you're here." The words sounded flat, but I really didn't know what else to say to the man I had not seen in two years, not since his transfer to his company's regional office in Osaka. I didn't think the years away from Norie had been good for him; he was heavier, and his face wore a tired, unhappy expression. I wondered if my aunt was still glad that she'd struggled for the right to marry him.

"What a pretty sight—my niece under the cherry blossoms." Uncle Hiroshi's voice sounded reassuringly the same—as deep and sonorous as my father's. The stress and accent in their speech were the same, although their languages were different. My father usually spoke English to me, while Hiroshi naturally preferred Japanese.

I spoke quickly to my aunt, making an excuse so that she wouldn't think I'd been following her. "Isn't this a nice place? I sometimes come here at lunchtime."

"Have you eaten already?" Norie surveyed the wooden boxes and paper wrappings around me with disapproval.

"No! This was left from the cherry blossom viewing parties, I'm sure."

"Well, it's terrible for a religious place to be littered! The partiers are allowed to drink on the streets only, not in here. We'd better clean up."

There was only one small trash can near the temple entrance and it had already overflowed with cherry blossom party leftovers. Without wastebaskets, there was supposed to be less chance that garbage would overflow onto the street. There was an unwritten rule that everybody carried their refuse home for disposal.

Uncle Hiroshi, Aunt Norie, and I wound up carrying an odious collection of garbage home. My building had a small area behind it for trash collection, so we threw the garbage on top of what was already there. Uncle Hiroshi hefted the largest bags up and over, making me worry about his back. The Shimuras tended to have weak backs. But Hiroshi and Norie were very satisfied to have performed their act of environmental do-gooding.

"Leave a place cleaner than when you arrived. That should be your guideline, Rei-*chan*," my aunt said.

"Well, it's certainly yours!" I was thinking of how she'd cleaned out my storage compartment and stolen my haiku evidence.

We slipped out of our shoes in the entryway, went inside, and washed our hands thoroughly. I put the water heater on to boil for tea and set out some rice crackers.

"Your apartment is very comfortable, Rei-*chan*. Did you find it by yourself?" Hiroshi asked.

"Well, Obasan was kind enough to sign the lease," I answered. "A foreigner can't rent an apartment without a Japanese citizen to vouch for her."

"It's a ridiculous law, considering all the good things Rei has done to the place," Norie said. "When I first saw it, the walls had peeling paper, the tatami mats were infested with bugs, and there was no bathtub. Our niece is a good home designer."

"It's certainly nice and clean," Uncle Hiroshi complimented as he accepted his cup of tea.

"It's all Obasan's hard work. Since she's been here, she's done so much cleaning, all the way from the windows to the *yukashita*." I was speaking in a way that seemed metaphorical but also expressed an awareness that my aunt might have snooped in the kitchen's underground storage drawer.

"Yes, I did a bit of spring cleaning. It was necessary because of the visitors during her illness. She is barely recovered—in fact, I really shouldn't have asked her to carry the park garbage." Norie sounded nervous. "Please forgive me, Rei-*chan*!"

Uncle Hiroshi, blithely unaware of the conversation's subtext, sipped his tea with relish. "Ah, I haven't had a tea like this in a long time. Is it from the beefsteak plant?"

"Yes, Obasan brought the tea during my illness— one of the many kind things she has done for me. Obasan, I have something small to give you in thanks for all you've done."

I handed her the wrapped bouquet of flowers, only slightly the worse for wear.

"Oh, you don't need to give me anything," Norie said, unwrapping the package anyway. "Is this mock orange? What an original combination, with the lotus leaves and cosmos." She smiled at me. "How nicely your taste is developing."

"I thought it would look great in one of the earthenware containers you have in Yokohama," I said.

"Yes, we can arrange it together there. Bring your

lesson book, so I can check off another step toward your first certificate."

I was upset at the implication that the flowers were going to be treated like mine, not hers, and that I was going to Yokohama. I asked in my politest voice, "Obasan, you're returning to your home, aren't you? Now that Uncle Hiroshi is here, you need to take care of him."

I beseeched them with my eyes. All the organizing Aunt Norie had done couldn't change the fact that there wasn't much room for three people in two rooms the size of fourteen tatami mats, total.

Aunt Norie put her cup down with a click. "Tsutomu says that the journalists are no longer at the house, and we have a free bedroom waiting for you. Please come home with us tonight. Spend one night and see how you feel tomorrow."

"The problem is that I have a meeting tonight with Mr. Ishida! You know how I've been neglecting my business. It's very important that I see him as planned."

"Why can't you do business during daylight hours? It is not safe for a young woman to be walking alone at night," Norie countered.

"Mr. Ishida is Rei's mentor. It's true that Rei cannot show him disrespect," Uncle Hiroshi said.

"Yes, it's just like your situation, Ojisan," I said, seizing the argument. "You want to live in Yokohama with Norie, but your company ordered you to Osaka, so you went. There was no choice."

Hiroshi and Norie looked at each other for a minute, and I wondered if I'd said something inappropriate.

Norie said, "Actually, that is no longer the case. Hiroshi's company is closing its Osaka operation."

"You'll be back in the Tokyo office! That's wonderful." It took me a few seconds to realize that I was the only one who seemed excited about that. Uncle Hiroshi looked as unhappy as he had at the temple, and Norie was staring into the red-brown depths of her tea.

"Well, it certainly will be a change," I continued.

"It is not our desire to put a burden on you when you have enough troubles already," Aunt Norie said.

"You're upsetting Rei," Hiroshi chided Norie. But he touched her hand, which I thought was a good sign.

"Rei is part of the family. She deserves the truth," Norie insisted.

"It's not so bad, really. I'm sure I'll find something new," Hiroshi said in a brisk voice. It was the way businessmen talked to one another on the subway — cool, dispassionate.

Now I suspected that Hiroshi's problem had something to do with work. Maybe the Tokyo move meant that he was getting demoted to a desk by the window. I looked at my uncle, but he wouldn't meet my eyes.

Aunt Norie walked across to the bathroom and turned her head, signaling for me to join her. I did. When she had closed the door and turned on the bathtub taps, she spoke in a voice so low that I had to strain to hear it.

"Ojisan cannot say it aloud to you, because he did not even say it to me. I found out from his supervisor that due to the economic crash, the bank is closing. Your uncle no longer has a job."

Chapter 17

A salaryman without a salary is Japan's unspoken nightmare. Hiroshi had started working for his bank in the early 1960s. My father had told me that these were tough years, when people still used hibachis instead of space heaters to warm their houses and babies wore diapers made from old *yukata* robes. And for the men who worked at reorganized or new companies, the order of the day, and the night, was work. Hiroshi debuted as a junior executive working sixty-hour weeks that turned into eighty-hour weeks as he progressed in responsibility. Three years ago he had left his family because the company wanted him to oversee a new office in Osaka. Now the bank he'd given his life to had let him down.

There was nothing shameful about the layoff, Aunt Norie said. He wasn't being fired because he had embezzled money or sexually harassed anyone. But given his age, fifty-eight, he would probably not be hired by another bank.

"Have you saved a lot of money?" I asked. Like most housewives, Norie paid all the bills and allotted her husband an allowance for daily necessities.

"Of course. I invested your uncle's extra salary along with my family inheritance in many different stock accounts. But the Asian stock market is so bad that our funds have lost over fifty percent of their value. We must leave them untouched and hope that they will regain their value." As she looked at me, the woman whose skin I'd recently admired was suddenly showing crow's-feet and shadows. I understood why she and Hiroshi had stopped to pray at the temple before coming to the apartment.

"Ojisan must not give up. I'm sure an employment agency would have something for him, maybe even in the same field—"

"Yes, perhaps he can work in a different bank as a floor walker, the man who directs customers to the correct place," she said without irony. "We must go back to him and be sweet and cheerful. Please don't ask him anything about the exact details of his job loss."

As she made a move to turn off the water, I said, "Before we leave, please tell me why you took that letter from the *yukashita*."

Norie sighed. "That haiku was meant not for you, but for me."

"How do you know that?"

"I have received such poems for many years. The

haiku are all famous classics, so they could not possibly be perceived as threats. But the messages!" She shuddered.

"The one you took applies to me," I said, feeling stubborn. "The message is about somebody wishing I would drink enough to go to sleep permanently."

"It is about death, but not yours. Don't worry."

"Don't worry? I reported it to Lieutenant Hata. He thinks it's worth worrying about!"

Norie took a shaky breath. "You shouldn't have done that. Say that you won't talk to him again."

"But there might be something about the notes that could identify Sakura's murderer."

"I'm sure there isn't! Don't you understand that this has been going on for a long time? It has everything to do with me and my reputation. Nothing else."

"Why don't you let the lieutenant see the other haiku that were sent to you? He might be able to catch whoever is doing it and save you a lot of future misery."

"I don't have them anymore." Norie sounded almost smug.

"Surely you tucked them away somewhere—"

"No, I flushed them down the toilet, just as I flushed the one that you tried to hide from me in the *yukashita*. It's the safest method of disposal, and the only way I can put the issue to rest."

Water washes everything away. My aunt's favorite saying was coming back to haunt me. I was so angry that I couldn't look at her. I stared into the tub, where the stream of water was being sucked down in slow, lazy circles, just as one of the few clues to Sakura's killer had been flushed away.

"Do you treat your own children this way, or do you do this because I'm the outsider? The one who doesn't know enough to take care of herself, despite her pathetically advanced age?"

"Don't talk that way." Aunt Norie was trembling against the door, as if I were liable to attack her.

"You want to take away my freedom of speech along with everything else? Well, I won't let you." I grabbed the doorknob, yanking open the door and storming out of the bathroom.

I grabbed my raincoat, backpack, and umbrella, not looking to see what was going on with Uncle Hiroshi. As far as I was concerned, Norie and he could have my place to themselves.

I still had four hours until my meeting with Takeo and Mr. Ishida, which was a good thing, because I was too shaken to be with anybody. I wanted to curl up alone in a quiet place and sob my heart out. But finding a public place to be alone in Tokyo is a tall order. The only thing I could think of was going to the movies, where it would be too dark to see people.

The Yebisu Garden Cinemas were showing a revival of *Mabaroshi no Hikari*. The film, the title of which meant "phantom light," told the story of a young woman struggling to build a life after her husband inexplicably kills himself. The action shifted from a depressed Osaka neighborhood to a beautiful fishing village. The woman struggled out of her sorrow and into a feeling of belonging in the new community.

When the lights came up, the mostly female audience gathered up their purses and raincoats. I stayed in my seat, watching the credits on the screen, hoping to delay my return to the reality of busy, noisy Tokyo. I knew very little about the old-fashioned places where people fished for their dinners and dried their own seaweed in the garden, but that fishing village looked like a far better world than the one I was living in. If Uncle Hiroshi and Aunt Norie sold their house and moved to the countryside, they too could have a second lease on life. Hiroshi could spend his days fishing and Norie could tend to a garden. They would worship at a small country temple with no litter problems. And if the new home was hundreds of miles from Tokyo, my relatives would never interfere with my life again.

I smiled sarcastically to myself, but my expression froze as I saw a willowy figure pass my seat. The woman was slightly hunched in the way girls are when they want to hide their height, or their developing chests, from the world. But I recognized her right away as Mari Kumamori, the shy fellow student I'd met at the Kayama School.

The moviegoers behind Mari must have thought I was smiling at them, because they bowed briefly, which forced me to bow, and in the end caused a lot of confusion. I cut into the aisle behind them so that I wouldn't miss Mari.

I spotted her outside the theater, moving slowly toward Ebisu Station. I didn't want to scare her, but

I was worried that I would lose her in the evening rush-hour crowd. I ran through the misty rain, not wanting to pause to stop to remove the compact umbrella in my backpack. I hadn't worked out much in the last week, and the exercise felt good. When I caught up with her, I wasn't even winded.

"Kumamori-san," I called, and she turned around.

"Miss Shimura." She looked startled and not particularly happy.

"I think we were at the same film."

"*Mabaroshi no Hikari?*" When I nodded, she said, "I've spent my day watching three films. It's a very lazy thing to do, but there was no ikebana class today, and I didn't have the heart to make any pottery."

"I'm sorry you've felt discouraged about working. Sometimes I have a bad day when I can't bring myself to get anywhere close to selling antiques. It's good to take time off."

"I'm thinking about quitting pottery forever," she said. "You saw how the headmaster broke my ceramics. Most of my work should be broken up like that. Sakura Sato once advised me that if I wanted to make good use of the pottery, I should smash it all and place the bits at the bottom of potted plants for drainage."

I could have told her that Sakura was just being nasty, but by now I understood Mari's style. She would never let herself feel like anything but the lowest garden worm. I thought carefully about how I should phrase my request. "I'm in a bad situation, too. The only thing I can think of is asking you for advice."

"It's hard to believe that a person such as myself could help anyone, but please tell me what you need." Mari stopped, as I guessed she would. A frenzied commuter rushed by, letting his briefcase swing out, and it bashed her pelvis. I gave him a dirty look while Mari swayed, trying to regain her equilibrium.

"I'd be grateful if you'd allow me to visit your pottery studio. I've been trying to figure something out about a set of plates that I am trying to sell. Since you collect ceramics from all periods, I think that if I could compare what I have to your collection, I would have a better idea about what I've got. I've tried to find something similar in shops, but . . ." I waved my hand in a vague movement suggesting despair.

"What period is your plate?" Mari asked. Her eyes looked a bit moist, perhaps from excitement. I hadn't realized how interested she was in collecting.

"I'm not sure," I hedged. "That's why I want to bring it to you for identification. And if you like the style, you could use it as a model for your work."

"My pottery collection is very humble, as is my home. It's in a small town called Zushi, south of Yokohama. I'm afraid it will be a long train ride for you."

"Oh, I know Zushi." I wrote Mari's number on the back of my theater ticket and slipped it into my pocket. My hand brushed against the haiku letter I'd hidden there, and I wondered if the delivery of it was the real reason that Mari had spent her day in Tokyo. Mari had been treated so terribly by Sakura that she had a definite motive to kill. Furthermore, her presence at the film was strange. I'd thought that I was chasing down Mari, but perhaps she was following me.

I was dreading finding out whether Norie and Hiroshi were still in my apartment, and I had a good excuse not to stop there, because I was almost late for my appointment at the Yanaka Tea Shop. I hoped that by now my cousin Tom had come over with his car, loading up his parents and all the bedding and kitchen implements Norie had brought.

Glancing into the old leaded-glass window of the tea shop, I saw Takeo, his dark hair falling over half of his handsome profile. Mr. Ishida was waiting at a table just beyond Takeo's. My aged friend, lacking interest in television and newspapers, would not have recognized Takeo Kayama, even though he knew the family's reputation.

I rushed to Mr. Ishida's table, murmuring apologies for my tardiness, despite the fact that I had just made it on time. On the way I nodded at Takeo, indicating that he should switch tables to join us. Etiquette-wise, it was the right thing to do; Mr. Ishida was old, and he was doing Takeo a great favor by meeting him outside of his shop hours.

Takeo bowed when I introduced him to Mr. Ishida—a polite but not extremely deep bow, the same movement that his father made. Mr. Ishida inclined his own head and shoulders slightly. He had no reason to stand up; he was the senior person.

"I'm so sorry for being late," I apologized once again.

"What do you want to drink, Rei?" Takeo asked. "I understand the stinkweed-seed tea is a specialty. Is that what you're drinking, Ishida-*sensei*?"

Mr. Ishida raised an eyebrow slightly, as if noticing Takeo's use of my first name without an honorific. Still, he replied cordially enough. "Yes, that is what I am drinking. Excellent for postprandial digestion."

"I had ginseng last time. I'll just go for a normal green tea this time around," I said, remembering the jitters I'd suffered.

"For me, it's between the ginseng and the stinkweed," Takeo said. "Both have their charms, but I think I'll follow *Sensei*'s choice."

I had begun to believe that the Kayamas wouldn't treat anyone outside their family as a superior, but Takeo was using a high honorific that meant the equivalent of "learned one" for Mr. Ishida. I gave Takeo the kind of look my aunt used to give me when I did things right.

Mr. Ishida began rattling on about various tea shops in Tokyo, and I felt frustrated for a few minutes before remembering that this was how he operated. It wasn't until I'd drunk about a third of my cup of green tea that he turned to the evening's real business.

"I imagine that I may owe Kayama-san an apology," Mr. Ishida said. I'd already warned him over the telephone that Takeo said the school's Kayama ware collection had been stolen. He had remained calm at the news, saying only that he would be interested in hearing the details from Takeo that evening.

"Not at all," Takeo assured him. "You were an easy mark for a criminal. I'm only sorry that she caused you so much trouble."

Was Takeo talking about the consignor or referring to me?

"Usually I never accept consignments from strangers. I broke my policy with this woman," Mr. Ishida said.

"Women can make you do things you wouldn't ordinarily," Takeo commiserated. I was annoyed enough to kick his leg lightly. When Mr. Ishida winced, I realized that I'd assaulted the wrong man.

"I'm so sorry!" I glanced at a folk art mouse adorning the shop's counter and added, "I thought something scurried under the table."

"Don't be afraid of mice. They're part of the ecosystem," Takeo said.

"There used to be a tea made from mice bones," Mr. Ishida said contemplatively.

"What?" Takeo and I exclaimed in unison. He was as disgusted as I was. That broke the tension, and we all laughed.

"That's right, children, I'm joking. Let me return to my point. I behaved contrary to my business policy because of two factors. One, the lady told me her name was Kayama, which seemed to make sense if she was offering me a consignment of Kayama ware. Two, this collection of ikebana containers, which a pair of deliverymen carried in the next day, was immense—two hundred pieces total. I asked the woman if she would be willing to share the cost with me of advertising the collection in *Ikebana International* and *Daruma* magazines, but she said no. At the time I thought it was because she did not want to spend money in advance, but now I must consider that it was because she did not want the school to learn about what she had done."

I dug into my backpack and pulled out a magazine that I'd bought at the subway station. "I wonder if you could find someone in here who looks a little bit like the woman. Or perhaps you could just show us her hairstyle."

"This is a typical magazine?" Mr. Ishida blinked as he slowly paged through.

"Not really. It's just a guide for women seeking better hairstyles." I began wondering how my own ragged locks were behaving after my mad dash from the train station to the tea shop. I tucked the ends behind my ears and hoped for the best.

"Yes, it was a typical woman's hairstyle. Like that," he said, nodding at a picture of a woman with a shoulder-length pageboy hairstyle.

"My mother wore her hair that way," Takeo said. "I used to watch her turn it under with a curling iron in front of the mirror."

Practically everyone I knew wore their hair in a pageboy: Aunt Norie, Eriko, Mari Kumamori. Sakura also was right on target—fifty-two years old, with her hair in a shellacked pageboy. Her hair had looked harder than anyone else's in class.

"Do you know the exact day that the woman came in?" I asked.

Mr. Ishida pulled a receipt out of the small man's

purse he carried. "She was here on January fourteenth."

Nobody needed to say that Sakura Sato was alive on that day.

"What were her clothes like?" Takeo asked.

"Ah, I've been waiting for you to ask. That was interesting. She was wearing an early-Showa-period silk kimono, orange and yellow with a pattern of the moon and stars woven into it. Most unusual." Mr. Ishida rubbed his chin.

"Why was it unusual?" Takeo asked. Mr. Ishida nodded at me, so I answered, sharing my knowledge of Japanese textiles. In the years of the Emperor Showa—the 1920s and 1930s—machine-woven kimono fabric was just coming into its own. Rising to the opportunity presented by the new machinery, designers went wild creating textiles that reflected the artistic influences of the period. Showa kimono were beautiful and usually available in near-perfect condition, but most Japanese people didn't think of them as treasures, the way I did. They bought new kimono. A middle-aged Japanese woman wearing a sixty- or seventy-year-old kimono would be considered eccentric.

I moved from the topic of the kimono to ask about the exact words the woman had used. Mr. Ishida replied that he could not remember the words, but the woman spoke politely and sounded as if she came from Tokyo or its suburbs. They had settled on the consignment percentages, and then the woman had taken a receipt for the goods and departed.

"Rei said you hadn't given the woman the money

for the nine Kayama ware pieces that were already sold," Takeo said.

"It was impossible for me, because the woman left a telephone number that doesn't work, and she hasn't been in contact. It's strange behavior, because private sellers usually buzz around me like mosquitoes until they get their money."

Takeo and I exchanged glances, and I was wondering if he was thinking, as I had earlier, that the mystery woman had to be Sakura Sato.

"I suppose there's no way to retrieve the containers that you already sold." Takeo sipped his tea. "It would be bad for your business to call people up and say they had to return something they bought."

"There are one hundred and ninety-one containers left in storage, so don't worry, Mr. Kayama. You still have the majority of the collection."

"You mean that you will return the collection to me? I am stunned by your generosity," Takeo said, smiling at Mr. Ishida.

"Yes. There's just the matter of the registry," Mr. Ishida said.

"What registry?" Takeo looked blank.

"Doesn't your family have a registry of all its possessions? I need a list with pertinent descriptions of each Kayama ware piece that was taken from your archive."

"I'll have to look for it." There was a waver in Takeo's voice, and I guessed that there was no list. The Kayama ware were all test pieces, items probably not considered valuable enough when they were put into the archives during World War II to be listed among the school's regular collection of ikebana ceramics. This meant that although Takeo had threatened to bring in the police, he hadn't a leg to stand on if he couldn't produce a registry.

"I hope you understand," Mr. Ishida said. "Imagine what would happen if the woman came back and I'd given everything in her consignment to you, without taking in money. Since we don't actually have proof that she's taken anything, we cannot accuse her of being a criminal."

"Of course not," Takeo said. "And I don't think this is a matter for the police. When she returns, would there be a way for you to telephone me immediately? I'd like to follow through myself."

"That's not a good idea," I interjected. "Takeo, you say that you live in the country. If you were there, you couldn't get to the store quickly enough. Mr. Ishida should just call the police."

"I'll get a beeper," Takeo said. "In the meantime, I'm going to search the Kayama Kaikan for a record of those containers. If I cannot find the record, I would like to purchase every piece of Kayama ware that you have. So I don't want you selling any more of them to anyone."

"I would not want to take advantage of you!" Mr. Ishida sounded anxious. "I haven't built my career stealing from people."

"Of course," Takeo said. "But the money isn't an issue for me."

Mr. Ishida nodded and made a movement to pick up the bill. I got to it first and went up to the tea shop counter. This was one check I wanted to pay, given that I'd brought two people together for an endeavor that had bombed. Besides, the cost of three cups of tea was less than a thousand yen. I could afford to be magnanimous.

When I returned, Takeo was helping Mr. Ishida on with his coat. "I'm giving him a ride back to West Tokyo. Come with us. My car has plenty of room."

"No, thanks. I live just around the corner." There was no way I was getting into a Range Rover in my neighborhood. It would ruin my image. To change the subject, I reached into my backpack and withdrew the ikebana container that had started all the trouble. "I've decided to give you the *suiban* I bought from Mr. Ishida. It obviously means more to you than to anyone else."

"I know," he said, picking up the *suiban*. "Thank you very much. I'll pay you back."

"Don't bother. Think of it as another donation to your school." Feeling a mixture of many things — sadness, worry, and the oddest tinge of desire — I slipped into my raincoat and out into the dark, rainy night.

Chapter 18

Norie's things were gone from my apartment. There wasn't a good-bye note. It seemed that lashing out at my aunt had done terrible damage. In fact, the message on my answering machine from my cousin Tom told me to call him at work the next morning instead of at home. Following Tom's gloomy request was a message from Mrs. Morita asking when she'd get the money for the plates she had given me. As Mr. Ishida had said, consignors liked to check on your progress.

Nine-thirty was too late to call her, I decided, and my stomach was empty and needed something. I was too tired to cook a real meal, so I decided to finish the refrigerated leftover *okayu*. As the gruel heated on the range, I watched small bubbles pop up from the depths, breaking its smooth gray surface. I was almost hypnotized by the rhythm of the breaking bubbles and watched them for some time before I smelled the burning bottom of the cereal.

I turned the gas off and poured the edible portion of the *okayu* into a saucer that I grabbed from the drying rack. The ceramic made an odd whining noise. I looked down and realized that I'd picked up not a saucer but one of Mrs. Morita's antique plates. The horrible sound was the glaze crackling under the boiling gruel.

Part of me raged at Aunt Norie for washing the plates and leaving them on the drying rack for me to make a mistake with. Even away from my apartment, my aunt caused me to screw up. I spooned the hot *okayu* off the plate and into a soup bowl. Then I turned my attention to rinsing the plate off with tepid water. After I was through, I couldn't see or feel the place where the finish had cracked. It wasn't damaged, but now I knew that it was heat-sensitive.

I stirred brown sugar into the *okayu* to make it tastier and ate quickly. Then I decided it was time to address the question that had nagged at me since the afternoon.

"Family Mart!" Mr. Waka answered cheerfully on the first ring.

"Waka-san, it's Rei. I telephoned with a haiku question. This one is about a beautiful girl being pushed."

"Ah, you are continuing your literary studies. I'm sorry, but I have many customers at the moment and can't chat."

"Cherry blossom viewers? I understand. Thanks—"

"No, there's been an accident. Some fool driving a Range Rover hit a light pole. What he was doing with such a big vehicle in a small street, I do not understand. An accident was bound to happen. My brother on the neighborhood council says vehicles over a certain weight should be banned, and I certainly agree." Mr. Waka rattled on, despite his initial protestation that he had no time to talk.

I felt a chill dance up my spine. "Were there two people in the Range Rover?"

"Yes, and wouldn't you know that a young man would be the driver? There is an old man in the passenger seat, maybe his boss or his grandfather. Nobody knows, because they haven't removed the bodies yet."

"The bodies! Are they dead?"

"To be honest, I don't know if they are dead or alive. I hope to hear from the ambulance staff."

I moved so quickly to pick up my coat, keys, and umbrella that I dropped the phone.

"Shimura-san? What happened?" Mr. Waka's voice bleated from the receiver lying haphazardly on the floor.

I picked it up. "I'm going there. It's in front of your store?"

"No, the little street that runs behind it. You cannot enter because the police have put up a safety barrier."

I thought for a second. "I'll come through the alley. Talk to you later."

❅　　❅　　❅

Conditions are perfect for an accident, I thought as I ran down the wet road, grateful for the rubber soles of my trusty Asics. A blanket of fog reminiscent of old Basil Rathbone movies hung over the streets, slick with rain.

Takeo should have taken well-lit, wide Kototoi-dori to get back to West Tokyo. Obviously he had been confused by the lack of street signs in the old section of Yanaka. If only I had been in the Range Rover to navigate.

My familiarity with the neighborhood's tiny alleys let me enter the accident scene from a different angle than the regular traffic. From the end of the block, I saw the light pole that had toppled over the crumpled front of the sport utility vehicle, which had veered crazily to the right side of the street. The only source of light was the ambulance. From behind the battered vehicle its lights flashed on and off, reminding me of the sparkling, multicolored lights decorating Salsa Salsa's dance floor. I recalled how grim I'd thought life was that night at Salsa Salsa. In comparison to this evening, that night had been wonderful.

Because the Range Rover was so tall, I had a good view from a block away of the cracked windshield and, behind it, a huge expanse of white. It was as if clouds had filled the front seat.

A rescue crew was trying to force open the driver's-side door. The passenger-side door was already open. Couldn't they just reach across to make the rescue? No, not with the big airbags.

Running at top speed toward the accident scene, I

nearly fell when something sliced right through my shoe and into my foot. It didn't hurt terribly but was bad enough to make me stop, leaning against a store-front to take off my shoe.

The rubber sole had been penetrated by a tack. Not the kind used for pinning posters to a bulletin board, but a very long and sharp one that was used for upholstery. I pulled out the offending item and put it in my pocket. As I moved forward more care-fully, my shoe glanced against another piece of metal. I bent down and swept my hand over the street. It was too dark to see much, but it was covered by masses of tacks.

There was no sidewalk, but I tiptoed along the edge of the street to avoid more hazards as I pro-ceeded toward the car. I heard two loud bangs come from the Range Rover.

The airbags that had been blocking the front wind-shield collapsed. I guessed that the emergency work-ers now pulling out Mr. Ishida had popped the bags. Mr. Ishida seemed able to move on his own. Soon he was standing on the street, with his hand over his face.

"Ishida-san!" I hurried forward, ignoring the emergency worker holding up his hand in the stop position. Who did he think he was, a traffic cop?

"My eye!" Mr. Ishida moaned.

A second paramedic coaxed him onto a stretcher and peered into Mr. Ishida's face with a flashlight. "The gentleman's eye has been hurt. Try to be calm, sir. We will take you to the hospital."

The airbag must have hit Mr. Ishida's eye. He was

only five feet tall, which meant that he sat lower than the dashboard.

"Will you take him to St. Luke's? They have an excellent emergency department," I suggested to the emergency worker.

"Nippon University Hospital is closer, and you may not come with us," he whined. "The public must stay behind the barricades."

"I'm not the public!"

"Are you a blood relative?" the emergency worker demanded.

"Not exactly," I faltered.

"She is like my granddaughter," Mr. Ishida said, and I squeezed his hand. He wasn't angry with me, despite the fact that I'd been the one to call him out of his safe home and into a near-death nightmare.

"You're going straight to the hospital, sir. Please let go of the woman's hand. She could cause you further injury."

The doctor's daughter in me saw several things the emergency workers had done wrong that could have hurt Mr. Ishida. They had pulled him out of the vehicle in a sitting position, let him stand, and then decided to put him on a stretcher. If he'd suffered a spinal injury in the accident, he could have been paralyzed. I didn't think that was the case, fortunately.

I glanced back at the Range Rover and saw that Takeo was standing on the driver's side talking to the police. I deduced that the airbag had hit his chest, because I saw him rubbing it.

A crowd of people—the "public" the emergency worker had referred to—suddenly began cheering from their position behind the barricades.

"They're both alive!"

"Do you want to drink a beer?"

The raucous cries went on. I had to strain to hear what Sergeant Mori, the nice young policeman from the Yanaka Cemetery police box, was saying to Takeo. From the way the sergeant bowed his head to me, I knew that he'd recognized me as the neighborhood girl who occasionally had a question about an address.

"Your registration?" Sergeant Mori asked.

"Registration? I don't know . . ." Takeo's voice faltered.

"Try the glove compartment," I suggested, hoping that it was there.

The sergeant went around to the left side of the car and rummaged around. When he came back, reading the paper by flashlight, he asked Takeo, "Do you reside at the Kayama Kaikan in Roppongi?"

"Yes, that is the official address."

"So you are . . . Takeo Kayama?"

"Yes. Here's my driver's license." Takeo pulled out his wallet, and I remembered how he didn't want to be recognized with me in public. Now he had—in the context of another bad situation.

"Mr. Kayama, may I ask you to describe the circumstances leading up to the accident?" Sergeant Mori was being very polite.

"Why is that woman still here?" interrupted the emergency worker who was my enemy.

"She could be a witness," Sergeant Mori said, surprising me. I wasn't going to argue with him. This was the first time that I'd ever wanted to be detained by the police.

"We were leaving the neighborhood after having tea with Miss Shimura," Takeo said, surprising me with both his cogency and his forthrightness. "There was a black truck ahead of me moving slowly. Maybe it was because it's a small street—I wouldn't have turned in here, but I wasn't sure of the way, and I thought that the truck would be headed toward the main street. Suddenly, bright spotlights came on from the top of the truck's cab. The light was blinding, so I honked briefly to encourage the driver to turn them off. People use those spotlights to trap animals and then shoot them. The lights usually face forward, but these were reversed."

I revised my opinion about Takeo's cogency. He was rambling about the environment now, a sign that he was possibly in shock.

"So it was because you were blinded that you drove straight into the light pole?" Sergeant Mori's assistant piped up.

"I think that my right tire blew out, and I lost control of the vehicle. I remember pulling to the right side of the road and then we crashed."

"What about the truck? Did you observe the license plate or at least the model? How about the people inside the truck? How strange that they did not stop to help you!" the assistant opined.

"It might have been a Nissan. That's all I know. I couldn't actually see if anyone was in the back of the truck. The light was too strong."

"You escaped injury, but your cross-country vehicle did not. And the streetlight is damaged," the police officer pointed out, as if Takeo hadn't noticed the tall steel beam knocked across his beloved Range Rover's hood.

"I'm very sorry. I'm willing to pay for any damage to the streetlight." Takeo drew a shaky breath. "And the street."

"Mr. Kayama, the sheer size of your vehicle helped protect you from a fatality. It's ironic that the dangerous factor is what ultimately saved you." Sergeant Mori was turning out to have a real philosophical bent.

In my mind I turned over Takeo's story and what I'd encountered when I ran toward the accident scene. I held out a tack to the police officer. Its sharp point glittered under the flashing ambulance lights.

"I think you'll find one of these in the tire that blew out," I said.

"But how could—did you—" Takeo sounded upset, and I realized that he thought that somehow I might have caused his accident.

Hastily I said, "I stepped on a few of these when I was running over. The street just beyond the car is covered by these tacks. The truck's driver must have spilled them onto the street, intending for an accident to happen."

Two other policemen ran forward with flashlights to investigate the area I'd mentioned. A chorus of painful cries led me to believe that the tacks were slicing through their shoes as well.

"Hold everything!" Sergeant Mori advised. "We need a spotlight and a photographer to document this possible crime scene. Until everything is cleaned up, this is a hazardous zone."

"I will take pictures for you!" A drunken cherry blossom viewer waved a trendy digital camera.

"Mr. Kayama, why don't you come along in the ambulance with Mr. Ishida to have your own injuries inspected?" Sergeant Mori asked.

I looked over to where Mr. Ishida had been lying, but his stretcher had been loaded onto the ambulance and the back doors closed. I'd lost track of him when he needed me.

"I'd rather get home," Takeo answered.

"I can telephone your family and tell them what happened," the sergeant persisted.

"No!"

"How will you get home?" Sergeant Mori asked. "Your vehicle cannot be driven."

"I'll go by taxi or subway. Whatever's closer."

Takeo was obviously dead set on avoiding the hospital. I had been thinking of following Mr. Ishida there but now changed my plan. My elderly friend had a bruised eye and would soon be in competent hands. Takeo, who was refusing a medical examination, could be at greater risk. He might have a concussion or other head injury.

I assured Sergeant Mori that I'd keep Takeo safe and led him back the way I'd come, close to the buildings on the side of the road where there weren't any tacks. Sergeant Mori's assistants backtracked around the block to start a search for the truck, which was no doubt far away by now.

Takeo walked at a normal pace until we could no

longer be seen by any police, emergency personnel, or cherry blossom partyers. Then he stopped, leaning against a building for support.

"You're not feeling that well," I said, growing nervous. He really should have gone to the hospital. He might collapse in the back alley, and I certainly didn't have the strength to carry a five-foot-nine-inch man who probably weighed 170 pounds.

"I'm just a bit shaken. Let me rest a minute."

What he needed was to lie down and be observed. Unfortunately, there was only one nearby resting place that I could think of. I offered, "You could stop at my apartment. Just to get your breath, and then I'll put you in a taxi."

"I'm going back to the Kayama Kaikan. I've got work to do."

"You almost lost your life!" I reminded him as we started walking.

"I can't rest after hearing Ishida-san's description of the woman who came in." We were standing near the Family Mart, and its fluorescent sign cast an unattractive glow on his angular features. Through the glass, I could see that Mr. Waka was involved in an animated discussion with a customer in the candy section.

"Do you think the woman who stole the Kayama ware was Sakura Sato?" I asked, offering him my conclusion.

He shook his head.

"Who, then?" We had started walking again, and Takeo still seemed slightly off balance. He didn't object when I took his arm.

"It sounds crazy. Especially since I've just come out of an accident. I don't think you'll believe me." Takeo's words came in a rush.

"Try me," I insisted.

"When Ishida-san mentioned the old kimono that the woman was wearing . . . well, after you explained about the age of the fabric, I understood. My mother collected old textiles, old poetry scrolls, the kinds of things you do." He stopped again to lean against a soft-drink vending machine. "In fact, that picture of her I showed you has her wearing an orange-and-yellow Showa-period kimono."

So that's why Takeo had given me a significant glance when Mr. Ishida had described the kimono. I'd thought that he just wanted to know more about textile history. Now it all came together. "Somebody stole your mother's kimono!"

"Perhaps. But now I believe the lady who visited Ishida-san really was . . ." He paused, as if unable to give me the last bit. "A Kayama."

"It can't be Natsumi. Mr. Ishida said the woman was in her fifties."

"No, I mean Reiko Kayama. My mother. I've been thinking for some time that she might be alive."

Chapter 19

Any child who had lost a mother might dream of her magical return. In my gentlest voice I told Takeo, "Let's sit down and talk this over. My apartment is nearby."

"No, I need to go home. I want to show you something tonight, when nobody's at the door to make a record of your visit. Tomorrow we'll go to Izu to look for some things in my family storehouse. You can drive, can't you?"

"Yes, but I'm busy tomorrow." I was also overwhelmed by his sudden, urgent flurry of demands. He was behaving irrationally. He had to be in shock.

"You're always busy! Very well, then, I won't force you to join me, but I'm getting that taxi." Takeo stepped into the road and lifted his arm to hail a car slowly driving down the street.

"I'm sure it's got passengers," I said, expecting the

laws of rainy nighttime taxis to be in force. But the taxi was free. Its door swung open, and Takeo got in.

"What do you think?" he asked.

"The rich have all the luck," I said, worry mixing with irritation. The taxi would not have stopped for me. I just knew it.

"The Kayama Kaikan," Takeo told the driver, who did a double take in the rearview mirror. He'd recognized the billion-yen boy. Takeo didn't seem to notice; he fell into a silence, staring out the window at lights blurred by rain. I sat on the far side of the taxi seat, pushing wet strands of hair out of my face. We couldn't really discuss Takeo's mother in front of the taxi driver, but I was anxious to hear what Takeo had to say.

When we disembarked, my thoughts turned to how one entered the Kayama Kaikan after hours. Would Takeo press his fingertips against a panel that would then shoot open the doors, or would a microchip card get him in? I imagined a few James Bond–like possibilities.

To my surprise, the utterly modern glass-and-steel tower had a very old-fashioned side door. Takeo used a regular key to unlock it. As I caught the heavy door—at least it was fireproof steel—I let Takeo go ahead of me. I expected him to turn off an alarm system, but it turned out there was none.

"This building is about as secure as one of those cardboard boxes the homeless live in at Shinjuku Station," I told him. "Even my apartment is better than this. I have three locks on my door and you have just one."

"It's convenient for me to come and go, but I suppose you're right. I'll speak to my father."

Takeo opened a door along the hallway, and as frigid air rushed at me I peered at tall buckets of flowers and branches. "This is where we keep some flowers for classes. We tend to rely on daily deliveries, so there's not that much stock here," Takeo said.

The next room he showed me had a humidifier, so it was as moist as the rainy evening outside, but not as cold as the refrigerated room. It was lined with floor-to-ceiling wooden shelves that were filled with labeled boxes. Takeo told me they held wooden ikebana vessels and ceremonial boxes that were used for entertaining.

"Is this where the Kayama ware was stored?" I asked, not seeing any empty spaces.

"Next room." As he snapped on the light in the next cool cell, he waved at a seven-foot-high-by-twenty-foot-wide section of shelving that was empty. "That's where the Kayama ware used to be."

"It's strange that your thief didn't leave the boxes behind to make it look as if nothing had been taken," I said.

"The Kayama ware would be worth more with the boxes. It had our school stamp, the year, and the artist's signature."

"I wonder why none of the staff noticed the containers were gone," I said. "Who goes into these rooms, anyway?"

"Almost all the employees. If you want to make a flower arrangement for the receptionist's desk, for example, you'd come here to pick up a *suiban* instead of taking one from the classroom stock. These pieces are older and more interesting than the pieces used for teaching. That's why we like to use them in ceremonial places."

The next room he showed was not humidified and contained short, thin boxes.

"These are my mother's poetry. Or rather, works that she copied. She was a calligrapher. She liked to copy haiku, especially those with flower themes."

I felt as cold as I'd been in the refrigerated room. "Has somebody been sending you haiku?"

Takeo stared at me. Then he walked quietly behind me and closed the door. When he came back, he said softly, "How did you know?"

"I've gotten two under my apartment door in the last two days. But my aunt's been getting them for years."

"For me it's been three months. It's usually in a rice-paper envelope tucked under the wiper blade on the Range Rover. Because the vehicle is parked behind the building, I just assumed the poetry was coming from a secretary or worker."

Someone who had a crush on him. I bet that was a common occurrence.

"Where else have you found poems?" I asked.

"The day that Sakura died, one was slipped under my office door. It was by Issa and read something like:

> *A daimyo! And what*
> *Thing makes him get off his horse?*
> *Cherry blossoms do.*"

"A *daimyo* is a nobleman," I said. "Maybe the poem is suggesting that Sakura's death has thrown an important guy such as yourself off your metaphorical horse. In this case, the horse should be swapped for a Range Rover."

"If that's the meaning—and I really don't know—it could be that my sister sent it. You know that we don't get along that well."

"Why?"

Takeo busied himself straightening the boxed scrolls on the shelves before answering. "When my mother was alive, Natsumi and I were together all day long. After the death, we started drifting apart. We were put in separate bedrooms, which I suppose makes sense for a boy and girl growing up, but we lost our connection. I started studying ikebana—wanting to be like my father, I suppose—and Natsumi was more interested in playing with little girls."

"Does she have an interest in haiku?" I asked.

"I don't think so. I mean, not in composing the poetry. Were the haiku you received original?"

"No. Right after I was poisoned, I was sent a haiku by Bashō that said, 'Intoxicated, slumbering amid pinks laid out on a rock.' This afternoon I received a poem that said 'The breezes of spring push the beautiful girl, arousing anger.' I haven't found out the poet's identity yet."

"Hmmm. My mother's calligraphy is organized by the flower, so I am able to show you the first poem you recited." He pulled out a long, slender wooden box and tucked it under his arm. "We probably don't have a scroll illustrating the second haiku because it doesn't mention flowers. Everything here must relate to ikebana."

Takeo opened a door that led to the stairs. I jogged up the first flight but then abruptly remembered Takeo had been in a car crash.

"We could take the elevator instead. Nine is pretty far up," I said.

"Impossible. The light would come on, and if Natsumi comes home from her date, she will see the light panel showing where we're going. It wouldn't be a problem for me to be seen going upstairs, but you wouldn't get away with it."

We continued up the stairs, Takeo keeping hold of the railing while I hovered by his side.

On the ninth floor the hallway was illuminated by only a red EXIT sign. Our shadows tailed us, leaping against the walls in a most sinister way. I was glad when Takeo unlocked his office and turned on his desk light. My gaze went around the room, which had been slightly straightened since my visit that afternoon. The magazines had been collected into a neat pile, and a small arrangement of camellias with insect-bitten leaves graced his desk.

"This is the picture," Takeo said, holding one of his mother playing with him and Natsumi at age four. Reiko Kayama was wearing an orange and yellow kimono patterned with the moon and stars, just like Mr. Ishida's visitor.

"Mr. Ishida should see it," I said. "Will you let me borrow it to show him?"

"His eye is injured, Rei. Have you forgotten?"

"He's got another one that's still working! Once he feels better, he will be able to make a good guess at whether your mother and the consignor are the same person."

"I don't want to give you that picture. It's the only one I have," Takeo said.

"I'll take care of it," I said. "I've never lost any of my consignments."

"Unlike me. I'm sorry to tell you this, but the Kayama ware container that you gave me earlier tonight smashed when my car hit the pole. I was too depressed to bother removing the shards."

I felt for him, but I knew we had to move on. "Will you show me your mother's calligraphy scroll?"

Takeo cleared off the remaining items on his desk and unrolled the scroll, weighting each end using a *kenzan* pin-holder. I joined in his scrutiny of Reiko Kayama's rendering of the "Slumbering amid pinks" poem. Her calligraphy was gracefully rounded and similar to that on the haiku that I'd received. But the scroll looked different from the note I'd gotten. I would never know why, because Aunt Norie had destroyed the note.

"Even though I don't have the copy of the pinks haiku anymore, I think the writer was obviously different from your mother. Look at the other note I have." I pulled out the poem I'd just received, about a beautiful girl being pushed.

Takeo read it silently, and I saw him shudder.

"What is it?" I asked.

"Just a bit cold."

"Do you have any other examples of your mother's

everyday handwriting?" I was still studying the scroll. In addition to the three short lines of writing, there was a small watercolor illustration of a pink flower head lying on a bed of gray river pebbles.

Takeo shook his head. "She was never separated from us, so there were no letters. I imagine that my father might have some letters, but I couldn't ask him. We're not close." He added, "Your aunt might have something from my mother."

"Aunt Norie was just a normal student in the school. Why would she get letters from your mother?"

Takeo slowly settled into his chair, and I remembered again that he'd just been in an accident. He was silent for a minute and then said, "Do you remember when we went to the *izakaya* for a beer and I asked you to give me some information about your aunt? You seemed to think I was trying to blame Sakura's murder on her. It wasn't that. I'm interested in how she and my mother got along."

"Why?"

"There was a bad feeling between your aunt and some people here. The rumor was that her teaching certificates were always speeded through, she always gets the best placement at exhibitions, and she was even offered a good teaching position within headquarters."

"But she never took that position," I said, feeling chilled. "She dropped out of flower arranging to spend more time when my cousin Chika was born."

"How old is Chika?"

I thought carefully. I hadn't seen Tom's little sister

more than once or twice in the last few years, because she was studying in Kyoto. "She's twenty-three."

"An interesting coincidence. My mother died twenty-three years ago," Takeo said. "Chika's birth was a convenient excuse for Norie to leave. Sakura once hinted that maybe . . . Chika was not really a Shimura. Do you understand what I'm trying to say?"

I turned away from Takeo and toward the window, the black night sparkling with rain and little lights from the windows of other buildings. I remembered the mirrored glass of the skyscraper and realized that now, because it was dark outside and light where we were, people could see in. I wondered why there were no shades in the room, nothing to hide me as I struggled to maintain my self-control.

"Sakura hated Norie," I said. "She would say anything to hurt her."

"I'm sorry," Takeo said from his distant armchair.

"If your mother is alive, why would she leave you?"

Takeo sounded weary. "There were two of us— Natsumi and me—the same age. I know we were a lot of trouble. Maybe she just wanted out."

"I'm sure that's not the case. The picture of your mother holding you shows such love. Look at her face." As I spoke, I remembered how Lila Braithwaite's children had overwhelmed me. Raising twins was probably as challenging as raising three children. But surely Takeo's mother wasn't the kind who would run away.

Takeo continued. "Or what if—because of my father's feeling for your Aunt Norie—my mother decided that she wanted to just leave the marriage? Divorcing him would be something the Kayama family wouldn't allow. Mistresses are considered all right—my grandfather and all my great-grandfathers had them. People say that my father hasn't remarried because it's too enjoyable to be an unmarried man."

"But didn't somebody find your mother's body? Surely that's irrefutable evidence she died."

"The coroner could have been bribed. He could have helped, maybe even providing the body of somebody anonymous who had died."

Takeo really wanted to believe that his mother was alive. The compassion I'd felt for him earlier swelled again. How could I get him to give up his ghost?

"Okay, say that your mother is still alive and she's been sending Norie poems all along to make her feel bad about breaking up the marriage. Why on earth would your mother send menacing haiku to my aunt? Or me?"

"She doesn't want history to repeat itself," Takeo said grimly.

"No need to worry. Your father has seen me only once, and it was when I was vomiting at his ikebana exhibition. He's not likely to ask me out."

Takeo snorted. "My father's not the one at risk of capitulation."

"Who is, then?" This entirely Japanese conversation about parents, love, and death was confusing me. I turned away from him to look out the window, thinking over his last words.

Takeo came up and stood directly behind me. When he spoke, I felt his breath on the nape of my neck. "Maybe you thought I was gay. Because I like flowers."

"Never. I know gay men," I said sharply. I was surprised by Takeo's revelation, but not by the way it made me feel. With the warmth of his breath on my skin, I felt my cold, celibate self start to thaw.

Takeo's hands touched my shoulders very lightly, and a current shot through me as his hands stroked down my bare arms. "It's been tough. I've grown up in this sterile tower with a father who won't talk to me, a sister with a shopping addiction, and a bunch of middle-aged women who want to be my mother. You've been the youngest, realest woman who has ever made it past the doorman."

"Don't call me *young*. We're the same age—"

"You are the only one who doesn't bow to me. And who looks beautiful in old clothes, instead of swaddling herself in Chanel and Escada."

"I didn't bow because I thought you were just a florist. And then, well, it didn't seem as if you liked me very much, so there was no point in courtesy." I babbled on, trying to figure out what was happening.

"I do like you. But it's hard for me to know what you're up to. I talked with Mr. Ishida for a while before I started the car. He said that you lived with a foreign lawyer, but that he left you last fall. Has it really ended?"

It was painful hearing Hugh described that way, but it was true that I had been more or less abandoned. I released my arms from Takeo's touch and turned around to face him. Instead of answering him directly, I said, "Being alone doesn't mean that I'm easy."

"On the contrary, I think you're rather hard." Takeo's eyes were on me, and I wondered if he was speaking metaphorically or had actually noticed that my nipples were standing out against my thin angora sweater.

I blundered forward, as much to move my breasts out of his line of vision as to get away from him, but he matched my move with one of his own. Kendo training. The next thing I knew, his arms were around me.

I parted my lips, receiving his kiss with some curiosity. I'd had Japanese boyfriends before, but none of them had ever tried to get close to me without insisting that we take a shower first. I had nothing against cleanliness, but it felt much sexier to be messed up from the rain, kissing someone who tasted faintly like tea.

Pretty soon my curiosity was replaced by urgency; he really was a delicious kisser, and I wanted to devour him. Our bodies moved into each other, a near-perfect fit with him only half a foot taller. As his fingers grazed my breasts, my own hands streamed up his body to explore his chest. He recoiled slightly, and I remembered that he was probably sore from the car accident.

"This isn't a good idea," I murmured, and broke away completely. We were visible in the silver tower. Anyone could see into the room, perhaps even the person who had killed Sakura and wanted Takeo and Mr. Ishida dead.

Takeo's face was as flushed as I imagined mine was. In a low voice he said, "I don't know you that well, but I like you. From the way you kissed me, I think you feel the same. We have this—thing—blossoming between us, and starting tomorrow we've got a lot to do. We'll find my mother and clear your aunt's reputation."

I couldn't bear to look at Takeo, so I stared at the cover of a *National Geographic* lying on the floor. I concentrated on a family of tigers and said, "It's pretty hard to clear someone else's reputation when your own is so bad."

"Rei, don't worry about being half American! I don't mind that, nor the fact that you made only two million yen last year. I just don't care." He came within inches of my face, and when I didn't lift my face to him, he stepped around me and simply put his arms around me again. I rested lightly against his wounded chest for a brief moment. I couldn't help it. It just felt perfect, despite the harsh words I had to say.

"The one with a reputation is you," I said. "Some people remember that you were kicked out of Keio University for almost causing some poor kid's death."

Takeo's body stiffened, but he didn't let go. "I voted against bringing kendo equipment into the lavatories, but I couldn't stop them. I spent two months making daily visits to the hospital to see the student. We all did. Did you hear that part of the story?"

I shook my head.

"I admitted it was my fault, so I was expelled. Then I enrolled at UC Santa Cruz, where I learned about organic horticulture and other things."

"Is that where you learned your moves, Takeo? When you were in the UC dormitory, with California girls similar to me?" I spoke fast because he was rapidly defusing all the arguments against him.

That did it. Takeo released me so quickly that I almost lost my balance. I didn't turn around but heard him ease back into his mother's chair.

"Sorry. My timing's bad. If there was one thing that my father's tried to hammer into me, it is the virtue of patience."

"I think I'd better go. The subway . . ."

"Of course," he said. "Thank you for seeing me home. Will you find your way downstairs by yourself?"

Going through the Kayama Kaikan in the dark was not a prospect I relished, but being with him in the dark was potentially just as bad, given my treacherous hormones.

I found the way down.

Chapter 20

I felt completely bereft when I woke up the next morning. I was alienated from Takeo and also from Aunt Norie. There was no savory smell of *miso* soup, no slap of my aunt's slippers against the floor as she walked to the door to pick up the newspaper. My aunt had been such a presence in the few days that she had lived with me, and now she was lost to me, along with all the other people I'd angered.

I crawled out of my futon. Perhaps it was just as well Norie wasn't around to see me in such a state. After returning home at one A.M., I'd felt so shaken by the night's events that I wound up downing a seven-hundred-milliliter bottle of Kirin beer. Instead of helping me sleep, the alcohol perversely caused me to awaken throughout the night. I spent long minutes staring at the digital display on my alarm clock while I ran through possible links between Sakura's death and Takeo's story about a mother who might still be alive.

My morning after felt lousy. While I waited for the electric teakettle to make my cup of tea, I called Mari Kumamori. I was beginning to worry that she had given me a false telephone number, but she picked up on the tenth ring. She agreed to see me at noon. Next I called Tom at the hospital. I was put on hold for a while, during which time I drank tea and did some leg-stretching exercises. I'd decided that even though I felt weak, I might as well go for a run. It could only make me feel better.

"Hello, Rei," Tom said when he finally came on. "You don't have to make up a phony doctor's name to get them to page me. Everyone in my department knows you."

"It's my accent, I bet." I was crestfallen.

"No, it's just that you're very polite. Nobody would think you're a physician."

There was a compliment somewhere in his self-deprecating joke, but I didn't want to kid around. "What's happening with your parents?"

"They told me about my father's job loss. It's hard, but we'll all get through it."

"And your mother?"

"She is actually more upset than he is."

"It's because of me. I tried to force her to tell me about something that happened long ago. She wasn't ready."

"Well, I'm ready. To tell you about Nolvadex, at least."

I stopped stretching my hamstrings and got out my notebook to write down the details.

"It's a drug used in treating breast cancer," Tom said. "Usually after a woman has the cancerous tissue removed, she will undergo a course of chemotherapy. And after that she might be prescribed Nolvadex to help keep the cancer in remission."

"Wow, isn't breast cancer here quite rare? I thought Asian women were practically immune," I said, reaching into my Jogbra to make a quick self-exam. Remembering Takeo's hands gave me a slight twinge.

"There are plenty of women with breast cancer in Japan, but they don't run around with pink ribbons pinned to their blouses and talk about it to everyone."

"Maybe they should. Anyway, do you think the drug could be prescribed to an older woman? Say around seventy years old?"

"Are you talking about Mrs. Koda?"

"Yes," I admitted. "But please don't say anything to your mother. I have a feeling that if she was hiding the drug in a Motrin container, she doesn't want people to know."

"You're probably right," Tom said. "Over the last few years I've noticed how frail Mrs. Koda has become. I'd always thought of it as old age. In hindsight, she might need the cane to help her walk, because dizziness and nausea are side effects of Nolvadex."

"It's a strong drug, then," I said. "Could someone overdose on Nolvadex and die?"

"If you're thinking that Nolvadex was what made

you sick at the ikebana exhibition, no, you don't need to worry. It's an estrogen receptor antagonist, and there are no known problems with overdose. You were definitely poisoned by arsenic."

I made reassured-sounding noises—though I wasn't, really—and hung up with Tom. Next I called Nippon University Hospital to speak to Mr. Ishida. I was relieved to hear that he'd been released, although when I telephoned his shop, he didn't answer. Maybe he was resting upstairs in his apartment. But I didn't know the number, and that made me worry.

It was time to run. I tried to pound away my worries, my feet hitting the potholed streets of my neighborhood with loud, angry thuds. Now I was sorry that I'd spent time with Takeo instead of trailing Mr. Ishida to the hospital.

I ran into the alley where Takeo's Range Rover had crashed. It was gone, and a city employee was sweeping up tacks while a few more worked on removing the toppled streetlight. Speeding around the corner, I continued thinking about the Nolvadex. Either Mrs. Koda had cancer or she was hiding someone else's anticancer drug in her desk drawer. The latter did not seem likely.

As I moved faster, my mind raced to the Stop Killing Flowers flyer about pesticide use in Colombia. Che's information about the workers who had gotten sick was the first part of the equation. Surely the pesticides tainting the flowers would remain present on the blooms after they were shipped overseas. Maybe the person at the Kayama School taking Nolvadex had developed cancer because of long-term exposure to pesticide-treated flowers. If Stop Killing Flowers knew about that detail, they would have an extremely convincing argument to give the Japanese public. Rumors about pesticides, dyes, and additives had stopped imports of food from North America many times.

I ran through the twisting streets crowded with parked scooters and vans, visualizing myself moving through a field of native grasses and wildflowers, nothing treated, everything real. After each step I took, the grass would spring up again, healthy and undamaged. Probably the Kayamas' country house was surrounded by fields like that—land they owned and had the luxury not to develop. It was all very nice for Takeo. I was suddenly angry at him for this, as well as for the casual way he'd unloaded Sakura's cruel stories about Norie. It was adding insult to injury that he had kissed me a few minutes later.

After the run, I showered and slipped into my favorite black jeans, which fit better than they had in years. My poisoning had taken off an inch. I tucked a ribbed T-shirt into the jeans and tied a scarf around my neck. My sneakers were still damp from the run, so I wore my penny loafers instead. Aunt Norie would have almost approved of the outfit I chose to wear to Mari Kumamori's.

I had a seat on the midday train to Zushi, so I was able to study the Kayama School teachers' certificate list, referring to my *kanji* dictionary to help me translate the spelling of some names. The trip took about an hour, and by the time I disembarked at Zushi Station, I had skimmed through a few hundred

Yumikos, Marikos, and Sachikos. The suffix *-ko*, which means "child," is common in women's names. I felt lucky to have been named Rei and not Reiko, which is a very popular Japanese name that means "beautiful girl-child." Takeo's mother's name was Reiko. *Beautiful girl.* The ominous haiku message came back to me, and I pushed it away. I wasn't classically attractive by Japanese standards, no matter what Takeo had said.

According to this list, Sakura's real first name was Shizuko, which means "quiet child." A ridiculous misnomer, considering the way she had raised her voice to Aunt Norie. I chided myself for being so uncharitable about a person who'd been killed. Everyone had something good inside them—even Sakura. Takeo had spoken of her with respect, recalling how she'd cared for him after his mother's death.

Mari had given me directions to her house via a bus, saying the trip would take seven minutes from the train station. I'd wanted to walk, but she had insisted that the streets were difficult for pedestrians. Once I was aboard the bus, zooming down an expressway, I could see why. Getting around in suburban Japan required wheels. During the short bus ride, I noticed several supermarkets with parking lots crowded with sport utility vehicles and minivans. There were few mom-and-pop stores, and no tea shops or tofu-makers.

Mari's house was in a hilly district of houses that looked like they'd all been built by the same architect in the late 1980s, before the bubble economy burst. The houses were built out of a yellow material that looked like brick but wasn't, with leaded-glass windows and shingled roofs—a hodgepodge of European house details that looked awkward, but very expensive.

I rang the doorbell and waited. I rang again, and after five minutes I decided Mari wasn't going to answer. I knew that I had the right address, because I recognized her surname on the mailbox on her gate.

I was gathering up my backpack when I caught a flash of movement along the side of the house. I peered over the faux brick wall to see Mari slowly carrying a cardboard box into a tin-roofed shack with windows. Her pottery studio, I guessed. There was a real brick kiln next to the shack that was also covered by a tin roof, and, to my surprise, there was also a small wooden shrine standing on a pole next to it. Under the shrine's tiny roof sat a family of bears, all fashioned out of clay and glazed a deep brown. Mari's last name, Kumamori, meant "bear in the forest."

Mari came out of the shack without the boxes and smiled tentatively at me. "I didn't expect to see you so soon."

"This is a lovely place," I said. "I never would have expected a shrine, though."

"Those bears are the gods protecting the kiln. I made them myself, so they're not very good."

"They're very cute," I said. "You could sell them."

Mari sighed. "Always you talk about selling. That isn't my interest."

"It's not that you need the extra income. It just might be fun for you to be a businesswoman."

"I have fun already," Mari said, waving me into the

pottery ahead of her. Sun flooded through the windows, lighting a large worktable. A potter's wheel and chair filled one corner of the small studio, and the walls were covered with shelves holding finished ikebana containers. I noticed a row of vases in the classic gray, cream, and brown hues the Kayama School favored, as well as a second row of brilliantly colored containers. They were all in shades of celadon ranging from pale aqua to a deep yellow green. I'd never seen celadon used at the Kayama School. Its strong color probably went against the "Truth in nature" coda, although celadon ikebana vases were featured in old wood-block illustrations. Mari's work was a rephrasing of tradition.

"The celadon is marvelous," I said. "And you've got so much variety in color. Was that difficult to achieve?"

"Some parts of the kiln are hotter than others, and that affects the color. I used the very same glaze for all of them." She gave me a nervous half smile.

"Well, let me show you what I've brought." I unwrapped my plate. I suspected that Mari wasn't going to buy a set of nine unlucky plates, so I'd only brought one of Mrs. Morita's plates and left the rest of the lot at home.

"This looks like *sometsuke* porcelain. A dinner plate of a good size. Do you have more?"

"Eight more, all identical. None of them has a stamp on the bottom. Do you think it looks like Imari?" I inquired.

"Yes. It's definitely Imari made during the Meiji period. I think that it should retail for about fifteen thousand yen per plate. If you have ten, you could sell the set for at least one hundred and eighty thousand."

"How do you know that?" I was amazed at the way Mari had ticked everything off so quickly.

"I grew up near the village of Imari on Kyushu. My family have been potters for six generations. We don't make blue and white porcelain, though; we specialize in celadon."

"Koreans are famous for celadon," I said, a bit confused.

"They are the ones who brought the tradition to Japan." Mari had opened up the box she'd carried in and taken out a long sausage of wet clay. She stood at her worktable, wedging the clay as she spoke. "The potters were kidnapped from Korea and set up in villages in Kyushu, where they were forced to make pottery for their Japanese lords."

"And your family learned the art from the Korean potters?" I sensed that she was deeply sympathetic to the group.

Mari continued pressing and turning the clay, fashioning it into a shape that looked something like a chrysanthemum. "We are Korean. Didn't you know?"

I was thrown for a loop. "But your name is Japanese!"

Mari shrugged. "I don't even speak Korean. None of my living relatives does, either. Yet I was fingerprinted in childhood. I don't have a regular passport. And I never could rent an apartment or buy a house without a Japanese guarantor."

These were the same hassles I went through as a

foreigner in Japan. But Mari had been born in Japan, so it seemed blatantly unfair.

"What's your maiden name?" I asked.

"Nagai. My family, like most, were given Japanese names, and throughout the years we have intermarried with some Japanese. But the government still has records showing our family line is Korean. I met a Japanese man who fell in love with me when he was on vacation in our region. We married and I moved to Tokyo. His family would not allow my name to be listed in their family registry. So even though I'm called Kumamori, it's not really official. And it's why I haven't had children. Because of his parents' feelings, they would not be allowed on my husband's Japanese family register."

Mari's story about unfriendly in-laws was similar to Aunt Norie's. However, because Norie was pure Japanese, her story had a happy ending. Now I wondered why my aunt, who had never said anything against Mari, had never become her friend. Could she be prejudiced?

"Shimura-san, don't look so sad." Mari seemed to sense my discomfort, because she smiled at me. "I'm proud to be a Korean Japanese. That's why I make celadon porcelain. It relaxes me, brings me closer to my family so far away."

"You've never brought the celadon to ikebana class."

"I bring the dull-colored stoneware ones that fit the motto 'Truth in nature.'"

Catching the resentment in Mari's voice, I ventured, "Do you think things at the school are harder for you because you're Korean?"

Mari slapped the clay hard. "Sakura never liked me, and I guess that she heard rumors or did some research. She asked me to stay after class one day two years ago. She told me that I should drop out and switch to one of the other schools because the Kayamas had never granted a teaching certificate to a Korean. Then she added something like, 'It's a matter of kindness that I'm sharing this information with you. I don't want you to waste your time.'"

"You could have gone to Mrs. Koda."

"Don't be naive. Koda-san comes from an old samurai family. She would feel the same way as Sakura-san."

"But you're so good—and the higher you rise in the school, theoretically the more money you bring to the Kayamas. Which student level are you at?"

"The final stage before the teacher's certificate. In fact, during the past two years, I have been repeating the lessons in book four. At the end of the lessons comes the examination for a teaching certificate. I've taken the exam three times but have never passed it."

"Is this the exam where your arrangement is identified only by number? Where you stand waiting outside the classroom while the teachers examine the flower arrangements?"

"That's just how it's done." Mari sounded glum. "The strange thing is that when I returned to the classroom after waiting outside, I saw that the flowers in my vase looked even worse than I remembered. Somebody tampered with the arrangement so that I wouldn't pass."

"Do you think it was Sakura?" I remembered how

she had rearranged my own awkward attempts with cherry blossoms and made the arrangement truly awful.

"Of course I've thought of it. But I had no proof." Mari took a rolling pin and began rolling out her clay. "And now, since she's dead, things should change for me, shouldn't they? I could take the examination in two months if I wanted to."

I changed the subject. "Did you ever hear of a type of ceramic called Kayama ware? Some containers were made in the 1930s for the school."

"I can't say I've heard of it." She didn't raise her eyes from the container she was hand-building. "Did you bring an example?"

"No, I gave mine away, and it broke. I think it would be more colorful than the containers the head-master prefers us to use. You might like it."

"My pottery is influenced by many periods, but the twentieth century is not one of them." She placed the container—a long, narrow vessel that reminded me of a canoe—on a plaster board and went to a sink to wash her hands. "If you like, I'll show you what I have in the house."

We left the pottery and went into the house through an unlocked back door. The interior was not as gaudily Western as the exterior. I noticed hand-some Korean *tansu* chests with typical butterfly met-alwork in the living room.

"I really like this furniture. Are they your family's pieces?"

"Some of them. Others we bought. Fortunately, my husband feels the same way about Korean furni-ture that I do." She slid open the door to one *tansu* to reveal tidy rows of old cups, plates, and bowls. Some of them were celadon, others were blue-and-white. It was a smaller collection than I had, but much older and finer.

"You chose these yourself?" I asked.

"Yes. You'll notice there aren't any sets. I buy singles, which brings the cost down." She reached into the back and pulled out a plate that was similar but not identical to Mrs. Morita's. "This is the other reason I'm so sure of the age of the plate you brought me."

"Too bad it doesn't match. We could make a larger set and sell it for a bit more money."

"I'm not interested in money," Mari reminded me.

"How admirable." Suddenly I felt embarrassed that I'd made the suggestion. She was different, far less materialistic than I.

"Your mission to see me was not very successful," Mari said. "I'm very sorry."

"Actually, I learned a lot. And don't worry about my problem with the Imari plates. I think I'll return the unlucky consignment to its owner."

"Won't you have a cup of tea before you leave?" Mari asked.

Something about the way she kept glancing out to the kiln told me that she was anxious to get her containers fired. I shook my head and said, "You've been very kind. I'll just see myself out through the garden."

On the way out I passed the little shrine with the ceramic bears. When I'd first looked at them I thought they were smiling, but on reexamination they looked as if they were snarling. I hoped it was just my paranoia.

Chapter 21

Back home in Yanaka, I popped into the Family Mart to see Mr. Waka. As I came through the door, he looked up from restocking the Lotte gum display and smiled.

"Busy last night, *neh*? I hear you solved a crime."

"Who told you that?" There had been nothing in the *Japan Times* about the car crash. One car colliding with a light pole didn't warrant a story.

"Some policemen came into the shop to ask about a towing service. I told them about my brother, of course. While they waited, they discussed among themselves how you had identified sharp tacks lying on the street. The litterbugs in this city are becoming a real menace!"

"The people who dropped the tacks wanted Takeo Kayama to crash his car. Did the police talk about that?" What a blessing it was to be able to listen in on police procedure through the careful eavesdropping of Mr. Waka.

"They were arguing about that idea. One policeman said he thought so, but the others thought it was just *chinpira* playing." He tore open a pack of strawberry-flavored gum and gave me a stick.

Chinpira were junior gangsters, the kind who were trying to become full-fledged members of the *yakuza*. I said, "If it was *chinpira*, they were hired by somebody to do the job."

"Between crime fighting and haiku study, I don't know how you have time to get your work done."

"I don't. It's a problem." I chewed the sickeningly sweet gum, wishing I could take it out of my mouth but not wanting to offend him.

"So, what's the new haiku? The one you telephoned me about?"

I didn't have the poem with me, but I knew the words and recited them.

"Oh, the old poem about the girl who gets caught up in the wind. I believe the poet is someone called Gyoutai. He lived in the eighteenth century."

"Tell me, do you find the line 'the girl is pushed' to be ominous?"

"No, the poem clearly states she is pushed by the wind. It means her hair and kimono were disorganized."

"Is that a normal kind of poem? Or do you think it could have another meaning?" I pressed.

"These poems are very common, as I told you before. They're in schoolbooks. Now, if you want to learn more haiku, you should take a night class at our community center. My brother is on the board and can give me a schedule."

"Thanks. Well, I'm sure I'll have another haiku to ask you about in a few days."

"What does that mean, in a few days? That's not a serious study plan. You must work at haiku every day. I would like to hear your own verses."

"Someday," I promised, thinking I'd be as likely to compose a poem about blossoms as to write an article on Kayama ware for *Straight Bamboo* magazine. In other words, not likely at all.

A new letter had been slid under the door of my apartment, I discovered when I went back home. I felt as sickened as ever, but at least now I could be certain that I was the intended recipient and not my aunt. Also, I would cross Mari Kumamori off the list of suspects. It was not likely that she had raced me back to Tokyo to plant the letter while I was spending five minutes with Mr. Waka.

I put on my gloves, opened the envelope, and read:

> *Gaikotsu no*
> *Ue wo yosoute*
> *hana-mi kana*

This haiku was the easiest yet for me to translate. It could have been written in homage to the innocent cherry blossom viewing taking place at Yanaka Cemetery. But I found it chilling.

Viewing the blossoms
Spread in festive apparel
Above the dead bones.

I placed the poem and its envelope into the plastic bag that held the earlier haiku about the beautiful girl being pushed. I didn't need help from Mr. Waka for this one. I thought of my other old friend, who needed my help: Mr. Ishida. I dialed Ishida Antiques once more, hoping that he would have recovered enough to answer. He did.

"You're home safely!" I said, so relieved that I forgot to say hello or identify myself.

"More or less. My eye is going to be fine. I have a corneal scratch, which is very painful, but with time it should improve. I am very glad, because for someone who makes his living with a magnifying glass, the loss of an eye would be catastrophic."

"I'm very sorry I dragged you out last night. If I had left well enough alone, nothing would have happened," I mourned.

"It was the right thing," Mr. Ishida replied. "When Kayama-san says that his family's Kayama ware is gone, I believe him. On the other hand, it could be true that the consignor brought me Kayama ware that was not in the school's archive. I need an official registry of the collection to make sure that I am not making a mistake."

"Why don't you just let Takeo buy the containers? He doesn't care what it costs to get the containers back."

"It would be unethical for me to sell to him,

Shimura-san. I could not keep my reputation if it became known that I forced a crime victim to pay for goods stolen from his own home!"

After more discussion, there was still no way out of this etiquette conundrum. I said good-bye. Then I telephoned one of the funeral florists in my neighborhood and asked them to deliver to Mr. Ishida a springtime arrangement that did not look funereal, with a get-well card from Takeo and me. Four thousand yen poorer, I made myself a cup of beefsteak-plant tea and brooded.

I needed money. Although I still had the equivalent of ten thousand dollars in my savings account, and much more in the untouchable Hugh Glendinning furniture fund, I hadn't earned money since my poisoning. I hadn't seen any private antiques buyers, and the antiques shop owners I'd talked to weren't interested in my inventory.

The Sunday morning shrine sale might be a good place to sell my wares directly to the public. I didn't really want to do it, because if my acquaintances saw me selling my wares from a tarpaulin laid out on the sidewalk, I could be pigeonholed as a lower-class dealer. My business card described myself as a purveyor of fine antiques, not flea-market goods.

I looked at my calendar. This weekend the traveling association of dealers who ran the sale was going to be at the Togo Shrine, a prime location near the international neighborhood of Omote-sando. If I could get in touch with the organizers, I might be able to make the Sunday sale.

My mind made up, I plowed on to the next item of

business: Mrs. Koda. I could not talk to her at the school, where other people might be listening. Now that I had the list of teachers from the school, it was easy to look up her home telephone number. Her address was in Hiro, a sedate and expensive neighborhood near the Kayama Kaikan.

It was seven o'clock. I pictured her cooking a small dinner for herself, maybe one fish and some rice and vegetables. I got a little bit hungry thinking about it. As a single person, I rarely went to the trouble of cooking such a meal for myself. Aunt Norie's culinary reign—*okayu* notwithstanding—had been a memorable one.

"Please forgive me if I am disturbing your evening meal," I said when she answered the telephone.

"I do not eat formal meals alone, Rei-san. But for you to be awake so late is not good! You must rest and recover from your illness."

"I'm recovering nicely, thanks to your concern. I even ran a few miles this morning, and I went out to Zushi to look at Mari's pottery."

"She is a talented potter as well as an excellent flower arranger. It is rare to be able to handle both the heaviness of clay and the lightness of petals. Her hands are a treasure."

It was on the tip of my tongue to bring up the fact that the Kayama School kept flunking Mari for the teacher's certificate exam. But it wouldn't do to be confrontational over the phone. I reminded myself of my goal, to get an audience with her.

"What is your schedule like?" I asked. "I would like to invite you for tea."

"How kind. I would enjoy it as well. There is a restaurant inside the Kayama Kaikan. Aren't you coming for class tomorrow?"

I hadn't been planning on it. "Actually, my days are so busy, packed with appointments and such, that I'd really like to spend an hour or so with you in the evening. I need to explain about what happened yesterday."

"Oh, with the Kayama ware? Don't worry. Takeo-san explained the situation."

"Mmm, there's a bit more to it." I paused significantly, hoping to arouse her curiosity. She didn't reply. "As you know, my Japanese is not very good. Especially on the telephone. I'd rather be able to explain it in person. I must make sure that there is no longer a terrible misunderstanding between myself and my aunt's most honored teacher."

"Your aunt is worried? Oh, she mustn't be that way!" Warmth flowed through the telephone line. "By all means, we must relieve her anxiety. Of course I will be happy to visit with you in my home when you have some free time."

"I'll be there in forty minutes. Thank you for your kindness." I hung up before she could make any kind of protest.

There was no way I was going to be late. I jogged downhill to Sendagi Station, flitting through groups of blue-collar workers and students. People here were used to my running and didn't break their stride or stare the way they did in Roppongi. The neighbors just called me the "Running Girl," according to Mr. Waka, which was an eccentric, but not particularly cruel, nickname. On the occasions when the young men from Tokyo University's running club saw me, they gave a quarter bow, shoulders only, so as not to break their stride.

A block ahead I saw a young man with short, spiked blond hair wearing a conservative blue blazer and gray trousers. He was walking with a taller, dark-haired man. From the backs of their heads, I guessed that the pair were Richard Randall and his new friend Enrique. We'd be able to ride the subway together.

I increased my pace, and when I reached Richard I playfully grabbed the back of his jacket.

My friend did not turn around but gave a small yelp. In the next moment his companion had slammed me against the station's grimy tiled wall. I stared into the angry face of Che Fujisawa, the environmental activist who had led the protest outside My Magic Forest.

"It's rude to surprise people," Che growled.

"*No problemo, neh?* I'm sure the young lady meant no harm. My jacket isn't even torn!" Richard jabbered in a bizarre mixture of Spanish and Japanese.

Belatedly I realized that I was in danger of blowing Richard's cover in Che's organization.

"*Gomen nasai, gomen nasai!*" I apologized, diving forward into a deep bow. Che was standing so close to me that my forehead knocked his jaw. The collision must have hurt him more than me, I thought, judging from the way he moaned and stepped back, clutching his mouth.

"You fool!" Che raged at me. "I know you from somewhere, I'm sure of it!"

"She's just a crazy girl who works at the Family Mart," Richard said quickly. "She has a crush on me, the owner says."

"*Gomen nasai.*" I bowed once more and darted off through the ticket wicket, glad I had a prepaid card. I looked over my shoulder and saw Richard searching for coins to pay for his fare at the ticket machine, no doubt causing a delay so that I could make a get-away on an earlier subway train. Richard was martyring himself for my cause. When Che had me up against the wall of the station, he'd seemed ready to beat me up. What he could do to someone smaller and less athletic than myself was too frightening to contemplate.

I'd believed that Richard's connection to Enrique would protect him within the ranks of Stop Killing Flowers, but I was wrong. I needed to get Richard out, and I was annoyed with myself for not grilling Takeo about his own connections with the group. Mrs. Koda might have a sense about whether Takeo felt more loyal toward his family's school or Stop Killing Flowers.

I rode the subway to Hiro; once on the street, I obtained the directions to Mrs. Koda's home from a policeman on duty in his box. He told me to look out for the apartment building with flower boxes at every window. It sounded charming, but when I saw the flowers they looked suspiciously fake—red geraniums at every window seemed too much to be true—and the building itself was a dumpy white tower faded to gray by pollution. I never understood why Japanese architects kept designing urban buildings in white. It was a losing battle with grime. In the early 1990s it seemed that a new white building went up in Tokyo every hour. Now the buildings all looked like ghosts with five o'clock shadow.

In a lobby decorated with European-style bouquets of artificial flowers, I found an intercom box and buzzed Mrs. Koda's apartment.

"You are downstairs? I wasn't aware you were coming tonight."

I'd thought that I'd been so clear. "Um, I can leave if it's not convenient. . . ."

"Please take the elevator to nine. I'll meet you there."

Outside the elevator doors stretched a hall covered in light green carpet. The pale blue walls were decorated with fluffy clouds and a depiction of the sunrise over Mt. Fuji.

"This is a very interesting building," I said to Mrs. Koda as we walked slowly together to her apartment. When she let me in, I was relieved to see it was a regular white-on-white apartment, clean and comfortable-looking and not excessively flowery. In fact, there weren't any flowers at all.

"I'm pleased to be here, in the middle of things. For a long time I was in the suburbs with my husband. I hated that!" she confided.

"I brought something small for you," I said, handing her a nicely wrapped box of strawberries that I'd picked up outside the station. I could not enter anyone's home in Japan empty-handed.

"Oh, you shouldn't have," Mrs. Koda said, refusing it three times before she accepted it. "I'll put these in the refrigerator to enjoy tomorrow. Would you like some tea?"

"No, thank you. I had some at home. . . . Really, no, I'm perfectly fine!"

Despite my protestations, she made me a cup of tea, placing it on a flowered cotton napkin atop a coaster set on a lacquered tray. I stared at the precise arrangement of china, textile, and wood, hoping Mrs. Koda wouldn't notice if I didn't touch the tea. She seemed like a nice old lady, but the fact was, I'd been poisoned while drinking tea with her before. I could pour my tea into a potted plant if she briefly left the room. Unfortunately, there were no potted plants.

"Let's sit down," Mrs. Koda said. "I'm sorry my sofa isn't very comfortable."

"Oh, it's soft as a cloud! This new furniture is so much nicer than the old pieces I have at home."

"Is your aunt still staying with you?" Mrs. Koda smiled at me.

Things were going so well in our etiquette match, it was a shame that I was going to have to get down to business. "I've recovered, so she has returned to her own home. My uncle is back from Osaka. He needs her." Plunging ahead, I said, "I should explain about the Kayama ware."

"Takeo informed me that you're writing an article about it. If you'd only said something to Miss Okada and me downstairs, we would have understood right away."

"Were you nervous because all the Kayama ware

was missing from the archives?"

Mrs. Koda looked startled. After a beat she said, "Yes."

"Who discovered the loss?" I asked.

"Miss Okada was the one who noticed it six weeks ago, because she goes into the archives regularly to find containers for display in the reception area. Then she came to me. I discussed it with Takeo, and he didn't have the heart to tell the *iemoto* about the loss. He'd thought maybe the containers were misplaced and that he could find them."

"I bought my piece of Kayama ware at an antiques store a few blocks away. There's more there, perhaps the rest of the collection. To get it back, the store owner needs proof that they're registered as school property."

"What kind of proof?" Mrs. Koda asked. I noticed that she didn't seem at all concerned about who might have brought the Kayama ware to the store.

"An itemized list. Takeo-san thinks that one doesn't exist."

"Of course there is a list," she soothed. "I make lists of everything. I compiled a list of Kayama ware twenty years ago. Don't worry, I'll find it for you. Rei-san, thank you for bringing this to my attention. You did the right thing."

"Speaking of missing objects, I found something else." I pulled the Nolvadex tablet wrapped with tissue out of my pocket and held it out to her. "I was worried that you lost this."

She squinted at the tablet, turning it over in her hand. "Where did you find it?"

"In the school office. It's Nolvadex, isn't it?"

"I must have been careless." Mrs. Koda put the tablet down with a click on a side table and refolded her hands. She looked defeated.

"Is it cancer?" I asked.

She gave the slightest nod. "Nobody except for Takeo-san knows."

"That's so hard on you. Everyone at the school cares—they would support you in every way they could."

"They would suggest that I resign," she said. "And then I would have nothing to do. Ikebana is my career. I want to continue as long as I can."

"Do you think that your cancer could have been caused by flower arranging?"

"I don't know." From her expression, I could tell she had heard the question before.

"Did your mother or aunt have breast cancer?"

She shook her head and stretched her hands out toward me. "How old my hands look now! In the beginning, when I was a young girl arranging flowers from my family's garden, my fingers were so soft and smooth. I did an ikebana demonstration for my future husband, and he always said that he fell in love with my hands."

"What a romantic man. But to get back to our discussion, if you have no family history of breast cancer, it might be an environmental factor that triggered the disease."

"My husband wanted control," she said, continuing her parallel conversation. "He did not allow me to work, although I had a wonderful invitation from Masanobu Kayama, who had taken over the school in the early 1960s from his father. Masanobu-*sensei* needed me, but my husband insisted that a woman of my station must not work. So I came to the school as a volunteer and worked here during the daytime while my husband was at the office. Only after he died could I become a true employee."

"You've been handling imported flowers for about thirty years?" I asked.

"A bit longer than that. The school became able to afford imported flowers in the late fifties."

Feeling like a member of Stop Killing Flowers, I told her, "Strong pesticides are still sprayed on flowers, especially roses and carnations from Colombia. That could have caused your cancer. Of course you should keep teaching flower arranging, but maybe only with organically grown plants."

"It is too late for me." She lightly touched the right side of her chest. "They cut it out. To stop working with flowers would cut out my heart as well."

"I'm terribly sorry about what's happened to you. And of course I'll keep your health private. But don't you think that sharing your illness with others could serve as some kind of warning?"

"Many of my friends who practice ikebana are fine. I'm an isolated case. I just happened to arrange more flowers than I should have. Maybe I did not wash my hands after each session. If people wash their hands, that should be enough. Takeo-san has ordered the staff to hang signs over the classroom sinks that encourage people to wash their hands after flower arranging. And at his suggestion, I live in this apartment with no living flowers."

"How did Takeo-san find out about your illness?" I asked.

"When Takeo-san was a student at Keio University, he had some trouble fitting in, so he came to me often to talk. When I was on vacation from school, undergoing chemotherapy, he came here unannounced. When he saw that I had lost much of my hair, he demanded to know what was happening. I could not keep a secret from the boy."

I began to put the pieces together. It was during the university years that Takeo had become a fervent environmentalist. Perhaps his worries about Mrs. Koda had led him in that direction.

"At that time, Takeo-san helped me make a plan to continue working. He found a wig that matched the hairstyle that I always had so that nobody would guess I was in bad health. He also allowed me to rest in his room whenever I wanted. Whenever anyone asked about my absence, I would say that I was doing a special project for him."

"Were you resting in his office when Sakura died?" I asked.

"Actually, I was at the doctor. But I have had so many absences lately that I couldn't bear to say that. It was just easier to pretend I was in the building."

I groaned. "Do you realize you have a perfectly decent alibi that you're not even using? By insisting you were in the building when nobody could find you, you're making yourself appear a lot more suspicious. The police may not have asked you much, but you have got to be honest with them."

"Rei-san, you don't think . . . that I hurt Sakura-san?" Mrs. Koda's sad eyes blinked rapidly. "Of course you must. That is why you haven't touched the tea."

I looked straight at her. "I became very sick the last time we had tea together. The police haven't caught the person who did it. Since then I've been careful."

After a slight pause she said, "That is sensible. It is what I would do myself if I were in your situation."

"I want to ask you one more thing. Why hasn't Mari Kumamori passed the teaching exam after trying it three times?"

"She's very good at her classwork, but when it comes to the examinations, she must get nervous. There is always a major flaw in the arrangements. I would like to give her a passing grade, but I cannot. The errors are too obvious."

"In testing, is there any time when nobody's in the room? I mean, between the time the students make their arrangements and leave the room, and when the judges come in."

"The room is always under supervision. We want to ensure that the students don't cheat, and also that they are treated fairly."

"Do you monitor the room during the time the students are waiting outside?"

"Up until about ten years ago, I did it. Then the *iemoto* asked that I give the responsibility to another teacher."

"Who is that?" I asked, although I could anticipate her reply.

"Sakura Sato. And now that she is gone, I suppose we'll need to find somebody else."

Chapter 22

J never touched a drop of tea, but when I left Mrs. Koda's apartment twenty minutes later, I felt totally wired.

I thought of telephoning Mari with the news that Sakura Sato had almost certainly kept her from passing the exam, but a train was just pulling in, so I decided to catch it and telephone from home. I sat on the train, tapping my foot restlessly as the stations went by. Even though it was nine o'clock, the train was filling up with salarymen just getting out of the office. The men slumped into their seats, newspapers falling out of their hands as they passed into sleep. No doubt some of them were absentee husbands who had been transferred away from their families, like Uncle Hiroshi.

I wondered if Hiroshi and Norie were home that night. I was starting to feel guilty about how we had parted. My aunt had taken care of me for three days, and I'd stormed out of the apartment without saying good-bye or thanking her. Calling her to apologize was going to be even more difficult, since I had heard Takeo's insinuation about her possible sexual relationship with his father.

When I arrived home, I called Mari Kumamori. She answered the phone herself, and when I told her the news about Sakura's intervention in her testing, she thanked me.

"I will try the exam again, Shimura-san. How strange that this time of tragedy has brought a benefit for me. Do you think that the police will be suspicious?" she asked.

"I don't think so!" Surely being held back from progressing in a flower-arranging hierarchy was not a serious enough motive for murder. Or was it?

After I finished talking to Mari, I dialed my aunt and uncle's home in Yokohama. Tom answered and told me that his parents had gone to bed.

"But it's only nine-thirty!" Japanese families routinely didn't go to bed until after midnight, based on the schedule of husbands and children coming home between ten and eleven.

"They're spending a lot of time together. It's a good thing, I think," Tom whispered.

"You mean they're . . ." He couldn't mean that my aunt and uncle were engaging in intimate activities.

"No, don't have a dirty mind. Mother's got Father talking, and now his emotions are spilling forth. The problem is that she has neglected me. I've had to do my own cooking, because they disappear for hours having their private conversations."

"Tom, just think about how your future wife will enjoy those cooking skills," I teased. "Are you far enough from your parents' room that they can't hear you?"

"Sure. I'm in the living room, and they're upstairs."

"I want to ask you something. Your mother mentioned that for years she has received anonymous letters. The letters were haiku by famous poets, but they seemed to send some kind of hidden message. Do you know about this?"

"She's never mentioned any notes to me. Although about a year ago, I did see her crying in the laundry room with a crumpled-up letter in her hand. I asked her why, and she made up a story about a high utility bill. But I'd noticed that the letter didn't have a company name or even a postage stamp on the outside."

"So . . . you just said okay and walked off?"

"What reason would my mother have to lie? I was more concerned with whether she was going to have my lunch ready to take to work. I'm afraid I was rather selfish."

I changed tactics. "Did she talk much about the *iemoto* when you were young?"

"Not really. Mother kept her flower-arranging world to herself. Besides, only since Chika went away to college has she been really active."

The phantom of my cousin Chika again. Baby Chika and adult Chika appeared like bookends surrounding the time that Norie had been involved—and uninvolved—with the Kayama School.

"Does the *iemoto* have something to do with the notes?" Tom asked.

"I think so," I said. "At the very least, can you keep an eye on your mother? I'm worried about her."

"I'm worried about you, Rei. It sounds as if you're off on a strange new tangent. What happened with the Nolvadex?"

"You were right. I asked Mrs. Koda, and it turned out that she is recovering from breast cancer. I promised that I wouldn't tell anyone, but of course you already knew."

"She will have confidentiality with me, I promise. Has she had a relapse? If she has any questions about her disease, I could make an appointment for her at our oncology department."

"She's still under the care of a doctor. I wouldn't mind speaking to someone in oncology, though. I want to find out whether there is a definite link between pesticides and breast cancer."

"Are you working with those environmental zealots who railed against my mother?" Tom sounded horrified.

"No, but it's a health concern your mother and all women who work with flowers need to consider."

"Listen, Rei, there are far worse things that could kill my mother." Tom's voice lowered. "They're opening the door upstairs. Someone's coming down. I've got to get off."

With that, he broke our connection.

I dreamed of oversized flowers emitting toxic fumes all night long, and I woke early the next morning, probably from the stress. It was 7 A.M., and since it was a Saturday morning, I wouldn't have to worry about morning rush-hour fumes. In fact, the streets were so free of traffic that I was able to jog from Yanaka to the Ocha-no-mizu district without having to slalom. I ran under a stand of cherry trees, thinking that it was interesting that people didn't sweep up fallen cherry petals the way they did leaves. The fallen cherry blossoms weren't considered litter, but a supreme ornamentation. Under my feet, the petals were crushed into pale pink polka dots, a sophisticated design against the dark gray of the sidewalk.

I was glad that Tom had recalled Norie crying over a letter. There was a good chance that it was a haiku. I was tempted to tell Takeo about this, but my recent experience with him had left me feeling unsure. Did he really want to clear my aunt and find Sakura's killer, or was he just out for an easy grope?

I told myself that I had enough men in my life: my cousin Tom, to give me medical advice and be like a big brother; Mr. Waka, to feed me gum and gossip; and Mr. Ishida, to supply me with wisdom. Not to mention Richard, who had been my best friend for years but now could be in serious danger from Che Fujisawa's environmental group. I had to talk to Richard before he got hurt.

I was headed for It's Happening! Language School, Richard's current place of employment. I ran down a few side streets before I found a small building that looked like the place that he'd dragged me to as his cover date for the previous Valentine's Day. An advertisement for the language school was in a second-floor window. It was early, but there was a chance a few workers were in—the perfect time for me to leave him a warning note. I buzzed the school office while my breathing slowed to a normal level.

"Hai?" a young man answered, sounding weary.

"I have a message for a teacher. May I come upstairs and leave a note?" I put a hint of desperation in my voice, as if I were a student rushing off to my workplace.

"Rei?"

There was only one person at It's Happening! who would recognize my voice so swiftly. But I wasn't taking any chances.

"Randall-*sensei*, could it be you?" I asked, still speaking Japanese.

"Who else? Come on up."

I ran up the steps and through the office door Richard was holding for me. He was wearing the same shirt and pants as the night before, with the jacket I'd almost torn slung over one shoulder. He looked as rumpled as a salaryman who'd missed the midnight train home, a sorry state for somebody who was fastidious about fashion.

"Richard." I fell into his arms, but he shrugged me off.

"You're all sweaty!" Richard picked up the can of Georgia Coffee he'd been drinking. He took a long sip and stared at me suspiciously.

"Is that hot coffee?" I asked.

"Mmm. It's from the machine in the hall. Want one?"

"No money. I was out jogging." I turned out the

pockets of my shorts to prove it.

"Okay, okay, I'll spring for one. I owe you for that last *caipirinha* at Salsa Salsa."

"Thanks," I said, taking it and sinking down on the floor, not wanting to leave damp traces on any of the office chairs. "I'm really sorry about everything. I never thought things would get so bad that you would have to sleep at work to avoid Che Fujisawa."

"That's not it at all." He yawned, revealing a tongue stud that I hadn't known he still wore. "I'm just trying to stay away from Enrique. He's moved into my apartment, and I'm starting to go mad."

"You mean you're still cool with Che?"

"Yes, that liaison is fine. It's pretty exciting, to tell the truth, though it was stupid of you to grab me at the station. You almost blew my cover!"

"Sorry. From the back, he looks a lot like Enrique."

"I'm not into Enrique anymore, okay?" Richard snapped.

"But your feelings were so strong. You said you were in love!"

"We had an argument," Richard said. "Enrique thought I was getting too involved in Stop Killing Flowers. He would rather go dancing than save lives."

I looked at Richard carefully, to see if he was kidding me. "Okay, I won't say the E-word again. Just tell me what's going on with Stop Killing Flowers."

"They talk Spanish half the time, which makes it hard, but from what I've been told by Che in Japanese, something really big is going to happen.

Something that will make national news headlines, given the season." Richard paused, clearly enjoying his effect on me.

"Cherry blossom season?"

"Exactly."

"I'm sympathetic to the cause of the workers. I just hope Che doesn't do anything too extreme."

Richard raised his eyebrows. "Well, the demonstrations they've had in the past have gotten some press attention, but the Japanese imports continued. They're going to do something major this time. It will make the Sunday night news, I'm sure."

"This action is something the police should know about. If Lieutenant Hata is on-site, he can make sure you don't get killed or arrested—" I was so agitated that my coffee can fell off the knee I'd been balancing it on and spilled a light brown puddle across the carpet.

"Don't you dare stop anything." Richard grabbed a wad of tissues and pressed it on the carpet. "You're such a mom. I would have told you, but now that you're threatening to bring Officer Friendly into the picture, I won't."

Mom! That was a truly rotten comment. I tried to keep from screeching when I told him, "If you're so loyal to your new friends, consider the fact that they might be the ones who almost killed Mr. Ishida and Takeo two nights ago. Or maybe you were part of it. Very nice. You've gone from teaching English to attempted murder!"

"We heard about the accident, but it wasn't us. Che told me last night. Why would we hurt someone who's a friend of the group?" Richard asked rhetorically.

"What does this 'friend of the group' business really mean? Is Takeo in or out?"

"Well, he's donated some bucks to the cause, but he will not join. Che told me that he considers joining us impossible, given his family background."

How self-destructive for Takeo to give money to an antiflower group—even though I had come around to believe that Stop Killing Flowers had an important agenda. I asked Richard whether he had heard that Takeo Kayama was in on their Sunday event.

"Of course not," Richard said smugly. "That event is being planned by members only."

"I see." If Richard wouldn't tell me something he knew, it was clear that I'd lost my best friend. I must have been looking glum, because Richard took my hand and gave it a quick squeeze.

"I know you've always thought of me as a supreme goof with no real ambition or social conscience," he said. "Things have changed since I've joined Stop Killing Flowers. But because you seem so committed to becoming a police informer, I'm not going to talk to you anymore. At least not about environmental things."

"Take care of yourself." I took one last look at the heart-shaped face topped with a slightly greasy halo of blond hair. My little angel was metamorphosing into someone else. I remembered the cult that had risen to prominence in the mid-1990s, transforming young Japanese college graduates into subway-gassing psychos. At least with environmentalists, I wouldn't have to worry about gas. Or so I hoped.

Chapter 23

I ran home and spent the rest of the morning going through the final administrative hurdles necessary for my flea-market debut. In Japan, it seemed impossible to do anything without a permit. Then I made a personal call on Mr. Ishida at his shop. After thanking me for the flowers I'd sent, he gave me some suggestions on what I should try to sell at the shrine sale. Since he wasn't going to be able to drive until his vision was better, he lent me his van to transport my wares to the shrine sale. I drove it to my neighborhood, parked legally, and spent two hours carefully transporting boxed china to it. Then I tucked it into bed in a parking garage two miles away that cost four thousand yen for overnight parking.

I returned home realizing that I'd forgotten to show Mr. Ishida the photograph of Takeo's mother.

I'd stashed it safely in my apartment, and now I transferred it into the money belt that I'd wear the next day at the flea market. Mr. Ishida had promised to stop by and see me there.

My Saturday afternoon mail had arrived. There was a gas bill that made me sorry I was still using my space heater on chilly days and something very unexpected: a creamy, square-shaped envelope that bore the Kayama School's address.

I opened the envelope and read the message, which was printed in English calligraphy on one side, Japanese on the other.

The *iemoto*, Masanobu Kayama, requests the pleasure of your company at a cherry blossom viewing party at the Garden of Stones, Sunday, April 7. The favor of a reply is requested by April 5.

April 5 had been the day before. Mrs. Koda could have said something about the party when I was visiting her, but she hadn't. Perhaps she didn't want me to go. I thought of the haiku I'd most recently received, the one that spoke of viewing blossoms dressed in festive apparel above dead bones. Was the writer speaking about the Kayamas' party?

The telephone rang, and to my surprise, Aunt Norie answered my greeting.

"Rei-*chan*, I'm sorry it's taken me this long to return your call. How are you feeling?"

"Perfectly fine. I'm embarrassed, though, about what happened between us. I apologize."

"No need to do that," Norie said briskly. "I called

to wish you well and also to see if you have something suitable to wear to the cherry blossom viewing party. It's going to be at the Garden of Stones, the Kayamas' country property."

"You received the invitation today?" I asked, guessing that she also had received an afternoon delivery. "Don't you think it's odd that the party is going to be held tomorrow?"

"Yes, the invitation is very late, but perhaps it's that way because it's hard to tell when the cherry blossoms will be at their best. The Izu Peninsula has a different weather pattern, you know."

"The Izu Peninsula has got to be hours away. Are you sure that it's worth going?"

"Now that Hiroshi's back, he will be happy to drive us. And the Kayamas' residence is really worth a look."

"I don't think we should attend. Another haiku was slipped under my door, and it seems to refer directly to the party. I think that's a bad sign."

Aunt Norie paused, and I guessed that she was debating whether to ask me what the haiku said. She didn't. Instead she said, "If I don't attend the party, the other women will think I've been thrown out of the school. I won't let that happen."

Shimura pride. It was a damnable thing to have, but I couldn't let her go alone.

"All right," I said.

"Very good. What we need to settle now is what you are going to wear. I can lend you a kimono that is too girlish for me. Do you have a pair of *zōri* that fit your great big feet? And *tabi* to wear underneath?"

"I have my own kimono . . . and is it a good idea for Uncle Hiroshi to come with us? He might be bored." I was angling for Tom, because I thought he was younger and stronger, better to have nearby in a confrontation.

"Your uncle is looking forward to attending, because he's always missed the party in past years. Tsutomu will be along as well, because I have my eye out to introduce him to some of the other teachers' daughters. I have already left an RSVP that we will be present: Hiroshi, Tsutomu, you, and me. The Shimura family!"

Once again Norie had conned me into doing something that I didn't want to do. Now I was torn. I wanted to stay in Tokyo and trail Richard to his rendezvous with Stop Killing Flowers, but I had a responsibility to protect my aunt. Although it might turn out that my aunt and Richard would both be at the same place—the Garden of Stones.

I pondered the problem while opening up the chest where I stored my vintage kimono. I had more than twenty to consider. I'd chosen the robes for their folk art value instead of fashion purposes. While many exhibited special tie-dye techniques and subtle organic colors, I knew they might not be fancy enough for the Kayamas. I lifted out layers of silk before I narrowed the selection to a few robes in springlike hues.

I started trying on the kimono over the pajama pants that I'd been wearing to relax. The party was going to take place at night, so I wanted to make sure the color of the robe I chose was vibrant enough not to get lost in the shadows.

I had decided on a pale pink kimono patterned with delicate green leaves and was trying to figure out which obi harmonized best with it when my doorbell rang. I moved the screen covering the window aside. I couldn't see who was standing at the door, but I did see a Range Rover filling up the street.

I didn't want to see Takeo, especially when I was half dressed like a courtesan. I called through the door for him to wait a minute, and I began unfurling the sash that I'd tied around my waist. I buttoned up my shirt all the way and smoothed my hair before opening up.

Takeo wasn't waiting outside; his sister, Natsumi, was.

"Were you sleeping?" Natsumi peered at me critically, and I realized then that I was wearing pajama bottoms with my button-down shirt, a typical evening-at-home outfit for me. Natsumi was wearing a shiny black patent leather coat with matching pants, Gucci stacked-heel loafers on her feet, and a black-and-gold police-style hat on her head. She looked like a storm trooper or a hostess at one of the S&M parlors targeted at businessmen seeking extracurricular abuse.

"You could say I was relaxing." I tried to look warmer than I felt. I didn't want to reveal that my sloppy outfit was par for the course, just as I didn't want her to know I'd been frantically trying on kimono to wear to her family's party. I wondered if Takeo had sent her in his stead because he was tired of dealing with me. Trying to get a feel for the situation, I asked, "Is that your Range Rover? It's not possible to leave it there in front of the neighbor's driveway. You might get towed."

"It's on loan from the dealership, so who cares? Besides, the car's bigger than most tow trucks, so it would take some effort to move it. When Takeo crashed our car here a few nights ago, the police had to find a special tow truck to remove it."

So despite Takeo's efforts to keep the accident a secret, she knew. Was that a good or bad thing? I said to Natsumi, "Why don't you come in?"

"Not many women our age have their own apartments," Natsumi said, stepping out of her shoes that I'd seen at her home. "Do your parents fund you?"

"I earn enough to support myself. And this place isn't that nice."

"Oh, don't talk like that. We Japanese say that kind of thing about our homes all the time—it's so ugly, it's so poor—but this place is really something. You've got a good eye for interior design."

"I'm terrible with flowers," I said, watching her examine the arrangement I'd made from the bittersweet her brother had brought me.

"It takes years to learn ikebana. Look at your aunt and her friends. They've been working at it for almost forty years."

"How long have you studied?" I asked, going into the kitchen and plugging in my small immersion water heater to make tea.

"Since I was sixteen. Takeo had to start when he was ten because he is going to take over the school." Natsumi's patent leather pants creaked as she settled onto one of the low chairs near my gas heater, which was glowing like a little fireplace. "I told them that since I was just going to get married, there wasn't any point in training me. But my father pointed out that no young man from a good family would marry a Kayama who couldn't arrange flowers. So I tried it, and I found that it wasn't as bad as I thought. I get to do some arrangements in department stores, which is a lot more fun than hanging around the Kayama Kaikan." Natsumi waved a slender hand with nails painted the color of blood. "No tea, it causes me to retain water. Do you have a ginseng soda?"

"Sorry, I don't have any. I could offer you water or grapefruit juice."

"Do you have Evian?" When I shook my head, Natsumi said, "Oh, well, I won't take anything then. Can't be too careful."

Even though I'd been the same way about drinking things at Mrs. Koda's, I was pretty irritated that she was hinting I might poison her. It would be rude to drink tea in front of her, so I left my freshly brewed cup of Darjeeling on the counter. I sat down across from her, moving aside the kimono that I'd tried on. The silk cascaded over the floor, a glossy waterfall of pink and mauve.

"Getting ready for a costume party?" Natsumi asked.

"Not exactly," I answered, not bringing up her

family's party for fear she'd tell me the kimono was all wrong. "You might find it interesting that the Victoria and Albert Museum in London had a major exhibit of old kimono last year. Other cultures seem to value the antique Japanese kimono more than we do here."

"Actually, I'm not here to talk to you about fashion," said Natsumi, overlooking the fact that it was she who had commented on the kimono in the first place. "I'm here because I want to warn you, girl to girl, about my brother."

"What's the warning?" She must have known that I had been in the office with him a few nights earlier. How much could she have heard through a closed door, though?

"I worry that your feelings might get hurt. He might play around with you, but it would never come to anything serious."

I felt my face becoming warm. She knew. How embarrassing.

"Oh, I understand the appeal. He's single, rich, and the right age, while you're not getting any younger." Natsumi's sneering face, underneath the military-style hat, reminded me of the meanest police chief I'd encountered in Japan.

"I'm the same age as you and Takeo. I consider both of us equally marriageable, and let me assure you, I have no designs on your brother."

"How dare you lie to me like that?" Natsumi's voice rose.

She wanted me to crawl in front of her pleading to be understood and bowing my head down to the tatami. But courtesy to a guest had its limits.

"Takeo is your brother, not a husband," I said. "He's not cheating on you if he spends time talking to other women. He doesn't love you any less."

"What do you know about love or family? You don't even live with your parents, probably because they threw you out! Yes, you and your aunt obviously share the same blood type." Natsumi was sitting bolt upright in her chair, glaring at me.

"My aunt wasn't thrown out of her home," I said. "And I must tell you that while I don't know whether Norie is type O, we are not genetically related. Her husband is the brother of my father."

"A Japanese father doesn't make you Japanese. You would never be accepted by my father, which means that Takeo will never marry you."

I did some deep breathing. "You're the only one who has marriage on her mind. I have better things to think about."

"Well, get back to your career then. Stop pretending to study flower arranging. And you're right, you're really bad at it! Some people have the knack; others don't. As for you, there's no hope, even if you studied every day."

While Natsumi went on spitting venom, I listened with one ear to the commotion in the street outside. I went to the window, casually shifting the *shoji* to look out. I slid it closed again and came back to Natsumi.

"Are you sure you don't want some tea? Your throat must be sore."

"No, I'm sure you'd poison it! You obviously know

just the way to do it, since you made yourself sick so easily at the Mitsutan exhibit. It might have fooled Koda-san and my brother, but not me!" Natsumi jumped up from the chair, knocking her leg against the gas heater. She swore, and I smelled something acrid.

"Are you okay? I don't want you to go up in flames," I cautioned.

"I'm melting!" Natsumi screamed, and shook her patent-leather-covered leg in distress. I made certain that there was no flame before I let my laughter release.

"You're just too hot, Natsumi-san."

She threw me an evil look and stormed out, squeezing her feet into the tight loafers as she slammed the door behind her. I slid the *shoji* aside to look out the window as Mr. Waka's brother's tow truck began hauling away the Range Rover. As the tow truck lumbered along, dragging the mammoth vehicle, Natsumi screamed. The truck kept going and Natsumi limped behind in her high-heeled shoes, flinging out obscenities that I would not have expected from a flower heiress's mouth.

My brother took that truck to his parking lot. That nasty little princess will have to pay forty thousand yen to get behind the wheel again," Mr. Waka said when I walked into the Family Mart an hour later.

"How did you know it was Natsumi Kayama who visited me?"

"She stopped to buy some cigarettes and asked

about your address. She had the building number but didn't know the streets."

"So you sent your brother and his tow truck after her?"

"Oh, no, nothing like that. It's just that I gave her an earnest caution, mentioning that a vehicle of that very size and make had been recently involved in an accident. I told her that there was no place to park a Range Rover on your street, and she called me a meddling little man! So I made a phone call to Yuji, and, well—" He giggled merrily. "My brother says that the Yanaka Neighborhood Improvement Society has no tolerance for illegally parked vehicles. Fate took its course."

"Well, I just hope she doesn't come back to haunt us."

"Yes, that young lady is trouble." He broke off when a middle-aged male customer came up to the counter and asked for a cup of *oden*, the murky, ever-simmering fish stew that was the Family Mart's signature dish. Mr. Waka ladled out a serving and rang it up with a smile and a comment about how nicely the customer's son had behaved when he came in the previous day. After the man's departure, the door chimed and Mr. Waka resumed our conversation. "Natsumi Kayama could have killed Sakura Sato. She was at the school the same evening it happened, and furthermore, she was at the exhibition when you were poisoned."

"How did you know about the poisoning? I never told you."

"Your aunt told me when she came to buy eggs.

She mentioned it when she told me that she needed the freshest food possible to restore your health."

"Don't tell anyone else about my poisoning," I said.

"Why? If you meet with foul play, this will be important evidence. I refuse to let a murderer get away with such a crime!"

"The police know everything already. I'd rather you didn't mention it to anyone because that would only further scandalize the Kayamas."

"And since when have you cared about them?" Mr. Waka exclaimed.

"I don't." I shifted uncomfortably. "It's just that the school has enough trouble with a murder at their headquarters and an environmental group trying to shut them down."

"And a daughter who breaks traffic laws. The *iemoto* must be ashamed," Mr. Waka said. "I wonder when he will remove her from the family register."

"Don't make me laugh," I said to Mr. Waka. "I've laughed too much already on this crazy afternoon."

"Laughing is good for the health, and so is this new gum made by Lotte! It's a mixture of cherry blossoms and St. John's wort that can freshen the breath while fighting depression. Won't you try some?"

I needed to maintain full alertness, so after I left the Family Mart I spat the gum into its paper wrapping and looked for a place to throw it away. There were a few more trash cans around since the cherry blossom parties had gotten into full swing, so I pitched my tiny bit of litter into one near the park.

"*O-neesan.*" A drunk laborer lying on a blanket under a tree called me "sister" in the way men did with girls they wanted to pick up. "Come have a beer. You look like you're ready for a nap—heh, heh."

"Yes, take a rest with us!"

I knew the men were harmless enough, but they had noticed what I'd forgotten when I'd left the apartment—that I was still wearing my pajama bottoms. I looked down at the pants' faded pink-and-green-checked print, wondering why Mr. Waka hadn't commented on them.

All I could do was put my chin in the air in the best imitation of Natsumi Kayama that I could muster, and pass. Laughter followed me like steam curling out of Mr. Waka's pot of *oden*.

I longed to run, but that would only inspire more hilarity, so I maintained a steady amble past the Yanaka Tea Shop, glancing in the window and hoping not to see Richard or anyone else that I knew. He wasn't there, but a pair of college-age girls pointed at my pants and giggled. I acknowledged them with a nod and continued on and around the corner to my apartment. Inside, I locked the door and collapsed. I poured myself a beer then and toasted the end of a very bad day.

Chapter 24

Loaded up at 6 A.M. on Sunday morning, I drove to the Togo Shrine and discovered that I'd been assigned a spot near the exit. Few of the dealers talked to me, and most of the market shoppers had spent their money by the time they came around to me. But a few people tarried, and after two hours I'd made about twenty thousand yen — approximately $160. At nine o'clock, when I was counting my cash, I noticed an old man with a patch over one eye trailing past. I called out his name, and Mr. Ishida stopped.

"I was looking for you, but I have only one eye to see from," he apologized, stooping to talk with me. We must have looked like two old-time villagers hovering over the old blue-and-white hibachi.

"How is your eye?" I asked.

"I still have a headache, and my vision is blurred.

The doctors tell me it will take time to heal." He lowered his voice so the dealers around me wouldn't hear. "I lent you the van because I wanted you to succeed in this venture, but now I'm wondering whether it was such a good idea. It's sad to see a purveyor of fine antiques sitting on a tarpaulin and bargaining! Maybe you should have asked someone else to do the selling for you. What about your friend Richard Randall?"

"Richard's more of a shopper than a seller," I said, not wanting to explain how troubled our relationship had become. "Why don't you sit down for a moment? There's something I want to show you." I unzipped my money belt and withdrew the photograph of Takeo's mother. "Imagine this woman twenty years later. Do you think she's the one who came into your shop?"

Mr. Ishida studied it for a long time, bringing it close to and away from his face. "The kimono is the same, but I am not sure. This young woman is so lovely. I don't think she would grow up to look like a typical middle-aged lady."

"Okay, next photo." I rummaged in my backpack and located a Kayama School brochure I'd been given when I started my studies. The brochure contained a picture of Sakura cutting flowers and the caption, "A flower master shares wisdom."

Mr. Ishida handled the brochure the same way he had handled the portrait of Takeo's mother. His face was expressionless, but after a minute he nodded. "This could be the woman I saw, but I cannot tell you for certain. My vision is not good now. Looking at the picture hurts my eye."

"I apologize. I'm asking you to do too much!" Feeling guilty, I put away the picture and brochure.

"Actually, my eye is tired because of some concentrated studies I was doing half an hour ago," he said. "Around the corner, where the better dealers are, a plate sold that was remarkably similar to the Imari plates that you have."

"Really?" If only I'd been able to walk around and shop. My position as a vendor restricted me.

"The dealer was asking five thousand yen. She didn't know what it was worth, and of course it was a single."

"What a deal," I said glumly.

"If you could sell ten plates instead of nine, you could achieve extra value. Sell the set for one hundred fifty or one hundred sixty thousand, perhaps," Mr. Ishida mused.

"But someone already bought the plate. You said it was sold."

"To me." Mr. Ishida held up a shopping bag. "Would you like to see?"

The plate was perfect. The blue and white underglaze was as creamy as on my pieces, and the green, red, and gilt depictions of birds, butterflies, and bamboo were all in the right places.

"Would you resell the plate to me?" I asked. "You were the middleman, so I'd be happy to pay you more than her asking price."

"Oh, just the cost is fine. Four thousand."

"But I thought the plate was five thousand."

"I bargained." Mr. Ishida held up a cautionary finger. "This is why I don't want you selling things in this market. It's too easy for the customers to bargain, and too hard for the dealers to make a profit."

I carefully wrapped my wonderful new dish with plenty of newspaper and put it in the van for safekeeping. I expected that I could sell the set of ten next week to one of the fancy stores for a price that would be much better than I'd get at the flea market. Mr. Ishida watched my goods while I went to the van, allowing me enough time for a rest-room break and a quick cup of coffee and a chocolate crêpe from a vendor in Harajuku.

When I returned to my position, I thanked Mr. Ishida and he went home to rest. I stared out at the crowd, realizing again how much I hated having to stay in one place. In the next hour, my only customer was a housewife who bought three blue-and-white saucers that she said matched two she had at home. "Now you have a perfect set of five," I complimented her, thinking about the terrific potential sale I had with my new set of ten plates.

Thinking about my improved business position was a distraction from what would happen later in the day. I wondered what Che was planning that would shake Tokyo. If it was something truly awful, would I be considered an accomplice for not sharing my scanty knowledge with Lieutenant Hata?

My reverie ended as a small foot slid onto my tarpaulin. It was followed by the body of a small blond boy who tumbled into the midst of my wares.

"Ow!" the boy shrieked, then broke into noisy tears. He'd landed on a grouping of antique baskets instead of my neat line of porcelain *soba* cups.

"You're okay, sweetheart," I said, straining at having to use such an endearment on someone who had nearly devastated my inventory. "Where's your mother?"

"Mummy's busy. Uncle Richard lost me!" the boy wailed. I looked at him more closely, taking in the Doraemon sweatshirt and pale blue eyes. I recognized the child as Lila Braithwaite's middle son, the one who had tried to cut his younger sister's hair with the toy scissors when I'd visited his home. The "Uncle Richard" he mentioned was my Richard, ecoterrorist in training.

"You're Donald, aren't you?" I asked, marveling at how he'd managed to slide into my display and not anyone else's. Richard had chided me for being as bossy as a mom. Obviously it showed.

"David!" the boy corrected.

"Okay, David. Did Uncle Richard bring you to the flea market?"

He nodded and cried harder. I thought of hugging him, but I really didn't want to, not with his runny nose. Instead I handed him the rest of my chocolate crêpe. He stuck it in his mouth.

It was such a mess, being with the chocolate- and mucus-streaked boy and not a helping hand around. I'd been hard on Lila for wanting her getaways from her three children, I realized now. I could barely deal with one. I needed to get David back to Richard.

"Excuse me, but could you please watch my goods for a little while? The prices are marked, and you could give anybody who wants one a ten percent discount," I said in a rush to the middle-aged dealer who had been scowling at me all morning from his display of nineteenth-century erotic cartoons.

"I'm afraid not." He only scowled harder. "You should keep your children at home, not bring them to the market."

"He isn't mine!" The snotty David and I looked nothing like each other, I hoped.

"If he's not yours, take him to the police." The man turned away from me firmly and went back to sorting his erotica.

"We are going to have to work together," I told David. "Do you like baskets?"

David tried all the baskets on his head or arms. Now that I had a small foreign boy amidst my wares, more people were stopping to look, and I even sold one of the drool-covered baskets, although David wailed when he had to part with it. My annoyance began to fade, because I knew that it was better that David Braithwaite had tumbled onto someone who recognized him rather than a non-English-speaking dealer. We spent an hour together, and I kept my eyes fixed on the crowd looking for Richard and Lila. No luck.

By one o'clock the market was slowing down and I decided that David's safe return took precedence over a few thousand more yen. I tied a kimono sash cord from my wrist to David's to keep from losing him as I made multiple trips carrying china to the van parked nearby. To some it might have looked inhumane, but David loved it when I told him that we were playing puppy and owner.

We walked the entire flea market twice, looking for David's family. I asked every vendor if a small blond man with two other children had been spotted. I finally had luck with a woman at the entrance to the flea market.

"A sweet blond angel dressed in black leather? He was pushing a stroller with a little girl in it, and there was another boy by his side. He asked me if I'd seen a little boy who looked like that." She nodded at David.

"Where did they go?" I asked.

"Through the market and then back. In the end they crossed the street and went to a police box."

"Great." I walked David across the street to the police box, where it turned out that Richard had in fact placed a missing-persons report. The policeman on duty looked David over while I explained that I knew the child and his mother and uncle. Seeming vastly relieved, the policeman suggested that I take the boy directly to Roppongi Hills. This seemed pretty trusting to me, but I guessed that the way David was barking and crawling made the officer afraid to remain alone with him.

By the time I'd secured David in the backseat of the van—with no child safety seat, I was praying for no accidents—he was still growling and yipping like a canine.

"I believe that you'll be the first dog to be allowed to live in Roppongi Hills," I said, feeling quite cheerful as I started driving. If Lila or no other family members were home, I knew that Mr. Oi, the building concierge, would look after him.

"Mummy say dogs dirty."

"Well, I can see how other dogs would suffer in comparison to such a handsome cocker spaniel as you."

"Doberman! David is a Doberman!" he shrieked.

At Roppongi Hills I left the van double-parked in the portico and went inside, holding David's hand.

Mr. Oi looked startled to see me with my new mate. "Mrs. Braithwaite is home, and I'm sure she has no idea that anything is amiss. Mr. Braithwaite is in Canada for the week, and I believe she is overwhelmed by the children."

"I noticed that last time. Three is a challenge."

"Well, she probably was looking forward to some quiet time to rest, but we will call her to announce David-*chan*'s arrival," he said, and called up over the intercom. He gave David a cherry-blossom-shaped lollipop to suck on while we waited.

"There's no answer," he said, looking at me with a puzzled expression. "The only explanation is that she is already on the telephone. She has two lines, you see, and if she is busy talking to somebody on one line, she may not want to answer our call. I let the telephone ring, but she is not answering. She must be home, because I sent up a guest earlier."

I had a similar phone system and was occasionally guilty of not answering an incoming beep when I was involved in something important. "Should I go upstairs and knock?"

"Yes, please, Miss Shimura. If she doesn't answer, please come downstairs with the child. I can entertain him with a small portable television."

"David watch Doraemon cartoon!" my charge demanded as I led him away.

Riding up in the elevator, I glanced at our appearance in the mirrored wall and straightened both of us up a bit. Last time I'd been in the elevator, I'd longingly looked there for the memory of Hugh. I didn't this time. Somehow the romantic feelings were gone.

When had I changed? Sometime between the night Takeo had followed me out of Salsa Salsa and our last awkward time together in his office, when he had stood close enough for me to feel his breath on my neck. Yes, I was thoroughly sunk, but for somebody who had been upset with me during our last encounter, and probably would be even more depressed when I suggested that the person fencing Kayama ware was not his long-lost mother but Sakura. It would be the loss of a dream that he had kept alive for so long.

David skipped toward his doorway on the seventh floor, and I hurried to catch up with him. I rang the doorbell. Lila didn't answer it, so after another minute I buzzed again.

I felt the first stirrings of fear. Mr. Oi had been certain that Lila was upstairs in her apartment, and if she wasn't answering, it might mean that she was injured. Or dead, I thought with a chill.

"David wants to wee!" David pressed his hands against the front of his pants.

"Just wait," I pleaded, mind flashing desperately

between two possible disasters: a deceased Lila Braithwaite or David letting loose on the cream-colored hallway carpet. I knew for certain that David didn't wear diapers, because I'd lifted him into the back of Mr. Ishida's van.

I knocked loudly and called Lila's name. David was moaning even more about needing the toilet. There was one thing left in my arsenal: my key ring. I'd never been asked to give up the copy of the key Hugh had made for me, and there was an off chance that it might fit Lila's door. I located the key in the bottom of my backpack, and when I put it into the lock, it didn't turn. However, the pressure I'd applied moved the door. I put my hand directly on the knob and turned it. The door had been unlocked the whole time.

David ran straight for the powder room, and I hoped that he wouldn't need my assistance there. I stepped into the apartment, which was as jumbled with child paraphernalia as I'd seen it before. There was a splendid flower arrangement on the coffee table, cherry blossoms stretching upward and draped artistically with gauze. It looked very Kayama. I passed into the kitchen looking for Lila. I saw a bottle of Cristal champagne and two goblets standing nearby—no doubt she was planning some kind of welcome home for her husband. I peered in the children's bedrooms and the master bedroom, where the bed was unmade. Still no sign of Lila.

David flushed the toilet and was skipping through the apartment.

"You and me can play all day," he chortled.

"We need to find Mummy, and she's not here. I'm afraid I'm going to have to take you back to Mr. Oi. You like him, don't you?"

"Lolly man?" David mulled over the suggestion.

"Why don't we take your favorite toy downstairs," I suggested. "What is it?"

"My Doraemon. He lives there." David led me back to his mother's bedroom and pointed toward the closet.

"Okay, let's liberate him." I flung open the door to the walk-in closet, looking for the toy that matched the cartoon show.

I don't know who screamed first, but suddenly the apartment was filled with sound. Instead of finding a stuffed animal in the closet, I'd found two: Lila Braithwaite, cowering in a black lace teddy, and Masanobu Kayama, the *iemoto* of the Kayama School, wearing nothing more than a towel.

"Mummy shouldn't play in the closet with Doraemon," David said with satisfaction, grabbing a big blue stuffed cat from behind the *iemoto*'s ankles. "He belongs to me."

Chapter 25

J escaped, but it was a disaster. Lila was sobbing about invasion of privacy while Masanobu Kayama shouted that if I breathed a word of foul gossip to anyone, I'd never get a teaching certificate. Through it all, David sang the *Doraemon* theme.

I was shaking as I rode the elevator back down and could barely acknowledge Mr. Oi when he called out good-bye to me. I got into the van and sat still for a few minutes trying to get a handle on things.

Lila was sleeping with the *iemoto*. Now I understood why she knew the way to the Kayamas' private floor—and why she had scratches on her midriff. They were marks of passion.

Had Sakura known? Most certainly, especially if the headmaster had made a habit over the years of seducing selected students. Lila was in her mid-thirties and extremely attractive—in the teddy, her aerobicized body had looked fit and fabulous. Poor Mr. Braithwaite, away in Canada. He probably was too busy to suspect his wife was involved with some-one else. Richard might have known. I imagined that he baby-sat when Lila needed time for her lover. How the woman had energy for a love affair when she had three small children around, I didn't understand. Although she had once said to me, "I like to have lots of things going on. It keeps life from being dreary."

I put the van in gear and headed toward Richard's apartment in Shibuya. The police had told me they would call him there with the news that I'd found David.

I was actually able to find a free parking place in a side street. I made sure that every door of the van was locked, given the antiques I had inside.

I walked around the corner to Moonbeam Villa. The building was more expensive than mine and housed many foreigners as well as Japanese tenants. I couldn't have afforded it with my unstable income, but that was all right with me. I liked Yanaka better.

A young man in a red baseball jacket was sitting on a fussy-looking faux Victorian chair in the lobby reading a Spanish-language newspaper. I hung back until I was sure that the person was not Che. It was Enrique, Richard's former boyfriend.

"Aren't you Enrique?" I asked in Spanish, and he looked up in surprise.

"Oh, Rei-san!" He smiled up at me. "I'm taking my siesta while Ricardo takes care of the children. They're too lively for me."

Remembering how energetically Enrique had danced, I rather doubted that. I sat down next to him and said, "So Richard kept the other two here with him? I wonder why the police told me to take David on his own to Roppongi Hills. What a mistake!"

"Yes, Richard was upset when the cops called him. Some miscommunication, obviously. What happened there?" From Enrique's expression, it was clear that he knew about Lila.

"I walked in on them," I said. "Now I feel like the biggest fool in the world."

"Che told us that the flower-arranging boss was a man of bad moral character. It's true, isn't it?"

"Well, he is a widower, so I suppose that his actions aren't hurting a spouse. But Lila's married."

"That is not the way love should be," Enrique said with vigor.

"What is your ideal?" I asked. It felt strange to be having this conversation. I was jealous when Richard had put Enrique ahead of me, but now I was determined to give him a chance.

"I believe that love is forever. You do not fall in love with one person and the next week or year with another! Love is difficult for Ricardo," Enrique said. "He falls madly, madly, and then he cools off. It is like being in a heat wave followed by snow. The only one he keeps a strong, consistent feeling for is *you*."

"Not really. He blew up at me, did you hear that? He's switched over to Che's world. He won't tell me what he's going to do later on today."

"Maybe he doesn't quite know himself," Enrique said. "If there's one thing I've learned about that boy, it's that he is more show than go."

I smiled at his use of the Western expression and asked, "Do you know what's going to happen later today?"

Enrique shook his head. "I'm not in the important circle. Richard, with his ability to speak to foreign journalists, is closer. But still not entirely there."

"It's such a shame. Such a waste of a good person. Well, I'm going upstairs. I need to talk to him about Lila."

"In front of the children?" Enrique sounded horrified.

"I'll be discreet."

Richard had always kept an immaculate apartment, with gleaming wooden floors, black leather furniture, and the only splash of color coming from bookcases lined with the bright covers of animation videos. I was worried that the Braithwaite children might have trashed the place. Donald and Darcy, however, were parked in front of his television set watching *Pocket Monsters*, the cartoon that achieved notoriety in the late 1990s when thousands of children in Japan went into epileptic seizures triggered by a cartoon character's flashing eyes. From the way Donald glanced away from the set, gave me a bored look of recognition, and stuck his finger inside his nose, I guessed that he was going to be okay—but I decided that I preferred his energetic and enthusiastic little brother, David. Darcy, the baby, was placid, ignoring me but alternating her attention between her sippy cup and a chocolate biscotti.

"You really know how to take care of children," I complimented Richard.

"No, you're the one! The police called, and I owe you everything for finding David. But where is he?"

"Long story. I'll get to that when we have some privacy. How did you ever lose David?"

"He slipped away when we were looking at vintage Levi's. I searched for half an hour before getting scared that somebody might have snatched him. That's when I made the police report." Richard crooked his finger, indicating that I should follow him into his bedroom in order to talk more freely. We kept the door open so that we could see what the children were doing.

"I left David at Roppongi Hills. Lila was home, and she had company." I raised my eyebrows, so he caught my meaning.

"You know." Richard sighed heavily. "In the beginning, I had no idea why she wanted me to baby-sit on weekends. When the children started talking about a flower man, I thought they meant he was a cute young delivery boy. Che and the rest of them in Stop Killing Flowers told me it was the headmaster."

"Are they in love?" I mouthed the last couple of words, because I too wanted to shelter the children. They had a father. For all I knew, Lila's marriage would survive and her relationship with the *iemoto* would wilt like picked violets.

"I don't think so. It's all about power. She gets to

be president of the foreign students' association and
has already got three certificates under her belt.
Garter belt, I should say. I'm sure she has great lin-
gerie."

"She does," I said.

"You didn't catch them in flagrante delicto?
Wow!"

"Uncle Richard, I want another biscotti!" Donald
whined.

"The jar is on the table, my sweet. Help yourself,"
Richard called back. To me, he said, "I'm trying to
teach him to be more self-reliant."

"The situation with the *iemoto* sounds like a potential case of sexual harassment. If he dropped Lila,
she might sue. Who knows?" I was trying to give
Richard's cousin the benefit of the doubt.

"How many members does the school have nation-
wide?" Richard asked.

"Twenty thousand. And twelve thousand of those
have teacher credentials."

"He'd have to be busier than a hooker in Bangkok
to sexually harass everybody up for a teacher's certificate."

I had to agree. "Most of the teaching candidates
never visit headquarters, because you can take classes at teachers' homes. So I guess it's not really a situation where a woman *has* to sleep with him to get
ahead."

"Sakura knew about them," Richard said. "Lila
told me that she was freaked out once when Sakura
followed her from the Kayama Kaikan all the way to
Roppongi Hills. Lila thought that Sakura wanted to

check out how fancy the building was, whether she was worthy enough to become the foreign students' president. In hindsight, I bet that Sakura was interested in knowing where the *iemoto* was dropping in for a matinee."

Lila and Masanobu Kayama had a definite motive to kill Sakura, but for them to be falsely accused would result in terrible things: disgrace to the Kayama School, and perhaps Lila's losing custody of her children in a divorce. The idea that the headmaster and Lila could be killers made me feel suddenly anxious about David.

"I shouldn't have left David. It was irresponsible of me." I leaned against Richard's wall.

"Look, you rescued him at the shrine; that was pretty damn amazing. Come over here and sit down. The longer you slouch against my Mapplethorpe print, the more glass cleaner I'll have to use to get off the smudges. You look like hell, babe."

"Well, I was at the shrine sale. Why were you there, anyway?"

"Don't you remember the good old days when I helped you carry things? I thought it might be a way to make up. Of course, I stopped looking for you after I lost David."

"You don't keep track of the shrine schedule. And I didn't tell you that I'd be at the Togo Shrine." I was disturbed by Richard's facile answer. It just didn't ring true.

Richard was silent for a minute. "I heard you might be there from Che."

"What is he doing, tapping my telephone?"

"Oh, no. What do you think we are, the government?" Richard bristled. "There's a lookout in your neighborhood, though. Stop Killing Flowers wanted to see if you really worked at Mr. Waka's Family Mart, as I told Che you did—"

"Oh, no!"

"Relax, Mr. Waka told them that you're his apprentice."

I was too worried to appreciate the irony in Mr. Waka's defense. "Has Che been slipping notes under my door?"

"No, but it's interesting that you mention that." Richard paused. "I really shouldn't be telling you this, but the Stop Killing Flowers lookout person saw a lady slip a letter under your door two days ago."

"Was there a physical description?" I asked, feeling excited.

"A middle-aged woman with flowers under one arm—a typical flower lover. I told them it was probably your aunt dropping something by, but they said no. They remember your aunt well from the protest outside My Magic Forest."

"If only they could just forget about the Shimuras—"

"If only you could forget about *them*. I mean us." Richard glanced at his oversized Swatch. "It's two-thirty. Lila asked me to have the kids back to her by three. Do you think you could drop us off in Roppongi Hills in Mr. Ishida's van?"

"There is no child safety seat. You'd be better off on the subway."

"I suppose so," he said grumpily.

"I hope this doesn't impact your, um, plans for today," I said with significance.

"You said you wouldn't ask me about Stop Killing Flowers," Richard reminded me.

"Right! Let's just hope we both live through the next twenty-four hours." I kissed the top of my friend's spiked head and gave the young Braithwaites an extra biscotti each on my way out.

Chapter 26

The art of kimono dressing is a bit like preparing for war. First there is underlying strategy: a struggle with an underskirt and a full-length, long-sleeved under-robe of the right color—I had one in blue that contrasted well with the pink and green kimono, but it took a long time to iron. Once it was on, I secured a silk collar around my neck, and I also tucked a rectangle of folded *washi* paper (in case I needed a napkin while drinking tea) and an ironed cotton handkerchief between my bra and the neckline of the under-robe. At last I slipped on the silk crepe kimono, and then the real battle began: tying a ten-foot-long obi, a silk brocade sash that was surely invented to confound anyone who ever had trouble folding an origami crane.

It took me an hour to get dressed and twenty minutes to powder my face and to figure out which of my lipsticks was subtle enough to work with the kimono—in the end, I picked a frost called Frenzy, which was pretty much the way I felt. I longed to sink down on my futon for a brief rest, but the huge, stiff bow I'd tied over my hips made that impossible. How could I ride in this condition to Izu? I was pondering this question when a car honked outside.

Aunt Norie slipped out of the Honda Accord's front seat, revealing her splendid purple silk kimono patterned with lacy plum blossoms. Her red obi was embroidered with gold. Norie shifted to sitting in the backseat with Tom. I tried to convince her to regain her rightful position next to Uncle Hiroshi, but she refused.

"Your stomach, Rei-*chan*. It will be easier for you up front."

"Okay, thanks." I guessed that she remembered all the bad trips to Lake Biwa when I was younger. "How long is the trip going to take?"

"Two hours. Do you think you can last?" Tom asked.

"Of course. I have a bag of crackers to eat if I feel queasy. Want some?" I held up the plastic bag I'd bought at the Family Mart.

"Rei, you'll get crumbs down your kimono. It's too loose, anyway. It reveals the nape of your neck, which makes you look like a geisha," my aunt chided. To fix things, she rose from the backseat and began tucking my kimono more tightly across my chest, which already had so many layers over it that it resembled a hard shield.

"I'm glad to see you have a handkerchief with you,

because the Kayamas usually serve the most delicious *chirashizushi,* and you may need to wipe your lipstick. It is the fluffiest rice, topped with little bits of green onion, sweetened egg, and shrimp. Now that you can eat normal food again, you'll enjoy it!" Norie chirped.

"I doubt Rei feels like eating any food served by the Kayamas. I wouldn't," Tom said.

"Don't be rude!" Uncle Hiroshi snapped, his first words since I'd entered the car. I wondered what was going on with the Shimura family.

After an hour's drive, the grimy, monster-sized buildings that made up Tokyo and Kawasaki gave way to smaller buildings spaced well apart, and then towering pine trees. Another hour and we had entered the Izu Peninsula. The scenery would have looked prettier if the sky hadn't been so gray. There was a storm warning on the radio, but before I could get the details of its path, Uncle Hiroshi abruptly switched it to a station playing Japanese oldies. As a high-pitched woman's voice crooned the popular song "Sakura," I closed my eyes. If the rain came, all the cherry blossoms would be washed out and we could make a quick round-trip home.

"The house is in the mountains. The *iemoto*'s grandfather was clever to build in such a remote area. Now the beaches of Izu are cluttered by mansions and souvenir shops. It's a horrible place to visit," Aunt Norie said.

"And outrageously priced," Uncle Hiroshi added. "For what you pay for a view of thirty snack shops, you could have an apartment in Hiro!"

"Mrs. Koda has an apartment in Hiro," I said.

"Oh? Did she invite you?" Norie seized on my comment.

"I stopped by for tea the other evening. I wanted to thank her for sending me the flowers."

"You should have asked her to your place for tea, not gone to her house. Rei, I hope you didn't invite yourself. That may be an American habit, but it's not proper in Japan."

"She has trouble walking, so I thought it would be unkind to make her visit me, especially with the subway stairs in my neighborhood—"

"How considerate!" Tom broke in. "Father, did you see the sign for the detour coming up? You must move into the left lane."

"This road was supposed to be improved because of tourism, but it's just one hassle after another," Uncle Hiroshi complained.

"Do you want to switch at the next rest stop? I like driving," Tom said. "I drove the car all the time when you were gone."

"Yes, and now that I'm back, you must be disappointed!" Hiroshi lashed out.

A rusted metal figure of a policeman with his hand outstretched clearly marked the detour. Hiroshi whipped the Honda into the turn so fast that the car's bumper hit the faux policeman. He fell over with a resounding clang into the roadway, but my uncle drove on.

"Other cars cannot get by. We must drive back and stand the figure back up," Norie fretted.

"You want to fix everything!" Hiroshi said. "Well,

this is not the same thing as carrying garbage out of a temple garden. We're on a one-way road! To turn around and drive back would be illegal."

The tension was making my stomach lurch a bit. I wanted out of the car. "Why don't you stop the car on the shoulder and I'll run back? Right now it's only a half-mile run. I can be there and back in ten minutes."

"In *zōri*?" Norie asked, referring to my fancy thong sandals.

"I'll take them off!"

Hiroshi never slowed. We debated the situation of the fallen policeman for the next ten miles, until we exited the paved road and started following a rough earthen track.

"Too bad we don't have a cross-country vehicle. Four-wheel drive would make me feel safer. Please reduce your speed," Norie instructed her husband.

I began dreaming of the Kayama family's Range Rover that had been smashed, and the loaner that Natsumi had been driving. The interior was probably wonderful—leather seats, walnut dashboard, CD player. Perfectly comfortable and quiet for a couple driving into the woods toward their assignation. I wondered if Masanobu Kayama had ever taken Lila to his country house. From what I'd read in classic Japanese novels, love affairs usually took place on a neutral ground such as an inn or a teahouse, not places where the husband's family lived.

"Didn't you hear me, Rei?" Norie broke into my thoughts.

"Sorry. What is it?" I asked.

"I asked you whether Mrs. Koda told you how she was planning to get to the party. The nearest train station is twelve kilometers from the house. I hope the Kayamas are giving her a ride. I would have offered our car, but with the four of us inside, there isn't much room."

"Perhaps she isn't coming," I said. "Mrs. Koda didn't mention a party at all."

"I see. Well, it is true that the invitations arrived very late. Usually the invitation arrives the day after the Tokyo cherry blossom season arrives, with the party date set for seven days later. Such terrible events happened at the school during those early cherry blossom days, it is no wonder that the invitation came late, and the RSVP number was to an outside line."

"What's that about the RSVP?" I asked, not understanding.

"In past years, the number given for RSVP purposes was Mrs. Koda's extension at the school office. But this time the number was that of a professional answering service. Don't worry, we will all be on the attendance list. I chatted with a young lady on the other end, and she said this party was the biggest ever. More than two hundred are planning to attend."

Takeo had probably arranged for the outside service to give Mrs. Koda a break. Despite all the bad things I'd heard about him, I couldn't help appreciating the way he was sensitive to the elderly woman's needs.

"Father, when's the last time you came to one of

the Kayamas' parties?" Tom asked.

"Mmm, it was the last year I was here before the transfer to Osaka. Must have been three years ago. Yes, that's right. But the party to remember was the one when Takeo and Natsumi were teenagers."

"I remember that party," Norie said. "Takeo did some kind of mischief with music. . . ."

"Yes, there was a classical music recital going on in the reception room. But when the musicians finished playing 'Sakura,' he blasted some kind of American new wave music."

"Really?" I liked new wave. "What was Natsumi like then?"

"Very beautiful," Norie said. "She was wearing a kimono from her mother's collection that was said to be worth more than eight million yen. She hasn't worn it since, come to think of it."

"She spent the whole party smoking on the verandah. It was disgusting to see a young woman with a cigarette hanging out of her mouth like that. You don't smoke, do you, Rei?" Uncle Hiroshi asked.

"No! I mean, I must confess I tried it when I was a teenager, but it made me nauseated."

"Of course it would." Tom chuckled.

I was still interested in the idea of the kimono. "How do you think the Kayamas store a kimono that's worth so much? In a vault?"

"Oh, no, the Kayamas have a *kura,* a storehouse for their valuables. They opened it for a tour about ten years ago. Each kimono is stored in an individual lacquered box. The system is very well organized."

"Like the archives at the school," I said.

"How do you know about the archives?" Norie asked. "I hope that you haven't been asking the school staff too many questions."

"I went on a tour," I said, popping a cracker into my mouth and chewing.

"Rei's obviously feeling sick, so let's not press her for conversation," Tom said. "Mother, if you don't mind, let's stay quiet for the rest of the ride."

"Which way is it now?" Uncle Hiroshi demanded. He stopped at the end of the dirt road.

"Oh, dear, I was talking so much that I didn't notice. I think we missed a turn, because I've never been to this place before," Norie said.

"All your gossip distracted me," Uncle Hiroshi told her.

"Father, I remember this area. I humbly ask that you let me take the wheel," Tom said.

"Fine! You do everything better than I do." Uncle Hiroshi unfastened his seat belt, threw his door open, and got out of the car. Tom left the back and took the driver's seat. Now the young ones were in front, the elders in the back. How odd that felt.

Tom turned the car around. The road was so rough that small rocks flew out from under the wheels. It was definitely bumpy enough to make me sick, but Tom continued at a slow, steady pace. We traveled back about two miles to a fork in the rough trail.

"Yes, that's where the correct turn is," Norie said. "It's a very subtle entrance. But look, up ahead there are pretty pink lanterns in the trees. And there is a car ahead of us! We must be on the right path."

The car's taillights vanished around a stand of tall

oaks. Tom continued at his measured pace, and when we rounded the bend the car was no longer in sight.

"Just follow the lanterns," Norie advised. "I'm sure they lead to the side of the house, where the gardens are."

I wished it weren't so dark. I wondered if we were passing Takeo's experimental garden—there was no way to tell. All I had a sense of was vast fields and trees, a luxury of space that I'd never before experienced in Japan.

"You see? Here we are!" Norie said.

Ahead of us lay a low, sprawling villa that reminded me of early-twentieth-century modernism. The house was built of stone, a material rarely used for houses in Japan, but had a traditional tiled roof. It looked very interesting. Now I didn't care about the long, uncomfortable car ride or my uncertainty about the party ahead. "Aunt Norie, did you bring a camera? I've got to take pictures!"

"Yes, yes." She passed me a pretty little silk bag that felt heavy. "You can use my Nikon, it's just point and shoot, *neh*? Just be sure not to use up the film. I'd like to have my photograph taken against the famous cherry trees."

"They haven't marked the parking," Hiroshi complained. "Last time we came, we parked on the grassy area over there."

"With Takeo-san's interest in environmentalism, he might want to save the grass," Tom said dryly. "I'll get a bit closer to the house, and maybe we'll see a parking valet."

But nobody was standing there. However, about a dozen cars were parked along the edge of the driveway. I recognized Lila Braithwaite and Nadine St. Giles, both dressed in sequined cocktail suits, emerging from a Mercedes and walking toward the house. Did Nadine know about Lila's affair? I wondered about that, as well as about who was baby-sitting the Braithwaite children that night.

"Well, I'm stopping here," Tom announced. He parked the car. After getting out, I arched my back with pleasure. The *obi*'s thick bow had forced me to sit ramrod straight the entire journey.

"Ah, look. Isn't that Natsumi at the door? I must say she doesn't look a day older than she did at nineteen," Uncle Hiroshi announced.

I looked and sure enough, Natsumi stood between two tall sliding doors. She was not wearing an eight-million-yen kimono—just a pair of black jeans and a T-shirt.

"You said I had to dress up!" I turned on my aunt in horror. If this was going to be a party full of young hipsters in black jeans, I'd feel ridiculous.

"I don't understand why she's dressed that way! And keep your voice down!" Aunt Norie whispered forcefully.

"*Ohairi kudasai,*" Natsumi called, the standard polite welcome that one made to guests. Her voice was slurred, and she leaned in the doorway as if to support her body.

"Drunk," Hiroshi said under his breath.

"Who cares? We all need a drink after that drive," Tom muttered.

Intoxicated. Slumbering amid pinks. I thought of the haiku as I trailed them toward the house. Lila was bound to notice me; I hoped it wouldn't be too awkward.

"Our house isn't very clean, and I'm afraid we haven't prepared the right food!" Natsumi spoke in a breathless singsong as we all bowed to her and passed into the house's entryway. In most Japanese homes, this was a space no larger than five feet square, but in this house, the fieldstone entrance was about thirty feet long and twenty feet wide. A cathedral ceiling marked by heavy beams soared above us. The house was very unusual for Japan. I longed to use the camera in the silk bag dangling from my wrist, but I'd have to wait until later, when the entryway wasn't so crowded. Also, I'd straighten it up a bit before taking the picture. A newspaper lay atop the hall table, where there was no flower arrangement of any sort. I would have expected some hint of cherry blossoms, since this was a cherry blossom viewing party.

"I wonder where the servants are," Aunt Norie said to me sotto voce as we peeled off the light silk *haori* coats. Tom and Uncle Hiroshi had worn business suits, so they had nothing to do but slip out of their shoes. Natsumi was rummaging in a long, low cabinet and then began tossing out dozens of slippers for us to wear.

I stepped out of my *zōri* and into a pair of woven straw slippers waiting for me on the polished oak floor. Then we all moved into a large reception room furnished comfortably with low chairs and sofas.

Bottles of hard liquor waited on a table made from a highly polished slab of zelkova, but the cups next to them were of oddly mixed sizes and included a plastic tumbler decorated with Doraemon, the magical cartoon cat that had stalked me throughout the day.

I choked back a laugh. At a minimum, I'd been expecting tuxedoed waiters handing around drinks on a tray to the forty guests who were already there. The house was beautiful, but the preparations were so awkward that even I could have done better.

The saving grace was the cherry garden, revealed by the room's three glass walls. The trees were in full splendor and softly lit with pink lanterns such as we'd seen on the path coming in.

In the garden, Norie's friend Eriko, who was wearing a dark blue kimono, was chatting with Lila Braithwaite. Norie immediately began making noises about wanting to talk to them. I thought it was better that I didn't come face-to-face with Lila, so I made an excuse about exploring the house. I made a drink for myself and then went into the dining room, where I had caught a glimpse of Takeo.

He was on the telephone, pacing around a striking dining table carved from a single huge slab of oak. He was wearing jeans, like his sister, and his beloved Greenpeace T-shirt.

"I understand that you're twenty kilometers away. You've just got to come." His voice had a hint of desperation. I must have made a sound, because he looked up at me. To my surprise, he motioned for me to come in and close the door. I sat down on the edge of a black leather chaise longue and listened.

"I need lots of *sashimi*—twenty platters of your best. I know this is an inconvenience. I'll pay extra." Pause. "Do you have *chirashizushi?* No? What else could you do on short notice?"

At that moment I knew why he and Natsumi were in jeans and the house wasn't ready. They hadn't known we were coming. We were all a big surprise.

Aunt Norie had commented on the unusual RSVP procedure. She had written it off to unrest at Kayama School headquarters. But it was obvious that someone who hated the Kayamas had sent the invitations and arranged for an answering service outside the school to take the RSVPs. Furthermore, the invitations had been mailed during the weekend, so there would be no danger of anyone chatting about it at headquarters. The event had been planned so that the Kayama family would not see it coming.

After he finished the call, Takeo put the telephone down. "Maybe I should call McDonald's. Do they deliver?"

"I don't know," I said.

Takeo leaned against the wall and shut his eyes. He spoke slowly, as if he were in a trance. "This is a total disaster. I can only imagine how many dozens more will arrive. I could kill my father for doing this to me!"

"Save your energy," I said, getting up and going over to him. "It's not his fault. I don't know whose it is yet, but I've a sense that's why we're all here. To find out."

Chapter 27

Before I earned a B.A. from Johns Hopkins and an M.A. from Berkeley, one of my top qualifications was a Girl Scout badge for emergency preparedness. I recalled the stay-calm, deep-breathing part while dealing with Takeo. I decided that now was not the time to hit him over the head with the unhappy news that his father was carrying on with Lila Braithwaite. I let him rant about how horrible it had been when guests had started arriving an hour ago, when he had been peacefully working on a compost pile and Natsumi had been painting her toenails in the living room.

"As the flower master designate, you can be as eccentric as you'd like," I told him. "Make them believe that you purposely were working outside and dressed in a Greenpeace T-shirt to communicate the message of the school's new green policy."

"There's no green policy," Takeo said, drinking obediently from the Doraemon tumbler filled with a bracing mixture of vodka and tonic that I'd given him.

"You are the next master," I repeated. "It's your duty to inform us about the direction the school is taking. And saying something from your heart about the school's future commitment to the environment might actually save the evening."

"You're crazy!"

"Not as crazy as your friends. Stop Killing Flowers is planning something so major that they assembled all of us to be their audience."

"But I gave them money! They were supposed to stay away from the school."

"Blackmail never works. When shopkeepers pay gangsters protection money, the fee always goes up. But in your case, the stake is something you care about. Right?"

Takeo didn't answer me. He seemed mesmerized by the crowd, which had swelled to about a hundred. A young deliveryman with dyed yellow hair and an earring was unloading cases of sake and beer.

"Sir, won't you stay to help serve?" Natsumi flashed cleavage along with her mournful expression as she bent to help him.

"I-I'm sorry, but that's impossible. I'm on duty," the deliveryman stammered.

"I'll make sure that you're well paid," Natsumi purred. "If it's a matter of calling your employer, I'd be happy to do that."

"Well . . . maybe for a little while." The man

stepped behind the table and unscrewed the cap of a bottle.

Good work, Natsumi. I shot her an appreciative look that she didn't acknowledge. I guessed that she was still angry about her visit to my apartment. I decided to reassure her brother instead. "Things are going to be fine," I told him. "Just greet your guests, and try to relax so that you can make a good speech in the next hour."

"Please don't leave!" Takeo gripped me by the arm as I started off.

"I just need to find a telephone. Is there one in a more private location than this?"

"Upstairs. We have one in each bedroom."

As Takeo and I headed upstairs together, we had to pass Aunt Norie standing in the hallway with her friend Eriko. Eriko smiled, but my aunt looked venomous.

"Rei-*chan*, don't you remember what I told you?" Norie was acting as if we were going upstairs for a quickie.

"I'm just making a telephone call," I said, and hurried on before she could find another reason for keeping me.

Takeo showed me into a charming small bedroom with exposed stone walls on two sides and a fireplace, a very unusual feature for a Japanese home. I knew it was his room from the stacks of environmental magazines on the floor. A calligraphy scroll that looked like his mother's work hung in an alcove above a vase of bittersweet.

"For propriety's sake, maybe I should call from another room," I suggested.

"Oh, is that what your aunt's so upset about?" Takeo asked. "She thinks I'm like my father."

I nodded, embarrassed because I now knew just how dreadful Takeo's father was.

"You have the same opinion." Takeo sounded bitter. "That's why you ran out on me the other night. You think I'm some sort of cad."

"Just let me use the phone, please." I knew that I sounded brusque, but now was not the time to go into my own confused feelings for Takeo. I resolutely turned my back on him and picked up the telephone receiver. By the time I'd reached Lieutenant Hata's home, Takeo had slipped out.

You're calling me on Sunday? The only day of the week that I don't have to work?" Lieutenant Hata grumbled after his wife put him on.

"Emergencies don't keep to a weekday schedule," I whispered. "Do you think you could make it to the Kayamas' cherry blossom viewing party? It's in Izu, and I can't give you directions, but maybe somebody on the police force here could help you find the Kayama family estate."

"That's the other problem, Miss Shimura. My territory is Roppongi, not the wilds of the Izu Peninsula."

"Please! This is serious."

Lieutenant Hata listened while I explained about the surprise party that I suspected had been orchestrated by Stop Killing Flowers. But at the end he sighed and said, "As far as this party goes, it sounds

like a comedy of errors. And we know what Stop
Killing Flowers' big plan was."

"What—what are they doing?"

"They are holding a festival in the Yanaka
Cemetery with mariachi bands, mimes, and various
other entertainers. Che Fujisawa is giving away free
organic cherry tree seedlings and asking people to
sign a petition. I saw a story about the festival on the
television news, and it looks like a fine event. The
group is collecting plenty of signatures, and three
senior politicians made a surprise appearance and
have pledged to sponsor legislation calling for safe
flower imports."

So Che's big surprise had been politicians? This
was the secret Richard had kept from me? I was
irate but not ready to give up. Trying to sound reasonable, I said, "You make it obvious that I'm wrong
about Stop Killing Flowers putting on this party. But
I still think it's a dangerous situation. Why would
somebody have brought together everyone from
Sakura's death scene? Could we be waiting for
somebody new to die?"

Lieutenant Hata was silent for a minute. "Are the
guests eating anything?"

"There is no food. People are complaining mighti-
ly about that. However, some sashimi is going to be
delivered, and I suppose an evil person could sprin-
kle something on it." I played up the last few words,
hoping it would make an impact.

"I'll call the district commander in Izu. But you
must understand that the peninsula is large, and
you've not given me much information about the

location of the Kayama estate. I can't promise that the local police will make a trip to this party. Without a crime having been committed, the only way I can entice them to go there is by saying someone called me to make a report of excessive noise and unruly behavior. Miss Shimura, would you agree that there is excessive noise and bad behavior at this party?"

I understood my cue. "Absolutely." So what if the guests were mostly in their fifties and extremely unlikely to swing from the rafters? Since the liquor delivery, the party *had* gotten slightly louder.

"Don't drink too much, and please give me the number there so I can check in on you."

As I recited the telephone number to him, I heard the clicking sound of somebody hanging up a telephone. Either the officer's wife had listened to our conversation—or somebody in the Kayama house had.

"Do you know where your wife is?" I asked Lieutenant Hata.

"Certainly. She is sitting at the table with me, shaving a bonito fish to use in our evening meal. Why do you ask, Miss Shimura?"

"Ah . . ." I didn't want to say that I thought somebody was eavesdropping. "I look forward to seeing the police force," I said, and hung up.

Downstairs I passed Takeo standing in the hall with Mari Kumamori.

"I want you to take the teacher's test again," Takeo was telling her. "And perhaps you would be kind enough to consider letting me borrow a few of your containers for an exhibit this fall."

"Oh, no!" Mari breathed in sharply, but although her words were negative, her face was filled with delight. "My work is so awful!"

"I think, it's in the vanguard. With our school's growing commitment to the environment, pottery with natural glaze is perfect." He changed focus from Mari to me as I passed him and stepped down into the entryway to put on my *zōri*. "Please don't leave us, Rei."

"I'm just going outside for a little while. Don't worry. I'll be back." Feeling like a female Arnold Schwarzenegger, I decided it was too bad that I had to step into my one-inch-high sandals instead of combat boots.

The line of parked cars stretched out for an eighth of a mile. The vehicles were mostly Japanese sedans, although there were a few trendy sport utility vehicles. I walked in the dark along the line of cars, examining the line of the guests still arriving. We all nodded at one another or made half bows. I didn't recognize any school employees.

The path curved around the back toward the ring of cherry trees. In between the trees were decorative stone lanterns and small boulders. The Garden of Stones appeared to be a hybrid of classic Zen gardening and American landscape design.

I saw my relatives and moved in for a quick read on the situation.

"I don't care about the flowers," Uncle Hiroshi was grumbling to Norie. "I just want something to eat. Where is the *chirashizushi* you promised they would serve?"

I came between them. "The food will come. There was nothing on hand because this whole party was unplanned."

"But how can that be?" Hiroshi asked.

"Somebody sent invitations for all of us to come, but the Kayama family didn't know."

"Who would do such a thing? To have guests when a house is not ready and food is unprepared is . . . a humiliation!" Aunt Norie said. Eriko leaned in from a nearby conversation and nodded in agreement.

"We don't know who did it," I said. "The important thing is not to let too many people know, because then they'd all feel bad for being here. Takeo has ordered some food to be delivered. It would be a great kindness if you would help put the dishes into something resembling a buffet when it all comes." I didn't add the request to stay and watch the food because I knew that would come naturally to her.

"Of course. It will be thrown together, but it shouldn't look too bad. I know exactly where the china is and how I should serve." Norie paused. "Rei-*chan*—is this why you went upstairs a little while ago? Just to help Takeo make a plan to save the evening?"

I nodded, and she smiled tenderly. "You *are* a good girl."

Peace restored, I walked back out to the driveway and then down a stone path curving toward a small white plaster outbuilding. When I came close, I realized that it was probably the *kura,* the storehouse used for family treasures. A vehicle was parked in front of it. When I walked closer, I stopped. It wasn't the Range Rover, but a black Nissan truck.

I moved to the hood, which was giving off some light pinging sounds, as if the ignition had been recently turned off. The hood was warm. The *geta* made me a bit taller, so I could see into the truck. In the pale light from the lanterns in the trees, I could make out the objects on the passenger seat: a fishing net, a ladder, and a few folded paper lanterns. So this was the vehicle of the person who had decorated the driveway. The secret party-giver might very well be inside the *kura* stealing the Kayama family's treasures.

I wasn't reckless enough to go in, but there was something I could do. I took out Aunt Norie's camera and snapped a picture of the items on the car seat and then one of the rear of the truck, making sure that the license plate was included. Then I headed back toward the house, wishing that I had a flashlight. The woods around the house seemed unbelievably desolate. I was probably only fifty yards from the house, but nobody could see me. I walked fast and was relieved when I came close enough to the house to see other guests leaving their cars.

I hadn't seen a single Kayama School staff person at the party; not Mrs. Koda, nor Miss Okada, nor any of the other important teachers or office ladies I'd seen at the headquarters. Certainly not Masanobu Kayama. Perhaps he was storming around his Tokyo penthouse, wondering how to punish me for discovering him and Lila.

But why would Lila have come to his house then? I tried to think of a motive. Had she masterminded

the whole party in order to ruin Takeo's chance to
take over the school? If so, that would mean she
wanted to marry his father and make her own children the new heirs. No. It wasn't worth anything to
be trapped in the Kayama family. Lila probably liked
her affair just the way it was.

I entered the Kayama house close on the heels of
a guest I recognized as the party page editor for the
Tokyo Weekender. If a candid description of the party
ended up in the biweekly tabloid, it would be
devastating to the Kayamas. I went in resolutely and
exchanged my shoes for slippers under Natsumi's
gaze. As I stepped up on the polished floor, she
grabbed my wrist. After the editor and his
entourage passed into the main room, she said, "I
want you to go upstairs, take off your kimono, and
give it to me."

The alcohol on her breath was so strong that it
made me step back. "Why?"

"I'm the hostess. I need to look beautiful," she said,
sounding as desperate as her brother had earlier.

"Don't you have your own clothing? What about
your mother's famous kimono?" I asked.

"I wore that a few years ago." She sneered, revealing dark lipstick on a front tooth. "I cannot repeat an
outfit."

"Well, you'd be repeating my outfit if I gave you
my kimono. And what do you propose I wear? I'm
too big for your black patent leather suit or even
those jeans," I said, examining them. They looked
like the equivalent of an American size two, while I
wore a six.

"There's a *kura* on the other side of the house where you can find one of my mother's old things to wear. You like vintage clothing! Take the key." Natsumi fished in a chest of drawers, then slammed it shut. "I can't find it. Well, that probably means that the *kura* is open. Maybe my brother's there." She wiggled her eyebrows at me. "You'd like that, wouldn't you? Some time with him?"

"You're drunk, and I'm not going to the *kura*," I said, thinking of the black truck parked outside it. "Please be reasonable. Everyone's already seen what you're wearing and thinks you look lovely. Just sit down quietly and you'll be fine."

"This is a semiformal party," Natsumi said in a slow, superior voice. "You don't understand Japanese etiquette. Clothing is very important. That's why I need you to give me yours."

I'd had *You don't understand Japanese etiquette* said to me so many times that it no longer hurt me. I looked straight back at her and said, "Very well, Natsumi-san. If you want to wear one of your mother's kimono, you're going to have to pick one out yourself."

"Girls, people can hear you arguing!" Aunt Norie came upon us like a small tornado. "I'll go with Rei to find the kimono. I know where the *kura* is."

"Oh, that would be so kind!" Natsumi delivered an exaggerated smile to my relative. "Be sure to find an underskirt and under-robe and an obi. I trust your judgment to choose things that match!"

"But you've got something else to do," I said in a low voice to my aunt. "The food."

"I'll get Tsutomu to set things out. He's become very good around the house."

"I'm going to go upstairs to get undressed and wait," Natsumi said.

"Of course," Aunt Norie replied.

I didn't like the deferential note in Norie's voice at all. When we got outside, I told her, "We're being set up. Something—I mean someone—is waiting for us in the storehouse."

"That's very silly, Rei-*chan*." Aunt Norie snapped on the flashlight and began walking down the dirt road toward where the black truck was parked.

"The storehouse is the root of all the trouble. Just as Sakura went into the school archives to borrow Kayama ware, she must have gone to the *kura* to borrow Takeo's mother's kimono. While she was there, she came across something that led her to be killed."

"What is this story about Sakura wearing Mrs. Kayama's clothing?" Norie stopped and looked at me strangely.

"Well, I'm not absolutely positive it was her," I amended. "But a middle-aged Japanese woman stole Takeo's mother's yellow kimono and called herself Mrs. Kayama when she went to Mr. Ishida's shop. She fenced some 1930s ceramics that were produced by the Kayama School."

Aunt Norie began breathing rapidly. "Oh, dear."

"What is it?"

"I think I've seen a woman dressed like that, but she was shrouded by early morning mist, so I couldn't see her face. I thought she was Mrs.

Kayama, come back from the dead to haunt me."

"Why?"

"She's come to my garden a few times, always around the anniversary of her death in early spring. I am sure that the woman who appears there is the one sending the haiku." Norie's words came out in a flood that had been held in too long.

"But how can it be Sakura if we've received haiku since her death?"

"It's a ghost who has come to haunt me for my sins," Norie said.

Just how bad was her sin? I cleared my throat and said, "You and the headmaster. Did you . . ."

"Yes, I did. I hurt him terribly." Norie's voice shook.

"Don't feel bad, Obasan. You were manipulated by him, and he does the same to other women in the school. These days they'd call it sexual harassment!"

"What?" Norie stopped and stared at me. "There was nothing romantic with the headmaster. What I mean is that I hurt him by causing his wife's accident."

"Takeo told me that she fell down a flight of steps in the garden. How could that be your fault?"

"I was at the bottom of the steps, cutting daffodils for a forthcoming exhibition. My scissors were too dull to do a good job, I realized. Because I was pregnant with Chika, I did not have the energy to go up the steps. Also, the weather had been rainy, so the stones were very slick, and that made me nervous. I called to Mrs. Kayama, who was on higher ground, asking if she could ask one of the other students to bring an extra pair of scissors. She called out that she would walk down herself and give me her own scissors. I called back an apology—my goodness, I hadn't expected the *iemoto*'s wife to do such an annoying errand—but she was very kind and insisted that she wanted to join me in cutting daffodils. But when she came, she fell head over heels down the steps. She landed, falling on the scissors she had been carrying for me. They pierced her throat."

"That's why, when you saw Sakura dead at the Kayama School, you were so devastated. You were remembering Mrs. Kayama's death."

Aunt Norie nodded. "Yes, and the others knew it, too. Twice I've found women dead with scissors in their necks. It's a bad record." She paused. "You don't think—you don't think there's a body lying in the *kura*? And I'm meant to discover it, just like the other times?"

"We should wait for the police." At my aunt's surprised look, I said, "I called Lieutenant Hata. He's going to send the local police out to look around."

"*Ara!*" my aunt exclaimed. "So when you were upstairs, you were not just calling a restaurant. You were calling the police!"

"Yes. Takeo was showing me where I could telephone privately."

"Are you sure you can trust him?"

I thought about Norie's question and the various guises in which Takeo had appeared to me. I'd first seen him as an arrogant rich boy, then a possibly dangerous environmentalist, and finally an emotionally needy young man who missed his mother.

"I guess so." I knew that sounded less than confident.

"Then you should ask Takeo-san to go into the *kura*. He is the man of the house."

Norie wanted to see how brave or honorable Takeo would be in the context of danger at his home. But this was the wrong test. Takeo would no sooner go hunting for a kimono for his spoiled sister than I would.

"Nobody's going in there until the police come," I repeated. "Come on, let's go back into the house. I'd feel better if the Shimura men were offering us support, wouldn't you?"

Aunt Norie did not argue.

Chapter 28

"I'm bored to death," Tom said when I came upon him pondering a calligraphy scroll in the house's grand hall. "Can we leave? The Kayamas have vanished, and I'm running out of things to do. I've already made six rounds of the cherry blossoms."

Norie and I exchanged glances, and I imagined she was thinking—as I was—that there were worse things to die from than boredom. After hearing about Mrs. Kayama's death, my cousin's exaggerated complaint was almost offensive.

"Tsutomu-*kun*, your services may be needed. We should stay a while longer," Norie murmured, smiling pleasantly at more party guests arriving.

"You mean, if somebody gets too drunk, as most of them are"—he waved his hand dramatically toward the crowd drinking on empty stomachs in the living room—"I will be asked by you to clean up the vomitus? Just because I'm the only physician here?"

"Nobody will ask you to do that," his mother snapped. "You don't have to do that at St. Luke's, do you? The tough jobs are given to nurses. To women!"

Was this a bit of feminist consciousness surfacing? I looked at my aunt in surprise, and the tense moment was mitigated by the arrival of the sashimi. Because Takeo didn't seem to be evident, I directed the deliveryman into the kitchen, and Norie and I swiftly moved the takeout food from its plastic trays onto the Kayamas' antique wooden trays. Norie asked Tom to carry out the food and stand guard over it.

"Guard against what, the guests eating?" Tom grumbled.

"No, against poisoners!" his mother shot back.

Tom raised his eyebrows but did as he was told.

Where was Takeo? I wondered about that when I got caught up in a dispute between Uncle Hiroshi and the deliveryman who wanted to be paid. In the end, Uncle Hiroshi handed over his credit card and said that he would guarantee the payment if the Kayamas hadn't made good on the bill by the next morning.

"That was very generous of you," I said to my uncle.

"I still have some money," he said stiffly. I had almost forgotten about his unemployment, and now that unhappy specter reared its head again.

As the elegant crowd stampeded toward the sashimi, I overheard a woman griping that there were no flowers garnishing the food. Aunt Norie and I had operated in a rush and overlooked this important detail.

As far as I was concerned, there were other priorities. I headed upstairs in search of Takeo, thinking that perhaps he had retreated to his room like an adolescent trying to avoid his parents' friends. But that would be out of character for someone who had been calm enough to order enough food for two hundred.

The door to the room he'd showed me earlier was closed, so I knocked lightly, not wanting to alert Natsumi in her nearby bedroom that I had come back to the house without a kimono. If Natsumi knew that I was upstairs, she was liable to rip off my kimono and stick me with her too-small jeans.

Hearing no answer, I cracked the door to Takeo's room a few inches. It was empty. I closed up the room and surveyed six other doors. One of them was slightly open, so I peeked in.

I'd found Natsumi. She was lying sprawled across a canopied bed in a matching purple lace bra and panty set that I would have envied if the situation had not been so dire.

This small bit of jealousy helped to quell the fear that was rising inside me. Natsumi couldn't be dead. I hurried forward and was greatly relieved to see the rise and fall of her tiny breasts under the lace. I shook her warm, smooth shoulder, and it flopped under my gentle grip. Looking at the jeans crumpled on the floor, I could figure out what had happened. She'd undressed to get ready to put on my kimono, and then she'd blacked out.

I shouldn't have felt glad that Natsumi was out of commission, but now at least she wouldn't be hassling Norie and me to go into the *kura* for her. Thank goodness for small blessings. I left the room, closing the door tightly to ensure Natsumi's privacy. I'd heard a door open and then close in the hallway.

I didn't think that it was a door to one of the bedrooms, but more likely the toilet. The tiny square window of patterned glass at the top corner of the powder room door indicated that someone was inside. Perhaps the unconscious Natsumi was going to be the first of many victims of too much drinking and too little food. The party columnist would have plenty to report on. I slipped into Takeo's vacant bedroom to wait, leaving the door cracked so I could catch sight of whoever came out.

Takeo's room was colder than the rest of the house; I wondered if he ever built a fire on cool nights like this one. There were no traces of logs on the grate, just a pile of environmental magazines. I was not a tidy person by nature, but not even I hoarded old publications to this extent. I turned my back on the clutter and toward the alcove where one of Takeo's mother's calligraphy scrolls hung above an arrangement of thorny branches.

I looked at the scroll he'd chosen to hang on the wall above the flowers. One of the nice things about Reiko Kayama's calligraphy was that her *hiragana* lettering and *kanji* were sketched clearly enough for me to decipher. Usually the lettering I saw in calligraphy artwork was unfathomable.

It also helped that once I'd read a few words, I

recognized the haiku as one I'd told Takeo about: *The breezes of spring push the beautiful girl, arousing anger.*

I'd first thought those words were a threat to me; now I understood that they were a recounting of the situation in which Reiko Kayama had fallen. Norie had told me that she thought Reiko slipped, but when she'd described the scene to me, she had only mentioned seeing Reiko falling. Norie hadn't said it aloud, but I thought it now: *Reiko Kayama could have been pushed.*

Who would have pushed the *iemoto*'s wife? Logic told me the pusher had to be the headmaster or Sakura or another person within the Kayama School. But I could think of a young boy who might have playfully bumped against his mother. She had been unable to regain her balance and tumbled down the long flight of steps. The boy would come to bear such guilt for the succession of events that he would spend years copying more of his mother's haiku and sending it to Aunt Norie, thinking she had seen him. How he managed to masquerade as his mother in a kimono I didn't understand. Had he faked his own car accident because he needed to make sure Mr. Ishida wouldn't connect him to the Kayama ware?

My vision blurred, and I realized that it was because there were tears in my eyes. How had I allowed myself to begin to become fond of Takeo? Norie had been right that he was the wrong person for me.

"What are you doing in here?" Lila Braithwaite's voice cut through my thoughts. I spun around and saw her standing in the doorway. In her white sequined cocktail suit, she resembled an ice queen.

"I'm waiting. And I'm sorry about what happened earlier today."

"So am I!" Lila's words tumbled out in a long, angry rush. "When I met you at first, I really thought you just wanted to sell me a few antiques. And I would have bought them, you know. Is that why you ruined my life—because you were angry that I didn't want your stupid plates?"

"Don't you think you're the one who designed your life's plan? It was your choice to be with the *iemoto*. If it wasn't that, well, you should tell the police. There are laws against sexual harassment—"

Lila closed the door behind her and came closer to me. "You're a regular little tour guide to Japan, aren't you, Rei? You speak the language. You sell the furniture. You even give legal advice! Well, be assured that Masanobu isn't harassing me. We're two adults who made a choice to do something together. Apart from our children. Just for us."

I was about to respond rather snappishly that she did have a husband somewhere, even if I'd never seen him, but I controlled myself. She was right. I'd opened first her apartment door and then her bedroom closet door. You couldn't get much more invasive than that.

"I'm not going to tell anyone." I meant that. I couldn't bear for Takeo to go through the embarrassment of knowing what his father had done. He had enough pain trying to work through the loss of his mother.

"I don't believe you." Lila's voice trembled.

"I promise." I kept my eyes on her. "As long as you don't have a connection with Sakura's murder."

"I—we—she—" Lila stammered a bit, then spoke in a dead tone. "Sakura knew. She was mean to me in class, and she hinted about her knowledge to Masanobu. But he just gave her a new promotion. He made her a super-grandmaster, with a new salary scale. Money solves everything, you know. Masanobu would never, ever lift a finger to hurt a woman."

"But he scratched you," I said, remembering the marks I'd seen when she was getting teacups in her kitchen. "I saw your back."

Lila was silent for a beat, then said, "I asked him to do that."

"You mean . . ." A vision of kinky sex flashed into my mind.

"You're not married," Lila said bluntly. "When you're a single woman, love is supposed to be hearts and flowers. Well, when you've been around for a while, sometimes you want to be pricked by thorns."

I must have been blushing, because Lila snorted. "You're embarrassed. You're so young, aren't you? Well, be assured that our love affair is over. He's no longer interested."

"He broke up with you?" I had to admit that I was pleased for her husband and children's sakes.

"Masanobu rushed off, saying the relationship would be impossible to pursue now that you'd found us out. I begged him to calm down and think it over, but he insisted he needed to leave. I assumed he would be coming here to oversee the final preparations. I think the only reason he isn't here is to avoid me. But it's a terrible party without him! I don't know how his children are going to carry on the show. They've failed miserably tonight."

"Did the headmaster mention this party to you?" I asked.

Lila looked startled by my question. "No. I received my invitation yesterday but didn't bring it up. I had other things on my mind. Our time together was so limited."

"If it's any consolation, he didn't know about this party," I said. "Natsumi and Takeo didn't know, either. It was set up with RSVPs taken by an answering service outside of the school so that none of the Kayama staff would get wind of it and tell the family. That's why Mrs. Koda isn't here."

"Then ... who sent the invitations?" Lila's eyes were wide.

"I don't know. My guess is someone who wants to devastate the family."

"Or who loves the family," Lila said softly. "If nobody had sent out invitations for tonight, there wouldn't have been a cherry blossom viewing party this year. The person who sent the invitation was saving the tradition—one hundred and forty-five uninterrupted years of cherry blossom viewing parties. For the Kayamas, tradition is everything."

I pondered Lila's theory after she left, hurrying down the stairs to her friend Nadine, who was calling for her to join in a group photograph.

Tradition. I thought about the years of Kayama

history as I found myself again looking at Reiko Kayama's scroll hanging in Takeo's bedroom alcove. I knew that I should go downstairs and try to find Takeo and ask him about this idea of tradition. Maybe he had noticed a teacher or student who had exhibited a strange fascination with the past.

But before I left the room, I wanted my own record of Reiko Kayama's artwork. I pulled Aunt Norie's camera out of the little handbag I'd been dangling from my wrist and focused on the scroll. I wanted to get a close view of her writing, so I zoomed in with the telephoto lens.

Looking at the scroll, I was struck once more by its dissimilarity to the haiku letters I'd received. The handwriting style would be different, but there was something else. As the flash went off, the answer came to me.

The difference was that in the text of Reiko's original scroll—the one that I was looking at now—there were four *kanji* characters: the ones for "spring," "wind," "beauty," and "woman." I had skimmed over them without a hitch because I was getting better at reading *kanji*. The notes that were slipped underneath my door were written completely in *hiragana*, the phonetic lettering.

Hiragana was used specifically for me. The person sending me the note thought that I couldn't read much Japanese and wanted to ensure that I understood the message.

Who knew that I couldn't read *kanji*? Not Takeo. I'd fibbed to him in the restaurant about being able to read the menu.

Who knew that I couldn't read? I repeated to myself, and then I remembered.

Where's your mother?" I asked Tom as I hurried up to him. He was standing tense and unsmiling over the emptying buffet table.

"Oh, there you are! She wanted me to tell you that she was going outside to get something for Natsumi."

"She went with Uncle Hiroshi?" I guessed.

"No, look at him!" Tom inclined his head toward the garden. I could just make out Uncle Hiroshi talking animatedly to a small man with a familiar-looking back. "He's talking to the president of Sendai Limited. Mother saw that, and she didn't want to disturb him."

"Oh, no!" I knew Masuhiro Sendai, one of Japan's captains of industry, through my ex-boyfriend Hugh. Sendai Limited had meant phone calls disrupting dinner and sleep on a daily basis. How ironic that Sendai was already distracting Hiroshi when his wife needed him.

"It doesn't hurt for my father to talk with Sendai-san. It can only help," Tom told me.

"But your mother shouldn't have gone out into the dark alone. Forget about watching the food, Tom— we've got to find her."

"I'm sure that she'll be safe. She's with Iwata-san." When I looked at him uncomprehendingly, he added, "That's right! You know Iwata-san by her first name. I'm talking about her friend Eriko."

Chapter 29

Several of the lanterns hanging in the trees had blown out, so it was even darker outside. A wind had come up from nowhere, and there was the feeling of approaching rain. I kicked off the cumbersome sandals and jogged in my silk-stockinged feet toward the *kura*. Carrying the little purse was a hindrance, so I set it down on a rock, taking out the camera and slinging it around my neck.

The *kura*, which had seemed small to me before, looked larger this time. It was a building the size of a typical house in Yanaka and appeared to be two stories, I guessed, from the bits of light seeping through a shuttered window set high above the door. Just like the tiny window in the Kayamas' toilet room, this window served an important function. The storehouse hadn't had a light on before.

Someone had been, or still was, inside.

I was glad to be without shoes as I crept up to the storehouse. The entrance was similar to a pair of barn doors, with a latch in the middle that had been opened. I pulled softly on the left door, cringing in expectation that it would creak. It was well oiled, though, and swung open without a sound.

I stood in the doorway, scanning the storehouse. Now I understood why there were no windows on the ground level. All the walls were lined by deep shelves filled with flat lacquered boxes, shelves that went up to the second level. That was accessed by a step *tansu*, a chest that was built in the form of a staircase. I'd seen step *tansu* used decoratively in houses, but not in a way such as this. The *tansu* didn't look like a staircase I'd trust, given that the treacherously narrow, steep steps were aged and dry wood. As I ventured a bit further into the room, I saw that a storage box close to the far wall had been opened. Red silk cascaded over the edge. Maybe it was one of Reiko's kimonos. But where was my aunt?

There was a crackling sound of lightning hitting something outside and the lights went out. I was left in stillness, and the *kura's* special fragrance, a mixture of old wood, fabric, hay, and earth, had been replaced by the smell of my own fear. Rain pounded on the tiled roof as musically as a *taiko* drummer. The storm was on.

I edged back toward where I remembered the door was. I was at an advantage, being downstairs and close to the exit. But as I moved, I became aware of a new scent, a heavy floral perfume.

I had lost my orientation in the darkness. I was no longer sure of the way back to the door or the distance to the shelves full of boxes. I stretched my hands out carefully, trying to gauge things and moved sideways. I had to be quiet.

After three minutes of moving very slowly, I bumped into a row of shelves. The sound of my hand knocking against wood was like the thunder outside. Remembering the layout of the shelving, though, gave me an idea. I crouched down and used my hands again to ascertain exactly how high and deep the bottom shelving was. It was probably large enough for me to crouch in if I could move one of the cumbersome kimono boxes out. I did that with very little noise and squeezed into the vacated space.

The temperature in the storehouse seemed to have risen a notch. I guessed it was my anxiety. The air was faintly smoky, as if somebody was smoking a cigarette.

Takeo smoked. I remembered his long-ago offer of a cigarette. I'd declined, and he had never smoked in my presence after that. Was he inside and smoking as he leisurely made his way toward me?

No, he wasn't the one. I knew that the danger was Eriko Iwata. I heard feet in *zōri* clipping carefully down the wooden-step *tansu* and onto the ground floor. My territory.

"Is it you, Rei-san?" Eriko's soft voice reached me. "Your aunt has had an accident up in the loft when we were looking for Natsumi's kimono. I need your help."

Nausea punched at my stomach as I thought of

what Eriko had done. The realization had come
when I was contemplating Reiko Kayama's calligraphy scroll written in *kanji*, not *hiragana*. I remembered Eriko noting my inability to read *kanji* at the
ikebana class. The woman running back into the
shadows of the refreshment area at the Mitsutan
exhibit had to have been Eriko. She'd tried to kill
me. Now she'd gotten my aunt.

The sound of steps came close, and I caught a glint
of something in the darkness. What was it? Civilians
weren't allowed to carry handguns in Japan.

Eriko coughed. She was being affected by the
smoke, too. But the cough was more distant—she
had passed me and gone in another direction.

"I'll help you, just as I helped the others.
Especially the headmaster," Eriko said.

"You made him miserable! And all of us as well!"
Takeo's voice rang out from somewhere above me.

Eriko didn't answer. I heard the sound of a bolt
slamming into place, and I realized the door had
been latched. Had she locked us in and left?

"Where are you?" I called to Takeo.

A flashlight's wide yellow beam flashed over the
shelves where I was hiding. I bumped my head in my
eagerness to get out of my hiding place, but I stopped
when I heard sandals clip-clopping back in my direction. Eriko had the flashlight, and she hadn't left.

"Thank you for speaking. Ah, there you are!"

The flashlight illuminated my face. She shone the
light so closely at me that I couldn't see much of anything except the shining steel samurai sword outstretched in my direction.

"This is one of the Kayama family's prized blades. I asked Takeo-san to take it out of storage for me," she said.

"I thought you'd use it on yourself," Takeo shouted from above. "Isn't that the honorable thing for someone to do after she's been revealed as a murderer?"

I wondered where Takeo was and how a woman only five feet two inches tall had overpowered a man significantly larger, stronger, and younger than herself.

"The sword is to make you move where I want you to go," Eriko said tightly. "Come out of that place, Rei-san. I don't want your blood to soil the premises."

"Is this how you trapped Takeo?" I guessed aloud. "You convinced him to give you the sword, and then you turned it on him? What about my aunt?"

"I'm with your aunt on the second floor," Takeo called down to me in English. "Eriko was trying to cut her with the ikebana scissors when I came in. She's still alive, but she's very weak."

My aunt was dying. I knew it without needing to see her. I felt something inside me break.

"Move," Eriko ordered me, waving the tip of the sword in front of my face.

I began edging my way out, and Eriko backed away slightly, keeping the flashlight and sword aimed at me. I unfolded myself and stood up, using my hand to keep myself steady. One of my feet had gone to sleep. Within a few seconds, as blood rushed back to it, it would prickle painfully.

"Go!" Eriko ordered me, waving the sword in my face.

"My foot went to sleep, so it will take a minute—"

"Believe her," Takeo called down from upstairs. "Her foot went to sleep the first time I took her out. It's the problem with Japanese raised in the United States. You're going to have to give her a few minutes to get her strength back."

I called back to Takeo in English, "How did you get caught?"

"I came in because I saw the light in the storehouse from my upstairs bedroom. I was thinking that if you were right about Stop Killing Flowers being here, I could calm them down. I walked right in and Eriko called from the loft that Norie was hurt. When I made it up the stairs, Eriko threw a fishing net over my head and said that if I didn't tell her where the swords were stored, she'd throw your aunt over the edge and down to the floor. She tied both of us together against one of the beams. She invited all the people here to embarrass my family and keep everyone occupied while she finished off your aunt and you."

"I understand English," Eriko spat back. "Don't talk behind me!"

"Good, we'll speak to you directly then." Takeo was using the icy delivery he employed with underlings, which worried me. If Eriko became very angry, she was liable to slash through me.

"Move in the direction I'm pointing you, please." Eriko continued speaking to me in formal Japanese, but her polite words were belied by the sword, which made a tearing sound as it sliced through my kimono and the silk under-robe.

"The sword is going to be sold along with all the other Kayama things," Eriko said. "You would be surprised to know that your work finding unappreciated treasures and selling them for high profits has been my inspiration."

"Really," I said. "Don't you think you'll get caught?"

"Not at all," Eriko said. "You will die from the small fire that is just smoldering now. A lantern that was hanging in the trees was knocked over by accident by Takeo and Rei when they came inside to enjoy a covert romance and were interrupted by Norie."

"I've been trying to tell you"—Takeo coughed—"that among the weeds you used as kindling is poison ivy. You pulled it from the back wall of the *kura*, didn't you? Your hands will be covered with a rash. You can walk back to the party, but within a few hours the evidence will be visible."

"Eriko, put the fire out at least," I begged. "The ivy releases dangerous fumes. It will kill you, too."

"We'd better hurry then," Eriko said. "Rei-san, you must walk up the *tansu* to the loft so that I can get everything arranged."

"That's how it was with Sakura, wasn't it?" I asked, stumbling in the dark as Eriko's sword tore a new hole in my kimono. "You poisoned Sakura first. Then, when she was dying, you used the shears to cut into her neck. You made a very . . . "—I searched for an appropriate word—". . . dramatic arrangement."

"I succeeded in reminding people of Norie's guilt in Reiko Kayama's death. She killed her, and nobody punished her!" Eriko cried.

"It was an accidental fall," I said as my foot knocked into the first step of the *tansu* staircase. "Norie feels guilty because Reiko fell in the process of bringing her some scissors. But it's not her fault."

"Your aunt was telling me that before she lost consciousness," Takeo said. "For years I refused to believe it was an accident, but now I do. Too late."

"Someone needs to remember," Eriko said. "I reminded Norie every year of the crime she committed. And I reminded you with letters, Takeo-san, when you were not following the correct path of your father. But you did not listen."

"What about me?" I asked. "Why did you poison me first and then start sending those notes? I had nothing to do with Reiko Kayama's death."

"You were too close to the truth. Just as she was." Eriko's voice softened. "Rei-san, please be careful climbing the stairs. Your body must be placed on the second floor with Takeo-san and your aunt. You must not fall down. That kind of accident would ruin my arrangement."

I lifted my skirts and stepped slowly up the staircase, which creaked ominously. Eriko's and my weight on the steps at once might be too much for the old wood to bear.

"Don't tell me that you killed Sakura because you were jealous of Norie!" Takeo's voice had become very weak, no doubt because he was so close to the poisonous fumes. If he got out of this alive, I bet he'd never pick up a cigarette again.

"Save your breath," I said to Takeo. "Sakura must have discovered that Eriko dressed up in Reiko Kayama's kimono and was masquerading as her while she was selling off the Kayama treasures." As I made my way up the steep steps, I was running through another good idea. It would be a risky move, but I did have the advantage of traction from my wet socks. "Sakura no doubt threatened to expose Eriko, so Eriko took the way out that seemed most logical. She murdered Sakura and tried to make it look like Norie did it."

"There's a danger in being too clever, Rei-san," Eriko's voice said from behind me.

"Ah so desu ka — Is that so?" I asked while making a giant stretch up two steps instead of one. As my left leg moved to join my right, I sensed Eriko's surprise at my departure. In the split second the sword slipped off my back, I whirled around and aimed my camera at her face. I pressed the picture-taking button and the flash went off with an explosion of glare.

Faced with the blinding white light, Eriko's mouth gaped in surprise and then horror, as she tripped backward away from the light and into nothingness. Almost immediately I heard Eriko's body hit the cement floor with a sickening thud. The sword made a jangling sound as it fell on the other side of the steps.

Eriko's whimpers turned into sobs. She begged me

to help her, first in Japanese and then in English. But I had other priorities. I needed to put out a fire, stop my aunt's bleeding, and untie Takeo. I had no time for Eriko's troubles. Instead, I put my hands on the edge of the loft and pulled myself up.

Chapter 30

My back was killing me as I bent forward and shoved a spade into yet another square of Aunt Norie's lawn. I'd never realized how hard gardening was.

"Be sure that you are reaching below the roots, Rei. Look how nicely Takeo-san is doing it. Just follow his example," Norie called from the chaise longue on the stone patio where she was supervising.

Takeo and I had been digging up the lawn for what seemed like hours under the strong May sun. Aunt Norie thought the storm that raged the night of our near tragedy at the Kayamas was a harbinger of the rainy season, and the second she had regained consciousness at the hospital, she had begged me to make sure her garden was planted in time to take advantage of the rain.

I was so grateful that Norie was alive that I would have done anything she asked. The lasting damage from Norie's struggle with Eriko were a large number of deep cuts on her forearms and hands. Over three hundred stitches had been needed to close her wounds, which meant that for the time being, Norie couldn't arrange flowers, cook, and certainly not put in the native plants that Takeo had given her. Fortunately, the poison ivy fumes hadn't hurt any of us.

I resettled the triangular-shaped straw hat on my damp head, imagining that I looked like a stereotyped Asian rice farmer. Takeo looked gorgeous under his hat, but then again, he looked that way in everything, his Greenpeace T-shirt notwithstanding. That T-shirt covered with Norie's blood had been seized by the late-arriving police as evidence for Eriko's murder trial. The police had also taken my torn kimono off my back and Norie's camera, which turned out to have taken a very good picture of Eriko holding the sword in front of her in the second before she fell and broke her back. The poison ivy rash that developed on Eriko's hands matched with the small burned pile of poison ivy plants in the loft—even more evidence against her, because she obstinately refused to confess.

Looking at the bittersweet bushes lined up against the stone wall, I thought about how sad it was that Takeo had lost his last hope that his mother might be alive. Aunt Norie had lost the woman she thought was a close friend. Tom and I could talk to her about the loss, but Uncle Hiroshi was not around much, since he'd started a new job with Sendai Limited.

I could see what was going to happen. Hiroshi would regain his sense of self but lose his chance to spend significant time with Norie. Well, at least he would spend his nights at home, not in Osaka.

"You're so lucky to live the way you do," I grunted to Takeo as I began turning the earth once again. "You have the ability to spend your days playing in dirt while retaining the title of flower master. After you're through redesigning Norie's garden, it may very well become a Yokohama landmark."

"I'm afraid not." He didn't look at me, but just kept digging. "I should tell you that my father decided that it would be better if Natsumi becomes the next master."

"That's not fair," I said. All along I'd thought that one of the problems with ikebana is that there weren't enough women as headmasters. But Takeo would have been a great headmaster. Even though the *iemoto* had broken off his relations with Lila, word about the ill-fated liaison had gotten around, and many of the students were demoralized. They needed a new leader.

"Natsumi didn't get in trouble at the party," Takeo told me. "She fell asleep upstairs like a good girl, instead of getting covered with blood, as I did. But don't cry for me, Rei. I've always had mixed feelings about whether I wanted to be the *iemoto*. After what we went through, I decided that life is too precious to waste. I talked to my father about my commitment to the environment. He and the board of directors thought I'd ruin their relationship with the entire floral industry. So I'm out."

"You're completely out of the Kayama School?"

"That's right. You won't be able to call me the

billion-yen boy anymore. Right now I'm an unem-
ployed gardener."

"You could go full steam ahead with Stop Killing
Flowers," I suggested. "You know Mrs. Koda is
doing that." The day after the disastrous party at the
Garden of Stones, Mrs. Koda had thanked me for
saving the Kayama School's treasures and reputation. In return she would do something to help all
women who loved flowers. She wanted to chair a
campaign to raise funds for the study of the effects of
floral pesticides on people.

When Richard and Enrique, who had reunited
during a date I engineered for them at Salsa Salsa,
told Che Fujisawa about the forthcoming cancer
study, the Stop Killing Flowers leader begged to be
allowed to be included in Mrs. Koda's press conference. Mrs. Koda agreed, in exchange for Che's
promise to praise the Kayama School for bringing
the serious health issue to the forefront. Mari
Kumamori had volunteered to design a celadon
suiban as a premium for the campaign's more generous donors. After her *suiban* was featured in the
lifestyle section of *Asahi Shinbun,* orders for all kinds
of pottery to be made by her began flooding the
Kayama School reception desk. The only one who
didn't have a great job future was Takeo.

"I just want to be a simple gardener. Isn't that
enough to fill my days?" Takeo had laid down his
shovel and was looking at me. Staring in my face,
searching for something. Reassurance, I guessed.

"My aunt will give you a good reference. You
could get a lot of nice jobs in the Yokohama sub-

urbs," I said, waving to my aunt as she got up from her lounge and disappeared into the house.

"Those aren't the kind of projects I'm interested in, Rei." He moved closer to me and looked deeply into my eyes. "After finishing this garden, the next one I want to do is in an old Tokyo neighborhood. It's a tough job that would involve blasting through concrete to make room for the smallest camellia seedling. I'm pretty sure the neighborhood association would let me do it, but I'm not sure how the tenant would feel."

"It might take a while to gain her approval," I said lightly. I had meant it teasingly, but when I saw Takeo's face fall, I saw that he hadn't understood. And suddenly I wanted him to know exactly how interested I was. Ignoring the fact that our bodies were flecked with earth and grass, I put my arms around him.

Our gardening hats bumped as our mouths came together. Takeo made an irritated sound and knocked both hats to the ground. We were lost in each other for what felt like hours, but then Aunt Norie's voice returned like a bee buzzing through the garden.

"*Gomen nasai!* Excuse me for interrupting!" she called out, the tone of her voice belying the words.

Feeling strangely unembarrassed, I turned my head to smile at my aunt. "We'll get back to work in a minute. After we're through getting reacquainted."

Norie clucked her tongue, but when I looked at her, she was smiling. I radiated my happiness back to her, then returned to Takeo and our wonderful work in progress.

It was going to take a while to plant Norie's new garden.

I had the time.

If you enjoyed *The Flower Master*,
then read on for a preview of
Sujata Massey's exciting new novel,

The Floating Girl

Coming Soon

Is the pain killing you? Shall I stop?"

I shook my head because the pain had eased temporarily. Miss Kumiko sighed, and stroked more sticky warmth over my inner thigh—a deceptively pleasant sensation. I knew that six more inches needed to be cleared. The aesthetician pressed a strip of cotton over my thigh, and I sucked in my breath as she began to pull.

"Oh!" I gasped as she yanked at least one hundred hairs from their follicles.

"Japanese women don't like to cry out," Miss Kumiko said brightly. "Not even when delivering babies. When my niece was born, my sister was silent. At moments of severe pain, she bit a handkerchief. Would you like a handkerchief?"

"No thank you, and this is hardly child birth. It's a bikini wax!" Damn my American half for making the process necessary. If I'd been fully Japanese, I would have inherited the hairless gene. But I was a hafu or hanbujin or konketsujin or whatever name Miss Kumiko secretly used for mixed race people. It was my own stupid vanity that had brought me into Power Princess Spa before the start of the July beach season. I had one final business appointment that afternoon, and then a drive the next day to the beach. But first, I had to get through the pain.

"Madam, it is not that I mind, but the manicurist in the next cubicle has problems," Miss Kumiko whispered. "Surprise screams from customers can cause her to lose rhythm."

"Maybe there's a reason your customers scream," I said.

"Ja, we are all done!" Miss Kumiko made a series of light slaps against my groin. This was more kinky than I'd expected, but then again, this was my first experience with waxing in Tokyo. I would live and learn.

I put on my skirt and limped out to the stylish black-and-white reception area.

"Rei Shimura?" The salon's bleached blond receptionist called me up to her stylish chrome desk.

"Yes?" I continued at my slow pace, thighs sticking together because of a few remnants of wax.

"We have two kinds of bikini wax, large and small," she announced so clearly that some of the other customers in the waiting area looked up from their magazines. "When we spoke on the phone, we thought you were a typical Japanese, so we quoted you the price for a small wax. However, Miss Kumiko reports that you required the large wax. Therefore the fee is a bit higher: six thousand yen. Is that fine?"

The entire reception room seemed to be leaning close to hear my embarrassed answer.

"Fine," I said glumly. With an exchange rate was about 120 yen to the dollar, making the price of hair removal about $50, twice the going rate in the United States. I paid up, thinking the only silver lining was that Miss Kumiko wouldn't require a tip. This was Japan, where you never paid extra for good service. It was expected.

I walk this uneasy line between pleasure and pain— and understanding and confusion— almost daily. Four years ago, I emigrated from San Francisco to Tokyo seeking a job working with Japanese antiques. Nobody would hire me, so I had to establish my own business. It's been a struggle at times, but I'm proud to say that at last I've leaped the poverty line. Miss Kumiko would not think of asking me to find her an antique chest, but plenty of older, wealthy Japanese have done that. Even in an economic downturn, I'd had some very lucky breaks.

As I struggled out of the Power Princess Spa, I was headed toward my latest lucky spot: the Gaijin Times, an English-language magazine aimed at foreigners living in Tokyo. Their editor, an ambitious young woman journalist called Whitney Talbot, hunted me down after she'd read my article on ceramics for a Japanese antiques magazine. Whitney had asked me to write similar articles with, as she put it, "an element of street sass." I was apprehensive, but when she named a price for a monthly column, I decided I had to try. My first article was a guide to haggling for antiques at the weekend flea markets held at Tokyo's Shinto shrines. It was supposed to be a do-it-yourself article, but my phone started ringing off the hook with insecure foreigners willing to pay me to haggle for them. It had become very good business.

I put my quick rush of pride away as I entered the narrow sliver of a building that was home to the Sanno Advertising Agency and the Gaijin Times. I rode the elevator up to the third floor and a hall painted a dull beige.

Throbbing music coming from speakers stationed on either side of the Gaijin Times office door was the first indicator that the magazine was striving to break free from a beige mold. Inside were chocolate-colored walls, chocolate brown tables, and a gray lump lying across the chocolate and strawberry print carpet.

I drew closer to the lump to identify it. Alec Tampole, an Australian who edited the magazine's copious nightclub listings, was stretched out on the floor, arms angled out from his side in an A shape, his knees curled snugly against his chest.

"What's wrong?" I asked, hurrying over.

"I'm doing some Pilates exercises. I forgot you were coming in today, Rye." He pushed his legs over his head in a move that looked like the yoga plow.

"My name is actually pronounced Rei. As in Sugar Ray," I said, striving for a pop music reference that he would understand.

"Come closer so I can hear you over the music—" Alec slowly lowered his legs, grunting with exertion.

I stood as closely to his ear as possible and shouted the correct pronunciation.

He laughed. "Right, Rye. Had an accident coming over?"

"No, what do you mean? Is something going on outside?"

"That's not the kind of accident I'm talking about. What's that gunk on your knickers?"

"You bastard!" I realized belatedly that the music maven had been angling himself for a perfect view up my skirt. I leaped away from him.

"Heh, heh. Had a hot wax for a hot date, eh?" As he swung his hips over his head once again, I kicked his large, khaki-clad behind. His anguished yelp was music to my ears as I left the reception area, heading into the tiny warren of offices and my next assignment.

Where's Whitney?" I aimed my question at Rika Fuchida, the magazine's college intern, who was standing with bare feet on Alec's desk taping up the edge of a Cibo Matto poster that had come loose. I was surprised Alec wasn't in the room watching Rika. Her skirt was shorter than mine.

"Oh, hello, Rei-san!" Rika was Japanese, so she had no trouble with my name. "Didn't you hear that Whitney-san is not here anymore?"

"No. Is she working from home?" I glanced at my watch. I had to be somewhere else in two hours, but I really had wanted to see the Gaijin Times editor for approval of my next column topic. I was proposing a do-it-yourself piece on how to buy and refinish a tansu chest for less than $1000.

Rika shook her head so vigorously that her trendy

short pigtails bounced. "Whitney quit."

"Oh, no!" I was aghast.

Alec leaned in the doorway and joined our conversation. "She took a job at the Asian Wall Street Journal. Going on to greener pastures, heh heh. Good thing for all of us that she did a bunk. This magazine needs to be more culturally connected. Whitney spoke the language, but she didn't know much about the pulse of modern Japan."

"If the Journal hired her, somebody obviously thinks she's good." I said. It was true that Whitney had only been in Japan for about six months, and she'd been quite open about how she needed a crash course in Japanese culture and history. That's why she'd hired me, in fact. But if management was unhappy with Whitney, they might not be excited about the contributors she had hired.

"Mr. Sanno, the magazine's owner, is sitting in on the story meeting today. He's the one who's going to select the new editor." Alec looked as if he would explode with excitement. "Don't get any ideas about showing off during the meeting. I saw your resume. The only journalism experience you've had prior to this is the Johns Hopkins University News-Letter."

"I'm not interested in the editor job," I replied coolly. His mention of the magazine owner had made me nervous—would Mr. Sanno even want to keep me on as a columnist? I was very grateful for the publicity that the Gaijin Times column had given my business. My net earnings were twenty percent higher since I'd started being published in the magazine.

"It's almost time for the meeting," Rika said. "May

I pause in your office redecoration, Alec-san, in order to serve the coffee?"

"I'll help you," I offered, not wanting to stand next to Alec for a minute longer. It was only when Rika and I were placing small glasses of iced coffee on wooden coasters around the conference table that I realized how foolhardy my move had been. I was acting like an obsequious office lady. This was not the way to reinforce my stature as a columnist to the magazine's owner.

I wondered what Mr. Sanno was thinking when he took the seat of power at the end of the battered steel table. The magazine's staff of six full-time editorial employees was a motley assortment of young people who perfectly reflected patterns of immigration to fin-de-siecle Japan. There was Joey, the half-Taiwanese, half-Japanese restaurant critic; Norton Jones, a fresh Columbia University graduate who covered national politics; Toshi Ueda, a recent Waseda University graduate who was the photo editor; my friend Karen Anderson, a former model who had put on weight and now wrote about fashion trends; the repulsive Alec, who did the music and entertainment listings, and Rika Fuchida, Alec's intern assistant. The gang wore assorted hues of patterned polyester, double-knit and jersey, vintage and new. Earrings swung from multiple pierce-holes, and heavy rings and bangles clattered against the table whenever anyone reached for their coffee. There was also an undeniable odor of tobacco hanging over the group. There was a ratio of one ashtray per person on the table, although nobody was smoking yet, perhaps in deference to the magazine's owner.

Mr. Sanno appeared about forty years old, but instead of the gray or navy suit that was de rigueur with men his age, was wearing a flashy green suit with wide lapels. He sat at the end of the table flipping through a large ring binder filled with pages of spread sheets. Numbers, I thought, tensing up. I suspected that he would talk about what had proven profitable in the past, and how we would need to change. "Thank you for allowing me to join your regular story meeting. You are kind to let me intrude into your busy day." Mr. Sanno's voice was surprisingly high. I wondered if this was because he found speaking English a strain. He spoke at the level of someone who did business on a daily level with English speakers, but not with the fluency of Japanese who had lived or studied overseas.

"Hey, no worries! I'd like to see a lot more of you," Alec said in his brash Australian way, and I sensed a stiffening around the table. Alec was trying to turn his role as de facto editor into a permanent promotion.

"Thank you, Mr. Tampon," Mr. Sanno said, smoothly botching the pronunciation of Alec's surname. I didn't hide my smile. "We shall all sorely miss the leadership of Miss Whitney Talbot. However, as we frequently say in Japan and China, the kanji character for "crisis" is made from two words: "danger" and "opportunity." Our challenging time offers a great chance to move forward, to create a larger circulation for Gaijin Times."

I stopped smiling. Mr. Sanno had turned to talking

about numbers even sooner than I'd expected.

"You may know that the Gaijin Times is the only magazine that Sanno Advertising owns. Perhaps you would like to understand why we created this magazine." He glanced around the table. "Because we own the Gaijin Times, we can run advertisements on its pages for free. Of course, we charge our clients the cost of our advertising services, and they agree that it is a fair system. If we have a Mexican restaurant client, so we run an ad for the spot, and in the same issue, Joey Hirota gives it a good review."

"Mr. Sanno, if I might say a few words, the magazine is more than a advertising circular. I report stories on the banking crisis, the yakuza, the future of the Diet," Norton interjected.

Norton didn't know the right etiquette for a conversation with a Japanese boss. I exchanged quick unhappy looks with Toshi and Rika. Joey Hirota was staring down in his lap, as if he'd been horribly embarrassed to be revealed as having written phony reviews. I should have figured out the reason for the review scam long ago. Personally, I never took much stock in anyone who thought you could buy a decent chimi-changa in Tokyo.

"With changes in the economy, however, our loyal advertisers have less money to spend. To keep the magazine alive, we need more subscriptions."

I did know that the business of being a working foreigner in Tokyo had gotten tough. Salaries for English teachers, bar hostesses and the like had dropped precipitously in the last seven years. Young gaijin were deeply skeptical of the length of time that they could make a living in Tokyo, which made the prospect of their paying 6,000 yen up-front for twelve magazines unlikely.

"I agree that we need to up our subscriber list," Alec chimed in. "We have to increase page space for music and clubs, things that remind gaijin kids of the things they left behind. A cover with the Beastie Boys or Fiona Apple would sell far more than one with a Japanese person on it. Get it?"

"I see your point," Toshi Ueda, the photographer, said. No Japanese person would blatantly tell another person he was wrong, but I had a sense that Toshi had something up his sleeve. "Speaking of musical culture, it is interesting that the Amuro Namie cover sold more than any other issue to date."

"Yes. Sales of that issue prove that Japanese idol singers appeal to foreigners. Foreigners come to Japan because they admire our popular culture!" Mr. Sanno's mild voice had become vehement, proving to me that Alec's brash, anti-Japanese comment had annoyed him.

I saw my chance to make a gentle comment to help my own cause along. "I agree. Another aspect of Japanese culture that foreigners love is Japanese antiques. Even if budgets are small, people will go out of their way to study and perhaps buy vintage Japanese furniture."

"What about original Japanese fashion?" Karen chimed in. "Why don't we point out some of the local designers who aren't yet in the department stores, and are thus less expensive?"

"So many good ideas." Mr. Sanno rubbed his

smooth chin. "In this case, I have looked at the Japanese publishing market for guidance. Can you identify the single largest selling category of book in Japan today?"

"Business," Norton said with a yawn.

Mr. Sanno shook his head.

"Pornography," Alec said with a sneer.

"No, I'm afraid it's something rather more innocent in its nature."

Rika raised her hand. When Mr. Sanno nodded at her, she said timidly, "Manga?"

He smiled expansively. "That's right. Forty percent of all written material sold in Japan are comics. Will the young lady please tell me her name? I'm afraid we haven't met."

"Rika Fuchida. I'm just the intern here from Showa College—"

"A fine school. I am a graduate." Mr. Sanno twinkled at her. "Do they still have the animation club?"

"Oh, yes. I'm a member."

Mr. Sanno flipped open the binder he'd been perusing, and read from it.

"As Rika-chan could probably tell you, there are several English language magazines aimed a fans of Japanese animation. But there has not yet been an English language comic book that tells foreigners how to live life in Japan."

Was he going to turn Gaijin Times into a comic book? No wonder Whitney had quit. Every face at the table was neutral. I could only imagine that the others were as shocked as I.

"When do you anticipate the change happening?"

Toshi's voice croaked. I imagined he was pondering what role his artsy, black-and-white photographs could have in a comic magazine.

"Since most of the three future issues' articles and art are already completed—yes, Miss Talbot was very efficient—that must not go to waste. However, I would like to see at least two articles in next month's issue that explore the idea of animation. We will also put out a call for cartoonists to audition their work, and begin running two or three different comics per issue. It's now July, so let's see, a full comic book format issue by December would be reasonable. With the hard work of everyone, it could happen. Joey will write his restaurant reviews as a comic strip—imagine the possibilities! The reader will not only read about what the food is like, but see it. Likewise for you, Miss Karen. Photographs don't work anymore."

"What do you mean?" Karen sounded confused, and I couldn't blame her.

" If a dress is not flattering to a woman, the real life appearance—" Mr. Sanno gestured to Karen's muumuu-like black dress—"makes it look bad. Likewise, photographs tell the true story, which can make the retailer look upset. A cartoon illustration, on the other hand, can make any dress look truly lovely."

I felt strange, as if I was hovering over the table and witnessing the beginning of a disaster. Karen felt badly enough about her weight gain, which Mr. Sanno was cruelly pointing out. What would happen to the rest of us, and to the publication? The Gaijin

Times had never been a prize-winning publication, but it had done a decent job imparting crucial lifestyle information to foreigners. I'd used Gaijin Times to search for apartments and jobs when I'd arrived. Come to think of it, I'd learned about the waxing specialists at Power Princess Salon after reading an article Karen had written in last month's issue. Could all that be scrapped for wasp-waisted, big-eyed androids carrying guns?

"I assume you'll bring in a new editor." Joey sounded glum. "One who is expert in comical matters."

"We Japanese always believe in promoting from within," Mr. Sanno said. "I am certain that one of you could easily rise to shine in the transition. We will decide on some projects for all of us today, and that will keep us busy before I select the editor."

There was a long silence, and I imagined everyone was trying to think of projects.

"I've heard there is an American scholar who is an expert on comic books aimed at salarymen. I could explore the changing ethos of work in Japan through animation," Norton suggested. "Toshi could take pictures of salarymen reading comic books on the subway to go with the story."

"The photos can be used as a basis for comic book sketches," Mr. Sanno said. "And if the salarymen are ugly, the drawing can make them look better. In my opinion, there have been too many ugly people in the magazine lately."

Mr. Sanno was not exactly a Japanese version of Hugh Grant, but of course, nobody could say that.

"Well, that salaryman idea take care of Norton and Toshi. But what about Karen-chan?"

Mr. Sanno was calling all the women in the room by the suffix 'chan' which meant little. I could tell that Karen thought it was demeaning, because her pale skin flushed. She spoke rapidly, another sign he'd rattled her.

"I was writing a story about fall cocktail dresses worn by some of the top bar hostesses in town. I will consult a fashion illustrator who can sketch the clothes on the girls. They're very, very attractive," she added, as if to head off further comments on ugliness versus beauty.

"What about sketching the clothes on well-known cartoon characters?" Rika, the intern, ventured.

"It might not be legal. Betty and Veronica are probably copy-righted," I said swiftly to avoid having Mr. Sanno slap Karen with an impossible assignment.

"Actually, it's different here," Rika replied. "Japanese manga publishers don't really care if amateur artists copy the figures. What the amateurs sell is called doujinshi, and when those doujinshi comics sell, it is believed to create publicity for the original series."

"Rika-chan is right." Mr. Sanno nodded at Rika, who promptly hung her head and mumbled how worthless she was. It was a perfect Japanese etiquette moment that I would have appreciated if Mr. Sanno had not swiftly turned his gimlet gaze to me. "Rei-chan, I know that you are only a part-time employee, but you will be a part of the transformation. Your column relates to antiques and fine arts, so you will have many possibilities."

"I know very little about animation," I said stiffly. "My background is in Japanese decorative arts."

"Manga are today's most important art form," Mr. Sanno said. "Can't you write that in your column?"

A battle raged inside me. I wanted to walk away from this stupid fantasy comic book of Mr. Sanno's, but I didn't want to give up seeing "Rei Shimura Antiques" in 14-point type once a month. I spoke carefully. "My goal is to help the Gaijin Times be the best that it can be. That is why I would be willing to resign if my writing doesn't fit the new format."

"Are you hoping to be fired, Rei?" Alec asked. I was really beginning to hate him.

"I know what you can do, Rei-san!" Rika offered. "Since you are a serious person, you can write a serious article about the history and artistic significance of Japanese animation. If you can present manga in a worthwhile light, the readers will become prepared for the switch to the new format."

"That's right, Miss Fuchida! Please help with Miss Shimura's assignment."

Rika, sitting across from me in her short pleated skirt, knee socks, and braids, still looked more like a junior high school student than a senior at Showa College. But at that moment I, and probably every other staffer in the room, could imagine what form she would emerge into as surely as Clark Kent transformed himself into Superman: she'd be Rika Fuchida, Gaijin Times' youngest ever editor-in-chief.